PRIZE STORIES OF 1951

THE O. HENRY AWARDS

DOUBLEDAY & COMPANY, INC., GARDEN CITY, NEW YORK, 1951

Prize
Stories
of
1951

 The
O. Henry Awards

SELECTED AND EDITED BY HERSCHEL BRICKELL

This, the thirty-third annual volume
of the O. HENRY MEMORIAL AWARD PRIZE STORIES,
is dedicated to the memory of
RING LARDNER
one of our greatest short-story writers,
of whom J. B. Priestley wrote in 1934:
"His short stories are grand.
They are funny, pathetic,
and devastatingly true.
What an ear that chap had!"

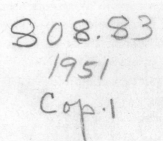
Copyright, 1951, by Doubleday & Company, Inc. All Rights Reserved
Printed in the United States at the Country Life Press, Garden City, N.Y.
First Edition

AFTER THE THREE PRIZE STORIES THE ORDER IS ALPHABETICAL BY AUTHOR

placed it third in her list of alternate choices. Mr. Jackson did not mention it in his selection, but the editor and his assistant thought it easily one of the best stories in the collection, so that it was awarded third prize.

Mr. Jackson wrote the longest report on the Downey story, and said of it, with great perspicuity:

"I have chosen 'The Hunters' for first place because it seems to me that Mr. Downey has realized more precisely than any of the twenty-four writers whose stories are here assembled the task he set himself.

"In this story, sharply and exactly presented, is both a lost man and today's Lost Man. Private Meadows has not merely lost his outfit, he has lost himself: 'He had left himself somewhere, and the farther he walked the terrain of war, the farther he went from himself.' He is so far lost, moreover, that he accepts with the automatism of the lost the leadership of the first soldier he meets. That this leadership carries him along to become the hunter-slayer, to perform acts of meaningless horror and uncaring violence which in turn take him to wanton killing under the leadership that is interested in nothing else—this, inevitably, is the story of all the lost, anywhere, who are so far gone that they take the first leader who utters a command, without thinking (or wanting to think) what they do.

"Mr. Downey does not forget, either, to show the momentary doubt of the lost, the momentary single chance to resist, to withdraw, the chance that is gone in a split second of irresolution, leaving the lost no choice: 'He turned and followed his leader.' Best of all Mr. Downey knows what is felt by the lost as they begin to sense what has happened to them when they turned to follow the 'beast that walks alone, that—among all the animals of the forest and in the meeting of its kind—is yet alone, the stalker of secret places, the hunter.'

"He comes to the heart of it when he writes, 'Private Meadows sensed the solitariness; but he thought it was the realization of his own loneliness,' and again when Meadows finds his company after his helpless assent to and participation in the hunter-leader's dreadful act, learns finally the enormity of what he has done, and realizes that he has been separated from his fellows for only part of a day: 'But his calculation gave him no assurance. He felt that he had been separated from his comrades for a campaign of time. And this—this feeling—was his real knowledge.'

"Aside from the fact that Mr. Downey has understood exactly what he is doing, that he has constructed and written his story almost faultlessly, and that he is saying something meaningful about men and war, he has also said something that has significance for everyone living in a world which is now discovering that when you walk the terrain of war you leave yourself somewhere, you get progressively lost, and when you are lost you are ready to accept any leader who speaks with what sounds like authority.

"That Private Meadows, when he came to himself, was shaken by regret—or by the desperate knowledge, at last, of how lost he now was—did not help him. It was too late.

"I have not intended to speak of Mr. Downey's story as though it were a stern and doleful sermon. All I mean is that, writing in simple, wonderfully precise terms of a small episode in a war, he has made his story say, unmistakably, something of universal importance and say it without stumbling, forcefully and clearly. The measure of his great ability is that his story, even aside from its implications, is a moving and powerful piece of work."

Miss Hale's comment on this story was:

" 'The Hunters' is a story of far-reaching implications. One might almost think of it as an allegory of lost, regimented man, the man of good will who is nonetheless bereft of will power when separated from his own group. I think the killer-soldier the protagonist meets in the woods—with his bets on bringing down goats and parachutists —is a perfectly ghastly conception and a sound one, which carries great weight."

Mr. Van Doren did not comment specifically on the story, although he listed it among the top twelve in the collection, saying that any story in the dozen might receive a prize with no objection from him.

Of the second prize winner, Miss Welty's "The Burning," Mr. Jackson wrote:

"This story seems to me in Miss Welty's best vein, which is, of course, very good indeed. It is a perfect example of her genius for suggesting so much more than her words actually say, which is what poetry does. Indeed her use of the mirror symbol is nearly pure poetry. As she has so often done, Miss Welty catches in this story the reflection of a collapse and a promise together, the mood of ending and beginning inextricably interwoven. Her device of presenting this through Florabel the slave, 'earth's most detached visitor,' is beautifully imagined and completed. And there is fundamental and genuine wisdom in the suggestion that the strongest may be those who 'let everything be itself, according to its nature—the animate, the inanimate, the symbol,' just as there is in the concluding declaration that the one who survives the ending of a world, who goes on into tomorrow, is the one who, with whatever burned bones may be left and with direct guidance gone, is yet willing to walk straight forward across the river that must be crossed, 'not considering that she, Florabel, one life, might step too deep and the river smile and take her.'

"To discover the beauty of Miss Welty's writing, with its finely laced, rhythmic patterns of word and symbol and idea, the reader had better absorb her story directly. I came very close to putting it first in this collection; I might have done so but for my admiration and respect for Mr. Downey's control of his story and, in my own view at least, the immediacy of his theme."

Miss Hale said of the Welty story: " 'The Burning' is a perfectly fascinating story. I like it better than almost anything I have read of Eudora Welty's. But, as bits of Miss Welty's writing always remain obscure in meaning to me, so has this story got passages whose sound I can admire but which, frankly, I simply don't understand. Toward the end, when the slave girl is wondering whether to carry off the mirror, there are passages mysterious to me. Perhaps that is how a slave girl's mind works. If so, it doesn't get across to me; it's not clear, and I am only bewildered in a mesh of beautiful words."

Mr. Van Doren placed the story at the top of his list of alternate choices, but without specific comment.

The editor is aware of Miss Hale's meaning in saying that the story seems obscure, as it does on a first reading, but it comes crystal clear by the third. Miss Welty goes very far indeed in this story in the use of symbolism, farther perhaps than in any other she has done, but the seeming obscurity is entirely superficial. One must read and reread to savor the full significance of a rare example of prose-poetry, which could not have been written by anyone living —or dead—except the author herself, and this is the highest praise.

Miss Hale's choice for the capital prize was Arthur Miller's magnificent "Monte Saint Angelo," of which she wrote:

"This is a completely fascinating story and to me a profound one. The 'unconscious Jew' in it seems to me to carry implications far beyond the plot meaning, of the carrying on of tradition through an alien atmosphere and culture. I think it a truly satisfying story. It is, of course, technically superb, but I shan't comment on this aspect of my top six ('Monte Saint Angelo,' 'The Hunters,' 'Peggety's Parcel of Shortcomings,' 'The Burning,' 'Old Century's River,' and 'The House of Flowers'), since I feel that all fourteen of the best (to me) stories have the quality which is achieved by writers who have mastered technique to the point where it is an instrument only, as one doesn't bother to speak of a great concert pianist's technique any more, but only of interpretation, feeling, et cetera."

Mr. Van Doren placed Mr. Miller's story seventh in his list of alternate choices, without comment, and Mr. Jackson had nothing to say about it specifically, either. This story is a masterpiece, and well deserved a prize, except that there were not enough to go around.

Mr. Van Doren rated Mr. Capote's cheerful and colorful "The House of Flowers" first, saying:

"I put Capote first because his story is at once the richest and most beguiling of the lot—with a humor in it that reinforces rather than betrays the delicate stuff with which he deals, and brings out better than any other ingredient would have done the exotic coloring so proper to the persons and the place."

Miss Hale, placing the Capote story sixth on her list of the top choices, said: "'The House of Flowers' is absolutely enchanting. Here again is a *known* character—not in any sense of a familiar figure, Heaven knows, but *artistically* known. The story is like an arrangement in the most delightful and airy taste of strange tropical objects—flowers, feathers, bits of sparkling mica—which seduces the reader completely. The innocent amorality of the story is part of its charm—it paints a real West Indian Garden of Eden, with its naïve prostitute, Eve."

Mr. Jackson made no comment on the Capote story, which was not in his first three.

Mr. Van Doren's choice for second place was Evan Connell's highly poetical "I Came from Yonder Mountain," of which he wrote: "I put Connell second because, although he is perhaps as skillful as Capote, he has less to tell: his somewhat defective heroine takes a wonderful walk and train ride, but she *is* defective. Nevertheless I do not expect to forget her and her baby, or, for that matter, the conductor of the train." Miss Hale put the Connell in her top fourteen, without further comment, and Mr. Jackson did not mention it.

Miss Hale's choice for third prize was John Hersey's delightful "Peggety's Parcel of Shortcomings," that very rare thing, a genuinely humorous short story. She wrote of it: "This one is, of course, awfully funny and for some time I hesitated to place so high a humorous story. But I think it a lot more than that. I think the extremely delicate, understated meaning of the story is remarkable—'That package . . . was all . . . my fleshiness, my unbeatable appetite for chocolate things, and my being without learning and no friends to speak of . . . and what good was I, anyhow? And I was embracing all these things in my arms like a dear beloved friend, and smelling to high heaven of the burden.' "

Mr. Van Doren did not place the story in his top dozen, and Mr. Jackson did not comment upon it.

Mr. Van Doren's choice for third place was Esther Patt's "The Butcherbirds," of which he wrote: "I put Esther Patt third for somewhat the same reason I placed Connell second. Again we have a remarkable idea or image, presented with perfect sharpness (though sometimes with overwriting); but the pathology lessens a little the importance of what is being told."

Miss Hale listed the Patt story among her top fourteen, all of which she thought of "A-1 quality," with this comment: " 'The Butcherbirds' is good and sensitive. I may be a prejudiced judge of this story, for I have an inescapable fatigue about stories of people's childhoods (even imaginary childhoods), which takes an awful lot of good writing to overcome."

This prejudice of Miss Hale is shared by both the editor and his assistant, the assistant feeling very strongly on the subject, but they both thought extremely well of Miss Patt's story. Her earlier story, "The Espalier," which appeared in the *American Mercury* was also excellent, and there is no doubt that she has exceptional talent.

Mr. Jackson placed Peggy Love's very appealing "The Jersey Heifer" third, with this comment:

" 'The Jersey Heifer' I have chosen because of its joyful—and also thoughtful—affirmation of the principle of acceptance. The author is fully aware that although 'the serpent is in the garden all the time,' the garden is still the garden—is all the garden that there is, and must be accepted whole, with the knowledge that the responsibility may not be evaded, no matter how one may struggle to justify or rationalize the evasion. This is a truth that does not grow old, and Mrs. Love has here restated it with freshness and beauty and conviction, and with a simplicity in the writing which does not conceal the underlying firmness and precision with which the theme is developed."

Miss Hale said of the Love story: "Really quite good. Almost in my top fourteen. Again it is a tinge of sentimentality which hurts it for me. Though I must say the picture of the jaunty heifer trapped and dying in the loft haunts me. This is one of the stories one feels one may be wrong about." The editor thinks Miss Hale is wrong, but he gladly admits that his own strong feeling for the story might very well have been colored by his early life on a stock farm, which made the experience unusually vivid to him. Mr.

Van Doren, himself a part-time farmer, did not place the story among his top twelve.

Among Mr. Van Doren's favorites, a judgment with which the editor and his assistant agree, was Oliver La Farge's remarkable "Old Century's River." Miss Hale placed it second in her list of alternate choices, with this comment: "I think 'Old Century's River' is one of the best *tales* I have ever read. It's got power and vitality and economy which are most impressive—a story where everything is so well-*known* that the story becomes vicarious experience. It is first-rate character drawing—the man is known and understood and wholly true."

Frank Rooney's "Cyclists' Raid" is a perfectly executed piece of work, glowing with technical skill of the highest degree. Miss Hale said of it: "This was another that I came close to putting at the top. I think the picture of mounting mass hysteria is tremendous. It, like my top three, has overtones of universal meaning. It is also beautifully done. If there were a fourth place, I should give it to this story." Mr. Jackson also rated it fourth, and again the editor deeply regrets that there are not enough prizes to go around. Mr. Van Doren gave the story ninth place in his top dozen.

Mr. Jackson placed James B. Hall's "In the Time of Demonstrations" fifth without comment, and Miss Hale said of it: "Another good story, with good feeling, but I thought it slight for its length." Mr. Van Doren omitted it from his top twelve, but the editor rates it well up among the best stories in the book, and considers it especially important as sure evidence of the appearance of another new talent of real promise and significance.

This completes the list of stories singled out for particular attention by the three judges, with the exception of Miss Hale's remarks on the following:

"'A Name for the City.' This is a fine example of Faulkner's wonderful private Americana. I don't know who else can create this feeling of the primitive backwoods past so vividly that the story is like something one has heard of one's own ancestors—*much* realer than historical reality. I think I would have placed this story up at the top except for its lacking elements of the 'exhibition story,' such as characterization. It is not really a short story, it is a legend." Neither Mr. Van Doren nor Mr. Jackson mentioned the Faulkner story.

Miss Hale continued: "'Sense of Direction.' A good story, but I think it has some fancy writing which hurts it. 'Homecoming.' This story, which for the most part seemed to me perilously near trash (saving your presence), has, however, an exceedingly good and valid ending."

Here the editor must disagree again with Miss Hale. He found "Homecoming" very far from even approaching trash, but rather a convincing and credible treatment of the universal problem of divorce and its frightening consequences. The story is too long for what it does, but it has great honesty and, as Miss Hale says, a particularly good ending. She adds, on this point: "A great number of even the best of the collection seem to me to have poor endings. Of course writing a good ending is as hard as drawing a good ear." Or a good hand, considering how few painters in the whole history of art have been successful with this telltale member, and none has equaled the Cretan-Spaniard El Greco, whose hands are veritable poems. The editor's assistant agreed with Miss Hale about "Homecoming."

Of "The Shadow of an Arm" Miss Hale wrote: "A good story, very touching, but it suffers from an effect of sentimentality which is really sound sentiment. The effect is unfortunate and not really the author's fault."

And of Carson McCullers' "The Sojourner": "I was very much disappointed in this story. It seemed to me that Mrs. McCullers was writing in a sort of slick, popular vein not characteristic of her at all. It's a good enough idea for a story (although a difficult one to make lucid) but I think it has been handled in an easy, almost flashy, way."

As much as the editor has always admired Mrs. McCullers' work, with the exception of "Reflections in a Golden Eye," a distasteful adventure in the purely pathological, he does not believe he was at all influenced by this in choosing "The Sojourner." These differences of opinion mean no more, of course, than that people disagree about short stories, as they most certainly do, often violently and vociferously.

Mr. Van Doren gave Jean Stafford's "A Country Love Story" second place on his list of alternates, without comment, and Miss Hale wrote of it: "This one has a lot of good stuff in it, and I remember liking it in *The New Yorker*. But on rereading I found myself confused by it. As subtle a meaning as this must be, somehow, made crystal clear (I don't mean obvious). The strong point, to me, of this story is that it is intensely feminine without being in the least a 'woman's story.'" The editor's assistant agreed with Miss Hale about the confusion in the story, leaving the editor alone in his opinion that the meaning is clear, and, more than that, the story the best thing Miss Stafford has yet written.

In addition to the stories already discussed, Miss Hale's fourteen "best" included John Cheever's "The Pot of Gold," a particular favorite of the editor's assistant too. Miss Hale also mentioned Robie Macauley's "The Invaders" and R. E. Thompson's "It's a Nice Day—Sunday," a prize winner in *Tomorrow's* College Contest. There have been too many stories about abnormal mental conditions recently, but Mr. Thompson does his tragedy very delicately, using muted strings, and the effect is quite powerful. Mr. Macauley and Mr. Thompson are two more of the new people who will be heard from in the future.

It seems curious that the Faulkner story did not receive more attention from the judges, granting that certain of this writer's most involved passages, if committed by anyone else, would deservedly be called just plain bad writing. The point about Mr. Faulkner's interminable sentences, which meander like one of his own Mississippi rivers, is that they do pile up effects in a manner reminiscent of Marcel Proust's more graceful arabesques. In other words, Mr. Faulkner is so gifted as to be able to break all the rules of style and to get away with it. Perhaps, as Miss Hale said of the story, it is really a legend, but if so it is a very good legend indeed, and who else except Mississippi's Nobel prize winner can create legends today? The answer is easy, Nobody.

Mr. Faulkner's story is of particular historical importance because it is concerned with the naming of Jefferson, the county seat of that mythical—and legendary—Mississippi county of Yoknapatawpha, the only creation of the kind achieved by a novelist in the whole history of American fiction, and incomparably the most complete. Several years ago, it was said in an O. Henry Introduction that Mr. Faulkner might very well turn out to be the most important novelist we have ever produced, and the only revision of this somewhat daring opinion that seems appropriate now is to remove any qualifying phrases. In other words, the editor firmly believes that Mr. Faulkner *is* the most important writer of fiction this country has yet produced.

Measured against the other two Nobel awards, those to Pearl Buck and Sinclair Lewis, Mr. Faulkner's stature looms as nothing short of titanic (we might toss in a few other novelists of Mr. Faulkner's generation without weakening his pre-eminent position).

This year, as has happened occasionally in the past, but never before to such a striking degree, a large number of first-rate stories had to be omitted because there is a limit to the size of this volume. Some may even say that better stories were left out than were included, and the only possible answer would be that choices must be made, no matter how arbitrary they may sometimes seem.

Several of the best stories of the year were omitted because of their length, which really put them in the category of the long short story, another literary classification from the short story. Three of these were Ray West, Jr.'s, "The Last of the Grizzly Bears" from *Epoch;* Caroline Gordon's "The Waterfall" from the *Sewanee Review;* and James Waffe's "Poor Cousin Evelyn" from the *Atlantic,* and now to be found in a volume of Mr. Waffe's excellent stories, called by the same title. The long stories of Mr. West and Miss Gordon will both appear, or may have already appeared, in Martha Foley's annual *The Best Short Stories,* and both deserved anthologizing.

Mr. West, who knows as much about the short story as anyone living, has written his best piece in his tale of the vanished grizzlies, with its acute comment on the change of character of the enemies of Man.

Also among the fine long stories was "The Road Home" by Margaret Lowery, from Mr. West's the *Western Review,* published at the University of Iowa, and the work of a talented new writer who is certain to be further heard from. The same magazine published David Sommers' "The Emperor of Ice Cream," which was on the final list of selections until the very last moment, and which was certainly good enough to rate inclusion even in an anthology of the high quality of this one. It is a sadly humorous piece about European exiles in the United States, and will not soon be forgotten by those who have read it. Mr. Sommers is another of the most gifted of the younger writers of short stories.

Kay Boyle's stories of occupied Germany, including such striking pieces as "Cabaret," which appeared in *Tomorrow,* were omitted because Miss Boyle, who has appeared here many times as a prize winner and otherwise, seemed more interested in a kind of super-reporting, which she does magnificently, one must admit, than in writing short stories. "Cabaret" is included in Miss Boyle's current volume, *The Smoking Mountain,* which is all about occupied Germany.

Other admirable stories that were left out included Wallace Stegner's "The Traveler" from *Harper's* for February of the present year; "Little Nolly's Blues" by Freeman Phillips from the *American Mercury* for March: James Cook's "Pastoral" from the *Mercury* for April; "Lady's Bet" by Hubert Saal, from *Town and Country* for May 1950, an excellent story by a new writer; and Elizabeth Coatsworth's "The Circle" and Esther McCoy's "High Heels" from *The Southwest Review* for the summer of 1950. Also, Susan Kuehn's "The Searchers" from *Harper's*, Miss Kuehn's only two previous stories having both appeared in this collection. All these stories, one repeats, were left out for no better reason than that those selected were liked a little better.

THE 1951 COLLECTION

While the judges have been comfortingly kind year after year in commenting upon the merit of the collections as a whole, 1951 marks the first year when all three of the members of the panel have agreed upon the outstandingly high quality of the anthology. Two of them, Miss Hale and Mr. Jackson, veterans at judging short stories, called the collection "the best yet," and Mr. Van Doren said: "I found the collection, down through Number Twelve, vivid and impressive. Each of these stories has a hard, bright kernel of idea or insight, and the development in every case is harmonious with the subject matter, so that the resulting whole will be difficult to forget."

Here is Mr. Jackson's highly optimistic comment:

"My feeling about this collection is that it constitutes the best yet put together for the annual Memorial in all the years I have been reading. Certainly the level is the highest of any of the three volumes —this is the third in sixteen years—that I have helped to judge. That this is true of the technical ability shown is obvious at the first reading; each writer in this list of twenty-four has looked squarely at his or her story problem, has taken pains to comprehend it, work it out, cut away extraneous matter, shape the story, make it do what it is intended to do. This is the proper task of any short-story writer, naturally. But the degree of competence here is plainly much greater than it has been over the years.

"As to reasons why, I do not believe that it is simply because there has been more instruction available, as some have recently suggested. True, there are more 'writing centers' at universities and colleges than ever before; there are the many fiction-writing conferences, and there is more individual teaching in the field of creative writing. Nevertheless I think there is another factor and an important one. I believe there is a new kind of editor at large in the magazine world in the last few years, a kind of editor who is not interested primarily in the various levels of technique or in showy ways with words, but instead prefers to look for maturity and responsibility in the writers whose work comes under his eye. Even the most dazzling display of virtuosity is not enough for this kind of editor. As a consequence in the magazines they edit there are fewer stories that depend chiefly upon such display. In this collection there is only one, and I have not included it among my first five, ably as it is written.

"If this notion has any validity, it accounts in considerable measure for the fact that more magazines are printing more stories that are not only well handled but have something worth saying and say it clearly.

"Along with this, too, the newer kind of editor does not shy away from what I can describe only as the short story that is also poetry. Two examples of what I mean by this are Eudora Welty's "The Burning" and James B. Hall's "In the Time of Demonstrations," evoking quite different moods, but both highly poetic nevertheless. To be sure, if stories like these were not being written editors would not be printing them; but what I am getting at is that even a dozen years ago they might very well have been written, yet found no willing editor.

"I do not wish to labor this aspect of it too strongly, though. Better stories are being printed and that is the point. The once familiar preoccupation with the trick-for-its-own-sake or with handsome writing for its own sake is vanishing. What we are getting, as collections like this amply demonstrate, is the short story written out of a probing, thoughtful, eager interest in life and how people live it, in problems and how people meet them, and especially in the significance in general terms of the problem-in-particular.

"John Donne's 'bell tolls for thee' has become a cliché, true; nevertheless the principle has now become automatically a part of the good short-story writer's way of looking at his material, and to a greater degree, I think, than ever before. Nor has this approach become an 'ism' for the short-story writer, at least not yet.

"Among the stories in this volume, an overwhelming proportion are mature, responsible evaluations of the world their writers see, each for himself. Not to be too solemn about it, the short-story writer today is no longer interested in vaudeville, as even the very best, many of them, used to be. And that is all to the good, especially if, as I think, editors have played a large part in bringing about the change."

Miss Hale wrote: "I found these stories for the most part of such high order that it was with the greatest difficulty that I was able to make judgments upon them. I am really excited by there being so many wonderful stories, and since I have reviewed the O. Henry collection for several years past, I can only say that I think this year's bunch is the best I've read as a whole."

Looking at this year's stories from the point of view of geographical origin, the most striking thing about them is that of the three prize winners, two, Messrs. Downey and Capote, are from Louisiana, and the third, Miss Welty, is from Mississippi. In times past the editor has joked, a little feebly, he suspects, about such matters, since he himself began life in Mississippi, as did Dr. Blanche Colton Williams. But the judges awarded the prizes, and they are, respectively, from New England, the Middle West, and the Pacific Coast.

What has happened is merely another striking example of how far the Deep South has come in the years since Henry L. Mencken let off his thundering blast about "the Sahara of the Bozarts" in the twenties and apparently aroused the ex-Confederates to frantic activity. They did not even pause to give the Rebel yell before going into action with pen and typewriter and now the war seems to be pretty well won, with Mr. Faulkner wearing the proud laurels of the Nobel Prize Committee.

Eight of the total of twenty-four stories were written by Southerners, or exactly one third. Seven were written by Middle Westerners and seven by Easterners, if one includes in the latter category John Hersey, who lives now in New York, but who was born in China. The other two are by Far Westerners. Fifteen of the writers included are making their first appearance in the O. Henry, which is about the usual proportion, and most of these are young people just embarking upon their literary careers. Seventeen of the contributors are men, including two prize winners, when some years the women have won all the awards.

Veterans of World War II include Messrs. Connell, Hall, Downey, Smith, Macauley, Casper, Phillips, Rooney, and Thompson. Teachers of literature, or specifically of writing, include Messrs. Hall, Phillips, Downey, Casper, Macauley, and Culver. Mr. Rooney is the only one of the group without a formal education, and many of the others have taken courses in short-story writing. Messrs. Hall, Downey, Macauley, and Casper are poets, and of course Mr. Faulkner began his career as a poet, which he still is in the larger sense of the word.

HAPPY HUNTING GROUNDS

The best places to look for good stories do not change very much from year to year. This year, for example, the *Atlantic Monthly* supplied three stories, *Harper's Magazine* three, and *Mademoiselle* the same number, with one prize winner, Mr. Capote's "The House of Flowers." Mr. Capote's first O. Henry story, "Miriam," also came from *Mademoiselle,* while his 1948 first prize winner "Shut a Final Door" appeared in the *Atlantic.* Magazines supplying two stories included *Epoch,* published at Cornell University, from which was taken Mr. Downey's first prize winner, *Tomorrow,* and *The New Yorker. Harper's Bazaar* published the Welty story.

From the *Western Review* came "In the Time of Demonstrations," and this magazine also supplied several very strong runners-up. One story came from *The Southwest Review,* the fiction in which has greatly improved recently, and the rest of the twenty-four came, one each, from the now-defunct *Flair,* the *American Mercury,* the *Yale Review,* the *Pacific Spectator, The Virginia Quarterly,* and *Charm. Charm's* fiction also showed a noteworthy upward tendency during the past year.

Thus the literary quarterlies were the source of seven stories, including the first prize winner, while the monthlies supplied fifteen, with two prize winners, and a weekly, *The New Yorker,* the remaining two. The *Prairie Schooner* published many good stories in the period covered and there were several noteworthy ones in the *New Mexico Quarterly.* It will be observed that the "big slicks" are missing from the list, and the reason is their fairly rigid adherence to formula, although *Collier's* publishes interesting stories quite frequently at present, the best in their class from the point of view of artistic merit.

Flair, with its eccentric make-up, provided material for many anecdotes, one of the best being the remark of an author who, on meeting a friend, said: "I had a short story in this month's *Flair,* but it dropped out." *Flair* published some excellent fiction, however, during its brief lifetime, and has been missed.

THE SHORT-STORY SCENE

The present position of the short story may be quickly summarized by saying that this form of fiction is in a highly flourishing condition artistically, with the anthology that follows offered as convincing evidence. The only fly in the ointment is that writing good short stories is far more likely to earn *kudos* than cash, since the market for this type of work is rigidly restricted and the prices paid range upward from exactly nothing in some literary magazines to about enough to keep an average family in groceries for two weeks, given the existing inflation, from the more opulent journals. The "little magazines," such as *Epoch* and the *Western Review,* cannot pay much, and neither can, or do, the other quarterlies, even those which enjoy subsidies from universities or colleges. Also, the total number of stories that can find places in the quarterlies is inevitably severely limited. Perhaps the market for quality stories might reach three hundred a year, but the figure is probably high rather than low. Also little magazines are already running into financial difficulties because of the high cost of everything.

In other words, the only way to make money directly from writing short stories is to master one of the familiar formulae and ring a few changes upon it, but not too many. The number-one formula, of course, remains that old, old biological-romantic one in which the Boy gets the You-Know-What, or vice versa, thus guaranteeing the survival of the human race and, incidentally, of the short story.

This year's collection, distinguished as it is in all respects, is especially notable for the large number of affirmative and cheerful stories it contains, the largest number this editor can remember. Short-story writers do not seem to believe the world is going to hell in a handbasket, at least not before the next issue of their favorite quarterly appears. This is even more remarkable because the tragic short story is easier to do than the cheerful one, since tragedy has a stronger and more direct impact than yea-saying. There is in the present volume one very funny story, an event of the first magnitude, since the editor can count on the fingers of one hand, forgetting the thumb, the number of humorous stories he has selected in eleven years. One would hardly have expected John Hersey, in the light of his fine serious novels and his classical report on Hiroshima, to turn up as a rare humorist. He has also written a story which, as Miss Hale said, fulfills all the other artistic requirements, particularly that of sharp characterization.

As this is being written, the Book-of-the-Month Club is offering for a current dividend *The Collected Stories of A. E. Coppard,* one of the all-time English masters of the brief narrative, which indicates a belief on the part of the canny people who run this famous institution that there are readers for first-class short stories. And in a fine article by Ray West, Jr., "The Craft of the Short Story: 1951," published in the *Western Review,* of which Mr. West was the founder, and still is the editor after fifteen years, he makes the statement that there are at present more volumes of collected short stories in print than at any other time in history. This is correct, beyond question. One of these is the *Collected Stories of William Faulkner,* which received the National Book Council's award for fiction last spring, and which has also been a book-club choice.

Some of the other collections include William Carlos Williams' *Make Light of It;* Mary McCarthy's *Cast a Cold Eye;* Walter Van Tilburg Clark's *The Watchful Gods and Other Stories,* several of which have appeared in this collection; Paul Bowles's *The Delicate Prey and Other Stories,* which also contains some O. Henry choices, as does Irwin Shaw's *Mixed Company* and Wallace Stegner's *The Women on the Wall.* Also, Mark Van Doren's *The Short Stories of Mark Van Doren,* one of which, "The Watchman," won an O. Henry award in 1949.

In addition to these there is James Farrell's *An American Dream Girl,* Mr. Farrell never having made the O. Henry because the editor does not think he is a good short-story writer, nor a very good novelist, either, for that matter. A number of critical anthologies are available, including *The Art of Modern Fiction,* edited by Mr. West and Robert Wooster Stallman, an exceptionally valuable anthology with critical analyses of short stories and novels; *The House of Fiction,* edited by Allen Tate and Caroline Gordon; Mark Schorer's *The Story;* and Robert B. Heilman's *Modern Short Stories.* Among the annual collections is *Stanford Short Stories,* edited by Mr. Stegner and Richard Scowcroft, with analyses of each story by their authors. Included in these volumes, published 1946–1950, with the exception of 1947 and 1948, are four stories that have appeared in the O. Henry, one of them, "Rest Camp on Maui" by Eugene Burdick, having been awarded second prize in 1947. The others were by Evan Connell, Jr., Clay Putman, and Donald Justice, and Mr. Putman's "The Old Acrobat and the Ruined City" (1950) was republished in Miss Foley's *Best Short Stories.* Knox Burger's *Collier's Best* contains an excellent introduction by a successful fiction editor, and many readable stories.

Mr. West continues his study with the interesting statement that he thinks "we can say the present-day story stems from James and Chekov, modified by Joyce and Kafka." He goes on: "Behind these four figures stand others as various as Poe, Hawthorne, and Melville in America; Goethe and Tieck in Germany; Gogol, Turgenev, and Dostoevski in Russia; Mérimée, Gautier, Maupassant, Flaubert, Daudet, and Zola in France; Scott and Kipling in England. Behind these stand a long line of tale tellers reaching four thousand years into history." Better make it six thousand years to be on the safe side, although just the other day bones of *homo sapiens* going back 75,000 years were found in Iran, and where man was, there were tale tellers.

Further comment from Mr. West bears directly upon the present O. Henry, in which the stories have form, quite definitely. He wrote: "By 'form' I do not mean the well-wrought miniature, the superficial limitations of structure, I mean the inclusion, by one means or another, of social density—firmness of tissue as well as the fine delineation of outline. The best of our modern short stories have it: Hemingway's 'The Short and Happy Life of Francis McComber,' Porter's 'Flowering Judas' and 'Pale Horse, Pale Rider,' Warren's 'Blackberry Winter.' . . . William Faulkner has it in the greatest abundance, and this is undoubtedly the final measure of his present importance as a writer of short stories."

Eudora Welty also has it, as anyone may observe by reading "The Burning," and it seems to the editor that Miss Welty and Mr. Faulkner are incomparably the present American masters of the short story. As for Mr. West's collection of "influences," he seems to err on the side of the all-inclusive. The truth, it seems to this commentator, is that the long shadow of the recluse of Salem, Hawthorne, falls across all the good short stories written in this country at present, with Chekov and Mansfield also in the background. But what we have done is to take Chekov and Mansfield at their best and improve upon them by this achievement of form of which Mr. West has spoken so penetratingly.

Once more it seems apropos to mention the unmistakable relationship of the short story to the lyric poem, or more particularly to the ballad. Mr. Van Doren, asked for comment on the point, since he is both a poet and a short-story writer, replied, very wisely: "The poem and the short story, yes; but neither should be *poetical*, and many contemporary writers make this mistake in both fields. The analogy is between the short story and the short poem, but it is wrong in this connection to mean by the short poem the lyric poem. That is where *poeticalness* comes from.

"The short story should be a little epic, or possibly a little drama, but never a lyric, if lyric suggests the static or merely stated. At its highest, lyric means something narrative or dramatic too; but we don't always find it at its highest. In verse as well as prose it too often degenerates into mere writing and attitudinizing. So with some of *these* (referring to some of the stories in the present O. Henry), and so with most of the things I read nowadays. A great short story is exactly what the name implies: a great little story. But it better be a story, just as a lyric poem had better be something like a story, too, in the last analysis."

Mr. Van Doren has said exactly what needed to be said on the relationship between the short story and the short poem, or, for that matter, what needs to be said every day about any kind of writing in the creative field. It was Goethe who said you had to have something to say when you wrote prose, but that with lyric poetry it didn't much matter. Of course it does matter, if the Sage of Weimar would not mind having one of his multitudinous dicta questioned. He was obviously smiling when he said it, anyway. . . .

The book of the year on the short story that the editor most enjoyed was Sean O'Faolain's *The Short Story,* and he regrets not being able to say more about it. Mr. O'Faolain thinks the Irish and the Americans write the best short stories, a sound judgment. His list of the most interesting modern short-story writers includes Joyce, Moore, O'Flaherty, Bowen, O'Connor, Dunsany, Bates, Coppard, Pritchett, Hemingway, Saroyan, Lardner, Steinbeck, and Welty, which gives the Irish six to our five, but with Faulkner thrown in, where he belongs, we would have an even break with the Gaels. Unless, that is, we add Mr. O'Faolain's own name to the Irish list, a deserved honor, but if we did we could match it with several of our own writers, so we would still be on an equal footing with the Irish, if not ahead of them. (Kay Boyle, Katherine Anne Porter, et al. . . .)

WHY ARE WE HERE?

As for the reason we have arrived at what looks like a high and extensive plateau in the art of the short story, the editor believes the existence of so many good courses in creative writing, most of them given by creative artists of the caliber of Messrs. Stegner, West, and a number of others, and of so many writers' conferences where the teaching is again in the hands of writers, not mere professors, may very well be the explanation.

At least it can be proved by *post hoc, propter hoc,* which one admits is not invariably a safe formula. But the simple fact is that the courses and the conferences do exist, and so does the striking, not to say sensational, rise, in the average quality of the current artistic story. There *are* many open-minded and discriminating editors, as Mr. Jackson has said, and these are essential, but their fortunate existence is hardly enough to explain what is now happening to the short story.

Reading the stories in the May magazines for 1951 is sufficient evidence that the high quality of this year's O. Henry is not in any sense accidental or fortuitous.

The future of the short story seems perfectly secure, and since at its best short fiction is a valid and vital commentary on life, there is reason to rejoice.

As usual, the editor wishes to thank magazine editors, literary agents, and many others, including readers scattered over the country, for their unstinting help in making this book a worthy memorial to O. Henry. The comments of all, favorable or otherwise, are welcomed and sincerely appreciated.

Herschel Brickell

ACORN COTTAGE
RIDGEFIELD, CONN.
MAY 16, 1951

from Epoch

THE HUNTERS

HARRIS DOWNEY *appeared in the O. Henry collection two years ago with "The Mulhausen Girls," one of his first published stories. Born and brought up in Baton Rouge, Louisiana, he was educated at Louisiana State University and New York University. He is now assistant professor of English at L.S.U. He served four years with the Air Corps in World War II, principally in the European theater. In addition to his short stories, he has published poetry and critical articles in a number of magazines.*

Private Meadows was lost. He had no idea which way his outfit had gone, had ever intended to go.

They were moving into France from the north. Naturally, their progress would be to the south. But during their fighting from Cherbourg they had moved in all directions. He did not know how long it had been since they left Cherbourg—three weeks, four weeks. It was some long, undeterminable stretch of time. Nor did he know how many miles they had come—forty, fifty, maybe two hundred. They had come through villages—slowly, ferreting snipers from the ruins that their own artillery made. Someone had named the names of the villages but he had not understood. He had asked the names again and again, feeling that he should establish something familia. ___ : memory, feeling that he might come to understand where he was going, what he was doing. But between question and answer he would fall back into the torpor that his life had been since Cherbourg. The answer, like a fragment slanting a helmet, would strike his mind obliquely and deflect away into the noisy and flashing anonymity of war.

He had traversed plow-furrowed fields when silence, imminent

Copyright, 1950, by Epoch Associates.

1

with violence, weighted him down like a pack. He had traversed shell-pelleted fields when fear tangled his legs like a barricade. He had seen his enemy and his comrades sprawled grotesque and cold in the neutrality of death, as impersonal as the cows among them, angling stiff legs to the sky. He had thrown grenades at hidden men; and once, staring into wide, stark eyes down the bead of his aim, he had sighed out his breath toward a union more intimate than love—and more treacherous than its denial. He had seen a dog, tethered at the gate, howl at the noise of destruction and die in terror; had seen bees swarm from their hives at the ground shake of cannon and hang in the air, directionless. He had seen Frenchmen return to their villages to gesticulate the glory of victory and, sobering, to peer from behind a silly grin at the rubbish that had been their homes. But these things had not touched him. He had left himself somewhere, and the farther he walked the terrain of war, the farther he went from himself.

He heard the spasmodic eruptions of war. He listened to silence hissing like the quick fuse of a bomb. Yet he felt nothing—unless it was weariness. He walked under the high fire of artillery as though it were a canopy against the rain. At first he had been unhappy and afraid; and perhaps, in the static musing, in the constant but unapprehended memory that was himself, he was yet unhappy and afraid.

Casually walking, talking to his friends, or running, crawling, squirming on his belly, looking ahead for cover, he had followed his leaders from sector to sector. The sun had come up on his left, on his right, from behind him, had sheered through the odd geometry of fields and had slid down the high summer clouds behind him, in front of him—always in a new tangent to the hedgerow. Twelve times, twenty times. How many times had he seen the sun point a surprising direction that was the west?

That morning he had seen the sun come up in the direction they were to move. Lying against the massed roots, he had looked through an opening of the hedgerow over a pasture that ran a quarter of a mile to a woods.

There near the woods he saw a farmhouse with spindly trees growing around it like a fence. He lay still, watching the sun slip above the treetops. To the right of him lay Barr, a replacement who had

2

been in the company only a week or so, a talkative fellow who some-how managed to hold his happiness and his identity about him. Be-yond Barr lay Pederson, whose twin brother had been wounded in his first skirmish and sent back. To the left of him was Harrod, whom Private Meadows had been with since induction. And beyond Harrod was Walton, a slow-talking, card-playing soldier who had come in with Barr. These men were his friends; by virtue of their position in the squad, they were his friends.

All along the row men lay with their heads in their helmets. Soon, from somewhere behind him, an order would be given and everyone would begin to move. But he would not comprehend the order. Even when it was passed on to him and he in turn passed it on, he would not consider its meaning. He had given up trying to understand words—orders, directions, cautions. He moved and lived in a channel of sounds, but his mind took them in as involuntarily as his lungs breathed the air. It was his eyes that activated him. He watched his leaders and his comrades. He followed. He did what they did. He listened acutely and unendingly but never accepted the meaning of sound. Consciously, he heard only silence—that dead silence which makes one feel that he has gone deaf.

As he looked through the hedgerow at the sun, he began to hear the silence gather. Even the men behind him, the lieutenant, the sergeants, had become silent. He could feel the silence creep along the hedgerow, turning the heads of his comrades. The sun, having cleared the trees, seemed to stick in the silence. The silence grew heavy. He could feel it on his back pressing him against the earth. The grass in the field was still, as though the silence were barrier against the wind. The silence swelled, grew taut, then violently burst.

It was the artillery from his own lines. The barrage was steady and strong. From beyond the woods the fire was returned, its shells fall-ing short in the field. The cows in the field had lifted their heads and now stood as still as stone. Two horses from the farmyard thundered across the level terrain. A fox bounding from the woods reached the clearing and raced round in a circle.

Private Meadows pulled his head away from the opening of the hedgerow and leaned back against the embankment of roots. His unit began to move down the hedgerow. He followed, on his hands and knees, dragging the butt of his rifle.

3

When they came to the end of the row, they bounded into the woods at the south. There in the woods they dispersed and moved to the east. It was there in the woods that he got lost. He had followed the others for a time and then, of a sudden, he was alone. The artillery had stopped. It was the silence that called him to consciousness. He walked on, listening. He could hear nothing but the crackle of twigs under his feet. There was no firing even in the distance. And but for the noise he himself made, the woods were quiet—no wind in the trees, no birds even. He sat down, leaned against the trunk of a tree, crossed his piece over his thighs, his finger on the trigger, and waited. He waited for a sound.

He had expected that other men would come from the direction he had come. But somewhere, skirting the trees, he must have got out of the line of advance, for no men came.

The woods were eerie. It seemed that all the men had walked off into another world, leaving him alone. He didn't like the silence. He got up and began to walk, taking a direction half left to the one that brought him to his silent place. He came to a cart path. But he would not enter it. He stayed in the woods, keeping the path in sight, following it; it was angling him again to the left. He walked slowly, cautiously, wondering whether he were approaching the enemy line. The woods were thick and dark. Each tree was watching him, listening to the sounds he made. Each step was a deepening into fear. It was not the sort of fear he knew under fire. There he was scared, but this was a worse fear—unrelenting and conscious.

He hardly moved at all, putting one foot carefully before him and looking about, listening with all his body to the silence, before he brought the other foot forward. Then he stopped still, like a man yelled into a brace. He had heard a voice. His heartbeat pounded the silence. Then, directionless, whispered, he heard distinctly: "Hey." It was an American word, he guessed. But German snipers used American words as traps. He started to walk on, and then a little louder this time: "Hey." The word spiraled through the silence like a worm in wood. He halted again. He was afraid to turn. He dared not lift his rifle. Whoever called had a bead on him. Tentatively he put a foot forward, took a step. "Hey." He was playing with him as a cat does a rat, teasing him before he put the bullet in his back or between his eyes, waiting for him to make some particular move—

to run, or turn, or lift his rifle, or gaze up into the barrel tracing him.

His enemy was all around him, saw him at every angle. He stood motionless, as though immobility forestalled the shot. He felt the sweat burst on his forehead. He was weak. In his memory he reviewed the sound, trying to divine its direction; and the voice came again. While he was listening to the voice in his memory, it came again, confusing him: "Hey there." It came from all sides of him, the voice of the forest itself. "Put down your gun." The command was clear and slow—behind him. He lowered his rifle to the ground, stepped backward, waited. "Turn aroun'." He turned slowly, holding his breath. He saw no one.

He watched the trunks of trees, expecting a head—and a gun—to slip round into the open. "Where you goin', bud?" At the foot of a tree to his left oblique, partly concealed under a bush, sat a man on his haunches, leaning forward on his rifle. It was an American: the helmet, the green jacket. "Whatcha scared of, bud?" The man stretched a foot forward and rose clear of the brush.

Private Meadows stood still. Was it a joke? He rather expected others to appear from the forest—from out of the brush, from behind the trees; expected all his lost comrades to appear from the silence that had swallowed them. He wondered whether he had not been lost in meditation; whether, as he followed his comrades through the trees, he had not fallen into a fearful dream and was now emerging into reality as one of his friends shook his shoulder, urging him on. He had been hypnotized by his fear. He wanted to cry but was too much exhausted to cry. The man standing before him, touching his shoulder with a thick, hairy hand, was strange. He and the man were alone. And the silence was real. "Come out of it, bud." But the man was not concerned. A grin stretched over his fat face like a painted mouth stretching over a tight balloon. He was enjoying the joke he had played. "Whatcha doin' here, soldier?" The voice was as cold as authority.

"I got lost," Private Meadows said.

Then the voice was as hooligan as persecution: "That's misbehavior before the enemy. They'd hang you for that. That's desertion."

Private Meadows didn't know the ensign of the man before him. Nor did he attempt to surmise it. It would be whatever the manner suggested it to be. In the man's manner there was some kind of

5

authority. So Private Meadows answered with the only defense he knew: "I was lost."

"Me too," the man said. "*I'm* lost."

The man pointed to the gun on the ground. Private Meadows picked it up. Then he looked at the man squarely. Vaguely in his mind were the questions: *Why did you make me put it down? Why did you scare me?* But he never uttered them. They hung wordless in his mind, expressed only as the straight, surprised, and momentary stare. Then they faded into his real being, that shadowy, remote musing, progressively growing dark since Cherbourg—and inaccessible. He looked off, into the direction he had been walking. "What are we gonna do?" he asked.

The man walked forward. His answer was a command: "Take it easy—till we know what's up."

Private Meadows put his arm through the sling, settled his rifle behind his shoulder, and followed. He was over his fright now, the weakness gone from his knees. He was safe again in the guidance of the Army.

He saw the broad round shoulders before him humping the air like an elephant's flanks and the heavy field boots scraping through the brush, flushing the silence. The noise of their progress was to Private Meadows an easeful shelter, like a low roof on a rainy night. Then there was the burst of a cannon—the slamming of a door in the giant structure of war, shattering the silence of the endless chambers that, for a moment, Private Meadows had forgot.

"A eighty-eight," the man said. They had both stopped at the cannon burst, had looked at each other and then in the direction of the sound. The burst came again, then again, as they stood motionless, listening. Then came the sound of rifle fire, pelleting the continuing bursts of the cannon. "Well, now we know where we are." The man spoke softly, his head, poked forward on the thick neck, malling up and down—a mechanical ram impelled by words. "Let's go," he said. He changed the direction nearly full right. They came to a dirt road. "You been on that road?" he asked. Private Meadows shook his head. "Must be mined. Or we'd be using it," the man said. "Sump'n comin'." Down the road, winding out from the trees, came a cart. They drew back, settled themselves behind a bush, and waited. The cart came slowly by, going in the direction from which they had come. A man walked beside the horse and from time to time put his hand at the bridle. In the seat of the cart was a woman holding a baby. In the back, among some baggage, sat a child, leaning her head against a mattress.

After the cart was out of sight, the two soldiers went again to the edge of the road. "Guess it ain't mined," the big one said. His eyes, nearly obscured under the net-covered helmet, were two little mice peering from under a crib. His grin was the lifting of a rake, and the mice scurried back into their holes. "Let's go," he said. He jumped the ditch and ran across the road.

Mechanically Private Meadows followed him. "Ain't we gonna try to get back?" he asked.

The man turned sharply and looked at him distrustfully. "You don't wanna go now, do you?"

"I don't know," Private Meadows said.

"We getting back, see. But we takin' the long way roun'." Private Meadows shrugged his shoulders. He was tired. The man had stuck his great round face close to his and was staring into his eyes. Private Meadows held his face against the stare but wearily closed his eyes. Sleep covered him like a breaker. His body swayed. Then he shook his head and opened his eyes. "Come on," the man said.

They walked through the woods, keeping within sight of the road. The distant rifle fire was continuous. The artillery had begun again, and from time to time a great cannon jolted all the other sounds to silence. Though they were walking oblique from the firing, Private Meadows wondered whether, on the tangent of their direction, they might not be approaching the enemy's lines. But this wonder was fleeting, like the recurrent sleep that blacked him out whenever he closed his eyes. Responsibility had gone the way of his fear; he was automaton again. He was following.

The man, who had been walking ahead, jumped to cover behind a tree, at the same time wagging a fat hand around his waist in signal to Private Meadows. Private Meadows was behind a tree almost as quickly as the man, and then, peering around, he saw the cause of alarm. A German soldier was coming toward them. He was unhelmeted, a cap pulled low over his forehead. Slung over his shoulder and hanging at his waist was a leather case. "Hey," the big man called in the whispering voice. The German was startled by the sight

7

of the man even before he heard the voice; for at the utterance he had already stopped, gazing first at the face and then at the rifle pointing from the fat round hip. "Hey," the man repeated—needlessly, for the German was standing frozen in the first attitude of shock.

Without turning his gaze from the German, the man called out to Private Meadows: "Is it clear?"

"Looks clear," Private Meadows said, shuttling his gaze among the trees.

The man approached the German until he stood within a few feet of him. "Search him," he said.

Private Meadows, holding his rifle at the waist, came beside the German, with his left hand felt the pockets of the uniform and, walking behind him, lifted the leather case from his shoulder.

"What's in it?" the man asked, still gazing at the German, thrusting the muzzle of his gun forward. The German, who had stood listless, his hands dropping to his sides after Private Meadows lifted the case from his shoulder, stared at his victor, as though in the uncomprehended words there was a new terror. Then quickly, as though guessing the meaning, he lifted his hands shoulder high in surrender. "Higher, you sonofabitch." The man motioned with the muzzle of his gun. The German understood the motion and lifted his hands above his head. "What's in it?" This time the voice was different. The German understood that the words were not for him. He cupped his hands behind his head.

"It's money," Private Meadows said. He held a handful of the bills in front of his companion.

"Christ! Kraut money," the big man said.

"It's filled with it," Private Meadows said, sliding the money back into the case.

"Where'd you get that money, bud?" the man said. The German became rigid. The terror returned to his eyes, but with it there seemed to be another feeling—of impatience, perhaps of injustice. "Where'd you steal that money, Kraut?" And at the question there came into the German's face a sense of outrage. The big man saw it. "You bastard," he said. "Can't you speak English?"

"*Nein*," the German said quickly. And he shook his head, "Nein." "Nein, nein!" The man mocked him. "You dumb bastard." He

8

lifted the muzzle of his gun and twice thrust it forward in the direction from which the German had come. "Get goin'," he said. "Vamoose." The German was doubtful. He turned his body slowly but kept shuttling his gaze from the gun to the fat, dark face above it. "Get the hell goin'." The German took a step tentatively, looked once at the fair-faced soldier who was adjusting the leather case at his waist. But in his eyes there was neither help nor corroboration—only indecision and doubt as great as his own. He started walking slowly away, his hands still cupped over his head. Then, just as he took the first step that was quicker and surer than the rest, the shot cracked through the woods. He fell forward on his face.

The big man lowered his rifle. Private Meadows, his mouth wide open, watched him open the bolt and push it forward again. He looked down at the ejected cartridge case, awesomely, as though it were a rabbit out of a hat, surprising and not quite convincing.

"Let's get the hell outa here," the man said. He walked quickly past Private Meadows.

Private Meadows looked again where the German had fallen. He saw an arm lifted, like a swimmer's in arrested motion. He saw it fall forward. He turned and followed his leader.

They came to a clearing, a series of fields surrounded by hedgerows and forming a rolling terrain.

"Better not go out there," the man said. Yet, if they followed through the woods, along the edge of the clearing, they would approach too directly the enemy line. "We gone far enough anyways." He listened to the distant crack of the rifles. He sat down and pulled his rifle over his fat legs crossed like a sawbuck. "Let's see that money." Private Meadows handed him the case and sat down beside him. The man dumped the contents on the ground. There was a tablet of forms printed in German. He tossed it away. "Musta been a pay sergeant . . . Suppose he was payin' men out on the goddamned *firin'* line?" The money was taped in seven tight bundles. "That sonofabitch was makin' way with somethin', you can bet your hat on that." He studied the numerals on the bills. He divided the money into two stacks and handed one stack to Private Meadows. He held up the case. "Want it?" Private Meadows looked at the case and then into the lariat eyes hesitantly. He shook his head. The man tossed the case beside the forms.

They both sat looking at the money in their hands. "Suppose it's any good?"

"It's German," Private Meadows said.

"Yeah, I guess so. But francs are good. We gonna get paid in francs. If ever we get paid."

"Maybe when we get to Germany——" Private Meadows said.

"Not me. I ain't go'n *get* that far," the man said. "Not me. Je-e-esus! Not me." He spread out his thick legs before him. "Look at them goats!"

In the clearing there were three goats. They had come through a break in the hedgerow or had climbed up some unnoticeable ravine, for they had not been there when the men first looked out. They neither grazed nor moved. It seemed that they were listening to the sounds of the firing.

"I'll take the one on the left," the man said. "You take the one on the right. And I'll bet you my stack of tens against it." He chunked out a bundle of the little bills.

Private Meadows spread the bundles of money fan-fashion, selected a bundle, threw it out, then turned toward the man—his look bending under the helmet to ask: *Now what?*

"We'll have to fire together or they'll be to hell and gone. Yours on the right." The man caracoled his arm into the sling and was adjusting himself to fire from the sitting position. Then Private Meadows understood.

"I . . . I don't think——" But the man was in position. Private Meadows thrust his arm through his sling quickly.

"Are you ready?"

"Say, do you think——?"

"Are you ready?"

Private Meadows jerked himself to the kneeling position and slid the gun butt into his shoulder, his face tight against the stock. He squinted his eyes as he leveled the sight. "O.K."

The man muzzled against his gun, and each of his commands was whispered in the respiration of a breath: "Ready—aim—fire."

The rifles cracked. The right goat fell, its front legs bending before it. The left goat sprang into the air, like a horse rearing, then rushed forward and crashed face first into the ground. The middle goat

10

lifted his head as though sniffing the air but did not move from where it stood.

"Look at that dumb bastard," the man said. He humped his shoulders over his rifle. "I bet I get him first shot." He turned his head toward Private Meadows, his chin sliding along the gun stock. "O.K.?" he asked impatiently.

"I——" But the man was straining in a flesh-taut position, ready to fire. "O.K.," Private Meadows said.

The man took aim. The goat started walking forward, his nose still in the air. The man shifted his gun, aimed again, fired. The goat bleated once, turned, and ran. The man shot again. The goat fell, gave three long trembling bleats, and was silent.

"Well, it's yours," the man said. He leaned back, picked up the money, and threw it to Private Meadows. "That bastard." He crawled back against the tree, put his gun on the ground beside him, and pulled a package from his knapsack. "Got a ration?" he asked.

"I got some choc'late," Private Meadows said. He stood up, holding the money out from him as if he might throw it back to the man or fling it into the woods. He looked down at the notes in his hand—thoughtfully, as though trying to recall how they came to be there. Then he slipped them into his jacket pocket. He sat down again and took out his chocolate. He took a bite of the hard cube, lay back on the ground, and immediately fell asleep.

"Hey. Hey, bud." The man was pushing his boot into Private Meadows's side. "Get up. The artillery's stopped."

Private Meadows sat up. The firing had almost stopped. "We musta taken the hill," he said.

"It's a town," the man said. "A village. We were after a village."

Private Meadows stood up. "You suppose we really took it?"

"Sounds like it," the man said. "We better get goin'. We better start findin' ourselves." He started walking down the edge of the clearing. The hulking form, moored to some narrow gaze, rode the slow steps heavily, in strenuous swells and sudden falls. Private Meadows followed. To their right the sun was halfway down the sky.

They came in view of a farmhouse. It stood in the clearing about fifty yards away. "Looks deserted," the man said. They stood looking over the field at the small squat house. "We'll see," the man said. He lifted his rifle and fired. Then they waited, but there was no sign of life from the house. "Can't tell if I even hit." He fired again. And as they stood waiting for whatever they expected might happen, an airplane loomed from the south. They ducked quickly into the woods and there from among the trees watched the plane. It was flying low and unsteadily. "Damned thing's fallin'," the man said. And as he spoke, they saw a figure drop from the plane—and then another. A parachute opened and then fell into the jolt of full bloom. The second opened, leapt up at the hinges of the air, jolted. Then a third. They had not seen the third drop from the plane but there it moved, in echelon, with the others.

"Brother!" the man said, lifting his rifle. "I'll take the one on the left again. Same bet."

Private Meadows stared as the man pivoted his gun on the floating figure and fired.

"Quick, you bastard," the man said, stepping closer to him, his mouth curling down from the utterance in anger. The impatient words were command.

Private Meadows shouldered his gun and, while still leveling the figure into his sight, fired. He saw a body twitch, the hands fall from the cords, the head lean back. As he lowered his gun across his chest, he drew his heels together and stood straight and stiff, gaping at what he had done.

"Same again on the middle one," the man said. He lifted his gun, but his target was already falling beyond the roof of the house. "God damn," he said, dropping his gun from his shoulder. "He's outa sight 'cause you waited so long. What were you waitin' for?"

"You don't shoot men when they're parachutin'."

"My ass! You don't shoot *prisoners*, do you?"

"You sure they were Germans?" His voice was almost supplication.

"How do I know?" He started walking into the woods. "Let's get the hell away from here."

Private Meadows stood holding his gun over his chest, his hand on the bolt. He looked over the field. The two white chutes, now lying on the ground, were barely visible. He drew his bolt, ejecting the cartridge case; thrust the bolt forward again; and, yet holding the gun across his chest, followed the man into the woods.

"Suppose they were *Americans!*" he called out.

The man stopped, turned back—the accusing, distrustful look again in his eyes. "American, French, Kraut, whatever they are, they're fly boys, playin' games in the air and sleepin' in a bed at night." His helmet was almost touching Private Meadows's own. "Look, bud, you shoot first and *suppose* afterward, or you'll get lead between your own eyes." He drew back a step. "Ain't you killed any before?"

Private Meadows remembered the terrified eyes staring into his own. He answered doubtfully, in the voice of conjecture: "But I knew who I was killin'."

The fat lips drew tight round a sibilant of contempt. Then, "Killin's killin'," he said. "How long you been in this push anyways?"

"Since Cherbourg."

The man looked him up and down. "It's a wonder you lasted this long."

Through woods, over the dirt road, and through woods again to the first fields. Down a hedgerow cautiously. Debris of the advance: cartridge belts, helmets, clips yet filled with bullets, a knit cap, a dog lying dead, a deck of cards scattered, and letters. The wounded and dead removed, but the signs of death in the wreckage. And then the main road, from which the night before they had deployed. Now an ambulance passing, now a jeep. A squad of soldiers, bearded, and fatuous with grime, shoveling dirt from an embankment to cover the carcass of a cow. Salvage of tanks and trucks. Trees broken and charred. A column of medics, walking with stooped weariness, into a side road. Trucks, filled with infantrymen, coming up from the rear. Then the village: "This town off limits for all military personnel." Really no village at all, only rubble: a tall mahogany armoire standing erect and unscratched among bricks and nameless jointures of wood like an exaggerated product in an advertisement; the horseshoe arches of four windows, like a backstage flat, signifying a church; the graveyard, a grotesquerie of holes, stone, and upturned coffins; and, sitting atop a fallen door, a yellow-and-white kitten washing an outstretched paw.

13

At the entrance of the village and even in the street beyond the off-limits sign there were soldiers. They stood in groups, but they were quiet, looking over the ruins of the village or down the wreckage-strewn road they had traversed, staring vacantly at the interpreter talking to a group of five Nazi officers or at the Military Police helping a sergeant line up a lengthening formation of prisoners. The scene was almost still, like a rehearsal of a play where everyone waits for the director to reach a decision.

The two soldiers stopped by an off-limits sign and surveyed the scene. "I gotta find my company," the big man said. He went up to a group of soldiers. Private Meadows watched him a moment and then followed after. He saw one of the soldiers answering the big man's question, pointing away from the village. And before Private Meadows reached the group the big man walked away. Private Meadows stopped, ready to lift his hand in farewell, but the man went lunging on without looking back—the heavy body, in its laboring gait, an enemy to the air it humped and to the ground it scuffed: the beast that walks alone, that—among all the animals of the forest and in the meeting of its kind—is yet alone, the stalker of secret places, the hunter. Private Meadows sensed the solitariness, but he thought it was the realization of his own loneliness that made him shudder.

He approached the group of soldiers and asked the whereabouts of his company. All the men looked at him blankly. And then one, interpreting the silence of the group, answered: "I don't know."

Private Meadows turned away. Beyond the formation of prisoners he saw some French civilians crossing the street. A fat woman, carrying a hamper, walked down the side of the formation, a little white dog following her, scurrying from one side to the other to sniff at the boots of the prisoners or at something in the rubble.

He was alone again. He was lost.

At home he had often had a dream of being late for school. The scenes of the dream were always different, but the dream was always the same. An unsuccessful effort to get to school: the determination, the hurry; running down the street, then caught in some void where time passed and he stood still; or still discovering himself at a strange corner, not knowing the direction, not knowing how he came to be there. The remembrance of the dream was fleeting but the familiar hopeless feeling of it remained. He felt that no one here would know his company, that his company would be in a distant place maneuvering through some different duty. He had left his company that very same morning after sunrise and only now was the sun beginning to set. But his calculation gave him no assurance. He felt that he had been separated from his comrades for a campaign of time. And this —this feeling—was his real knowledge.

He went from soldier to soldier, from group to group, asking the position of his company—his question automatic and hopeless, but persistent like a sick man's fancy. And when a soldier answered "Yes" and named the directions, his mind was filled with only the realization of the soldier's knowing, so that he had to ask again.

His company was bivouacked less than a mile from the village. It was still twilight when he walked among his platoon.

"Meadows! Man, I thought you'd found your number." It was Barr. He was sitting on the ground, leaning against the wood fence. He touched the ground beside him in invitation for Meadows to sit.

"What happened to you?" Harrod, too, was leaning against the fence. He was smoking a cigarette. His face was black with grease and dirt.

"Guess I musta got lost," Private Meadows said. He leaned his gun against the fence, dropping his helmet to the ground, and sat down.

Without looking around Barr stretched his hand to his left and said: "They got Pederson." Private Meadows looked up at him. "And Walton was shot in the hip but he'll get all right, lucky dog." He put his feet out before him, crossed them at the ankles, said wearily: "We 'bout all would have got it if it wasn't for those bombers. Zoom. Bang. And not another eighty-eight booped after that."

"Those *what?*" Private Meadows asked.

"The bombers. The lucky dogs. Sleeping in England tonight."

"I got lost," Private Meadows said.

Harrod and Barr both looked at him.

"Well, you're home now, chum," Barr said. "Good ole Easy Company. Gonna have hot stuff tonight—outa mess kit. And a sleep, I-hope-I-hope-I-hope, here against a soft, warm fence."

"Wish they'd hurry with chow," Harrod said. "If I close my eyes, I'll never make it. . . . How much longer they gonna keep us in the line anyhow?"

15

"Couple of more days, I guess," Barr said. His tone was now flat, as if he had no interest in what he said.

"I wonder if I'll live that long," Harrod said. There was nothing in his voice; it sounded like a routine speculation, as if he wondered whether he would be in town long enough to send his clothes to the laundry.

It was almost dark.

Private Meadows was bent forward, his arms lying against his thighs, his eyes pressed against his wrists. Barr noticed that each hand clutched a stack of notes and, as he started to ask what they were, he heard the sobbing. It simpered like a fuse and then burst. The shoulders shook convulsively. "What the hell, kid?" Barr sidled close to him and put his hand on his arm.

Harrod looked over at him, then flipped away the dead cigarette that he had been absently holding between his fingers. A whistle blew.

"Snap out of it, kid," Barr said, rising. "It's time for chow." He stepped back and picked up his mess kit. Then he and Harrod stood on each side of Private Meadows and waited.

from Harper's Bazaar

THE BURNING

EUDORA WELTY *has appeared frequently in this collection. She won second prize in 1941 with "The Worn Path"* from The Atlantic, *and first prizes with "The Wide Net" in 1942 from* Harper's Magazine, *and with "Livvie Is Back" in 1943 from* The Atlantic. *Her "The Petrified Man" from* The Southern Review *was reprinted here in 1939; "A Sketching Trip" in 1946 from* The Atlantic; *and "The Whole World Knows" in 1947 from* Harper's Bazaar. *Miss Welty was born April 13, 1909, in Jackson, Mississippi. She attended Mississippi State College for Women and received her A.B. from the University of Wisconsin in 1929. Her books are* A Curtain of Green, 1941, *a collection of stories;* The Robber Bridegroom, *a novel, 1942;* The Wide Net, 1943, *stories;* Delta Wedding, *a novel, 1946; and* The Golden Apples, *more stories, in 1949. She has been a fellow at Bread Loaf, was awarded Guggenheim Fellowships in 1942 and 1949, and received a $1000 award from the American Academy of Arts and Letters in 1944. She was an O. Henry judge in 1949. Miss Welty was in Europe in 1949, 1950, and 1951.*

Florabel was out in the back hall, running after the kitten. That's how it happened that she was the one to see. A horse was coming in the house. She could look up the hall through the big front door, and a crowd with a long tail of dust was following up their road behind.

Florabel ran both ways, then ran up the front hall into the parlor where they were. But they had their backs turned, both ladies, standing up with their sewing over their feet.

"Back you go, Flora," said Miss Theo's deep voice. "I see you there in your dirty apron," and as though to show her everything, Flora held poor kitty up to the back of Miss Theo's head, where she had her eyes.

There were running feet all over the house, Ophelia and all had heard, the dogs sounded now, late but loud—here was commotion come. Miss Theo and Miss Myra, keeping their backs to whatever commotion—as long as it was still in the yard, or coming up the steps, or crossing the porch, and even with two tremendous bangs planting itself in the front hall—still had to see it when it did come, the white horse. It drew up in the parlor door. Miss Theo was touching Miss Myra; it was in the gold mirror over the mantel those two saw it.

It was a rough, white, wet, grimacing horse, not so pretty. It brought two soldiers with red eyes, one on the horse, breathing hang-jawed, and the other by his side, smoking a little pipe. The charmed horse could pass right through a door and find ladies at home. The sisters—there was one minute while they touched their hair—turned with linked hands and faced the men when the blue rider began to get down.

"W-will you take me on the horse?"

Miss Myra, interrupting him, spoke so fast that she might have been secretly racing Miss Theo, or even placating her—Miss Theo with shut eyes was preparing what to say. But Miss Theo now said, "Florabel, what is it?" As if the horse was not real.

The rider-soldier, who had closed his mouth to begin speech again at the same time as Miss Theo, now stopped trying. It was so bright outside and so dark inside that at first the men couldn't see—nobody could see well. But that soldier took a step on the carpet and creaked the floor. Hearing that, he took another step, and with his red eyes sticking out he went as far as Miss Myra and took her around that little set waist. Before he knew it, he had picked her up half as high as he was—she was so light. The other soldier went to Miss Theo. From the back hall, down the back stairs, came a bang—baby Phinny threw down his cup.

"Step back, Flora, keep out of harm's way," said Miss Theo, in such a company voice Florabel thought harm was one of the two men.

She stood back in the doorway magically holding the horse that loomed there in the mirror, while more blurred and swift between, the Union soldier ran after Miss Myra and before long pushed her down. There was the parlor, enclosed with pictures and shuttered tight against the heat and that smell of smoke, full of dim, precious things, the bare gleam of the hall behind, the front stairs' shadow big as a tree and empty. Nobody went up there and nobody came down. Outside the mirror, the flat of Miss Theo's hand came down on mankind with a boisterous sound.

Then Miss Myra lay in the center, fallen in a turned-around chair —a round red velvet chair like a box.

"You presume—you dare," said Miss Theo's voice. Her bands of black hair awry, she made her way to the center, too, with a rustle of clothes, all to stroke her sister's hanging head in a forbidding rhythm. Maybe it was to keep her there, asleep in the heart and with her brighter hair loose and so sad; as she would still come at nighttime to the quarters when somebody called sick. Phinny threw down his plate; but Florabel still would not go.

"Dare right ahead," said Miss Theo. "No man in the house to prevent you. Brother—no word. Father—dead, mercifully—so of course . . ." She spoke in an almost rough-and-tumble kind of way used by ladies who didn't like company.

The horse, anxious, nudged at Florabel who was holding him there, a good obedient slave in her fresh-ironed dress and her striped turban, or so she would have been got up had she known it all ahead, like Miss Theo. "Never is Phinny gone," her lips tried making the words across to the mirror and back. "Phinny here. He a he."

"Afraid you've found the ladies of this house a little out of your element. My sister is more delicate than I, as you see," said Miss Theo.

Both soldiers were aback, in corners, shut out of it, then suddenly no longer; both hats were snatched from the parlor organ where they had been tossed; one had been turning itself on a candlestick on that soundless box, the hat that looked like forever. Kitty came picking her way among the horse's feet, but Florabel did not speak to her. "May I offer you this young kitchen Negro, as I've always understood . . ." Miss Theo, rooted as she was, swayed there.

The Northerner gave Miss Theo a serious, recording look as though she had given away what day the mail came in. "My poor little sister," Miss Theo said low to Miss Myra, "don't mind this old world," and she drew back her hand and brought out smelling salts—which

19

she now showed she carried in her bosom. But Miss Myra carelessly pushed back the bottle and said, "Oh, I just want to sit here."

One soldier then spoke freelike to the other. "What was you saying when we come in?"

"I said they wasn't gone yet—after all."

"Wasn't they?"

They laughed, but jolted each other so hard back and forth as they walked to the door that each seemed determined to be the first out, and then one turned back—the smoker, and said, "The devil . . ." (it seemed he never wanted to stir the nest again). "We come with orders to set the house afire, ma'am. General Sherman."

"Of course."

"Well, we done burnt up Jackson twice," the other soldier said, loud by the empty hall, "if that'll make her take notice." The horse whinnied loudly and moved his feet.

"You ladies ought to been out. You didn't get no word here we was coming?" The man pointed his little pipe at Miss Theo.

"I never will satisfy you on that," said Miss Theo.

"Lady, they told you. And when your own people tell you somebody's coming to burn your house down, the businesslike thing to do is get out of the way. I ain't going to tell you no more now."

"Then go, please."

"Burnin' up people's further than I go yet."

Miss Theo stared him down. "I see no degree."

So it was he that jerked Florabel—hand from the bridle—and turned her around, talking to the Bedlamlike horse which began to beat the floor boards behind. She listened, but Phinny did not throw anything more down; of course he was scared, if not of horses, then of men. And the horse did get loose; he took a trip through the hall and dining room and library.

Florabel looked back over her shoulder through the doorway to where Miss Theo stood at the mirror pressing her cheeks against the bones, until at last, when the rider caught the horse, Miss Theo shivered away. She crossed over to the chair where Miss Myra was. The big sister looked down at the little nodding sister and then brought back by the hair the peaked face with its purple eyes and slapped it.

"Myra," she said, "collect your senses. We have to go out before them."

Miss Myra slowly lifted her white arm, like a lady who has been asked to dance, but she only called "Flora," because that was the one she saw being lifted with a sweep of a big traylike hand onto the horse's back and taken off through the front door. And then kitty, following, trotting fast, running out ahead to the woods, where she was never seen again; but Florabel, from where she was, didn't speak to kitty, either.

For soon this poor set-up black girl's rising screams began outside, low in the yard and around that house, springing up everywhere she ran, like all the green in the world after a hard rain, that poor people, any other July, would have had to start chopping on right away.

The ladies kept them waiting.

Miss Theo finally brought Miss Myra out of the house through the wide-open front door and the rustling porch with the vine shadows. There were some catcalls and owl hoots from under the trees.

"Now hold back, boys. They's too ladylike for you."

"Ladies must needs take their time."

"And then they ain't no damn good at it!" came a clear, youthful voice like a banjo singer's.

The sisters showed no further surprise by now to see the Negroes of the place (old Ophelia in the way, talking, talking) running in and out all the doors of the house to carry off beds, tables, washstands, with their backs bent double; or the horses ready to go; or the food bolted down—and so much thrown away, this must be a second dinner; or the unsilenceable dogs, the old pack mixed with the strangers and fighting wonderfully over bones. The blue jays shrieked from tree to tree for a mile around. There was a bellowing like a bull, but it was Phinny inside. The last skinny sacks were thrown onto the wagons—the last flour, and all from Ophelia's shelves, even her pepper grinder. The silver Florabel could not count was counted on strange blankets and then, even the teapot, rolled together, tied up like a bag of bones. A drummer boy with his drum around his neck caught both Miss Theo's peacocks and wrung their necks in the yard. Nobody could look at those bird corpses; nobody did.

So most of the soldiers were smoking among big bushes in the yard, when the sisters left the porch like one, and in step, hands linked, came through the high grass in their crushed and only dresses and

21

walked under the trees. They came to a stop as if it was moonlight under the leafy frame of the big tree with the swing, without any despising left in their faces which were the same as one, as one face which didn't belong to anybody. This one clarified face, looking both left and right, could make out every one of those men through the bushes and under the trees, and mark every looting slave also, as all momently stood fixed like serenaders lighted by the moon; and agree with company that there was trouble in the world, every kind of trouble—but not Phinny. Old Ophelia was talking all the time, all the time, telling everybody in her own way. But nobody was ever to ask.

"What are they fixing to do, Theo?" asked Miss Myra, with a frown about to come on her too-white forehead, as if she wasn't going to understand any torches moving forward now to go into Rose Hill.

"Wait and see," said Miss Theo, folding her arms.

To Florabel that house they were about to set fire to was like the showboat that slowly came through the trees just once in her time, at the peak of high water—bursting with its secret, sparking in ruddy light, with a minute to go before that ear-aching cry of its calliope.

But when she drew close, with Miss Theo's skirt to peep around, the face looked down like death itself and said, "Remember this, you black monkeys," as the blaze outdid them all.

A while after the burning Miss Theo and Miss Myra, finding and taking hold of Florabel who was holding still in a ditch, did at last go beyond the place and proceed through the grand worthless fields down their own road. It was a hot afternoon like the others, but it played a trick on them with a smell and prophecy of fall—it was the burning. The pool standing among the stumps in the cracked cup of the old pond tasted as hot as coffee and as bitter. There was still and always smoke between them and the sun.

After all the July miles, there Jackson stood, burned twice, facing them in the road. You could see through it like a haunt; it was all chimneys and hollow places. There were soldiers among the ashes; these ashes were cold. Soon even these two ladies, once knowing their way everywhere, declared they were lost. While some soldiers watched them, they pointed at what they couldn't see, traced spires, while a horse without his rider passed them and ran down a black alley softly and did not return.

They walked here and there, sometimes over and over the same track, holding hands all three, like the time it snowed, that winter, and all the Negroes went to play together in the woods. They turned loose only to point.

"The State House."—"The school."

"The Blind School."—"The penitentiary!"

"The big barn."—"The deaf-and-dumb."

"Oh! Remember when we passed three of them, sitting on a hill?" They went on matching each other, naming ruin for ruin.

"The lunatic asylum!"—"The State House."

"No, I said that. Now where was Mrs. Calloway's, that was surely her hitching post."

"But why would it be standing and the rest not?" asked Miss Theo. "And ours not?"

"I think I should have told you, Myra. Word *was* sent to us to get out when it was sent to the rest. Two days' warning. I think it was a message from General Pemberton."

"But you didn't answer. Oh no, of course we couldn't go, dear." Miss Myra paused in the ashes and although a distant soldier watched, recited:

> "There was a man in our town
> And he was wondrous wise,
> He jumped into a bramble bush
> And scratched out both his eyes."

She stopped, looking at the soldier.

"And when he saw his eyes were out," prompted Miss Theo.

> "With all his might and main,
> He jumped into that bramble bush
> And scratched them in again."

"He sent word," Miss Theo went on, "our General Pemberton, you remember, for us all to get out ahead of this. What were you doing when it came, I forget. It was two days' warning—have I said? But time caught up with me, and I couldn't ever bring myself to tell you, Myra. I couldn't quite believe it—that they meant it—to come and do that *destruction* to us."

"Poor Theo. I could have."

"No, you couldn't. I couldn't believe it, take it in any more than Florabel there could have. I can reproach myself now, of course, with everything," and they began to walk on boldly through and boldly out of the burnt town, still single file.

"Not everything, Theo. Who had Phinny?" cried Miss Myra ardently.

"Hush. Of course that was what I was *thinking* of when . . ."

"If I hadn't had Phinny, then Phinny wouldn't have . . ."

"Hush, dearest, that wasn't *your* baby, you know. It was Brother Benton's baby. I won't have this."

". . . perished. Dear Benton. So good. Nobody else would have felt so *bound.*"

"Not after I told him what he owed a little life! Each little life is a *man's* fault; I said that. Oh, who'll ever forget that day?"

"Oho, Benton will. He's dead, I know. So good, too, never married."

"Stayed home, took care of his sisters. Only wanted to be forgiven."

"There has to be somebody to take care of everybody."

"I told him, when I said all that, he must never dream he was *inflicting* his sisters. That's what we're for."

"He didn't have anybody else; and it never would have inflicted us. We could have lived and died. Until *they* came, and tore things open . . ."

"Riding in the house on horseback," said Miss Theo. "Another reason was, I always wanted something of him to *remain,* you know."

"And I'll never know what possessed them, riding in like that," said Miss Myra, almost mischievously; and Miss Theo turned.

"And *you said* . . ."

"I said something wrong," said Miss Myra.

"I blame myself only—that I let you stay an hour in that house, after they told me it was doomed. I was equal to it, but not you."

"You let them holler at me. Oh, to my shame you led me, dear! Why did you say it wasn't my baby?"

"Phinny?" said Miss Theo, going around a hole.

"I had Phinny. Are you going to take Phinny away from me?"

"Now that's one thing I wouldn't dispute anybody else's claim to!"

Miss Theo, after just saying how Phinny mattered, pressed her cheeks with her palms and showed her pressed smile as she glanced around—the same old smile that in the dimmest picture would make anybody say, That was Miss Theo.

Miss Myra said, "Oh, don't I know who it really belonged to, who it loved the best, that baby?"

"You mustn't perjure yourself," said Miss Theo in a new voice.

"Theo, it's not what I'm doing."

They both sighed.

"You're still that young girl you were, that's your trouble." Miss Theo walked in front, but she was looking at Miss Myra through the eyes in the back of her head and seeing her blush.

"I claim him. You hide him if you want to. I had him, dear. It was some soldier, no, one of our beaux that used to come out and hunt with Benton. I'm impetuous and always so high-strung and easily carried away. And if Phinny *was* mine . . ."

"Don't you know he's black?" Miss Theo had stopped and blocked the path.

"He *was* white." Then, "He's black *now*," whispered Miss Myra, darting forward and taking her sister's hands.

But Flora knew that the next moment from drawing together they could have struck each other with sharp nails, the sisters, like poor feeble cats in the street full of breaking sticks, except for remembering who walked behind.

"If I only had something to eat!" sobbed Miss Myra, and once more clung to her sister and let herself be embraced. One eye showed over the tall shoulder. "Oh, Florabel."

"Could be he got out," said Florabel in a high voice. "He strong, he."

"Who?"

"Look yonder. What do I see? I see the Richards' perfectly good hammock still under the old pecan trees," Miss Theo said, and spread her hand.

There was some little round silver cup familiar to them in the hammock when they came to it down in the grove. Lying on its side, with a few drops in it, it made them smile.

The yard was full of butterflies. Miss Myra, as if she could no longer wait, climbed into the hammock and lay down with ankles

25

crossed. She took up the cup like a storybook she'd begun and left there yesterday, holding it before her eyes in those freckling fingers, slowly picking out the ants. Both sisters were great readers, and could read books, cups, or anything.

"So still out here and all," Miss Myra said. "Such a big sky. The figs dried up. I wish it would rain."

"Won't rain till Saturday," said Florabel.

"Florabel, don't go 'way."

Miss Theo sat down, too, rested awhile, though she did not know how to sit on the ground and was afraid of grasshoppers, and then she stood up, shook out her skirt, and beckoned to Florabel who had backed off far to one side where some chickens were running around loose with nobody to catch them.

"Come back here, Flora! You know it takes three," she was telling Miss Myra. "We've got Flora, and as long as we've got her we won't do without her."

Miss Myra let the cat die in the hammock. Then she gave her hand to climb out, Miss Theo helped her and without any help for herself untied the hammock from the tree trunks. She was long bent over it, and Miss Myra watched the butterflies. At last she held up, for a long look, two long strands of cotton rope, of red and white untwisted from each other, bent rigid like the hair of white ladies taken out of plaits.

Florabel, at a touch, darted up the tree and, hooking her toes, made the ropes fast to the two branches not far from each other, where Miss Theo had it in mind. When she slid down, by the good rope, she stood waiting while they settled it, until Miss Myra repeated, "I'll go first, sister," in a spoiled and prissy way. Then Florabel squatted under the good rope, made a basket, and Miss Myra tucked up her skirts and stepped her torn shoe in the black hands.

"Tuck under, Flora."

Miss Myra, who had said that, stepped over Florabel's head and stood on her back with her careful feet, and Florabel felt her presence like a fish on the line, each longing she had to draw away from Miss Theo, draw away from Florabel, away from that tree.

"Who're we doing this for?" she asked once, as if she'd always needed reminding. Florabel turned her head around to see the rope get tied better and better by Miss Theo's puckered hands, like a bonnet on a very windy day, and Miss Myra looking out.

"I learned this from an engraving in Captain Billy's *Journal* in Papa's bookcase," said Miss Theo, turning up her eye. "As a child."

Then Miss Theo, going from bragging into sudden movement, took Florabel around the ribs and drew her giggling out from under. Just then Miss Myra kicked her—a brutal kick, almost as if that were Miss Theo or a man hanging in the tree.

Miss Theo stood holding Florabel and looking at that face—helping herself to grief. No wonder Miss Myra used to hide with her book. Hidden in the summerhouse, still she screamed sometimes when Florabel threw the dishwater out on the ground.

"Now I'm smarter than you," said Miss Theo to Florabel, dragging her. "And now I know what I'd always suspicioned: I'm brave as a lion. If I ordered you back up that tree to help down my sister, you'd run and leave me here, sure as you're living. I know your minds! So I don't ask you to be merciful. In fact I won't tolerate mercy. You're to leave us both just as we are, and that's the way they'll find us—so much the worse for them," and she pushed Florabel down and stepped on her shoulders, where she weighted her like a rock.

Miss Theo had studied and learned how to tie her own knot up there. She was quicker now, and Florabel was quicker too. Then Flora started to run.

"Stay up! Stay up up up!"

Florabel ran, crying. Miss Theo was so powerful she came down. She sailed down like a spider on its thread, which snapped, and she reached in the grass. Even those hens were flying up with a noise, as if they felt a shadow on their backs.

If it had been Miss Myra. Florabel had not done what she thought she did when she gave the good rope to the good sister and the bad rope to the bad.

There was nothing to do but hide, down in the jungly grass choked with bitterweed and black-eyed Susans, wild to the pricking skin, with many heads nodding, cauldrons of ants, with butterflies riding them, grasshoppers hopping them—down in the loud and lonesome grass that was rank enough almost to mat the sky over. There she held like a mantis until the grass had folded and spread apart at the falling of dew to let shine the one sharp star. This was after the chickens had gone to roost in a strange uneasy tree against the cloud where the guns still boomed and the way from Vicksburg was red. Then Florabel could find her feet.

She knew where Miss Theo was. She could see only Miss Myra now—the last white, the stockings. In a wading bird tucked in his wing for sleep, she saw her ghost, down by the river.

After being lost for a while, moving by day, still crouching, stealing through briar bushes she saw the place again. Above, the cloud had turned. Like a big black bird that had flown all the way to the West, it was flapping home now, with it all in its mouth. Florabel knew the house by the chimneys and by the crape myrtle tree off to one side, where the bottom of the summerhouse stood empty as an egg basket. Some of the flowers looked tasty, like chicken legs fried a little black.

Climbing over the barrier of the big doorsill, and wading in ashes, she was lost still inside that house; she was lost when it had walls. She found an iron pot and a man's long boot, a doorknob and a little book fluttering, leaves spotted and fluffed like guinea feathers. She stood up with the book and read aloud like Miss Theo. "Ba-ba-ba-ba-ba-ba-ba." Then she saw that parlor mirror down in the chimney's craw, flat in the cinders, its gleam addled. It made her smile. She started toward it.

Behind her the one standing wall of the house held notched and listening for the first word, like the big ear of King Solomon into which went the repeated asking of birds. The tree stood and flowered. Weren't people to carry it all away; what had she come for? Dropping suddenly to the ground, she heard the solid cannon, the galloping and rolling in her ear, heard the low drum of burning. She rubbed the bruised, swollen glass with spit on her apron and leaned over it, and saw a face suddenly, all neck and ears, then gone. She drew the closer, kneeling and persuasive. She had seen Miss Myra do that: before its eye she opened and spread her arms.

Though the mirror did not know Florabel, she would have known the mirror in the middle of a desert because it was set like a door between black men. Their arms were raised, just so, holding up the mirror's roof, which now the mirror brimmed, among gold leaves and little heads—dressed up in gold, looking almost in, themselves, to see what they carried there—men now split away, flattened with fire, bearded, noseless as the moss that hung from swampy trees.

Men had said that day that people were turned loose—that they were to cry Jubilee and take what they wanted—whether it was heavy as a feed sack or light as Phinny—a good child. Perhaps Florabel had been told to carry off this very mirror; perhaps, but she still liked to think she could go hide if her burden was too much and the step too perilous; any brimming bucket from which not one drop was to be spilled was always meant for Ophelia's other girl, Lavonia.

Where the mirror did not swell and cloud like the trampled spring, gold gathered itself from the winding water, and honey under water started to flow, and then the gold fields were there, hardening gold. Should she take it? Through the water, gold and honey twisted up into houses, holding them up like arms, trembling, by the canals; through its door a floor with the scales of a snake, a window like pigeon eyes, church. She saw them walking the streets in early light with hives or houses on their heads, men in dresses—some with red birds. And monkeys in velvet; companies in boats like birds. And ladies looking from the pointed windows. Florabel supposed that was Jackson before Sherman came.

Should she take the mirror? When she pulled at it, it was as heavy as she was; her back ached already. She wondered if they would not rather she left it here, safe, where nobody came any longer; all had passed by, unless indeed they had gone in. The cloudy bottom sent up wiggle-tails against that brim where now a face pure as a water-lily shadow was floating. More wiggle-tails, lizards, hatched with tiny sun flashes to strike up and meet in turmoil, and soon their heads were flying. Deep down, they were climbing and aping old things Florabel had seen done in this world already, sometimes what men had done to Miss Theo and Miss Myra and the peacocks and slaves, and sometimes what a slave had done and what anybody now could do to anybody.

She put her arms over her head for she knew they all must be coming again, gathering below her and all around her, bees saddled out of the air, butterflies harnessed to one another, bats with the masks on, birds together, all with their weapons bared. She dropped flat and lay over the mirror hiding it and hiding her face and her breasts and hands.

She listened for the hissing, the blows, and dreaded that army of flies, birds, serpents, their flying enemy faces and bright kings' dresses never dreamed of, that banner of colors forked out, that rainbow, all who were flying, striking, stricken, falling, gilded or blackened, all splitting and falling, turbans unwinding, turning like the spotting leaves of fall and spiraling down; she dreaded the fury of all the butterflies and dragonflies in the world riding, swords unconcealed and at point—descending, and rising again from down under with an echo that shook her bones, one whale made of his own bed, rising to open his mouth and swallow Jonah still alive one more time.

If she were not weak and complaining, if she could look in once more, she might surprise poor Jonah's face in the foam—a homely face to her, which could look back from its long red lane even if it was too late to speak. He was her Jonah, her little old monkey, she worshiped him still, though it was long ago he had to be given up. How long ago!

Then Florabel got to her feet, stiffly, as if told to.

Florabel, with no last name, was a slave. By the time of that moment on the hill, her kind had been slaves in a dozen countries and that of their origin for thousands of years. She let everything be itself according to its nature—the animate, the inanimate, the symbol. She did not move to alter any of it, not unless she was told to and shown how. And so she saw what happened, the creation and the destruction. She waited on either one and served it, not expecting anything of it but what she got; only sooner or later she would seek protection somewhere. Herself was an unknown, like a queen, somebody she had heard called, even cried for. As a slave she was earth's most detached visitor. The world had not touched her—only possessed and hurt her, like a man; taken away from her, like a man; turned another way from her and left her, like a man. Her vision was clear. She saw what was there and had not sought it, did not seek it yet. (It was *her* eyes that were in the back of her head, her vision that met itself coming the long way back, unimpeded, like the light of stars.) The command to loot was one more fading memory. Many commands had been given her, some even held over from before she was born; delayed and miscarried and interrupted, they could yet be fulfilled, though it was safer for one once a slave to hear things a second time, a third, fourth, hundredth, thousandth, if they were to be carried out to the letter. In that noon quiet after conflict there might have been only the two triumphant, the mirror which was a symbol in the world and Florabel who was standing there; it was the rest that had died of it.

In Florabel's eyes no tears formed but a brightness came. She cocked her head, looked sharp at the mirror, and the image was caught—head in the flayed forehead of a horse with ears and crest up stiff, the shield and the drum of skins of big swamp birds, the horns of deer sharpened to cut and kill with. Florabel showed her teeth. She left that mirror the way she found it in those cinders that were already springing weeds. Let the mockingbirds look in, and the buzzards crack it.

She looked well in the ashes and found Phinny's bones all right. She ripped a square from her skirt and tied up the bones in it, and directly left that place.

She set her foot in the road; in one hand was the bag of bones, in the other a stick to drive the snakes. Without being sure, Florabel believed that on the day it happened, Miss Theo (two stones the sisters were) twisted like a snake till the sun went down. Hearing something like words come out of her mouth once, a mysterious croaking, she had ventured near and asked her what was going to happen, where would she go, she, Florabel, and Miss Theo would not part with an answer to that.

To follow the smell of horses and fire, to keep in the wheel tracks, Florabel had to cross the river. She made her way down the bank, where under the burned and fallen bridge she sat on a stump and chewed the comb of a dirt-dauber. She took a drink out of the Big Black, then waded into it. She went slowly, gradually submerging herself to the waist and to the breast, stretching her throat like a stalk, holding her treasure over her head, not considering that she, Florabel, one life, might step too deep and the river smile and take her.

At that time it was only Friday, so it hadn't rained.

from Mademoiselle

THE HOUSE OF FLOWERS

TRUMAN CAPOTE, *whose name is pronounced with an accented e, was born in New Orleans September 30, 1924, into a family of Southerners on both sides. He attended six different schools in five sections of the country. He began to write very early, and has said that little interests him except writing. His "Miriam" was published in the 1946 edition of this collection, and in 1948 his "Shut a Final Door" won first prize. Others of his stories that have been anthologized include "The Headless Hawk," "The World Within," and "My Side of the Matter." A collection of his stories was published in 1949, under the title of* A Tree of Night, *and in 1948 his first novel,* Other Voices, Other Rooms, *which became a best seller, was brought out.* Local Color, *made up of travel sketches, appeared in 1950. Mr. Capote is now living in Taormina in the house once occupied by D. H. Lawrence, and is finishing his second novel.*

Ottilie should have been the happiest girl in Port-au-Prince. As Baby said to her, look at all the things that can be put to your credit. Like what? said Ottilie, for she was vain and preferred compliments to pork or perfume. Like your looks, said Baby: you have a lovely light color, even almost blue eyes, and such a pretty, sweet face—there is no girl on the road with steadier customers, every one of them ready to buy you all the beer you can drink. Ottilie conceded that this was true, and with a smile continued to total her fortunes: I have five silk dresses and a pair of green satin shoes, I have three gold teeth worth thirty thousand francs, maybe Mr. Jamison or someone will give me another bracelet. But Baby, she sighed, and could not express her discontent.

32

Baby was her best friend; she had another friend too: Rosita. Baby was like a wheel, round, rolling; junk rings had left green circles on several of her fat fingers, her teeth were dark as burnt tree stumps, and when she laughed you could hear her at sea, at least so the sailors claimed. Rosita, the other friend, was taller than most men, and stronger; at night, with the customers on hand, she minced about lisping in a silly doll voice, but in the daytime she took spacious, loping strides and spoke out in a military baritone. Both of Ottilie's friends were from the Dominican Republic, and considered it reason enough to feel themselves a cut above the natives of this darker country. It did not concern them that Ottilie was a native. You have brains, Baby told her, and certainly what Baby doted on was a good brain. Ottilie was often afraid that her friends would discover that she could neither read nor write.

The house where they lived and worked was rickety, thin as a steeple, and frosted with fragile, bougainvillaea-vined balconies. Though there was no sign outside, it was called the Champs Elysées. The proprietress, a spinsterish, smothered-looking invalid, ruled from an upstairs room where she stayed locked away rocking in a rocking chair and drinking ten to twenty Coca-Colas a day. All counted, she had eight ladies working for her; with the exception of Ottilie, no one of them was under thirty. In the evening, when the ladies assembled on the porch, where they chatted and flourished paper fans that beat the air like delirious moths, Ottilie seemed a delightful dreaming child surrounded by older, uglier sisters.

Her mother was dead, her father was a planter who had gone back to France, and she had been brought up in the mountains by a rough peasant family, the sons of whom had each at a young age lain with her in some green and shadowy place. Three years earlier, when she was fourteen, she had come down for the first time to the market in Port-au-Prince. It was a journey of two days and a night, and she'd walked carrying a ten-pound sack of grain; to ease the load she'd let a little of the grain spill out, then a little more, and by the time she had reached the market there was almost none left. Ottilie had cried because she thought of how angry the family would be when she came home without the money for the grain; but these tears were not for long: such a jolly nice man helped her dry them. He bought her a slice of coconut, and took her to see his cousin, who was the proprietress of the Champs Elysées. Ottilie could not believe her good luck; the jukebox music, the satin shoes and joking men were as strange and marvelous as the electric-light bulb in her room, which she never tired of clicking on and off. Soon she had become the most talked-of girl on the road, the proprietress was able to ask double for her, and Ottilie grew vain; she could pose for hours in front of a mirror. It was seldom that she thought of the mountains; and yet, after three years, there was much of the mountains still with her: their winds seemed still to move around her, her hard, high haunches had not softened, nor had the soles of her feet, which were rough as lizard's hide.

When her friends spoke of love, of men they had loved, Ottilie became sulky: How do you feel if you're in love? she asked. Ah, said Rosita with swooning eyes, you feel as though pepper has been sprinkled on your heart, as though tiny fish are swimming in your veins. Ottilie shook her head; if Rosita was telling the truth, then she had never been in love, for she had never felt that way about any of the men who came to the house.

This so troubled her that at last she went to see a *Houngan* who lived in the hills above town. Unlike her friends, Ottilie did not tack Christian pictures on the walls of her room; she did not believe in God, but many gods: of food, light, of death, ruin. The Houngan was in touch with these gods; he kept their secrets on his altar, could hear their voices in the rattle of a gourd, could dispense their power in a potion. Speaking through the gods, the Houngan gave her this message: You must catch a wild bee, he said, and hold it in your closed hand . . . if the bee does not sting, then you will know you have found love.

On the way home she thought of Mr. Jamison. He was a man past fifty, and an American connected with an engineering project. The gold bracelets chattering on her wrists were presents from him, and Ottilie, passing a fence snowy with honeysuckle, wondered if after all she was not in love with Mr. Jamison. Black bees festooned the honeysuckle. With a brave thrust of her hand she caught one dozing. Its stab was like a blow that knocked her to her knees; and there she knelt, weeping until it was hard to know whether the bee had stung her hand or her eyes.

It was March, and events were leading toward carnival. At the Champs Elysées the ladies were sewing on their costumes; Ottilie's hands were idle, for she had decided not to wear a costume at all. On rah-rah week ends, when drums sounded at the rising moon, she sat at her window and watched with a wandering mind the little bands of singers dancing and drumming their way along the road; she listened to the whistling and the laughter and felt no desire to join in. Somebody would think you were a thousand years old, said Baby, and Rosita said: Ottilie, why don't you come to the cockfight with us?

She was not speaking of an ordinary cockfight. From all parts of the island contestants had arrived bringing their fiercest birds. Ottilie thought she might as well go, and screwed a pair of pearls into her ears. When they arrived the exhibition was already under way; in a great tent a sea-sized crowd sobbed and shouted, while a second crowd, those who could not get in, thronged on the outskirts. Entry was no problem to the ladies from the Champs Elysées: a policeman friend cut a path for them and made room on a bench by the ring. The country people surrounding them seemed embarrassed to find themselves in such stylish company. They looked shyly at Baby's lacquered nails, the rhinestone combs in Rosita's hair, the glow of Ottilie's pearl earrings. However, the fights were exciting, and the ladies were soon forgotten; Baby was annoyed that this should be so, and her eyes rolled about searching for glances in their direction. Suddenly she nudged Ottilie. Ottilie, she said, you've got an admirer: see that boy over there, he's staring at you like you were something cold to drink.

At first she thought he must be someone she knew, for he was looking at her as though she should recognize him; but how could she know him when she'd never known anyone so beautiful, anyone with such long legs, little ears? She could see that he was from the mountains: his straw country hat and the worn-out blue of his thick shirt told her as much. He was a ginger color, his skin shiny as a lemon, smooth as a guava leaf, and the tilt of his head was as arrogant as the black and scarlet bird he held in his hands. Ottilie was used to boldly smiling at men; but now her smile was fragmentary, it clung to her lips like cake crumbs.

Eventually there was an intermission. The arena was cleared, and

35

all who could crowded into it to dance and stamp while an orchestra of drums and strings sang out carnival tunes. It was then that the young man approached Ottilie; she laughed to see his bird perched like a parrot on his shoulder. Off with you, said Baby, outraged that a peasant should ask Ottilie to dance, and Rosita rose menacingly to stand between the young man and her friend. He only smiled, and said: Please, madame, I would like to speak with your daughter. Ottilie felt herself being lifted, felt her hips meet against his to the rhythm of music, and she did not mind at all, she let him lead her into the thickest tangle of dancers. Rosita said: Did you hear that, he thought I was her mother? And Baby, consoling her, grimly said: After all, what do you expect? They're only natives, both of them: when she comes back we'll just pretend we don't know her.

As it happened, Ottilie did not return to her friends. Royal, this was the young man's name, Royal Bonaparte, he told her, had not wanted to dance. We must walk in a quiet place, he said, hold my hand and I will take you. She thought him strange, but did not feel strange with him, for the mountains were still with her, and he was of the mountains. With their hands together, and the iridescent cock swaying on his shoulder, they left the tent and wandered lazily down a white road, then along a soft lane where birds of sunlight fluttered through the greenness of leaning acacia trees.

I have been sad, he said, not looking sad. In my village Juno is a champion, but the birds here are strong and ugly, and if I let him fight I would only have a dead Juno. So I will take him home and say that he won. Ottilie, will you have a dip of snuff?

She sneezed voluptuously. Snuff reminded her of her childhood, and mean as those years had been, nostalgia touched her with its far-reaching wand. Royal, she said, be still a minute, I want to take off my shoes.

Royal himself did not have shoes; his golden feet were slender and airy, and the prints they left were like the track of a delicate animal. He said: How is it that I find you here, in all the world here, where nothing is good, where the rum is bad and the people thieves? Why do I find you here, Ottilie?

Because I must make my way, the same as you, and here there is a place for me. I work in a—oh kind of hotel.

We have our own place, he said. All the side of a hill, and there at the top of the hill is my cool house. Ottilie, will you come and sit inside it?

Crazy, said Ottilie, teasing him, crazy, and she ran between the trees, and he was after her, his arms out as though he held a net. The bird Juno flared his wings, crowed, flew to the ground. Scratchy leaves and fur of moss thrilled the soles of Ottilie's feet as she lilted through the shade and shadows; abruptly, into a veil of rainbow fern, she fell with a thorn in her heel. She winced when Royal pulled out the thorn; he kissed the place where it had been, his lips moved to her hands, her throat, and it was as though she were among drifting leaves. She breathed the odor of him, the dark, clean smell that was like the roots of things, of geraniums, of heavy trees.

Now that's enough, she pleaded, though she did not feel that this was so: it was only that after an hour of him her heart was about to give out. He was quiet then, his tickly haired head rested above her heart, and shoo she said to the gnats that clustered about his sleeping eyes, shush she said to Juno who pranced around crowing at the sky.

While she lay there, Ottilie saw her old enemy, the bees. Silently, in a line like ants, the bees were crawling in and out of a broken stump that stood not far from her. She loosened herself from Royal's arms, and smoothed a place on the ground for his head. Her hand was trembling as she lay it in the path of the bees, but the first that came along tumbled onto her palm, and when she closed her fingers it made no move to hurt her. She counted ten, just to be sure, then opened her hand, and the bee, in spiraling arcs, climbed the air with a joyful singing.

The proprietress gave Baby and Rosita a piece of advice: Leave her alone, let her go, a few weeks and she will be back. The proprietress spoke in the calm of defeat: to keep Ottilie with her, she'd offered the best room in the house, a new gold tooth, a Kodak, an electric fan, but Ottilie had not wavered, she had gone right on putting her belongings in a cardboard box. Baby tried to help, but she was crying so much that Ottilie had to stop her: it was bound to be bad luck, all those tears falling on a bride's possessions. And to Rosita she said: Rosita, you ought to be glad for me instead of standing there wringing your hands.

It was only two days after the cockfight that Royal shouldered Ottilie's cardboard box and walked her in the dusk toward the mountains. When it was learned that she was no longer at the Champs Elysées many of the customers took their trade elsewhere; others, though remaining loyal to the old place, complained of a gloom in the atmosphere: some evenings there was hardly anyone to buy the ladies a beer. Gradually it began to be felt that Ottilie after all would not come back; at the end of six months the proprietress said: She must be dead.

Royal's house was like a house of flowers; wisteria sheltered the roof, a curtain of vines shaded the windows, lilies bloomed at the door. From the windows one could see far, faint winkings of the sea, as the house was high up a hill; here the sun burned hot but the shadows were cold. Inside, the house was always dark and cool, and the walls rustled with pasted pink and green newspapers. There was only one room; it contained a stove, a teetering mirror on top a marble table, and a brass bed big enough for three fat men.

But Ottilie did not sleep in this grand bed. She was not allowed even to sit upon it, for it was the property of Royal's grandmother, Old Bonaparte. A charred, lumpy creature, bowlegged as a dwarf and bald as a buzzard, Old Bonaparte was much respected for miles around as a maker of spells. There were many who were afraid to have her shadow fall upon them; even Royal was wary of her, and he stuttered when he told her that he'd brought home a wife. Motioning Ottilie to her, the old woman bruised her here and there with vicious little pinches, and informed her grandson that his bride was too skinny: She will die with her first.

Each night the young couple waited to make love until they thought Old Bonaparte had gone to sleep. Sometimes, stretched on the straw moonlit pallet where they slept, Ottilie was sure that Old Bonaparte was awake and watching them. Once she saw a gummy, star-struck eye shining in the dark. There was no use complaining to Royal, he only laughed: What harm was there in an old woman who had seen so much of life wanting to see a little more?

Because she loved Royal, Ottilie put away her grievances and tried not to resent Old Bonaparte. For a long while she was happy; she did not miss her friends or the life in Port-au-Prince; even so, she

38

kept her souvenirs of those days in good repair: with a sewing basket Baby had given her as a wedding gift she mended the silk dresses, the green silk stockings that now she never wore, for there was no place to wear them: only men congregated at the café in the village, at the cockfights. When women wanted to meet they met at the washing stream. But Ottilie was too busy to be lonesome. At daybreak she gathered eucalyptus leaves to start a fire and begin their meals; there were chickens to feed, a goat to be milked, there was Old Bonaparte's whining for attention. Three and four times a day she filled a bucket of drinking water and carried it to where Royal worked in the cane fields a mile below the house. She did not mind that on these visits he was gruff with her: she knew that he was showing off before the other men who worked in the fields, and who grinned at her like split watermelons. But at night, when she had him home, she'd pull his ears and pout that he treated her like a dog until, in the dark of the yard where the fireflies flamed, he would hold her and whisper something to make her smile.

They had been married about five months when Royal began doing the things he'd done before his marriage. Other men went to the café in the evenings, stayed whole Sundays at a cockfight—he couldn't understand why Ottilie should carry on about it; but she said he had no right behaving the way he did, and that if he loved her he wouldn't leave her alone day and night with that mean old woman. I love you, he said, but a man has to have his pleasures too. There were nights when he pleasured himself until the moon was in the middle of the sky; she never knew when he was coming home, and she would lie fretting on the pallet, imagining she could not sleep without his arms around her.

But Old Bonaparte was the real torment. She was about to worry Ottilie out of her mind. If Ottilie was cooking, the terrible old woman was sure to come poking around the stove, and when she did not like what there was to eat she would take a mouthful and spit it on the floor. Every mess she could think of she made: she wet the bed, insisted on having the goat in the room, whatever she touched was soon spilled or broken, and to Royal she complained that a woman who couldn't keep a nice house or her husband was worthless. She was underfoot the whole day, and her red, remorseless eyes were seldom shut; but the worst of it, the thing that finally made

39

Ottilie threaten to kill her, was the old woman's habit of sneaking up from nowhere and pinching her so hard you could see the fingernail marks. If you do that one more time, if you just dare, I'll snatch that knife and cut out your heart! Old Bonaparte knew Ottilie meant it, and though she stopped the pinching, she thought of other jokes: for instance, she made a point of walking all over a certain part of the yard, pretending she did not know that Ottilie had planted a little garden there.

One day two exceptional things happened. A boy came from the village bringing a letter for Ottilie; at the Champs Elysées postcards had once in a while arrived from sailors and other traveling men who had spent pleasant moments with her, but this was the first letter she'd ever received. Since she could not read it, her first impulse was to tear it up: there was no use having it hang around to haunt her. Of course there was a chance that someday she would learn to read; and so she went to hide it in her sewing basket.

When she opened the sewing basket, she made a sinister discovery: there, like a gruesome ball of yarn, was the severed head of a yellow cat. So, the miserable old woman was up to new tricks! She wants to put a spell, thought Ottilie, not in the least frightened. Primly lifting the head by one of its ears, she carried it to the stove and dropped it into a boiling pot: at noon Old Bonaparte sucked her teeth and remarked that the soup Ottilie had made for her was surprisingly tasty.

The next morning, just in time for the midday meal, she found twisting in her basket a small green snake which, chopping fine as sand, she sprinkled into a serving of stew. Each day her ingenuity was tested: there were spiders to bake, a lizard to fry, a buzzard's breast to boil. Old Bonaparte ate several helpings of everything. With a restless glittering her eyes followed Ottilie as she watched for some sign that the spell was taking hold. You don't look well, Ottilie, she said, mixing a little molasses in the vinegar of her voice. You eat like an ant: here now, why don't you have a bowl of this good soup?

Because, answered Ottilie evenly, I don't like buzzard in my soup; or spiders in my bread, snakes in the stew: I have no appetite for such things.

Old Bonaparte understood; with swelling veins and a stricken,

40

powerless tongue, she rose shakily to her feet, then crashed across the table. Before nightfall she was dead.

Royal summoned mourners. They came from the village, from the neighboring hills and, wailing like dogs at midnight, laid siege to the house. Old women beat their heads against the walls, moaning men prostrated themselves: it was the art of sorrow, and those who best mimicked grief were much admired. After the funeral everyone went away, satisfied that they'd done a good job.

Now the house belonged to Ottilie. Without Old Bonaparte's prying and her mess to clean she had more spare time, but she did not know what to do with it. She sprawled on the great brass bed, she loafed in front of the mirror; monotony hummed in her head, and to drive away its fly-buzz sound she would sing the songs she'd learned from the jukebox at the Champs Elysées. Waiting in the twilight for Royal she would remember that at this hour her friends in Port-au-Prince were gossiping on the porch and waiting for the turning headlights of a car; but when she saw Royal ambling up the path, his cane cutter swinging at his side like a crescent moon, she forgot such thoughts and ran with a satisfied heart to meet him.

One night as they lay half-drowsing, Ottilie felt suddenly another presence in the room. Then, gleaming there at the foot of the bed, she saw, as she had seen before, a watching eye; thus she knew what for some time she had suspected: that Old Bonaparte was dead but not gone. Once, when she was alone in the house, she'd heard a laugh, and once again, out in the yard, she'd seen the goat gazing at someone who was not there and twinkling his ears as he did whenever the old woman scratched his skull.

Stop shaking the bed, said Royal, and Ottilie, with a finger raised at the eye, whisperingly asked him if he could not see it. When he replied that she was dreaming, she reached for the eye and screamed at feeling only air. Royal lighted a lamp; he cuddled Ottilie on his lap and smoothed her hair while she told him of the discoveries she'd made in her sewing basket, and of how she had disposed of them. Was it wrong what she'd done? Royal did not know, it was not for him to say, but it was his opinion that she would have to be punished; and why, because the old woman wanted it, because she would otherwise never leave Ottilie in peace: that was the way with haunts.

41

In accordance with this, Royal fetched a rope the next morning and proposed to tie Ottilie to a tree in the yard: there she was to remain until dark without food or water, and anyone passing would know her to be in a state of disgrace.

But Ottilie crawled under the bed and refused to come out. I'll run away, she whimpered. Royal, if you try to tie me to that old tree I'll run away.

Then I'd have to go and get you, said Royal, and that would be the worse for you.

He gripped her by an ankle and dragged her squealing from under the bed. All the way to the yard she caught at things, the door, a vine, the goat's beard, but none of these would hold her, and Royal was not detained from tying her to the tree. He made three knots in the rope, and went off to work sucking his hand where she had bit him. She hollered to him all the bad words she'd ever heard until he disappeared over the hill. The goat, Juno and the chickens gathered to stare at her humiliation; slumping to the ground, Ottilie stuck out her tongue at them.

Because she was almost asleep, Ottilie thought it was a dream when, in the company of a child from the village, Baby and Rosita, wobbling on high heels and carrying fancy umbrellas, tottered up the path calling her name. Since they were people in a dream, they probably would not be surprised to find her tied to a tree.

My God, are you mad? shrieked Baby, keeping her distance as though she feared that indeed this must be the case. Speak to us, Ottilie!

Blinking, giggling, Ottilie said: I'm just happy to see you. Rosita, please untie me so that I can hug you both.

So this is what the brute does, said Rosita, tearing at the ropes. Wait till I see him, beating you and tying you in the yard like a dog.

Oh no, said Ottilie. Royal never beats me. It's just that today I'm being punished.

You wouldn't listen to us, said Baby. And now you see what's come of it. That man has plenty to answer for, she added, brandishing her umbrella.

Ottilie hugged her friends and kissed them. Isn't it a pretty house? she said, leading them toward it. It's like you picked a wagon o flowers and built a house with them: that is what I think. Come in out of the sun. It's cool inside and smells so sweet.

Rosita sniffed as though what she smelled was nothing sweet, and in her well-bottom voice declared that yes, it was better that they stay out of the sun, as it seemed to be affecting Ottilie's head.

It's a mercy that we've come, said Baby, fishing inside an enormous purse. And you can thank Mr. Jamison for that. Madame said you were dead, and when you never answered our letter we thought it must be so. But Mr. Jamison, that's the loveliest man you'll ever know, he hired a car for me and Rosita, your dearest loving friends, to come up here and find out what had happened to our Ottilie. Ottilie, I've got a bottle of rum here in my purse, so get us a glass and we'll all have a round.

The elegant foreign manners and flashing finery of the city ladies had intoxicated their guide, a little boy whose peeking black eyes bobbed at the window. Ottilie was impressed, too, for it was a long time since she'd seen painted lips or smelled bottle perfume, and while Baby poured the rum she got out her satin shoes, her pearl earrings. Dear, said Rosita when Ottilie had finished dressing up, there's no man alive that wouldn't buy you a whole keg of beer; to think of it, a gorgeous piece like you suffering far away from those who love you.

I haven't been suffering so much, said Ottilie. Just sometimes.

Hush now, said Baby. You don't have to talk about it yet. It's all over anyway. Here, dear, let me see your glass again. A toast to old times, and those to be! Tonight Mr. Jamison is going to buy champagne for everybody: Madame is letting him have it at half-price.

Oh, said Ottilie, envying her friends. Well, she wanted to know, what did people say of her, was she remembered.

Ottilie, you have no idea, said Baby; men nobody ever laid eyes on before have come into the place asking where is Ottilie, because they've heard about you way off in Havana and Miami. As for Mr. Jamison, he doesn't even look at us other girls, just comes and sits on the porch drinking by himself.

Yes, said Ottilie wistfully. He was always sweet to me, Mr. Jamison.

Presently the sun was slanting, and the bottle of rum stood three-quarters empty. A thunderburst of rain had for a moment drenched

43

the hills that now, seen through the windows, shimmered like dragonfly wings, and a breeze, rich with the scent of rained-on flowers, roamed the room rustling the green and pink papers on the walls. Many stories had been told, some of them funny, a few that were sad; it was like any night's talk at the Champs Elysées, and Ottilie was happy to be a part of it again.

But it's getting late, said Baby. And we promised to be back before midnight. Ottilie, can we help you pack?

Although she had not realized that her friends expected her to leave with them, the rum stirring in her made it seem a likely assumption, and with a smile she thought: I told him I would go away. Only, she said aloud, it's not like I would have even a week to enjoy myself: Royal will come right down and get me.

Both her friends laughed at this. You're so silly, said Baby. I'd like to see that Royal when some of our men got through with him.

I wouldn't stand for anybody hurting Royal, said Ottilie. Besides, he'd be even madder when we got home.

Baby said: But Ottilie, you wouldn't be coming back here with him.

Ottilie giggled, and looked about the room as though she saw something invisible to the others. Why, sure I would, she said.

Rolling her eyes, Baby produced a fan and jerked it in front of her face. That's the craziest thing I've ever heard, she said between hard lips. Isn't that the craziest thing you've ever heard, Rosita?

It's that Ottilie's been through so much, said Rosita. Dear, why don't you lie down on the bed while we pack your things?

Ottilie watched as they commenced piling her possessions. They scooped her combs and pins, they wound up her silk stockings. She took off her pretty clothes, as if she were going to put on something finer still; instead, she slipped back into her old dress; then, working quietly, and as though she were helping her friends, she put everything back where it belonged. Baby stamped her foot when she saw what was happening.

Listen, said Ottilie. If you and Rosita are my friends, please do what I tell you: tie me in the yard just like I was when you came. That way no bee is ever going to sting me.

Stinking drunk, said Baby; but Rosita told her to shut up. I think, said Rosita with a sigh, I think Ottilie is in love. If Royal wanted her back, she would go with him, and this being the way things were they might as well go home and say that Madame was right, that Ottilie was dead.

Yes, said Ottilie, for the drama of it appealed to her. Tell them that I am dead.

So they went into the yard; there, with heaving bosoms and eyes as round as the daytime moon scudding above, Baby said she would have no part in tying Ottilie to the tree, which left Rosita to do it alone. On parting, it was Ottilie who cried the most, though she was glad to see them go, for she knew that as soon as they were gone she would not think of them again. Teetering on their high heels down the dips of the path, they turned to wave, but Ottilie could not wave back, and so she forgot them before they were out of sight.

Chewing eucalyptus leaves to sweeten her breath, she felt the chill of twilight twitch the air. Yellow deepened the daytime moon, and roosting birds sailed into the darkness of the tree. Suddenly, hearing Royal on the path, she threw her legs akimbo, let her neck go limp, lolled her eyes far back into their sockets. Seen from a distance, it would look as though she had come to some violent, pitiful end; and, listening to Royal's footsteps quicken to a run, she happily thought: This will give him a good scare.

from Southwest Review

SENSE OF DIRECTION

LEONARD CASPER *is a native of Fond du Lac, Wisconsin, where he was born in 1923. He took his B.A. and M.A. at the University of Wisconsin and is now teaching there while working at the same time for a Ph.D. He went into the Army in 1943 and served three years, part of the time in Czechoslovakia and Germany. He has published stories in* Story, Cronos, *and* The New Mexico Quarterly Review, *besides* The Southwest Review. *His poetry has appeared in* Interim, Bard Review, Accent, Western Review, *and* The Kansas Magazine. *The poetry, he writes, "has helped to inform the prose, but so far this affection does not seem to be returned."*

Where was he running?

"Go'n outside. Git out now! Go'n outside and play." Long Kever's fierce eyes subtracted his son's twelve years from his own forty and asserted authority. "You're not mopin round here. I got trouble enough."

J. W. hated him then. "He's my brother," he said, his lips barely moving off his teeth.

Long made a backhand motion. "Sass?"

"He's my brother!" The boy slid around the doorway of the farmhouse and backed into the kitchen. With his dinner pail and schoolbooks he felt defenseless.

"Forget about Meade." Long curved over his son in contempt. "What're you after, anyway, a ride in the car?" he added hastily. Nothing was wasted in his face; the bones were compact under thin skin. Even his clothes were worn to the stubborn shape of his body. "We're go'n in t'Arkana tonight and pick up Meade and you're stayin

46

put here. You're gonna be in bed by the time the wake begins. You hear?"

J. W. looked around for help. But there was no one in the kitchen except Gran, who was swiddling water meaninglessly over some boiling eggs. And he was too old to make any difference.

"Now don't go faunchin around. Just you git out and gimme some peace!"

The boy was almost crying, but not for his brother, as he turned away and walked through the house. He saw his mother stretched out on her bed as if she were holding her breath; there was only the slightest tick of the mattress under her heartbeat. Milo, the hired hand, was out with the shoats. The house was so quiet that it frightened J. W., hanging over his head like a deadfall.

He went upstairs to the little room that he had shared with Meade until last year. He missed his brother because he'd been the only one with push enough, finally, to stand up to their daddy. J. W. hoped to be like Meade that way. Otherwise, they were nine years apart, with little to bring them together. (In fact, once Meade had offered to skin J.'s dog, Josha, alive.)

In memory of Meade, however, and of anger that Meade had trained in him, J. W. walked to the part of the room closest to the kitchen and slammed his books onto the floor. Then just as deliberately he dropped his lunch pail, feeling caving mad and mean.

Specially mean because last week end the Beaudettes had been over and his daddy had been so nice to their kids, and it struck him that Daddy was always nicer to other people's kids than he was to his own. Usually Long was far away and sulky and all he talked about was farm, farm, until the words ran out of J. W.'s ears, the way they had run out of Meade's. He felt mean because, remembering Meade, he knew how to act now.

He changed clothes quietly, sweating in the compact heat that had bunched under the rafters; quietly he pulled himself together with a bradded belt and padded back downstairs. From the foreroom he could see that his daddy was watching him, drumming lean fingers nervously on the boiler of cistern water he was heating on the range for his bath. His face was like bobwire now, after all that upstairs ruckus; and J. W. wisely just slid himself out the front doorway.

Up the road he could see four boys strung out, walking, with their books and dogs. J. W. reached under the front porch and pulled out a coffee sack of colored rags that he'd been saving. Then he still had time to whistle up Josha.

But the shrill sound also brought Long Kever to the front door. His narrow chest was drawing in and out with the effort to control himself. But at the same time that J. W. was worried by him, the boy was wondering just how far he could go before his daddy got out the razor strop.

He whistled again, this time not so shrilly. There was commotion in the far cornfields which were heavy and ready for snapping and shaking thunderously; then a red-haired beagle came tearing across the brooding stretches of cowpeas, grinning and sticking out her tongue. J. W. looked up innocently in the direction of the front door. "We're gonna play."

Long nodded, his mouth locked. He's my son, take it easy, he told himself and tried to reconcile this older J. with the little tad in Sunday rompers and bangs, and the quiet boy sucking his collar tip. I won't hit him while I'm mad; but if I let him mojo me much more, he'll be like Meade in a few years, gettin stuck with some Georgian's cotton knife or stickin someone else. *What hath God wrought?*

The blasphemy came so suddenly and revealed his weakness so surely that his anger flared up in self-defense, and he had to look back toward the kitchen to keep himself from shouting.

Damned old man there: thinkin he can cook, good for nothin, just cootin round! Broken veins like fungus on his face; eyes the color of blue-john.

Then it was safe to look outside again. He wouldn't ask J. W. where those rags came from, though Mary Elizabeth could have made a nice throw-rug out of them.

Two of the schoolboys were Beaudettes; the others were neighbors farther down the line. They all ran toward J. W. on the road and held handsawing parleys while their dogs circled one another and sniffed. Long could hear them talk about playing fox and saw them looking at the woods across the road. Then J. W. went into the shed to get ropes for the dogs.

As usual, Lindy Beaudette had Booger with him, a little bench-legged feist-dog who was always complaining. The other dogs were sooners, too, but didn't seem to mind so much.

Long couldn't help thinking how satisfied the boys looked, standing there surrounded by their own; and J. W. looked just as content, as he joined them. But Long had an inkling of what could go on behind glad faces. Just last week end the Beaudette tribe had been over and they'd talked all night and J. W. had seemed to be paying no attention to the grownups and had played with Lindy and Snub, but afterward he had asked Mary Elizabeth some searching questions that showed he'd been on to them all the while. They'd been talking babies.

When J. was suckin, Long thought, I wasn't any use to him; now he's growin up and I still ain't much help, but I'm cockier and I don't know it always. He's gettin on and he's liable to pass me up if I don't stop backtrackin and start findin out where this-all is headin. Little whipsnapper!

Be back for supper, Long thought, holding back on his irritation. "Be back for supper," he yelled, letting it slip, angrily.

J. W. faced him. "I don't choose any boiled aiggs," he whimpered. Supper table was a foreign land to him now, which he saw in his mind's eye webbed with silent gravestone faces.

"Be back, you hear!" Long shouted. He didn't bother to say there'd be applesauce and coffee and corndodger, too. Gran might spoil everything.

A cross-pollinating windful of fluff and seed swept suddenly from the opposite tree line, joining father and son for a moment in a wilderness of gusts.

Then J. dropped his eyes. Without answering he handed Josha's rope to one of the boys, tore the coffee bag on a fence nail so that it made two ties to twist around his waist, and started off through the weeds and into the woods. The other boys waited ten minutes and then followed, Booger leading the pack.

Remember to take J. huntin, Long noted, and went back to check the boiler of bath water. Everything seemed important that day, even the smudges on the wallpaper, and he was afraid he would miss what was most important. He stopped in the parlor to turn on the radio, hoping to get some music to soothe Mary Elizabeth.

There's a hundred patterns of radio waves crisscrossin the air, he thought. When I pick just one here, or here, I forget about the others bein there. Now could I open the dial all the way at once . . . But

49

everthin comes to us piecemeal, bite-size. No wonder I can't get a handhold.

He remembered catching himself many times sitting dully at the supper table while Meade and Mary Elizabeth had included him out of their talk and he had tried to trigger it out, trying to be fair, trying not to get mad, almost kicking Mary Elizabeth, and then becoming indifferent and stony because, after all, he was only himself and couldn't get into the others without their say-so.

There was a storm in the air, and static ran razorback-wild. He snapped the radio off entirely.

And a strange bird sounding like steel on whetrock and the ripshin thickets and hardwood shelter crowns. J. W. dropped a colored rag of spoor each time he changed direction. He stopped to scratch his back against the bark of a tree, trying to think up a new trail to follow. They had played this game so often that, to keep him*self* interested, he had to populate the underbrush with wild animals, like pariah and carrion. He didn't know exactly what pariah and carrion were, except that he'd met them in a book once; but he imagined that their color was black and they took on sudden-awful shapes, like a sea change. Black was the right background for being a silver fox. Meade was dead, stabbed in a fight with Georgia cotton pickers. And J. felt that somehow his daddy was mostly responsible. Black. His mama had an angel's face and laughed a great deal with her sons.

Then he heard Josha's bugle getting too close; he spat into the palm of his hand, slapped it, and followed the meager pointer to the right.

While Long: opened the cold-water tap from the windmill pump reservoir and let a trickle of water into the metal tub in the room next to Mary Elizabeth's. He pulled at his face in the mirror while he waited, decided he wouldn't have to shave again before next morning. He'd been unreasonable toward J. W., he realized, but it irritated him to think that the boy liked his brother for all the wrong reasons.

He felt he had no friends in the house: his sons, sometimes indifferent, often dissatisfied, and occasionally hating deeply; Mary Elizabeth, with her more subtle avoidance of him.

Long hated to think of the hours he would spend sitting with

Meade's body that night and the thoughts he would think. If he had let J. watch with him, it would have been even worse, he was afraid. J. was on the way to being like his brother, and Long preferred not to face him.

I'd rather be a kid, twistin rabbits in the woods *any* time!

And chickarees dropping nutshells from oak branches and the crawl of black emmets on a slickery ellum and a pariah cobra with a flecked hood that rose up and up until it overmassed the stacked clouds. *I see a fox. The fox runs. The fox eats grapes. My teeth are set on edge to the seventh generation. The fox is . . .* J. W. Kever, impressing on himself the importance of being sly and fast and wicked. This was no game.

He didn't need a compass, because long ago he had noticed that the forest was a mixture of hard and softwoods, and almost always the softwood sections were poleward from the hard. So he knew his directions even when the sun couldn't filtrate through the treetops, knew them as well as a mother's hand knows the shape of her baby's head. He dropped a blue rag and ran on.

While Long: turned off the tap and went to the kitchen to dipper out the hot water into his bucket. Gran had the makings of the corn-dodger in the skillet ready to bake, he noticed. "Looks right good," Long said, making the effort. There was no answer. Well, maybe he was deaf. A piece gone here, a piece there.

On the way to the tub Long cut eyes at his wife's bedroom. She was still stretched out, the way she'd been since noon, since he had finally told her that Meade was dead. He himself had known it for several days and had arranged for shipment of the body. Every time he had seen Mary Elizabeth, he had meant to tell her; but each time she had looked away, as usual, with that puzzling little smile of the untouchable, until finally he had lost his temper and shouted, "Well I hope you're happy now your son went and got three inches of cold steel between his ribs that's what you get for encouragin him to leave yes it's a fact and you can smile to yourself all you want now."

No one deserved to be spoken to like that. Had *he* said it? To his *wife?*

He felt an urge to go in and comfort her. Once he had actually gone to the door and called softly, "Honey?" But she didn't even move. He would never enter her room again; he acknowledged that their bed rites were over.

He remembered when he had first started tenanting next to her father's farm. She was eighteen. Was there more to come? he had wondered. She had seemed perfect as a circle. Then the night of their first quarrel: she was crying while he stood by, too proud to speak, too ashamed to leave. Mary Elizabeth had said, through a welter of weeping, "These should be your tears on my face." And, startled, he had loved her with certainty.

Now he could remember only being startled; now, as then, he disbelieved that she was capable of feeling as deeply as she had spoken. Where had she borrowed that expression? What slip of the dial picked something real, revealed, then overruled?

More clearly he recalled the first two years of marriage, and his futile attempts to prolong love. After Meade was born, he had given up: she couldn't, or wouldn't, be both mother and wife. She had decided to love her child and, Long suspected, had decided that her child was to love no one but her. She had succeeded.

Long had been involved in seasons, sickness, crops, and payments, and he would have found it difficult to be a friend of his son even if Mary Elizabeth hadn't interfered. Still he had done his best, with J. W. as well as with Meade, trying to curb his temper, trying to do what was right even though the boys couldn't understand, trying to give them things he had done without, yet trying not to spoil them. But he didn't have a chance.

How many times had he wanted to beat Meade (as Gran had whipped *him*) when he saw him growing up with a smart mouth full of back talk! But he had held back, even when he was sure he was right, had clinched his hands behind him and ruled by overbearing, because he knew that as it was his reasons were being twisted by his wife and she was winning their children at his expense by siding with them; and because he himself wanted their affection so badly. Until at last he had slapped Meade's smart mouth and they had cuss-fought and then fist-fought in the kitchen, the boy almost as strong as the man twice his age; had broken dishes, cracked the table, clinched and struck against the walls and kitchen stove, and rolled in a deadlock, panting, swearing, weak with anger, on the hardwood floor; with Mary Elizabeth pretending to cover J. W.'s eyes and holding him so he couldn't run out of the room and whispering that his daddy was a brute but she would care for him always.

They had rolled apart, crying; and without a word Meade had taken his things, kissed his mother, and walked down the road. She had defeated Long: and he began to wonder if she had married him just to be married. Who can remember?

Then not a word from Meade for a year, not a word as far as *he* knew. Might as well be dead! Long had thought.

Next day, the letter came.

Angrily Long threw the hot water into the tub and went back for more. He felt Gran's presence an insult: he never told me; if I'd known it could be like this . . .

A hawk of spittle flew from Gran's mouth and sizzed on the forefront of the stove. Damned old man! with his rooty hands and otherworld air. He'd already outlived his brain by years.

Chewing the inside of his mouth furiously, Long turned away.

And frogstools in a glom of weeds and a clutch of fat pine and civvy-cats green-eyed over carrion and medlars singing through the grass. J. W. let the whicker of an owl lead him down the foxpath from the anxious hunting cries of Booger and the Beaudettes. He was sweating hard underneath his bradded belt, and his armpits dripped. Loss of breath made him dizzy; and when the wilderness opened and closed too often, he had to stop for air and pick a new path. The ragbag was getting lighter and he barely felt it. But the baying shouts behind him pressed him forward, hunted. Clouds like plagues of ferros drove eastward with him toward the Mississippi.

He struck a glade where the longleaf were scarce, and he bolted across it, dodging from tree to tree, frightened—like a rabbit, he thought, wishing he could see behind him like a rabbit too. Then he remembered to be a fox, and he clicked his teeth and was mean again. He threw himself down a covered draw cut by a creek. He broke through the bushes and left a red rag, like a drop of blood, on the bank before heading upstream.

The wind excited the bearded trees overhead, and he shivered a little, not from the shallow cold of the water but from his wild sense of solitude. When he left the creek, forty feet up, he was no longer a silver fox but a timberwolf with cold eyes. He cut back at the razor-grass with angry supple feet.

In broad evening and bedside, the cancer feeds on crocodile, bow-shot.

While Long: sank into the tepid bath water and tried to relax. Tried not to think, but *felt* his thoughts anyway. Felt: I planned for Meade to run this farm someday and have it his own. He could still have had it if he'd apologized. No; if he had lived.

Gran was singing in the kitchen, without words, without tune, in a retching voice like a tin shovel scooping water off a concrete barn floor. Exactly.

Long shivered. Why did Mary Elizabeth think she had to kill me piece by piece this way? What am I scapegoat for in her life?

Whose boy are you, sonny? Mommy's boy.

Someday J. W. will likely understand and be grateful. That's all I care about; what happens to me meantime don't matter. He'll realize. (But kids never do. Long thought of his own father.) Well, maybe J. W. will be different; he'll understand, when he has kids of his own; (shrug) or maybe not.

I'm never gonna figure on him, that's a cinch; then I won't ever be disappointed.

This is my problem, and I got to trigger it out all alone.

But I can't. Not alone. It'd take more than *I* got to sweat it out by myself and maybe be stoned and hope someday to be stamped with approval, after I'm gone.

Mercy!

No; a man can't stop feelin, any more than he can shave off his beard, once and finally. *But, mercy!*

And white scud and young lions couched in dens and old birches watered with sunshine and freckled leaves and the laughing call of mockers. Flight, like a black pariah, the smell of daylight no longer bouncing so handily from the soft, packed shatters. Flat, lying head-less in the tussocks, panting, while laughing boys and dogs run by within bowshot. Ain't they tired, why'm I so winded, am I lost? Just one chance more, just a breather, then I'll run—what was that? I thought I heard . . . There's a skeeter in my ear!

In what pits of the body a yellow taste is brewed. Trees repeat themselves for tortured eyes. The siffle of air through the grass like the rut of waves, a sound of grating bone, of teeth. Who can lie alone, unfeeling, denying there's an insect in the ear?

With a cry J. W. leaped to his feet and raced for the other bend of the creek. He knew he was heard, and that the hunters would close in, but he didn't care. He howled once, in a triplet of terror, like a coyote, and broke cover. Then a wicker of saplings protected him. He was fierce and proud and angry, tired and hurt, but mostly angry, at everyone, at anything. He snarled at the wild goats of the rock.

The coffee sack was empty; all the red rags of blood were gone. Now the dogs must follow by the spoor of J. himself. And they did. Booger smelled a track of fear and Josha bugled imminent siege.

Then Mary Elizabeth: over and over, rolling stationary. It was an assault on my body, every time, not at all like I had imagined, not at all like brotherly love, like a clean-limbed young-man courtship, but foul, physical, and no saving grace, frightful, worse than bestial, cruel.

Meade was different—sweet, wholesome, affectionate, giving me the advantage, letting me be private again, a protection, giving no occasion to hurt, brotherly. *Lover boy.*

I didn't keep him, so I killed him. (He would have loved me.) Now everyone will slay me, unless there's put a mark upon me; make a mark of grief upon my face, that asks compassion, then they'll hold their hand. (Oh, let me hold you.)

While Long felt: tension of the water surface throwing reflections. He saw samaras from the cistern, like a manswarm of seeds against his unprepared body; made an open-closing hand to catch them, and lost them in the swirl. Searching inward parts, in what pit of the body pity?

Felt: what relation am I to my sons?

Felt fear, like a taste of rennet in his mouth.

What quitclaim have I got on them, or them on me? May be I need them; but the day they don't need me, what then? Do I take up with someone else's cubs, like Beaudette's, for instance, because I can't feel human by myself? Like scratchin a cat's back because you kinda like the feel of fur on your hand, and her humpin: as long as you're both satisfied, it's a bargain. But when Meade disinherits me, when he says, "Now I'm my own ancestor; I don't want you," what lie can I tell him about blood or instinct to keep him mine?

What's a wife? What's a grandfather? *Don't you think he looks like his daddy?* What's a family? Can't act like human beins, it's all over. What law ever enforced affection? No relation lasts forever; that's why it's relative.

I could go on pettin a cat that scratches. But martyrs are better off dead; livin martyrs risk they might become holier-than-thou and self-satisfied and whiny.

Where am I runnin?

We broke new ground—for a burial. Tomorrow we're gonna plant hope, for final.

I'll go t'Arkana, see about a settlement. (Shrug) Man does what he can—then tries to save the pieces.

But the crack's still in the kitchen table.

And I'll be by myself.

Felt: fear of being too reasonable again; afraid of being afraid.

And the sour smell of humus and the twinkle of needles and flutter of cambered leaves and a hardened ostrich lurching her eggs in the dust as though they weren't hers. J. W. tasted his hatred as he sped blindly through the forest, no longer careful, making a thousand criss-cross noises because he had heard Snub and Lindy call each other to break off saplings for clubs. Now sunless and solitary despite the nearness of pursuit, he panted carefully, on the brink of losing control, and made snap judgments with his rolling wild eyes.

He struck another clearing and, rather than risk back-tracking, ran straightforward across it, thinking over and over, "Dog eat dog, dog eat dog," not knowing where the words came from. Bushes scuffled against his legs. The sun was going down behind him, going past and around, the wind was sinking, but he couldn't turn. Wearing a pelt of sweat and grinding his palms with his raggled claws till they ached and his fingers groaned.

Three crows suddenly chased a blinded, rutching owl low in the air before his face. The frantic owl, fugitive and vagabond, paddled heavily in the leaden air, the crows shrill, vicious, driving it ahead with rapid slashes at its eyes and body. They passed together through the walls of hemlock.

J. W. drove forward with increased cruelty, refusing to spare himself, smashing the underbrush with his body, feeling driven, feeling hunted, fugitive and vagabond. This was the way Meade would run, half-Indian half-deer, half-man half-legend, with lips drawn back over the teeth, supple-tense, not a brother but an idol, with a body like a landmark, with ropes of smoke disdaining from his nostrils, and a heart that ran up and down within the cage of ribs like a restless panther.

J. W. licked his chapped lips. Overhead swallows were falling through the trees like leaves. The ground was sozzling. With an inrush of prone gray light, like layered clay, he found himself ringed in by sycamore and gum trees and the windless stinging weeds of river bottoms, and then he was in loblolly, red and thicker than water, with no north-south distinction of trees, and looking for all the world like everywhere else.

Where am I runnin?

He had to stop anyway: there was a big wild hog blocking his path. Its back was lean but powerful and hunched with waiting, muscled with readiness; its eyes were the eyes of a brass statue; it straddled his way like a boulder, soundless and unsearchable. Breathing heavily but with what he thought was a smile, J. approached his kin. The brass liquefied; the wild hog inched backward, and suddenly was no longer there.

J. W. brushed away sweat and hair and tears from his eyes, feeling solitary and rejected, raked with fear and the force of his own imagination. He looked for landmarks and could recognize none. Not knowing which way to turn, he was turning all ways, spinning and sobbing, when the dogs came up, no longer on ropes, baying and hooting and down at the mouth. He could barely see them. Booger was ahead and overran him; then they were all around him snapping, a foot away, eager but puzzled and cringing.

"I'm a mean wild animal," J. W. explained, scarcely recognizing his own voice, because it was his brother's and he hadn't heard it for a year. But he wasn't just a wild animal because if he had been, they would have fallen on him and torn him up, and instead they were almost terrified, and he had been running for nothing. Josha, who had too much courage for her own good and would have run a bear, looked away bewildered when J. knelt and stretched out his hand. His heart toppled when Josha bugled once down in her throat, piteously. He saw himself with their eyes and he was Meade, Cain-faced and mocking, so cruel and terrifying that even J. felt unwelcome and could not stand him, and he remembered how the wild hog had disclaimed him and then he knew that the hog was real. Darkness came and went, throughout the river bottom. His separate cells were panic-stricken and dispersed, and there was a taste of rennet in his mouth.

Before he realized it, J. W. had taken a branch from the ground, kicked his way through the dogs, and was pummeling the boys who had come up hollering, with their saplings uplifted half in fun. The aftereffects of his unbearable fear and loneliness and grief and forced iconoclasm clubbed them powerfully, and shouting, sobbing, whining they pounded back at him.

Long Kever stood against the doorjamb, listening to the rain-crows, feeling corroded with thought but thinking he had triumphed. Hellfire and pain were everlastin, he decided, but heaven was indrawn, it was a whipstitch. Though if it was the real thing, it still outweighed. There was no reason to think of heaven as quantity-bulk in the first place. Love was like heaven, a brief possession, unsearchable, hard to reconstruct with two-by-fours and buildin blocks; but love was like heaven. There was no use lookin for it from anyone he already knew. He'd have to start over. Man does what he can: the rest is the wake.

He grinned sourly, halfway pleased with himself (*at least I reached me a startin point*), and looked over at Gran. That old bag of body noises! Old tenderhead! He felt, for a moment, as wise as Gran and all old men were supposed to be. Why *wasn't* Gran? Because, thought wise Long Kever, men forget. Body cells keep flushin and changin, they tell me, and so is it any wonder that before we all die, we been a lot of persons too? It takes a great man to be himself and still *be* somebody, and to remember, when he should.

Gran (old J. W., W. for Walton but J. for Job) was still at the stove, his ten thumbs burning themselves and knocking off noisy potlids. Although he knew he was being watched, he showed no concern, but basked in the warmth of his activity. For ten years he had carried on a running interior talk with his dead wife, and he had long ago reached the point where he could change the subject without apologizing.

"Y'see now, Long thinks he's thinkin, Mama, but that's jis his way of grief. So let it come out, ain't that rahght? Much study, seth the Good Book, is a weariness of the flesh. Ol' skin an' bones parahh dogs is they own carr'n, eatin off they own fat. He's wrong, but let him suffuh his own way. Younguns jis ain't got no respeck no more, is all, gittin too fahn-heered an' thinkin they's first-folks a'ready. It's all done now: one snappuh carryin on the name, is all. It ain't the same as what we all spected, is it, Mama? But Ah c'n say Ah done did mah sheer, put mahse'f up as scapergoat, tangled mahse'f in the bramblers rahght handy foh him to cuss at and heap mah back with dislahkin, go on, let'm take it outen me, Ah'm old, hopin he wouldn sacrifahce the boy, cause boys is hahd to come by sometahms. Ah done mah sheer, an' when it all breaks up, Ah'll take keer this ol' self, too, don' worry, Mama. Ah puts mah trust in the Lawd and looks to the hah't foh comfo't."

He began to set places at the table, forgetting and then adding one for Milo who came in silently and scrubbed at the washbasin, then sat with his head hung on his hands, feeling no grief but in sympathy with the silence.

The stillness of first dark, too early for crickets, slowly drained Long of all facsimile of satisfaction. *We close our hands on water.* Reason said it had to be so. He gripped the scarred wood of the door-jamb, wondering if it gripped him back or whether those little whirl-ing molecules were running around and running away.

The air was momentarily aflash, the sun as seen through copper screening, just before it dropped below the western twilight hills. It trembled among the trees across the road, then passed.

The trees split, the quiet frazzled off, as a clout of boys and dogs distinguished themselves from the forest, their voices frightened and worried, tired feet driven by the memory of the fight that had wrung them with its vicious senselessness, their sudden grasp that they were lost, and J. W.'s saving sense of direction which even he had doubted but which had brought them, sobbing, to their startup.

Looking at them, Long wondered starkly, "What's this got to do with me?"

The boys all flung themselves and their dogs down among the books around the bridal-wreath bush, except J. W. who was afraid to stop. Eyes closed with tears, hands hanging open at his side, J. ran to the man in the doorway and sheltered his face in the pit of Long's stomach. Long's own hands were working; finally one of them came around awkwardly, came up fearfully, and chucked J. W. on the nape of the neck.

He stood silently. He stood silently in the dark. He stood silently in the dark with his own.

from The New Yorker

THE POT OF GOLD

JOHN CHEEVER *was born in Quincy, Massachusetts, in 1912. He attended Thayer Academy in Braintree, and has lived since in
Washington, D.C., and New York City. His stories have appeared in* The New Yorker *over a period of years, as well as in*
Harper's Bazaar, Mademoiselle, Collier's, The Atlantic Monthly,
New Republic, Yale Review, *and* Story. *He has made two previous appearances in this collection, with "I'm Going to Asia" in
1943 and "Vega" in 1950. Asked to bring his biography down to
date, Mr. Cheever said he "had two children and a new pair of
shoes," but was not certain either fact was relevant.*

You could not say fairly of Ralph and Laura Whittemore that they
had the failings and the characteristics of incorrigible treasure hunters, but you could say truthfully of them that the shimmer and the
smell, the peculiar force of money, the promise of it, had an un-
toward influence on their lives. They were always at the threshold of
fortune; they always seemed to have something on the fire. Ralph
was a fair young man with a tireless commercial imagination and an
evangelical credence in the romance and sorcery of business success,
and although he held an obscure job with a clothing manufacturer,
this never seemed to him anything more than a point of departure.

The Whittemores were not importunate or overbearing people,
and they had an uncompromising loyalty to the gentle manners of
the middle class. Laura was a pleasant girl of no particular beauty
who had come to New York from Wisconsin at about the same time
that Ralph had reached the city from Illinois, but it had taken two
years of comings and goings before they had been brought together,
late one afternoon, in the lobby of a lower Fifth Avenue office build-

ing. So true was Ralph's heart, so well did it serve him then, that the moment he saw Laura's light hair and her pretty and sullen face he was enraptured. He followed her out of the lobby, pushing his way through the crowd, and since she had dropped nothing, since there was no legitimate excuse to speak to her, he shouted after her, "*Louise! Louise! Louise!*" and the urgency in his voice made her stop. He said he'd made a mistake. He said he was sorry. He said she looked just like a girl named Louise Hatcher. It was a January night and the dark air tasted of smoke, and because she was a sensible and a lonely girl, she let him buy her a drink.

This was in the thirties, and their courtship was hasty. They were married three months later. Laura moved her belongings into a walkup on Madison Avenue, above a pants presser's and a florist's, where Ralph was living. She worked as a secretary, and her salary, added to what he brought home from the clothing business, was little more than enough to keep them going, but they never seemed touched by the monotony of a saving and gainless life. They ate dinners in drugstores. She hung a reproduction of van Gogh's "Sunflowers" above the sofa she had bought with some of the small sum of money her parents had left her. When their aunts and uncles came to town—their parents were dead—they had dinner at the Ritz and went to the theater. She sewed curtains and shined his shoes, and on Sundays they stayed in bed until noon. They seemed to be standing at the threshold of plenty; and Laura often told people that she was terribly excited because of this wonderful job that Ralph had lined up.

In the first year of their marriage, Ralph worked nights on a plan that promised him a well-paying job in Texas, but through no fault of his own this promise was never realized. There was an opening in Syracuse a year later, but an older man was decided upon. There were many other profitable but elusive openings and projects between these two. In the third year of their marriage, a firm that was almost identical in size and character with the firm Ralph worked for underwent a change of ownership, and Ralph was approached and asked if he would be interested in joining the overhauled firm. His own job promised only meager security after a series of slow promotions and he was glad of the chance to escape. He met the new owners, and their enthusiasm for him seemed intense. They were prepared to put him in charge of a department and pay him twice what he was getting then. The arrangement was to remain tacit for a month or two, until the new owners had secured their position, but they shook hands warmly and had a drink on the deal, and that night Ralph took Laura out to dinner at an expensive restaurant.

They decided, across the table, to look for a larger apartment, to have a child, and to buy a secondhand car. They faced their good fortune with perfect calm, for it was what they had expected all along. The city seemed to them a generous place, where people were rewarded either by a sudden and deserved development like this or by the capricious bounty of lawsuits, eccentric and peripheral business ventures, unexpected legacies, and other windfalls. After dinner, they walked in Central Park in the moonlight while Ralph smoked a cigar. Later, when Laura had fallen asleep, he sat in the open bedroom window in his pajamas.

The peculiar excitement with which the air of the city seems charged after midnight, when its life falls into the hands of watchmen and drunks, had always pleased him. He knew intimately the sounds of the night street: the bus brakes, the remote sirens, and the sound of water turning high in the air—the sound of water turning a mill wheel—the sum, he supposed, of many echoes, although, often as he had heard the sound, he had never decided on its source. Now he heard all this more keenly because the night seemed to him portentous.

He was twenty-eight years old; poverty and youth were inseparable in his experience, and one was ending with the other. The life they were about to leave had not been hard, and he thought with sentiment of the soiled tablecloth in the Italian restaurant where they usually went for their celebrations, and the high spirits with which Laura on a wet night ran from the subway to the bus stop. But they were drawing away from all this. Shirt sales in department-store basements, lines at meat counters, weak drinks, the sooty jonquils he brought her up from the subway in the spring, when jonquils were cheap—these were all unmistakably the souvenirs of the poor, and while they seemed to him good and gentle, he was glad that they would soon be memories.

Laura resigned from her job when she got pregnant. The reorganization and Ralph's new position hung fire, but the Whittemores talked about it freely when they were with friends. "We're *terribly* pleased with the way things are going," Laura would say. "All we need is patience." There were many delays and postponements, and they waited with the patience of people expecting justice. The time came when they both needed clothes, and one evening Ralph suggested that they spend some of the money they had put aside. Laura refused. When he brought up the subject, she didn't answer him and seemed not to hear him. He raised his voice and lost his temper. He shouted. She cried. He thought of all the other girls he could have married—the dark blonde, the worshipful Cuban, the rich and pretty one with a cast in her right eye. All his desires seemed to lie outside the small apartment Laura had arranged. They were still not speaking in the morning, and in order to strengthen his position he telephoned his potential employers. Their secretary told him they were both out. This made him apprehensive. He called several times from the telephone booth in the lobby of the building he worked in and was told that they were busy, they were out, they were in conference with lawyers, or they were talking long distance. This variety of excuses frightened him. He said nothing to Laura that evening and tried to call them the next day. Late in the afternoon, after many tries, one of them came to the phone. "We gave the job to somebody else, sonny," he said. Like a saddened father, he spoke to Ralph in a hoarse and gentle voice. "Don't try and get us on the telephone any more. We've got other things to do besides answer the telephone. This other fellow seemed better suited, sonny. That's all I can tell you, and don't try to get me on the telephone any more."

Ralph walked the miles from his office to his apartment that night, hoping to free himself in this way from some of the weight of his disappointment. He was so unprepared for the shock that it affected him like vertigo, and he walked with an odd, high step, as if the paving were quicksand. He stood downstairs in front of the building he lived in, trying to decide how to describe the disaster to Laura, but when he went in, he told her bluntly. "Oh, I'm sorry, darling," she said softly, and kissed him. "I'm terribly sorry." She wandered away from him and began to straighten the sofa cushions. His frustration was so ardent, he was such a prisoner of his schemes and expectations, that he was astonished at the serenity with which she regarded the failure. There was nothing to worry about, she said. She still had a few hundred dollars in the bank, from the money her parents had left her. There was nothing to worry about.

When the child, a girl, was born, they named her Rachel, and a week after the delivery Laura returned to the Madison Avenue walkup. She took all the care of the baby and continued to do the cooking and the housework.

Ralph's imagination remained resilient and fertile, but he couldn't seem to hit on a scheme that would fit into his lack of time and capital. He and Laura, like the hosts of the poor everywhere, lived a simple life. They still went to the theater with visiting relatives and occasionally they went to parties, but Laura's only continuous contact with the bright lights that surrounded them was vicarious and came to her through a friend she made in Central Park.

She spent many afternoons on a park bench during the first years of Rachel's life. It was a tyranny and a pleasure. She resented her enchainment but enjoyed the open sky and the air. One winter afternoon she recognized a woman she had met at a party, and a little before dark, as Laura and the other mothers were gathering their stuffed animals and preparing their children for the cold journey home, the woman came across the playground and spoke to her. She was Alice Holinshed, she said. They had met at the Galvins'. She was pretty and friendly, and walked with Laura to the edge of the Park. She had a boy of about Rachel's age. The two women met again the following day. They became friends.

Mrs. Holinshed was older than Laura, but she had a more youthful and precise beauty. Her hair and her eyes were black, her pale and perfectly oval face was delicately colored, and her voice was pure. She lighted her cigarettes with Stork Club matches and spoke of the inconvenience of living with a child in a hotel. If Laura had any regrets about her life, they were expressed in her friendship for this pretty woman, who moved so freely through expensive stores and restaurants.

It was a friendship circumscribed, with the exception of the Galvins', by the sorry and touching countryside of Central Park. The women talked principally about their husbands, and this was a game that Laura could play with an empty purse. Vaguely, boastfully, the two women discussed the irons their men had in the fire. They sat together with their children through the sooty twilights, when the city to the south burns like a Bessemer furnace, and the air smells of coal, and the wet boulders shine like slag, and the Park itself seems like a strip of woods on the edge of a coal town. Then Mrs. Holinshed would remember that she was late—she was always late for something mysterious and splendid—and the two women would walk together to the edge of the woods. This vicarious contact with comfort pleased Laura, and the pleasure would stay with her as she pushed the baby carriage over to Madison Avenue and then began to cook supper, hearing the thump of the steam iron and smelling the cleaning fluid from the pants presser's below.

One night, when Rachel was about two years old, the frustration of Ralph's search for the goat track that would let him lead his family to a realm of reasonable contentment kept him awake. He needed sleep urgently, and when this blessing eluded him, he got out of bed and sat in the dark. The charm and excitement of the street after midnight escaped him. The explosive brakes of a Madison Avenue bus made him jump. He shut the window, but the noise of traffic continued to pass through it. It seemed to him that the penetrating voice of the city had a mortal effect on the precious lives of the city's inhabitants and that it should be muffled.

He thought of a Venetian blind whose outer surfaces would be treated with a substance that would deflect or absorb sound waves. With such a blind, friends paying a call on a spring evening would not have to shout to be heard above the noise of trucks in the street below. Bedrooms could be silenced that way—bedrooms, above all, for it seemed to him then that sleep was what everyone in the city sought and only half captured. All the harried faces on the streets at dusk, when even the pretty girls talk to themselves, were looking for sleep. Night-club singers and their amiable customers, the people waiting for taxis in front of the Waldorf on a wet night, policemen, cashiers, window washers—sleep eluded them all.

He talked over this Venetian blind with Laura the following night, and the idea seemed sensible to her. He bought a blind that would fit their bedroom window, and experimented with various paint mixtures. At last he stumbled on one that dried to the consistency of felt and was porous. The paint had a sickening smell, which filled their apartment during the four days it took him to coat and recoat the outer surface of the slats. When the paint had dried, he hung the blind, and they opened the window for a test. Silence—a relative silence—charmed their ears. He wrote down his formula, and took it during his lunch hour to a patent attorney. It took the lawyer several weeks to discover that a similar formula had been patented some years earlier. The patent owner—a man named Fellows—had a New York address, and the lawyer suggested that Ralph get in touch with him and try to reach some agreement.

The search for Mr. Fellows began one evening when Ralph had finished work, and took him first to the attic of a Hudson Street rooming house, where the landlady showed Ralph a pair of socks that Mr. Fellows had left behind when he moved out. Ralph went south from there to another rooming house and then west to the neighborhood of ship chandlers and marine boardinghouses. The nocturnal search went on for a week. He followed the thread of Mr. Fellows's goings south to the Bowery and then to the upper West Side. He climbed stairs past the open doors of rooms where lessons in Spanish dancing were going on, past whores, past women practicing the "Emperor" Concerto, and one evening he found Mr. Fellows sitting on the edge of his bed in an attic room, rubbing the spots out of his necktie with a rag soaked in gasoline.

Mr. Fellows was greedy. He wanted a hundred dollars in cash and 50 per cent of the royalties. Ralph got him to agree to 20 per cent of the royalties, but he could not get him to reduce the initial payment. The lawyer drew up a paper defining Ralph's and Mr. Fellows's interests, and a few nights later Ralph went over to Brooklyn and got to a Venetian-blind factory after its doors had closed but while the lights of the office were still burning. The manager agreed to manufacture some blinds to Ralph's specifications, but he would not take an order of less than a hundred dollars. Ralph agreed to this and to furnish the compound for the outer surface of the slats. These expenditures had taken more than three fourths of the Whittemores' capital, and now the problem of money was joined by the element of time. They put a small advertisement in the paper for a housewares salesman, and for a week Ralph interviewed candidates in the living room after supper. He chose a young man who was leaving at the end of the week for the Midwest. He wanted a fifty-dollar advance, and pointed out to them that Pittsburgh and Chicago were just as noisy as New York. A department-store collection agency was threatening to bring them into the small-claims court at this time, and they had come to a place where any illness, any fall, any damage to themselves or to the few clothes they owned would be critical. Their salesman promised to write them from Chicago at the end of the week, and they counted on good news, but there was no news from Chicago at all. Ralph wired the salesman twice, and the wires must have been forwarded, for he replied to them from Pittsburgh: "Can't merchandise blinds. Returning samples express." They put another advertisement for a salesman in the paper and took the first one who rang their bell, an old gentleman with a cornflower in his buttonhole. He had a number of other lines—mirror wastebaskets, orange-juicers—and he said that he knew all the Manhattan housewares buyers intimately. He was garrulous, and when he was unable to sell the blinds, he came to the Whittemores' apartment and discussed their product at length, and with a blend of criticism and charity that we usually reserve for human beings.

Ralph tried to borrow money, but neither his salary nor his patent was considered adequate collateral for a loan at anything but ruinous rates, and one day, at his office, he was served a summons by the department-store collection agency. He went out to Brooklyn and offered to sell the Venetian blinds back to the manufacturer. The man gave him sixty dollars for what had cost a hundred, and Ralph was able to pay the collection agency. They hung the samples in their windows and tried to put the venture out of their minds.

Now they were poorer than ever, and they ate lentils for dinner every Monday and sometimes again on Tuesday. Laura washed the dishes after dinner while Ralph read to Rachel. When the girl had fallen asleep, he would go to his desk in the living room and work on one of his projects. There was always something coming. There was a job in Dallas and a job in Peru. There were the plastic arch preserver, the automatic closing device for icebox doors, and the scheme to pirate marine specifications and undersell Jane's. For a month he was going to buy some fallow acreage in upstate New York and plant Christmas trees on it, and then, with one of his friends, he projected a luxury mail-order business, for which they could never get backing. When the Whittemores met Uncle George

68

and Aunt Helen at the Ritz, they seemed delighted with the way things were going. They were terribly excited, Laura said, about a sales agency in Paris that had been offered to Ralph but that they had decided against, because of the threat of war.

The Whittemores were in their thirties when the war began. They were apart for two years. Laura took a job. She walked Rachel to school in the morning and met her at the end of the day. Working and saving, Laura was able to buy herself and Rachel some clothes. When Ralph returned at the end of the war, their affairs were in good order. The experience seemed to have refreshed him, and while he took up his old job as an anchor to windward, as an ace in the hole, there had never been more talk about jobs—jobs in Venezuela and jobs in Iran. They resumed all their old habits and economies. They remained poor.

Laura gave up her job and returned to the afternoons with Rachel in Central Park. Alice Holinshed was there. The talk was the same. The Holinsheds were living in a hotel. Mr. Holinshed was vice-president of a new firm manufacturing a soft drink, but the dress that Mrs. Holinshed wore day after day was one that Laura recognized from before the war. Her son was thin and bad-tempered. He was dressed in serge, like an English schoolboy, but his serge, like his mother's dress, looked worn and outgrown. One afternoon when Mrs. Holinshed and her son came into the Park, the boy was crying. "I've done a dreadful thing," Mrs. Holinshed told Laura. "We've been to the doctor's and I forgot to bring any money, and I wonder if you could lend me a few dollars, so I can take a taxi back to the hotel." Laura said she would be glad to. She had only a five-dollar bill with her, and she gave Mrs. Holinshed this. The boy continued to cry, and his mother dragged him off toward Fifth Avenue. Laura never saw them in the Park again.

Ralph's life was, as it had always been, dominated by anticipation. In the years directly after the war the city appeared to be immensely rich. There seemed to be money everywhere, and the Whittemores, who slept under their worn overcoats in the winter to keep themselves warm, seemed separated from their enjoyment of this prosperity by only a little patience, resourcefulness, and luck. On Sunday, when the weather was fine, they walked with the prosperous crowds on upper Fifth Avenue. It seemed to Ralph that it might only be another month, at the most another year, before he found the key to the prosperity they deserved. They would walk on Fifth Avenue until the afternoon was ended and then go home and eat a can of beans for dinner and, in order to balance the meal, an apple for dessert.

They were returning from such a walk one Sunday when, as they climbed the stairs to their apartment, the telephone began to ring. Ralph went on ahead and answered it.

He heard the voice of his uncle George, a man of the generation that remains conscious of distance, who spoke into the telephone as if he were calling from shore to a passing boat. "This is Uncle George, Ralphie!" he shouted, and Ralph supposed that he and Aunt Helen were paying a surprise visit to the city, until he realized that his uncle was calling from Illinois. "Can you hear me?" Uncle George shouted. "Can you hear me, Ralphie? . . . I'm calling you about a job, Ralphie. Just in case you're looking for a job. Paul Hadaam came through—can you hear me, Ralphie?—Paul Hadaam came through here on his way East last week and he stopped off to pay me a visit. He's got a lot of money, Ralphie—he's rich—and he's starting this business out in the West to manufacture synthetic wool. Can you hear me, Ralphie? . . . I told him about you, and he's staying at the Waldorf, so you go and see him. I saved his life once. I pulled him out of Lake Erie. You go and see him tomorrow at the Waldorf, Ralphie. You know where that is? The Waldorf Hotel. . . . Wait a minute, here's Aunt Helen. She wants to talk with you."

Now the voice was a woman's, and it came to him faintly. All his cousins had been there for dinner, she told him. They had had a turkey for dinner. All the grandchildren were there and they behaved very well. George took them all for a walk after dinner. It was hot, but they sat on the porch, so they didn't feel the heat. She was interrupted in her account of Sunday by her husband, who must have seized the instrument from her to continue his refrain about going to see Mr. Hadaam at the Waldorf. "You go see him tomorrow, Ralphie—the nineteenth—at the Waldorf. He's expecting you. Can you hear me? . . . The Waldorf Hotel. He's a millionaire. I'll say good-by now."

Mr. Hadaam had a parlor and a bedroom in the Waldorf Towers, and when Ralph went to see him, late the next afternoon, on his way home from work, Mr. Hadaam was alone. He seemed to Ralph a very old man, but an obdurate one, and in the way he shook hands, pulled at his ear lobes, stretched himself, and padded around the parlor on his bandy legs Ralph recognized a spirit that was unimpaired, independent, and canine. He poured Ralph a strong drink and himself a weak one. He was undertaking the manufacture of synthetic wool on the West Coast, he explained, and had come East to find men who were experienced in merchandising wool. George had given him Ralph's name, and he wanted a man with Ralph's experience. He would find the Whittemores a suitable house, arrange for their transportation, and begin Ralph at a salary of fifteen thousand. It was the size of the salary that made Ralph realize that the proposition was an oblique attempt to repay his uncle for having saved Mr. Hadaam's life, and the old man seemed to sense what he was feeling. "This hasn't got anything to do with your uncle's saving my life," he said roughly. "I'm grateful to him—who wouldn't be?—but this hasn't got anything to do with your uncle, if that's what you're thinking. When you get to be as old and as rich as I am, it's hard to meet people. All my old friends are dead—all of them but George. I'm surrounded by a cordon of associates and relatives that's damned near impenetrable, and if it wasn't for George giving me a name now and then, I'd never get to see a new face. Last year I got into an automobile accident. It was my fault. I'm a terrible driver. I hit this young fellow's car and I got right out and went over to him and introduced myself. We had to wait about twenty minutes for the wreckers and we got to talking. Well, he's working for me today and he's one of the best friends I've got, and if I hadn't run into him, I'd never have met him. When you get to be as old as me, that's the only way you can meet people—automobile accidents, fires, things like that."

He straightened up against the back of his chair and tasted his drink. His rooms were well above the noise of traffic and it was quiet there. Mr. Hadaam's breath was loud and steady, and it sounded, in a pause, like the heavy breath of someone sleeping. "Well, I don't want to rush you into this," he said. "I'm going back to the Coast the day after tomorrow. You think it over and I'll telephone you." He took out an engagement book and wrote down Ralph's name and telephone number. "I'll call you on Tuesday evening, the twenty-seventh, about nine o'clock—nine o'clock your time. George tells me you've got a nice wife, but I haven't got time to meet her now. I'll see her on the Coast." He started talking about baseball and then brought the conversation back to Uncle George. "He saved my life. My damned boat capsized and then righted herself and sunk right from underneath me. I can still feel her going down under my feet. I couldn't swim. Can't swim today. Well, good-by." They shook hands, and as soon as the door closed, Ralph heard Mr. Hadaam begin to cough. It was the profane, hammering cough of an old man, full of bitter complaints and distempers, and it hit him pitilessly for all the time that Ralph was waiting in the hallway for the elevator to take him down.

On the walk home Ralph felt that this might be it, that this preposterous chain of contingencies that had begun with his uncle's pulling a friend out of Lake Erie might be the one that would save them. Nothing in his experience made it seem unlikely. He recognized that the proposition was the vagary of an old man and that it originated in the indebtedness Mr. Hadaam felt to his uncle—an indebtedness that age seemed to have deepened. He gave Laura the details of the interview when he came in, and his own views on Mr. Hadaam's conduct, and, to his mild surprise, Laura said that it looked to her like the bonanza. They were both remarkably calm, considering the change that confronted them. There was no talk of celebrating, and he helped her wash the dishes. He looked up the site of Mr. Hadaam's factory in an atlas, and the Spanish place name on the coast north of San Francisco gave them a glimpse of a life of reasonable contentment.

Eight days lay between Ralph's interview and the telephone call, and he realized that nothing would be definite until Tuesday, and that there was a possibility that old Mr. Hadaam, while crossing the country, might, under the subtle influence of travel, suffer a change of heart. He might be poisoned by a fish sandwich and be taken off the train in Chicago, to die in a nursing home there. Among the people meeting him in San Francisco might be his lawyer, with the news that he was ruined or that his wife had run away. But eventually Ralph was unable to invent any new disasters or to believe in the ones he had invented.

This inability to persevere in doubting his luck showed some weakening of character, but he was nearly forty and his head was gray. There had hardly been a day when he had not been made to feel the power of money, but he found that the force of money was most irresistible when it took the guise of a promise, and that years of resolute self-denial, instead of rewarding him with reserves of fortitude, had left him more than ordinarily susceptible to temptation. Since the change in their lives still depended upon a telephone call, he refrained from talking—from thinking, so far as possible—about the life they might have in California. He would go so far as to say that he would like some white shirts, but he would not go beyond this deliberately contrite wish, and here, where he thought he was exercising restraint and intelligence, he was, instead, beginning to respect the bulk of superstition that is supposed to attend good fortune, and when he wished for white shirts, it was not a genuinely modest wish so much as it was a memory—he could not have put it into words himself—that the gods of fortune are jealous and easily deceived by false modesty. He had never been a superstitious man, but on Tuesday he scooped the money off his coffee and was elated when he saw a ladybug on the bathroom window sill. He could not remember when he had heard money and this insect associated, but neither could he have explained any of the other portents that he had begun to let govern his movements.

Laura watched this subtle change that anticipation worked on her husband, but there was nothing she could say. He did not mention Mr. Hadaam or California. He was quiet; he was gentle with Rachel; he actually grew pale. He had his hair cut on Wednesday. He wore his best suit. On Saturday he had his hair cut again and his nails manicured. He took two baths a day, put on a fresh shirt for dinner, and frequently went into the bathroom to wash his hands, brush his teeth, and wet down his cowlick. The preternatural care he gave his body and his appearance reminded her of an adolescent surprised by early love.

The Whittemores were invited to a party for Monday night and Laura insisted that they go. The guests at the party were the survivors of a group that had coalesced ten years before, and if anyone had called the roll of the earliest parties in the same room, like the retreat ceremony of a breeched and decimated regiment, "Missing. . . . Missing. . . . Missing" would have been answered for the squad that had gone into Westchester. "Missing. . . . Missing. . . . Missing" would have been spoken for the platoon that divorce, drink, nervous disorders, and adversity had slain or wounded. Because Laura had gone to the party in indifferent spirits, she was conscious of the missing.

She had been at the party less than an hour when she heard some people coming in, and, looking over her shoulder, saw Alice Holinshed and her husband. The room was crowded and she put off speaking to Alice until later. Much later in the evening Laura went into the toilet, and when she came out of it into the bedroom, she found Alice sitting on the bed. She seemed to be waiting for Laura. Laura sat down at the dressing table to straighten her hair. She looked at the image of her friend in the glass.

"I hear you're going to California," Alice said.

"We hope to. We'll know tomorrow."

"Is it true that Ralph's uncle saved his life?"

"That's true."

"You're lucky."

"I suppose we are."

"You're lucky, all right." Alice got up from the bed and crossed the room and closed the door, and came back across the room again and sat on the bed. Laura watched her in the glass, but she was not watching Laura. She was stooped. She seemed nervous. "You're lucky," she said. "You're so lucky. Do you know how lucky you are? Let me tell you about this cake of soap," she said. "I have this cake of soap. I mean I had this cake of soap. Somebody gave it to me when I was married, fifteen years ago. I don't know who. Some maid, some music teacher—somebody like that. It was good soap, good English soap, the kind I like, and I decided to save it for the big day when Larry made a killing, when he took me to Bermuda. First, I was going to use it when he got the job in Bound Brook. Then I thought I could use it when we were going to Boston, and then Washington, and then when he got this new job, I thought maybe this is it, maybe *this* is the time when I get to take the boy out of that rotten school and pay the bills and move out of those bum hotels we've been living in. For fifteen years I've been planning to use this cake of soap. Well, last week I was looking through my bureau drawers and I saw this cake of soap. It was all cracked. I threw it out. I threw it out because I knew I was never going to have a chance to use it. Do you realize what that means? Do you know what that feels like? To live for fifteen years on promises and expectations and loans and credits in hotels that aren't fit to live in, never for a single day to be out of debt, and yet to pretend, to feel that every year, every winter, every job, every meeting is going to be the one. To live like this for fifteen years and then to realize that it's never going to end. Do you know what that feels like?" She got up and went over to the dressing table and stood in front of Laura. Tears had risen into her large eyes, and her voice was harsh and loud. "I'm never going to get to Bermuda," she said. "I'm never even going to get to Florida. I'm never going to get out of hock, ever, ever, *ever*. I know that I'm never going to have a decent home and that everything I own that is worn and torn and no good is going to stay that way. I know that for the rest of my life, for the rest of my life, I'm going to wear ragged slips and torn nightgowns and torn underclothes and shoes that hurt me. I know that for the rest of my life nobody is going to come up to me and tell me that I've got on a pretty dress, because I'm not going to be able to afford that kind of a dress. I know that for the rest of my life every taxi driver and doorman and headwaiter in this town is going to know in a minute that I haven't got five bucks in that black imitation-suède purse that I've been brushing and brushing and brushing and carrying around for ten years. How do you get it? How do you rate it? What's so wonderful about you that you get a break like this?" She ran her fingers down Laura's bare arm. The dress she was wearing smelled of benzine. "Can I rub it off you? Will that make me lucky? I swear to Jesus I'd murder somebody if I thought it would bring us in any money. I'd wring somebody's neck—yours, anybody's—I swear to Jesus I would——"

Someone began knocking on the door. Alice strode to the door, opened it, and went out. A woman came in, a stranger looking for the toilet. Laura lighted a cigarette and waited in the bedroom for about ten minutes before she went back to the party. The Holinsheds had gone. She got a drink and sat down and tried to talk, but she couldn't keep her mind on what she was saying.

The hunt, the search for money 'that had seemed to her natural, amiable, and fair when they first committed themselves to it, now seemed like a hazardous and piratical voyage. She had thought, earlier in the evening, of the missing. She thought now of the missing again. Adversity and failure accounted for more than half of them, as if beneath the amenities in the pretty room a keen race were in progress, in which the loser's forfeits were extreme. Laura felt cold. She picked the ice out of her drink with her fingers and put it in a flower vase, but the whisky didn't warm her. She asked Ralph to take her home.

After dinner on Tuesday, Laura washed the dishes and Ralph dried them. He read the paper and she took up some sewing. At a quarter after eight the telephone, in the bedroom, rang, and he went to it calmly. It was someone with two theater tickets for a show that was closing. The telephone didn't ring again, and at half-past nine he told Laura that he was going to call California. It didn't take long for the connection to be made, and the fresh voice of a young woman spoke to him from Mr. Hadaam's number. "Oh yes, Mr. Whittemore," she said. "We tried to get you earlier in the evening but your line was busy."

"Could I speak to Mr. Hadaam?"

"No, Mr. Whittemore. This is Mr. Hadaam's secretary. I know he meant to call you, because he had entered this in his engagement book. Mrs. Hadaam has asked me to disappoint as few people as possible, and I've tried to take care of all the calls and appointments in his engagement book. Mr. Hadaam had a stroke on Sunday. We don't expect him to recover. I imagine he made you some kind of promise, but I'm afraid he won't be able to keep it."

"I'm very sorry," Ralph said. He hung up.

Laura had come into the bedroom while the secretary was talking. "Oh, darling!" she said. She put her sewing basket on the bureau and went toward the closet. Then she went back and looked for something in the sewing basket and left the basket on her dressing table. Then she took off her shoes, treed them, slipped her dress over her head and hung it up neatly. Then she went to the bureau, looking for her sewing basket, found it on the dressing table, and took it into the closet, where she put it on a shelf. Then she took her brush and comb into the bathroom and began to run the water for a bath.

The lash of frustration was laid on and the pain stunned Ralph. He sat by the telephone for he did not know how long. He heard Laura come out of the bathroom. He turned when he heard her speak.

"I feel dreadfully about old Mr. Hadaam," she said. "I wish there were something we could do." She was in her nightgown, and she sat down at the dressing table like a skillful and patient woman establishing herself in front of a loom, and she picked up and put down pins and bottles and combs and brushes with the thoughtless dexterity of an experienced weaver, as if the time she spent there were all part of a continuous operation. "It did look like the treasure . . ."

The word surprised him, and for a moment he saw the chimera, the pot of gold, the fleece, the treasure buried in the faint lights of a rainbow, and the primitivism of his hunt struck him. Armed with a sharp spade and a homemade divining rod, he had climbed over hill and dale, through droughts and rain squalls, digging wherever the maps he had drawn himself promised gold. Six paces east of the dead pine, five panels in from the library door, underneath the creaking step, in the roots of the pear tree, beneath the grape arbor lay the bean pot full of doubloons and bullion.

She turned on the stool and held her thin arms toward him, as she had done more than a thousand times. She was no longer young, and more wan, thinner than she might have been if he had found the doubloons to save her anxiety and unremitting work. Her smile, her naked shoulders had begun to trouble the indecipherable shapes and symbols that are the touchstones of desire, and the light from the lamp seemed to brighten and give off heat and shed that unaccountable complacency, that benevolence, that the spring sunlight brings to all kinds of fatigue and despair. Desire for her delighted and confused him. Here it was, here it all was, and the shine of the gold seemed to him then to be all around her arms.

from Flair

I CAME FROM YONDER MOUNTAIN

EVAN S. CONNELL, JR., *was born in Kansas City, Missouri, twenty-seven years ago. He was a student at Dartmouth and Williams Colleges, a navy pilot two years, took his A.B. at the University of Kansas, and studied at Stanford and Columbia Universities. He was represented in the 1949 collection by "I'll Take You to Tennessee," which appeared in* Tomorrow, *and was his first published story. It won the Edith Mirrielees $500 first prize, the $100 second prize in the 1948 Midwestern Writers' Conference, and was the number-one story in Wallace Stegner's anthology,* Stanford Short Stories. *He has since published stories in* The American Mercury *and elsewhere. Mr. Connell writes that his most serious frustration is he would like to be an opera singer, but cannot.*

Beyond the upcountry of the Carolinas, farther back in the hills where the clay looks blue and the wild carrot and yellow lily cover the scars of crumbled sawmills, where thunder has the high rattling sound of pebbles in a wood bucket, there the ridges are laden with scented air in the heart of the afternoon, and there if you wander into a hollow sometimes you'll catch a far-off smell of sweet bay or see the pendent bells of a honey cup swinging in the wind. There the red spruce and the paintbrush grow, bordering trails that spiral down the mountains, and if the long silver clouds that look like snakes arise in the west soon there will fall drops of rain big around as acorns.

It was on such a day that a girl wound down the trail to a town called Keating, which was a town shaped like an oak leaf with a railroad track for a stem. The girl's name was Laurel Wyatt and she

78

carried under one arm, wrapped in a crazy-patch quilt, her baby which did not very often move. She did not look at the baby, but once in a while she spoke to it as though it were a person.

" 'Tis a piece," she said in that fashion, looking mildly ahead.

A breeze shook the sides of her raisin-colored sweater and twisted those strands of her hair not bound by the ribbon behind her neck. Her hips were narrow and her legs short, and were it not for her abrupt breasts she would have looked like a man. At her mouth corners, beneath the sockets of her cheeks, glistened shreds of fried pork.

Cinnamon squirrels sailed across the tree limbs considering her through quick eyes, while in the woods flickers called and blood-heads knocked with sudden impatience, and were answered by thunder sounding far in the west. Overhead the sun filtered through the mountain pines: in its light flickered insects with wings as thin as tissue.

A raindrop thumped the crazy-patch quilt. Another pounded into the trail, thereby causing a dust umbrella to open beside the girl's foot.

"Powerful day," she said.

Across log bridges where excited water popped and slipped on rocks, past raccoons who stopped their dark and slender hands to watch her, softly on a pad of brown pine needles Laurel moved down on the town of Keating. The streams as she passed over them were marbled in white and green, and moss tails which were stuck to the bottom swayed in the current; once one pulled free and wriggled quickly downstream as though it were alive. Once, as she crossed a log bridge, her footsteps jarred loose a fat beetle which floated gravely away. Water spiders skated in a hidden pool behind the rocks, ignoring twigs and a dried pine cone that revolved in the center.

She came to a cold stream where on the far side a baby hog bear sliced the water again and again and each time looked in wonder at its empty paw. Laurel stood by a charred stump until at last the bear sat up, and, seeing her, trundled off into the woods.

Thunder rattled as she moved over a bald. Stones in her path were speckled with mica, and by them copper thorns which overhung the trail grabbed at her ankles, but her skin was stiff as parchment so each thorn skidded by. In the woods again she laid her baby on a rock while she fastened the little buttons of her sweater. Then on she went, and down.

When she came to the clearing of a cabin she stopped at the cistern and with a porcelain dipper took water from the bucket. A column of brown smoke rose a few feet above the cabin and then expanded like a toadstool. A long, tired man in cocoa overalls who sat in the cabin doorway raised one hand to her but she did not see him. She hung the dipper on its nail, walked across the clearing and on down the trail.

A flare hawk coasted over with beak hooked bitterly and talons doubled; on the ground small patterings stopped. Wandering electric clouds crackled, shot quick forks at one another which sometimes bent down to test the strength of the red spruce trees, and once as Laurel Wyatt crossed a charred tract there floated silently from one cloud a ball of green fire.

"The heart of Judas," she said. And scarce looked at it though the fire followed her to the trees.

Beyond another bald a shower swept by; her sweater sagged with water. On she walked, across ridges where the false loblolly grew and down the tangled hollows, by a preacher's counsel painted on a tablet of stone, on until at last she came to the doorstoops of Keating whereon lay bent rakes and barrel hoops and dozing hounds with wet mange. Through the town she went to the railroad platform, and there she laid the baby beside her on a bench, crossed her thighs, and sat looking straight ahead.

A candle-shaped man stood at one corner of the platform; beside him sat a woman with a body like a gourd and face blistered by the sun.

"Oh, stop clowning," this woman said when the man began to imitate Laurel Wyatt.

He stalked back and forth, his lips pressed together.

"Must you eternally, eternally pace?" she asked.

"Here comes the train! It can't get up the hill."

"Something funny every minute of the day," she said. Her voice was exhausted.

The train squawked and chuggled over the hill, feathers of steam spurting from its engine wheels. The number on its hood was 7. The steam feathers vanished and emerged again as the train prepared to stop. When this had been done all that moved was the iron bell atop the cab which swung drunkenly back and forth emptying itself over the platform. From the pistons drops of water fell hissing into the cinders. Suddenly a coach door clanked and the conductor jumped down, a tiny man with hook-and-lace shoes and a nose like an orange rind.

The man picked up two alligator suitcases; the woman quickly wedged a parcel and a raincoat under his arms.

"Sweetheart, you're tired?" he asked. She climbed the steps while he followed, staring at the back of her head. "You're tired, maybe?" he asked, disappearing into the coach.

The conductor's eyebrows were as white and crisp as scrolls of birchbark. He smelled of stout tobacco. He walked across the fly-blown boards of the platform dragging one foot and rubbing his arms while the iron bell on the cab clanged and rolled north, clanged and rolled south.

" 'What you going to wear for a wedding coat?' " caroled the conductor in a sharp voice. He limped to the end of the platform where he spit across the tracks and stood looking at the mountains which were dim in the haze. Sparks and ashes settled on his collar. He turned around and limped back along the platform, still rubbing his arms. " 'Old chin whiskers of a billy goat,' " he sang. He stood at the other end of the platform, then, considering a bulging gold watch, he came back and jumped aboard the train.

Laurel Wyatt sat on the bench gazing straight ahead. The conductor looked suspiciously at her knees which the polka-dotted dress was too short to cover. He banged the coach door and at this noise Laurel's eyes focused.

"I am locally," she said.

"Too late! Too late!" he called with laughter in his voice.

"I have come to train travel," she said.

The conductor slowly opened the door; Laurel Wyatt went into a coach and sat down, dropping the baby onto the seat beside her. She sat as on the bench, with hands folded tranquilly in her lap.

The couplings rattled, clanked, the coach jumped backward, then forward, and began to move.

The toes of the baby curled but it made no sound. About its wrist was tied a string with seven knots.

" 'For I'm a-going—I'm a-going away——' " In came the conductor, the black leather of his hook-and-lace shoes squirking. "Whereabouts you folks headed?"

"Out of these queer hills!" exclaimed the man. "They give me the creeps." And looking toward Laurel Wyatt he said, "That girl's cracked. She gives me the creeps."

"Dearie, everything gives you the creeps."

"You're tired, sweetheart? You're not feeling so good again? You've got the cramps again?"

"They're like that. Yes, sir. They are. I seen them time and again, time and again do it. They think the train waits specially for them. But it don't. No, sir!" The conductor went along the aisle patting the top of each seat. " 'For to stay—a little while——' "

He stopped beside Laurel. "Them folks inform me you been sitting there nearabouts an hour waiting on this train. You deef? What's the matter with you? We set by that station there eight entire minutes, you didn't get on. I expect you be a deef one. Hey? This train come up the hills, set by eight entire minutes, you don't fleck a muscle. Only got a number of minutes in Keating. They's a storm fixing to swamp us. People think trains set by all day long waiting for them specially, they don't, don't do nothing specially. Not for nobody. I expect you know that. Hey? Don't you? Don't that appeal to you? Eight minutes is all. You be deef? Ain't you? What's the trouble with you?"

"I presume I forgot it," Laurel said, but she did not look at the conductor.

"You do! You do! Ahahah!" The conductor pinched the end of his nose in rage. "Give me your money. Whereabouts you headed? Tipton? You people always go to Tipton. I don't know why. That's where you be headed. Tipton costs you a dollar and ten cents more."

Laurel cautiously folded her hands.

"Whereabouts you headed? Tipton. That's where."

But she did not answer.

"You be headed for Tipton. Hey?"

"I came from yonder mountain."

The conductor bent his knees and sank down a little to peer out the

82

window. "That mountain there resembles an eagle's beak. Now give me your money."

"I have that money," Laurel said, reaching into the pocket of her sweater. "And here. 'Tis the money for a train travel to Tipton town." She added: "I have quite a considerable of this money." And then she sucked in her lips and looked at the floor of the coach.

The conductor put the money in his coat pocket and moved along, dragging one foot. " 'But I'm a-coming back—if I go ten thousand mile—if I go ten thousand mile.' "

Laurel rested her hands in her lap and quietly swung her crossed leg. She did not move, but sat mile after mile in that same fashion while the train clicked along with the rhythm of a galloping horse's hoofs, and all that showed she was not a stone girl was when the train screeched around a curve and the late afternoon sun brushed the pale hairs of her cheek.

As the train descended, moving south, the clay cutbacks became stippled with gravel and changed in color; they became almost white, then pink, and when the train clacketed over a bare patch the clay broke suddenly through the topsoil in a scarlet web. The train rolled between two wooden sheds on which were nailed crusty tin signs for medicine and baking soda and snuff, and crossed a street where bells were ringing and a man swung a red lantern. Then the coach was dark, for clay banks rose beside the windows, and when these banks unfolded to admit the sun there was no town.

Laurel Wyatt stood up. The coach swayed and she fell on the baby. She stood again and thrust her fingers up through the baggage mesh above the seat.

"Tipton town?" she asked very low.

Her body swayed with the train and as she dangled by her fingers the pale, dotted dress lifted above her knees. Her legs were thick, with ankles tan and stiff. But higher they became soft and white, like twin birch logs.

"Oh, my Lord!" she said.

As the train sped around a curve her hips bumped the window and then swung into the aisle. She looked over her shoulder toward the corridor at the rear where the conductor had disappeared. Then she gazed ahead.

" 'Twas Carleton," she said, and unhooking her fingers from the mesh she dropped into the seat.

It was as she sat down that there came tapping gently upon her window the long, thin fingers of rain, and the sky which had been vacant was carefully braided with clouds. Fields that had lain flat beside the wheels humped into ridges and became the sides of a trough wherein the ashes of the train collected, and the coach tipped forward with squealing wheels while orange sparks flicked by. Through the trough with windows rattling, couplings banging, went the train. Then onto plowed fields it rushed. And there was Tipton.

The iron bell rang and turned west and rang and turned east.

" 'What'll the wedding supper be?' " the conductor sang. Laurel's sweater caught on the door handle and he pulled it free for her to step down, singing, " 'Dogwood soup and catnip tea.' "

Far in the distance rose the eagle-beak mountain. Turning until it overhung her left shoulder, Laurel Wyatt entered the city of Tipton, cheeks sucked in, dropping each foot as though into a deep hole. A hedge grew before her; she pushed through it while people paused to watch. Then on through patterns of flowers bound to stakes, past the stoppered mouth of a cannon, by a red iron tablet of poetry, and under the broken sword of a stone horseman riding north.

Across lines of yellow paint she moved, and in the street she stopped, looked over her shoulder for the eagle's beak, and went on until a building blocked the way. She stopped, struck once at the door, and stood waiting.

There came through the shutters above a woman's irked voice: "Yes?"

"I am here."

"What do you want?" When there was no answer the woman's voice called again: "His office is closed! Come back tomorrow."

The day darkened and filled with the scent of rain, and later there was a sound at the shuttered window and the voice called out again: "I told you to go! I said tomorrow!"

Laurel looked at the door.

"Oh, all right! I'll tell him, I'll tell him." A window slammed. And in time by the landing window a candle was carried, a lamp turned on.

In the doorway the doctor buttoned his vest. "Well, girl?" He peeled off his glasses, twirled them by the white rubber earpieces, glanced at the baby. "You know that child is dead. You know that."

To the door came a nurse dressed in a robe. Her throat was like the stem of a mushroom and her mouth was tight. She looked carelessly at the baby. "I should think it is dead."

"Blister plasters," muttered the doctor. "If it wasn't dead before you'd have murdered it with those plasters. You know that, don't you?"

"I doubt if she does," said the nurse.

"Somebody ought to go back in those hills and teach you people. Everybody knows I'm too busy, but somebody ought to."

"I told her. I said, 'Come back tomorrow.'"

Though Laurel spoke, her words could scarcely be heard: " 'Tis dead."

They watched her.

"Why didn't your husband come along with you, girl?"

The nurse laughed like a mare. "If she got one he's likely drunk."

"Where are you from, girl?"

"She doesn't know."

"You're a long way out of those hills, my girl. A long way. You got enough money to get back? You do, don't you?"

"She hasn't got any money. Look at her. She hasn't got anything."

"You take that child back, hear? You give it a fine burial."

"She's not listening."

"Nobody ever listens to what I say. Nobody ever does. What's the use? All right, girl. Give it here to me. I'll see it's done."

"She'd drop it in a ditch."

The lamp in the hall darkened the sockets of Laurel's cheeks, caught a glisten like flakes of mica in her eyes. Slowly, slanting into the doorway, rain began to fall. A drop slid down her temple, rolled over her cheekbone and came to rest on her jaw. Water streamed down her arms and curved through her empty palms, dripped steadily from her fingertips. The dress with its thousand dots grew wet as moss and wrapped around her powerful legs.

She turned away from the silent doctor and nurse. Through the rain she walked, past the sloshing window ledges, through boundaries of sticks and paint, beyond the settling cannon, beyond awn-

85

ings and wires whereon the bulbs of Tipton weakly flickered, upon the black and silent cinders until they had sunk in clay, and on, with the rhythm of a slow pulse beat, into the edge of a forest, and there among trunks of spruce the sound of her footsteps dissolved in the rain.

from the Atlantic Monthly

BLACK WATER BLUES

MONTY CULVER *was born in Pittsburgh, February 22, 1929. His father was a professor at the University of Pittsburgh, and he received his B.A. there in 1949, taking a writing major under Professor Edwin Peterson. "Black Water Blues" was written in his senior year and won the 1949* Atlantic Monthly *college contest. Ada McCormick, without knowing of the* Atlantic *prize, recognized the merit of "Black Water Blues." She bought it, released it to appear in the* Atlantic *as a "first," and will publish it in* Letter, *her magazine of research and recognition in Tucson. After taking an M.A. at the University of Pittsburgh in 1950, Mr. Culver moved to the University of Illinois, where he is a member of the rhetoric staff, and is working for his Ph.D. He lives in Urbana with his wife, Beverly, and spends his spare time working on short stories. "Black Water Blues" was his first published story.*

His name was Rohrs. They called him the Lion, of course; they could not be expected to do much else. The name was out there with the others, on the big poster by the box office: Bump Roxy and his Famous Blue Band. Featuring Adelia Roxy, Step-Up Tate, "The Lion" Rohrs.

He sat in front of the dimly lighted hall and chorded lightly with long, knobby fingers on eighty-eight keys. The hall was beginning to fill. Couples straggled through the door, circling timidly around the vastness of the bare dance floor, staring at the young white man who sat on the piano stool. A few were young: tall buck Negroes in high-hitched pants and bulging shoulder pads; girls in gay dresses, giggling up at their grinning escorts. But most of the early comers were the older folks, who came to listen only and not to dance. They came before eight o'clock to get the choice seats underneath or at the ends of the footlights. Often they sat without moving for the whole five or six hours, tapping their shoes along with the big bass, flashing grins that gleamed weirdly in their black and brown faces.

The Lion Rohrs sat alone on the big stage, playing gently, quietly, to the early comers. He had learned that it took the Negroes a little time to get used to the idea of a white man playing in a colored man's band. He usually managed to get up on the stage while the others were unpacking the paraphernalia.

He looked up from the keyboard and into the eyes of a staring young couple across the lights. He grinned at them—a savage grin, a grin of joy born of the chords that chortled under the long hands. And the couple grinned back.

He pressed the loud pedal and did a sudden trick in the bass, watching an older couple sitting near the stage. As they jerked their heads up, he winked at them, into their startled faces, and heard their laughter, clear and relieved.

Tonight a few white men were out there to listen. That would be a nuisance. Bump Roxy hated to play to white men. But there was no sense worrying about it now.

Bump strode from the wings, nodding curtly to Rohrs. Stagehands followed him on and began setting up the traps on the platform in center stage.

"Here sits the Lion, warmin' up the audience," said Sam Lester. The others straggled in: Hadley the number-one horn man, LeRoy Bunner with his guitar, Clarence Jackson, the incomparable Step-Up Tate. Tate and Willie Shepherd stopped beside the Lion. He cocked an eyebrow at them and rolled the treble playfully.

"M-mmm," Willie sighed. "That Lion, you just never know what he's gonna do next."

"Lion, he don't know what he'll do his damn self." Step-Up chuckled and touched Rohrs lightly on the arm before moving away.

It was funny, the Lion thought, funny how easy it was to get along —with everybody but Bump, at least. All you had to do was smile most of the time and play music all the time. The music was the thing, of course; it sometimes thawed even Bump Roxy's scowling distrust. He had sold himself to Bump by sitting on a piano stool and touching the keys as he talked.

"Man, it wouldn't work," Bump had said. "It wouldn't work at all. I ain't taking on no white man. . . . Man, play some more. Play that damn thing some more."

Rohrs looked up at Bump, sitting up on the high chair behind the traps, the sticks in his hands. Oh, Lord! thought the Lion, for Bump was glaring across the lights at the little knot of white men in the near corner of the floor. Most of them were all right—kids, college kids maybe, who paid their way into a colored dance hall to hear the music they wore out on records. But a couple of them, big smirking men in sport coats, looked mean. The lights distorted their faces, but Rohrs could see the coats and the sport shirts with the tight-buttoned, long-pointed collars—the uniform of the toughs.

It was bad enough when there were just decent white men out there for Bump to glare at. A couple of mean ones might spoil the whole show. They might make cracks at Adelia, and that would really be something. Bump usually tolerated a white audience, but it was different when his wife came into it. He had raised a lot of sand in St. Louis when a white man had just whistled at his wife. And he had snapped at the Lion for a week afterward.

The Lion watched Bump grip the sticks. Bump Roxy was a great drummer and a great musician. He told them when they overdid it or underdid it; he mapped the order of the solos. He held the band together.

It was worth holding together, the Blue Band. They were one of the few low-down outfits left in the country, perhaps the only great one. To Rohrs they were a way of life. He had left home to play piano against his family's wishes. When he joined the Blue Band, a year ago, he had written of it to his father. There had been no reply.

He watched Bump drop his eyes to the drums, touch the sticks to the snare. The muttering roll grew slowly, rising, fading, then higher still. Rohrs, although he had heard the theme a thousand times, held his breath until he heard the alto wail, the shuddering note of Step-Up's break.

It was a loafer for the Lion, nothing but rhythm and a couple of quick breaks. He glared from Adelia's empty chair to the wings, wondering where she was, what the hell was she doing. Bump always got sore when she was late getting on, and Bump would be sore tonight as it was, with those two nasty-looking white fellows out there. Besides, she had to do "It Ain't Necessarily So" in the first set.

Then, while he worried, Adelia came. She glided out of the shadows of the wings in her bold red gown, dazzling band and audience with her smile. The dance hall sighed.

And she spoiled Bump's big drum break. She walked on and grabbed at the eyes and minds of the audience just when they should have been fixed on the wooden blur over the tomtoms. The Lion thought, I wonder if she did that on purpose.

As she sat down, someone in the white corner whistled. Bump jerked his head up and stared dead-pan over the lights. Rohrs heard Clarence Jackson's fingers stumble on the big fiddle.

They played a couple of pops for the dancers, and it was time for "It Ain't Necessarily So"—the bawl of Hadley's muted trumpet, Lester's slim, clear notes on the clarinet. And Adelia with her head bent a little to one side, Adelia calling to the lovers in her husky voice. When she finished and the band started another dance tune, she came and stood by the piano. As the saxes played, she leaned down and gave the Lion that brilliant smile.

"How was I?" she asked. "Better than usual?"

"There's nothing better than your usual," he replied, and she laughed and touched his shoulder. Even as she did it, as the brown hand rested there for a second, he saw her eyes flicker over his head, up to Bump on the high chair, looking for a reaction.

Damn it, Rohrs thought, I wish she'd cut that out. He gets sore at me often enough as it is. Aloud he said, "Why don't you put that thing away?"

"What thing?"

"That needle you're stickin' in him all the time," Rohrs said. She giggled, and he grinned at her. He went on, "No kidding, you better lay off him. There's a couple guys out front he don't seem to like the looks of."

"He just frets about them on account of me," she said. "If he ain't got sense enough to know better, let him worry."

She walked away and sat down in her chair; it stood at the end

90

nearest the white corner, the Lion noticed. He shook his head, worrying.

He had been warned about that situation when he first joined the band. On the night of his first trip with them, he had ridden alone in the coupé with Sam Lester. He had asked questions by the dozen, anything about the band that came into his head. And naturally he asked about Adelia.

"Bump and Adelia married?"

Lester looked sidewise at him. "Yeah, they're married. That's a good thing for you to remember."

"Jesus! Do I look like forgetting it?"

"Lots of white men do," Lester grunted. "Lots of white men come to hear the band try to make her forget it. Lots of colored men too. We had a horn player once, tried to fool around with Adelia. Bump damn near kill that man. Hard to tell what he'd do to a white man. Damn if I ever want to see."

Rohrs had remembered that. He was friendly when he talked to Adelia, but he only did it when he had to, and he was always careful to avoid giving any impression of talking confidentially to her. Even then, Bump sometimes resented it.

Clarence Jackson once told the Lion that Bump had a sister who ran off with a white man. That would explain a lot. If Adelia knew that, she ought to have more sense than to dog him all the time.

Another time Step-Up Tate had said, "That man crazy about that woman. He ought to tell her so more often." The Lion was still thinking about that as they wound up the fox-trot. Bump Roxy shoved a handkerchief across his scowling face. He sat staring at the drums.

Rohrs was suddenly concerned. Bump always wanted to play loud when he was mad; he liked to hit the drums as he would hit the heads of the whistling white men; he liked to hear the horns open up and blast, maybe blow the leering faces off the floor.

That was all right, but they weren't in shape to blast. It was nine o'clock and they had nothing but a few dance numbers behind them. They would blow their brains out on anything like "High Low Jack" or "Shattered Slumber." . . .

Bump lifted his head and called it. " 'Shattered Slumber.' "

The Lion said, "Hold it now." He slid off the stool, grinning, seeing the startled faces of the band staring up at Bump. When he stood by the drums, he said, "Man, you know better than that."

"Goddamn it, Lion . . ."

"Man, it ain't ready, it ain't ripe," the Lion went on. "We ain't ready and the audience ain't ready. You got to build up to a thing like that. You know that." It was true; the boys would kill themselves and the audience wouldn't give a damn.

"That's right, Bump," Sam Lester said. "You know that."

"I figured it was Lion's time," Bump said lamely. There was a long piano solo in "Shattered Slumber." "I figured it was Lion's time for a big one. Everybody else had one."

" 'Crosstown,' then," said the Lion. " 'Crosstown,' if it's my time. It's too early for the other."

Bump's face was sullen. Rohrs grinned at him and said confidentially, "Man, we can't all warm up as quick as you do."

He walked away, chuckling at the relief in the faces of Hadley and Step-Up, winking at Willie Shepherd. He wondered how mad Bump would be.

They played the "Crosstown Blues." Nobody would ruin himself on melancholy "Crosstown," but it was something, just the same. The horns started: Hadley, Step-Up, and Lester, in turn, wailing the mournful one-bar phrase, then together. They held one, cut it off.

The Lion broke, with tingling chords. He talked to Step-Up for a while, piano and sax alternating and then mixing in dialogue. There were little appreciative chortles from the faces that crowded each other and peered over the edge of the stage.

The horns swept it up again and carried a chorus, fading, dying into silence. Bump took a rimshot. The Lion rolled one, high on the keyboard, held it, did tricks with it. He broke it, walked his hand down the board. With the left he reached deep down for the boogie bass.

They said that the Lion had it; everyone who knew, who had ever heard him, said so. He had the touch, they said: the touch of the great ones that had gone before; the touch that twitched the muscles and boiled the blood. There is music that can grow only of the love of music, and its greatest and supreme thrill is in its playing. This the Lion knew.

He gave it back to the horns, and the yells at the solo's end drowned even the trumpet. He wiped sweat from the corners of his eyes and swiveled on the stool to watch the boys finish it up. As his head swung, he saw the ugly smiles on the faces of the two white men who stared up at Adelia.

It was midnight, fourth intermission time. The Lion, alone, leaned against the wall outside the stage door and watched the rain drizzling into the alley. It pattered in the puddles and dribbled from the roof's edge over his head. He knew that the puddles were dirty, black with the soot and grime of the mill town, and he grinned, singing his song to himself.

> "I wake up in the mornin
> Black water drippin from the eaves
> I wake up in the mornin
> Black water drippin from the eaves
> It's runnin in the gutters
> Soakin down the grass and leaves"

Bump Roxy said, "Move youh goddamn chair!"

The Lion jerked away from the wall. The voice was so close that he was sure it spoke to him, but when he looked around the edge of the door he saw Bump and Adelia in the tiny vestibule.

"What you talking about?" said Adelia.

"You hear what I say. I say move that goddamn chair!"

"Why should I?"

"You know why. You know I don't like them men lookin' at you," Bump said. His fingers clenched.

"What harm that do you?"

"That's all right. I don't like the way you look at them, either!"

"How can you tell how I look when you sittin' up there behind me?" Adelia was angry now, Rohrs realized. "You talk like you crazy. In the first place, I move my chair, those men move right with me if they want to. In the second place, I can't move my chair anywhere without sittin' right in front of somebody. You must be out youh head."

She stalked back toward the stage. Bump, following, yelled, "And stay away from that goddamn Lion too!"

Rohrs shook his head. He thought of Step-Up saying, "Crazy about her. Ought to tell her so more often." He shrugged and walked back to the stage, flopping his hands loosely from the wrists, wriggling and drooping the fingers, trying to relax them. The last set was coming up.

The last set was the big one. It was mostly their own stuff, and it was all what they loved to play. The fox-trotters had heard their last ballad, and they knew it; they moved from the edges of the hall and crowded toward the stage.

The last set had "Shattered Slumber"—the shouting horns, the thunder of the drums, the hilarious vocal dialogue between Jackson and Shepherd. The last set had "Basement Stuff," and "High Low Jack," and Adelia singing the haunting "Ride On." The crowd gulped it and howled for more. They groped over the edge of the stage with their hands, trying to pull more music from the grinning, sweating players.

Bump did a specialty. Rohrs turned and watched admiringly. That man is great, he thought, great enough that this white-audience business is going to hurt him someday. . . .

It was time for Adelia's last song, "The Man I Love." Hadley stood up and scatted it, and the bawl of the trumpet filled the hall, made the Lion shiver. And Adelia sang.

The guitar carried the accompaniment alone, and the Lion had turned to look. Oh, Jesus! he thought. . . .

She was singing it at the toughs, at the two leering white men who stood directly below her. She swayed her body, and smiled and flicked her eyes at the two men.

This is going to be bad, the Lion thought as he had to swing back to the piano. This is going to be hell.

And when, at the end of the number, he fearfully turned again, what he saw was so unexpected that he literally rubbed his eyes and looked again. The two men were gone.

He didn't have much time to wonder about it. Bump called them into a huddle. He was wet all over; he wiped his eyes and cheeks as he talked. " 'Now Black Water,' " he said hoarsely. " 'Black Water,' and then we got to slack it off. We got to tone it down or they'll never let us out of here."

"Black Water Blues" was the Lion's favorite specialty. He had writ-

94

ten it himself, and it was a little poetry, and a lot of sadness, and all the old-time blues scheme and rhythm. It was the only thing he ever sang. He was no Cab Calloway, but he carried a tune well enough, and he could put the mourning in his voice.

> "Black water is somethin
> Lord that I sure do hate
> Black water is somethin
> That I sure do hate
> Fortune teller told me
> Black water gonna be my fate"

He stroked the keyboard and listened to the soft play of the band. The thing was his and theirs at the same time. They had taken it in; they played it happily, lovingly. And the audience strained forward over the lights.

> "I wake up the mornin
> Black water in my bed
> I go to eat my breakfast
> Black water in my bread
> Well I believe
> Believe I better go my way
> Black water gonna haunt me
> Until my dying day

> "I had myself a woman
> She liked to dress in red
> I found her in black water
> Found her lyin dead
> Well I believe
> Believe I'll go far far away
> Black water gonna dog me
> Until that judgment day"

The crowd yelled and clapped. The boys were grinning. Jackson leaned over and hit him on the back. Rohrs gave LeRoy the flat-hand sign of approval for the guitar solo. It was all good: the joy of playing it and the sadness of hearing it; the way the crowd clapped and the boys grinned.

A stagehand stood in the wings, trying to get Adelia's attention. She heard his whisper and walked to him. He said something, pointing offstage, and she nodded and went off, out of sight. The Lion watched her go out, wondering.

They played three more, quietly and sweetly, tapering-off tunes to calm the audience so that they could quit. Then it was closing time, theme time, and Adelia had not returned. Bump was scowling again. The Lion shook his head in disgust. She was going too far, not being on stage at theme time.

The drums rolled again, and Step-Up broke. He had finished, and Hadley was standing, when the terrified face of the stagehand appeared over the piano. "Man! Man, there's trouble!" He was almost crying.

"What's wrong?"

"End it! End it, man, quick!"

"Start the curtain down," said the Lion, and called out, in the singsong, syncopated voice that they used for communicating during numbers, "Knock it off, right now! There's trouble brewin'!"

They stared at him, but Hadley cut the solo, and they blew the final blare as the curtain fell.

Then everything happened fast. The stagehand cried out, "I didn't mean nothin'! I didn't know nothin' was wrong!" and the manager, calmer, said, "Mistuh Roxy, I'm afraid youh wife hurt bad."

Then they all charged off and were in time to see two stagehands carrying Adelia through the hall backstage—Adelia with her red gown torn mostly off, and what was left smeared and dripping with the dirty water from the alley; Adelia crying in little gasps of amazement and horror. . . .

Bump Roxy roared and the stagehand gibbered and the manager soothed; a doctor followed the bearers into a dressing room, and Bump plunged after them.

"Two white men," the guilty stagehand babbled to the frozen band. "Two white men told me ask Mrs. Roxy come out 'n' autograph . . ."

"You know you hadn't ought to do nothin' like that!"

"I didn't know nothin' was wrong! They gimme five dollahs. Jesus, I didn't know nothin' was wrong!" The manager guided him gently away.

There was an old piano in the end of the tiny hallway, near the dressing-room door. The Lion sat heavily on the stool. A stack of folding chairs was heaped against the wall; the band opened them and sat down, lined along the hall, waiting for the door to open.

Rohrs was staring at the keyboard when someone touched his arm. LeRoy Bunner's face was grave. "You better get out of here, man."

The Lion shook his head.

"Lion, you crazy. Don't you know what them men done to Adelia? It ain't gonna be safe out here for no white man."

"You might be right," said the Lion. He touched the keys softly, hit a B-flat chord.

"I tell you that man like to kill somebody," LeRoy said. He looked around for support.

"Let him be," Step-Up said. "The Lion, maybe he know what he's doin'."

"Bump gonna go for the first white man he sees!"

"That's all right," the Lion said. "This way he won't have to go out in the street and chase one." Old Step-Up, he thought, he sees it, he sees it like I do. He started to play quietly. He took a simple, four-note walking bass figure and worked over it gently, playing sadness. LeRoy looked around, licked his lips, and then sat down.

The Lion played, waiting.

It was for Bump, so that he wouldn't go raging the streets and get arrested. But it was for more than that; Rohrs knew it and Step-Up had seen it. It was for the great Bump Roxy, who might never be able to face another white audience if this wasn't handled right. It was for the music: for "Crosstown" and "Shattered Slumber," and the "Black Water Blues" that might never be played again; for the grins and flat-hand signs when they finished one. It was for Adelia, and for himself. It was for Bump Roxy and his Blue Band.

He did not look up when the door opened and the footsteps came out slowly and then stopped. He heard Bump move toward him, felt him standing directly behind. He made himself stay loose when the huge hand touched his shoulders and the back of his neck.

The hand did not move; it lay there gently. He did not let himself sigh; he sat and played the blues. He did not look up even when the hand began to tremble and he heard the ugly, harsh sobs.

The chords rippled the stillness of the room.

from Harper's Magazine

A NAME FOR THE CITY

WILLIAM FAULKNER *is now a Nobel Prize winner, in addition to the many other honors that have come his way recently, including the 1951 National Book Award in fiction for his* Collected Short Stories. *In 1949 he was awarded the first prize in the O. Henry competition for "The Courtship" and ten years before received a similar award for "Barn Burning." Other stories of his that have appeared in this collection include "Wash," 1934; "Lion," 1936; and "Two Soldiers," 1942. Mr. Faulkner was born fifty-four years ago in Oxford, Mississippi, the seat of the state university, which he attended briefly before serving in the Canadian Air Force during World War I. Most of his many novels and short stories are linked in one way or another with the legendary history of the imaginary North Mississippi county of Yoknapatawpha and its county seat, Jefferson. Mr. Faulkner lives in a white-columned house near Oxford, pursuing his hobbies of farming and hunting. He continues a lifetime practice of staying as far away from the so-called literary life as he can.*

"Experience," Uncle Gavin said, "is not in the senses, but in the heart. I cite you the world travelers, the tense and furious circumnavigators: first, three years, then one year, then three months, and then one month, and then ninety hours, and now—or am I wrong?—thirty hours, and who knows but what perhaps at this very instant somebody with still more money, for whom somebody has invented a still faster machine, has just departed to do it in three hours, leaving behind him, embalmed in cosmos-flung television to beat among the very stars themselves, his immortal epitaph: 'Good-by, Ma, and may the best man win.' I cite you blind Homer, unable to quit the Athenian stone he sat on without a child to lead him, yet plumbed

98

and charted the ultimate frontiers of passion and defeat and glory and ambition and courage and hope and fear." And as he—Uncle Gavin—grew older, he began to spend more and more of his time trying to prove this to me. I mean, he used to tell me the old tales about Jefferson and the county in order to explain something I had seen, or that he and I had seen together; now he began to tell them for their own sake, as though he himself had been there a hundred or a hundred and fifty years ago; he, the middle-aging country lawyer in the second half of the twentieth century, was the *I was* and *I did* and *I saw* of a time when some of the progenitors of America still lived and breathed, and General Andrew Jackson's political star had not even risen yet, and even old Issetibbeha, the Chickasaw King, still existed in the memories of living men. Which was where this one came from about the ancient clumsy monster of a home-made iron lock which came all the long way overland by horseback from Carolina to Mississippi, and not only named a town but even created it.

Jefferson was not even Jefferson then. It was not even a town. It was a Chickasaw agency trading post: a store, a tavern, a jail or calaboose, a half-dozen log cabins set in a disorderly huddle in the middle of the wilderness domain which Ikkemotubbe, old Issetibbeha's successor, was ceding to the white men for land—peace, escape, whatever he and his people called it—in what was to be Oklahoma territory. There was no church, no school, least of all a courthouse. Because although they probably knew from the first that they wanted, needed, would someday have a church and a school, it would be almost a quarter of a century before they would discover suddenly that they not only had to have a courthouse, but they had to have it quick. They had something to put in it, of course, as a kind of nest egg; even the simple dispossession of Indians begot in time a minuscule of archive and record, not to mention the normal litter of man's ramshackle confederation against environment—that time and that wilderness. In this case it was a meager, fading, dog-eared, uncorrelated, at times illiterate, sheaf of land grants and patents and transfers and deeds, and tax- and militia-rolls, and bills of sale for slaves, and counting-house lists of exchange rates and spurious currency, and liens and mortgages, and rewards for escaped or stolen Negroes and other livestock, and diary-like annotations of births and marriages and deaths and public hangings and land auctions, accumulating slowly in a sort of iron pirate's chest in the back room of the post-office-trading-post-store, until one day, twenty-five years later, when, because of a jail break compounded by the ancient monster Carolina lock, the box was removed to a small lean-to room like a wood- or a tool-shed built two days ago against one outside wall of the mortised-log, mud-chinked shakedown jail; by which fortuity was born the Yoknapatawpha County courthouse, the box containing the records not moved from any place but simply to one, removed from the trading-post back room not for any reason inherent in either the back room or the box, but on the contrary since the box was not only in nobody's way in the back room, it was even missed when gone since it had served as another seat or stool among the powder and whiskykegs and firkins of salt and lard and molasses about the stove on winter nights, and was moved at all for the simple reason that the settlement (overnight it was a town without having been a village; one day in about a hundred years it would wake frantically from its communal slumber in a rash of Rotary and Lions clubs and Chambers of Commerce and City Beautifuls: a furious beating of hollow drums toward nowhere, but simply to sound louder than the next tiny human clotting to its north or south or east or west, dubbing itself city as Napoleon dubbed himself emperor, and defending the expedient by padding its census rolls—a fever, a delirium in which it would confound forever seething with motion and motion with progress) found itself faced with a problem—or rather, under the Damocles sword of a dilemma—from which nothing could save it except the consecration or ordination or whatever you call it, of a courthouse.

Even the jailbreak was fortuity: a gang—three or four—of Natchez Trace bandits (twenty-five years later legend would begin to affirm, and a hundred years later would still be affirming, that two of the bandits were the Harpes themselves, Big Harpe anyway, since the circumstances, the method, of the breakout left behind like a smell, an odor, a kind of Gargantuan and bizarre playfulness at once humorous and terrifying, as if the settlement had fallen, blundered, into the notice or range of an idle and whimsical giant. Which—that they were the Harpes—was impossible, since the Harpes and even

100

the last of Mason's ruffians were dead or scattered by this time, and the robbers would have had to belong to Murrell's organization—if they needed to belong to any at all other than the simple fraternity of rapine) captured by chance by a band of militia and brought in to the settlement jail because it was the nearest. Or a chance band of militia rather, since the presence of the band was a third fortuity, it having been part of a general muster at the settlement two days ago for a Fourth of July barbecue, which by the next day had boiled down into one drunken brawling which rendered even the last hardy survivors vulnerable enough for the residents of the settlement to eject them, this particular band having been carried, still comatose, in one of the evicting wagons, to a swamp four miles away known as Hurricane Bottoms, where they made camp to regain their strength or anyway their legs, and where the bandits, on their way across country to their hideout after their last exploit on the Trace, stumbled onto the campfire. And here report varied, divided; some said that the sergeant in command of the militia recognized one of the bandits as a deserter from his corps, others said that one of the bandits recognized in the sergeant a former follower of his, the bandit's, trade. Anyway, on the following morning all of them, captors and prisoners, returned to the settlement in a group, some said in confederation now seeking more drink, others said that the captors brought their prizes back to the settlement in revenge for their eviction because these were frontier, pioneer, times, when—as Uncle Gavin said—personal liberty and freedom were almost a physical condition like fire or flood, and no community was going to interfere with any mere amoralist so long as he practiced somewhere else, and the settlement, being neither on the Trace nor the river but lying about midway between, wanted no part of the underworld of either.

But, like it or no, they had some of it now. They put the bandits into the jail, which until now had had no lock at all, its clients so far being amateurs—local brawlers and drunkards and runaway slaves—for whom a single wooden bar in slots across the outside of the door like on a corncrib, had sufficed. But they had now what might be four—three—Dillingers or Jesse Jameses of the time, with rewards on their heads. So they locked the jail this time. They did it right. They bored an auger hole through the door and another through the jamb

101

and passed a length of heavy chain through them, and sent a messenger at a run back to the post-office-store to fetch the old Carolina lock from the latest Nashville mail-pouch—the lock, the iron monster weighing almost fifteen pounds, with a key almost as long as a bayonet, not just the only lock in that part of the country, but the oldest lock in that cranny of the United States, brought there by one of the three men who were what was to be Yoknapatawpha County's coeval pioneers and settlers, leaving in it the three oldest names— Alexander Holston, who came as half groom and half bodyguard to Dr. Samuel Habersham, and half nurse and half tutor to the doctor's eight-year-old motherless son, the three of them riding horseback across Tennessee from the Cumberland Gap along with Louis Grenier, the Huguenot younger son who brought the first slaves into the country and was granted the first big land patent and so became the first cotton planter; while Dr. Habersham, with his worn black bag of pills and knives and his brawny taciturn bodyguard and his half-orphan child, became the settlement itself (for a time, before it was named, the settlement was known as Dr. Habersham's, then Habersham's, then simply Habersham; a hundred years later, during a schism between two ladies' clubs over the naming of the streets in order to get free mail delivery, a movement was started, first, to change the name back to Habersham; then failing that, to divide the town in two and call one half of it Habersham after the old pioneer doctor and founder)—friend of old Issetibbeha, the Chickasaw chief (the motherless Habersham boy, now a man of twenty-five, married one of Issetibbeha's granddaughters and in the thirties emigrated to Oklahoma with his wife's dispossessed people), first unofficial, then official Chickasaw agent until he resigned in a letter of furious denunciation addressed to the President of the United States himself; and—his charge and pupil a man now—Alexander Holston became the settlement's first publican, establishing the tavern still known as the Holston House, the original log walls and puncheon floors and hand-mortised joints of which are still buried somewhere beneath the modern pressed glass and brick veneer and neon tubes.

The lock was his: fifteen pounds of useless iron lugged a thousand miles through a desert of precipice and swamp, of flood and drought and wild beasts and wild Indians and wilder white men, displacing that fifteen pounds better given to food or seed to plant food or even powder to defend with, to become a fixture, a kind of landmark, in the bar of a wilderness ordinary, locking and securing nothing, because there was nothing behind the heavy bars and shutters needing further locking and securing, not even a paperweight because the only papers in the Holston House were the twisted spills in an old powder horn above the mantel for lighting tobacco; always a little in the way, since it had constantly to be moved: from bar to shelf to mantel then back to bar again until they finally thought about putting it on the bimonthly mail pouch; familiar, known, presently the oldest unchanged thing in the settlement, older than the people since Issetibbeha and Dr. Habersham were dead, and Alexander Holston was an old man crippled with arthritis, and Louis Grenier had a settlement of his own on his own vast plantation now, half of which was not even in Yoknapatawpha County, and the settlement rarely saw him; older than the town, since there were new names in it now even when the old blood ran in them, and you no longer shot a bear or deer or wild turkey simply by standing for a while in your kitchen door, not to mention the pouch of mail—letters and even newspapers —which came from Nashville every two weeks by a special horseman who did nothing else and was paid a salary for it by the federal government; and that was the second phase of the monster Carolina lock's transubstantiation into the Yoknapatawpha County courthouse.

The pouch didn't always reach the settlement every two weeks, nor even always every month. But sooner or later it did, and everybody knew it would, because it—the cowhide saddlebag not even large enough to hold a full change of clothing, containing three or four letters and half that many badly printed one- and two-page newspapers already three or four months out of date and usually half and sometimes wholly wrong or misinformed to begin with—was the United States, the power and the will to liberty, owning allegiance to no man, bringing even into that still almost pathless wilderness the thin, peremptory voice of the nation which had wrenched its freedom from one of the most powerful peoples on earth and then again within the same lifespan successfully defended it; so peremptory and audible that the man who carried the pouch on the galloping horse didn't even carry any arms except a tin horn, traversing month after month, blatantly, flagrantly, almost contemptuously, a region where for no more than the boots on his feet, men would murder a traveler and gut him like a bear or deer or fish and fill the cavity with rocks and sink the evidence in the nearest water; not even deigning to pass quietly where other men, even though armed and in parties, tried to move secretly or at least without uproar, but instead announcing his solitary advent as far ahead of himself as the ring of the horn would carry. So it was not long before Alexander Holston's lock had moved to the mail pouch. Not that the pouch needed one, having come already the three hundred miles from Nashville without a lock. (It had been projected at first that the lock remain on the pouch constantly. That is, not just while the pouch was in the settlement, but while it was on the horse between Nashville and the settlement too. The rider refused, succinctly, in three words, one of which was printable. His reason was the lock's weight. They pointed out to him that this would not hold water, since not only—the rider was a frail, irascible little man weighing less than a hundred pounds— would the fifteen pounds of lock even then fail to bring his weight up to that of a normal adult male, the added weight of the lock would merely match that of the pistols which his employer, the United States Government, believed he carried and even paid him for having done so, the rider's reply to this being succinct, too, though not so glib: that the lock weighed fifteen pounds either at the back door of the store in the settlement, or at that of the post office in Nashville. But since Nashville and the settlement were three hundred miles apart, by the time the horse had carried it from one to the other, the lock weighed fifteen pounds to the mile times three hundred miles, or forty-five hundred pounds. Which was manifest nonsense, a physical impossibility either in lock or horse. Yet indubitably fifteen pounds times three hundred miles was forty-five hundred something, either pounds or miles—especially as while they were still trying to unravel it, the rider repeated his first three succinct—two unprintable— words.)

So less than ever would the pouch need a lock in the back room of the trading post, surrounded and enclosed once more by civilization, where its very intactness, its presence to receive a lock, proved its lack of that need during the three hundred miles of rapine-haunted Trace; needing a lock as little as it was equipped to receive one, since it had been necessary to slit the leather with a knife just under each jaw of the opening and insert the lock's iron mandible through the two slits and clash it home, so that any other hand with a similar knife could have cut the whole lock from the pouch as easily as it had been clasped onto it. So the old lock was not even a symbol of security: it was a gesture of salutation, of free men to free men, of civilization to civilization across not just the three hundred miles of wilderness to Nashville, but the fifteen hundred to Washington: of respect without servility, allegiance without abasement to the government which they had helped to found and had accepted with pride but still as free men, still free to withdraw from it at any moment when the two of them found themselves no longer compatible, the old lock meeting the pouch each time on its arrival, to clasp it in iron and inviolable symbolism, while old Alec Holston, childless bachelor, grew a little older and grayer, a little more arthritic in flesh and temper, too, a little stiffer and more rigid in bone and pride, too, since the lock was still his, he had merely lent it, and so in a sense he was the grandfather in the settlement of the inviolability not just of government mail, but of a free government of free men, too, so long as the government remembered to let men live free, not under it but beside it.

That was the lock; they put it on the jail. They did it quickly, not even waiting until a messenger could have got back from the Holston House with old Alec's permission to remove it from the mail pouch or use it for the new purpose. Not that he would have objected on principle nor refused his permission except by simple instinct; that is, he would probably have been the first to suggest the lock if he had known in time or thought of it first, but he would have refused at once if he thought the thing was contemplated without consulting him. Which everybody in the settlement knew, though this was not at all why they didn't wait for the messenger. In fact, no messenger had ever been sent to old Alec; they didn't have time to send one, let alone wait until he got back; they didn't want the lock to keep the bandits in, since (as was later proved) the old lock would have been no more obstacle for the bandits to pass than the customary wooden bar; they didn't need the lock to protect the settlement from the bandits, but to protect the bandits from the settlement. Because the prisoners had barely reached the settlement when it developed that there was a faction bent on lynching them at once, out of hand, without preliminary—a small but determined gang which tried to wrest the prisoners from their captors while the militia was still trying to find someone to surrender them to, and would have succeeded except for a man named Compson, who came to the settlement a few years ago with a race horse, which he swapped to Ikkemotubbe, Issetibbeha's successor in the chiefship, for a square mile of what was to be the most valuable land in the future town of Jefferson, who, legend said, drew a pistol and held the ravishers at bay until the bandits could be got into the jail and the auger holes bored and someone sent to fetch old Alec Holston's lock. Because there were indeed new names and faces, too, in the settlement now—faces so new as to have (to the older residents) no discernible antecedents other than mammalinity, nor past other than the simple years which had scored them; and names so new as to have no discernible (nor discoverable either) antecedents or past at all, as though they had been invented yesterday, report dividing again: to the effect that there were more people in the settlement that day than the militia sergeant whom one or all of the bandits might recognize.

So Compson locked the jail, and a courier with the two best horses in the settlement—one to ride and one to lead—cut through the woods to the Trace to ride the hundred-odd miles to Natchez with the news of the capture and authority to dicker for the reward; and that evening in the Holston House kitchen was held the settlement's first municipal meeting, prototype not only of the town council after the settlement would be a town, but of the chamber of commerce when it would begin to proclaim itself a city, with Compson presiding, not old Alec, who was quite old now, grim, taciturn, sitting even on a hot July night before a smoldering log in his vast chimney; his back even turned to the table (he was not interested in the deliberation; the prisoners were his already since his lock held them; whatever the conference decided would have to be submitted to him for ratification anyway before anyone could touch his lock to open it) around which the progenitors of the Jefferson city fathers sat in what was almost a council of war, not only discussing the collecting of the reward, but the keeping and defending of it. Because there were two factions of opposition now: not only the lynching party, but the militia band, too, who now claimed that as prizes the prisoners still belonged to their original captors; that they—the militia—had merely surrendered the prisoners' custody but had relinquished nothing of

106

any reward: on the prospect of which, the militia band had got more whisky from the trading-post store and had built a tremendous bonfire in front of the jail, around which they and the lynching party had now confederated in a wassail or conference of their own. Or so they thought. Because the truth was that Compson, in the name of the public peace and welfare, had made formal demand on Dr. Peabody, old Dr. Habersham's successor, and the three of them—Compson, Peabody, and the post trader, Ratcliffe—added the laudanum to the keg of whisky and sent it as a gift from the settlement to the astonished militia sergeant, and returned to the Holston House kitchen to wait until the last of the uproar died; then the law-and-order party made a rapid sortie and gathered up all the comatose opposition, lynchers and captors, too, and dumped them all into the jail with the prisoners and locked the door again and went home to bed—until the next morning, when the first arrivals were met by a scene resembling an outdoor stage setting: which was how the legend of the mad Harpes started: a thing not just fantastical but incomprehensible, not just whimsical but a little terrifying (though at least it was bloodless, which would have contented neither Harpe): not just the lock gone from the door nor even just the door gone from the jail, but the entire wall gone, the mud-chinked, ax-mortised logs unjointed neatly and quietly in the darkness and stacked as neatly to one side, leaving the jail open to the world like a stage on which the late insurgents still lay sprawled and various in deathlike slumber, the whole settlement gathered now to watch Compson trying to kick at least one of them awake, until one of the Holston slaves —the cook's husband, the waiter-groom-hostler—ran into the crowd shouting, "Whar de lock, whar de lock, ole Boss say whar de lock?"

It was gone (as were three horses belonging to three of the lynching faction). They couldn't even find the heavy door and the chain, and at first they were almost betrayed into believing that the bandits had had to take the door in order to steal the chain and lock, catching themselves back from the very brink of this wanton accusation of rationality. But the lock was gone; nor did it take the settlement long to realize that it was not the escaped bandits and the aborted reward, but the lock, and not a simple situation which faced them, but a problem which threatened, the slave departing back to the Holston House at a dead run and then reappearing at the dead run almost

107

before the door, the walls, had had time to hide him, engulf and then eject him again, darting through the crowd and up to Compson himself now, saying, "Ole Boss say fetch de lock"—not send the lock, but bring the lock. So Compson and his lieutenants (and this was where the mail rider began to appear, or rather, to emerge—the fragile wisp of a man ageless, hairless, and toothless, who looked too frail even to approach a horse, let alone ride one six hundred miles every two weeks, yet who did so, and not only that but had wind enough left not only to announce and precede but even follow his passing with the jeering musical triumph of the horn: a contempt for possible—probable—despoilers matched only by that for the official dross of which he might be despoiled, and which agreed to remain in civilized bounds only so long as the despoiler had the taste to refrain) repaired to the kitchen where old Alec still sat before his smoldering log, his back still to the room, and still not turning it this time either.

And that was all. He ordered the immediate return of his lock. It was not even an ultimatum, it was a simple instruction, a decree, impersonal, the mail rider now well into the fringe of the group, saying nothing and missing nothing, like a weightless desiccated or fossil bird, not a vulture of course nor even quite a hawk, but say a pterodactyl chick arrested just out of the egg ten glaciers ago and so old in simple infancy as to be worn and weary ancestor of all subsequent life. They pointed out to old Alec that the only reason the lock could be missing was that the bandits had not had time or been able to cut it out of the door, and that even three fleeing madmen on stolen horses would not carry a six-foot oak door very far, and that a party of Ikkemotubbe's young men were even now trailing the horses westward toward the river and that without doubt the lock would be found at any moment, probably under the first bush at the edge of the settlement: knowing better, knowing that there was no limit to the fantistic and the terrifying and the bizarre, of which the men were capable who already, just to escape from a log jail, had quietly removed one entire wall and stacked it in neat piecemeal at the roadside, and that not they nor old Alec neither would ever see his lock again.

Nor did they; the rest of that afternoon and all the next day too, while old Alec still smoked his pipe in front of his smoldering log, the settlement's sheepish and raging elders hunted for it, with (by now: the next afternoon) Ikkemotubbe's Chickasaws helping, too, or anyway present, watching: the wild men, the wilderness's tameless evictant children looking only the more wild and homeless for the white man's denim and butternut and felt and straw which they wore, standing or squatting or following, grave, attentive, and interested, while the white men sweated and cursed among the bordering thickets of their punily-clawed foothold; and always the rider, Pettigrew, ubiquitous, everywhere, not helping search himself and never in anyone's way, but always present, inscrutable, saturnine, missing nothing: until at last toward sundown Compson crashed savagely out of the last bramble-brake and flung the sweat from his face with a full-armed sweep sufficient to repudiate a throne, and said,

"All right, God damn it, we'll pay him for it." Because they had already considered that last gambit; they had already realized its seriousness from the very fact that Peabody had tried to make a joke about it which everyone knew that even Peabody did not think humorous:

"Yes—and quick, too, before he has time to advise with Pettigrew and price it by the pound."

"By the pound?" Compson said.

"Pettigrew just weighed it by the three hundred miles from Nashville. Old Alec might start from Carolina. That's fifteen thousand pounds."

"Oh," Compson said. So he blew in his men by means of a foxhorn which one of the Indians wore on a thong around his neck, though even then they paused for one last quick conference; again it was Peabody who stopped them.

"Who'll pay for it?" he said. "It would be just like him to want a dollar a pound for it, even if by Pettigrew's scale he had found it in the ashes of his fireplace." They—Compson anyway—had probably already thought of that; that, as much as Pettigrew's presence, was probably why he was trying to rush them into old Alec's presence with the offer so quickly that none would have the face to renege on a pro rata share. But Peabody had torn it now. Compson looked about at them, sweating, grimly enraged.

"That means Peabody will probably pay one dollar," he said. "Who pays the other fourteen? Me?" Then Ratcliffe, the trader, the store's proprietor, solved it—a solution so simple, so limitless in retroaction, that they didn't even wonder why nobody had thought of it before; which not only solved the problem but abolished it; and not just that one, but all problems, from now on into perpetuity, opening to their vision like the rending of a veil, like a glorious prophecy, the vast, splendid, limitless panorama of America: that land of boundless opportunity, that bourne, created not by nor of the people, but for the people, as was the heavenly manna of old, with no return demand on man save the chewing and swallowing since out of its own matchless Allgood it would create, produce, train, support, and perpetuate a race of laborers dedicated to the single purpose of picking the manna up and putting it into his lax hand or even between his jaws—illimitable, vast, without beginning or end, not even a trade or a craft but a beneficence as are sunlight and rain and air, inalienable and immutable.

"Put it on the Book," Ratcliffe said—the Book: not a ledger, but *the* ledger, since it was probably the only thing of its kind between Nashville and Natchez, unless there might happen to be a similar one a few miles south at the first Chocktaw agency at Yalo Busha—a ruled, paper-backed copybook such as might have come out of a schoolroom, in which accrued, with the United States as debtor, in Mohataha's name (the Chickasaw matriarch, Ikkemotubbe's mother and old Issetibbeha's sister, who—she could write her name, or anyway make something with a pen or pencil which was agreed to be, or at least accepted to be, a valid signature—signed all the conveyances as her son's kingdom passed to the white people, regularizing it in law anyway) the crawling tedious list of calico and gunpowder, whisky and salt and snuff and denim pants and osseous candy drawn from Ratcliffe's shelves by her descendants and subjects and Negro slaves.

That was all the settlement had to do: add the lock to the list, the account. It wouldn't even matter at what price they entered it. They could have priced it on Pettigrew's scale of fifteen pounds times the distance not just to Carolina but to Washington itself, and nobody would ever notice it probably; they could have charged the United States with seventeen thousand five hundred dollars' worth of the fossilized and indestructible candy, and none would ever read the entry. So it was solved, done, finished, ended. They didn't even have to discuss it. They didn't even think about it any more, unless perhaps here and there to marvel (a little speculatively probably) at their own moderation, since they wanted nothing—least of all, to escape any just blame—but a fair and decent adjustment of the lock. They went back to where old Alec still sat with his pipe in front of his dim hearth. Only they had overestimated him; he didn't want any money at all, he wanted his lock. Whereupon what little remained of Compson's patience went too.

"Your lock's gone," he told old Alec harshly. "You'll take fifteen dollars for it," he said, his voice already fading, because even that rage could recognize impasse when it saw it. Nevertheless, the rage, the impotence, the sweating, the *too much*—whatever it was—forced the voice on for one word more: "Or——" Before it stopped for good and allowed Peabody to fill the gap:

"Or else?" Peabody said, and not to old Alec, but to Compson. "Or else what?" Then Ratcliffe saved that too.

"Wait," he said. "Uncle Alec's going to take fifty dollars for his lock. A guarantee of fifty dollars. He'll give us the name of the black-smith back in Cal'lina that made it for him, and we'll send back there and have a new one made. Going and coming and all'll cost about fifty dollars. We'll give Uncle Alec the fifty dollars to hold as a guar-antee. Then when the new lock comes, he'll give us back the money. All right, Uncle Alec?"

And that could have been all of it. It probably would have been, except for Pettigrew. It was not that they had forgotten him, or even assimilated him. They had simply sealed—healed him off (so they thought)—him into their civic crisis as the desperate and defenseless oyster immobilizes its atom of inevictable grit. Nobody had seen him move; yet he now stood in the center of them where Compson and Ratcliffe and Peabody faced old Alec in the chair. You might have said that he had oozed there, except for that adamantine quality which might (in emergency) become invisible but never insub-stantial and never in this world fluid; he spoke in a voice bland, reasonable, and impersonal, then stood there being looked at, frail and child-sized, impermeable as diamond and manifest with portent, bringing into that backwoods room a thousand miles deep in pathless wilderness, the whole vast, incalculable weight of federality, not just representing the government nor even himself just the government; for that moment, at least, he was the United States.

"Uncle Alec hasn't lost any lock," he said. "That was Uncle Sam."
After a moment someone said, "What?"

"That's right," Pettigrew said. "Whoever put that lock of Holston's
on that mailbag either made a voluntary gift to the United States,
and the same law covers the United States Government that covers
minor children: you can give something to them, but you can't take
it back; or he or they done something else."

They looked at him. Again after a while somebody said something;
it was Ratcliffe. "What else?" Ratcliffe said. Pettigrew answered, still
bland, impersonal, heartless, and glib:

"Committed a violation of Act of Congress as especially made and
provided for the defacement of government property, penalty of five
thousand dollars or not less than one year in a federal jail or both.
For whoever cut them two slits in the bag to put the lock in, Act of
Congress as especially made and provided for the injury or destruction of government property, penalty of ten thousand dollars or not
less than five years in a federal jail or both." He did not move even
yet; he simply spoke directly to old Alec: "I reckon you're going to
have supper here same as usual sooner or later or more or less."

"Wait," Ratcliffe said. He turned to Compson. "Is that true?"

"What the hell difference does it make whether it's true or not?"
Compson said. "What do you think he's going to do as soon as he gets
to Nashville?" He said violently to Pettigrew: "You were supposed to
leave for Nashville yesterday. What were you hanging around here
for?"

"Nothing to go to Nashville for," Pettigrew said. "You don't want
any mail. You ain't got anything to lock it up with."

"So we ain't," Ratcliffe said. "So we'll let the United States find the
United States' lock." This time Pettigrew looked at no one. He wasn't
even speaking to anyone, any more than old Alec had been when he
decreed the return of his lock:

"Act of Congress as made and provided for the unauthorized re-
moval and/or use or willful or felonious use or misuse or loss of government property, penalty the value of the article plus five hundred
to ten thousand dollars or thirty days to twenty years in a federal jail
or both. They may even make a new one when they read where you
have charged a Post Office Department lock to the Bureau of Indian
Affairs." He moved; now he was speaking to old Alec again: "I'm

going out to my horse. When this meeting is over and you get back to cooking, you can send your nigger for me."

Then he was gone. After a while Ratcliffe said, "What do you reckon he aims to get out of this? A reward?" But that was wrong; they all knew better than that.

"He's already getting what he wants," Compson said, and cursed again. "Confusion. Just damned confusion." But that was wrong too; they all knew that, too, though it was Peabody who said it:

"No. Not confusion. A man who will ride six hundred miles through this country every two weeks, with nothing for protection but a fox-horn, ain't really interested in confusion any more than he is in money." So they didn't know yet what was in Pettigrew's mind. But they knew what he would do. That is, they knew that they did not know at all, either what he would do, or how, or when, and that there was nothing whatever that they could do about it until they discovered why. And they saw now that they had no possible means to discover that; they realized now that they had known him for three years now, during which, fragile ard inviolable and undeviable and preceded for a mile or more by the strong, sweet ringing of the horn, on his strong and tireless horse he would complete the bimonthly trip from Nashville to the settlement and for the next three or four days would live among them, yet that they knew nothing whatever about him, and even now knew only that they dared not, simply dared not, take any chance, sitting for a while longer in the darkening room while old Alec still smoked, his back still squarely turned to them and their quandary too; then dispersing to their own cabins for the evening meal—with what appetite they could bring to it, since presently they had drifted back through the summer darkness when by ordinary they would have been already in bed, to the back room of Ratcliffe's store now, to sit again while Ratcliffe recapitulated in his mixture of bewilderment and alarm (and something else which they recognized was respect as they realized that he—Ratcliffe—was unshakably convinced that Pettigrew's aim was money; that Pettigrew had invented or evolved a scheme so richly rewarding that he—Ratcliffe—had not only been unable to forestall him and do it first, he—Ratcliffe—couldn't even guess what it was after he had been given a hint) until Compson interrupted him.

"Hell," Compson said. "Everybody knows what's wrong with him. It's ethics. He's a damned moralist."

"Ethics?" Peabody said. He sounded almost startled. He said quickly: "That's bad. How can we corrupt an ethical man?"

"Who wants to corrupt him?" Compson said. "All we want him to do is stay on that damned horse and blow whatever extra wind he's got into that damned horn."

But Peabody was not even listening. He said, "Ethics," almost dreamily. He said, "Wait." They watched him. He said suddenly to Ratcliffe: "I've heard it somewhere. If anybody here knows it, it'll be you. What's his name?"

"His name?" Ratcliffe said. "Pettigrew's? Oh. His Christian name." Ratcliffe told him. "Why?"

"Nothing," Peabody said. "I'm going home. Anybody else coming?" He spoke directly to nobody and said and would say no more, but that was enough: a straw perhaps, but at least a straw; enough anyway for the others to watch and say nothing either as Compson got up, too, and said to Ratcliffe, "You coming?" and the three of them walked away together, beyond earshot then beyond sight too. Then Compson said, "All right. What?"

"It may not work," Peabody said. "But you two will have to back me up. When I speak for the whole settlement, you and Ratcliffe will have to make it stick. Will you?"

Compson cursed. "But at least tell us a little of what we're going to guarantee." So Peabody told them some of it, and the next morning entered the stall in the Holston House stable where Pettigrew was grooming his ugly hammer-headed iron-muscled horse.

"We decided not to charge that lock to old Mohataha, after all," Peabody said. "That so?" Pettigrew said. "Nobody in Washington would ever catch it. Certainly not the ones that can read."

"We're going to pay for it ourselves," Peabody said. "In fact, we're going to do a little more. We've got to repair that jail wall anyhow; we've got to build one wall anyway. So by building three more, we will have another room. We got to build one anyway, so that don't count. So by building an extra three-wall room, we will have another four-wall house. That will be the courthouse." Pettigrew had been hissing gently between his teeth at each stroke of the brush, like a professional Irish groom. Now he stopped, the brush and his hand arrested in midstroke, and turned his head a little.

"Courthouse?"

114

"We're going to have a town," Peabody said. "We already got a church—that's Whitfield's cabin. And we're going to build a school, too, soon as we get around to it. But we're going to build the court-house today; we've already got something to put in it to make it a courthouse: that iron box that's been in Ratcliffe's way in the store for the last ten years. Then we'll have a town. We've already even named her."

Now Pettigrew stood up, very slowly. They looked at one another. After a moment Pettigrew said, "So?"

"Ratcliffe says your name's Jefferson," Peabody said.

"That's right," Pettigrew said. "Thomas Jefferson Pettigrew. I'm from old Ferginny."

"Any kin?" Peabody said.

"No," Pettigrew said. "My ma named me for him, so I would have some of his luck."

"Luck?" Peabody said.

Pettigrew didn't smile. "That's right. She didn't mean luck. She never had any schooling. She didn't know the word she wanted to say."

"Have you had it?" Peabody said. Nor did Pettigrew smile now. "I'm sorry," Peabody said. "Try to forget it." He said: "We decided to name her Jefferson." Now Pettigrew didn't seem to breathe even. He just stood there, small, frail, less than boy-size, childless and bachelor, incorrigibly kinless and tieless, looking at Peabody. Then he breathed, and raising the brush, he turned back to the horse and for an instant Peabody thought he was going back to the grooming. But instead of making the stroke, he laid the hand and the brush against the horse's flank and stood for a moment, his face turned away and his head bent a little. Then he raised his head and turned his face back toward Peabody.

"You could call that lock 'axle grease' on that Indian account," he said.

"Fifty dollars' worth of axle grease?" Peabody said.

"To grease the wagons for Oklahoma," Pettigrew said.

"So we could," Peabody said. "Only her name's Jefferson now. We can't forget that any more now."

from the Western Review

IN THE TIME OF DEMONSTRATIONS

JAMES B. HALL *comes from near Blanchester, in southern Ohio, and has been a farm boy, merchant seaman, and soldier. As a seaman he sailed off the West Coast to the Orient, and during World War II he was a chief warrant officer. He was in a parachute outfit and then in an anti-aircraft battalion "that made a specialty of being detached from everyone else and then being scattered all over North Africa, France, and Germany." Since returning to civilian life in 1946, Mr. Hall has, he writes, had an intense literary education at the University of Iowa and at the Kenyon Summer School of English. He is now teaching fiction writing and poetry in the Iowa Workshop Program. He has published stories, poetry, and criticism in* Western Review, Perspective, Story, Poetry, Experiment *and other magazines. Mr. Hall is married and the father of two girls "just big enough to stand and look out the lower panes of glass in the barracks doors of the student housing area in Iowa City."*

Sunday morning at nine I always come up from my room in the basement of our church and open all the doors, from the inside. Then I stand in the vestibule and look out into the township and up the roads where the cars are already coming out of barnyards and out of lanes: from Striders and Batesons, from Turner Tedricks and Old Man Culbersons and the Baker Boys. The first ones park with their car bumpers pressed against the stone foundations of the church and everyone else parks behind them. Finally all of Second Creek has come to hear this older preacher.

Everyone this morning, except Joe Strider. When he finally stopped at the front steps the Baker Boys stood up to help. Joe handed them the little things: the fan and the sailor hat and the fly swatter with the red handle. Then he opened the back door and handed out the black cane with the white crook, and the crutch.

Joe reached into the back seat and began pulling. The boy's head came out first: face up, his hair plastered down with water and dripping. While the boy leaned on the Baker twins, Joe bent to straighten the leather strap on the leg brace. Brother was pale and right at two hundred. My oldest boy might have been that big maybe.

"Tell the Boys thank you," Joe said.

Brother puckered up and trembled in the sunshine. I was still watching for our young preacher and this older preacher, but I could hear Brother shuffle and stomp down the aisle to the Striders' pew in front. Without looking inside I knew everyone was staring at him until he finally would hunch into the pew and bend down his head to look at the floor.

But from the vestibule, with one hand holding to the bell rope, you can think. (But you can only think this thing if you are the one who unlocks the front door from the inside and raises the east windows for circulation, or in winter keeps the furnace; and then only if you have set out the metal collection plates with the bottoms made of velvet.) You can think then suddenly of how old you are and how you have stared at the years and of what you need. And the one thing I needed was for this morning to be different because the forty-eight times I pull the bell rope each Sunday brings that thump into my chest and brings that ache into the elbow sockets. Yet there was no tiredness when I first came up from Clermont County, for my people were all fur trappers and sawmill hands and Ohio rivermen. They had all walked north and across that river from the pinch of war in '65, from old Kentucky.

I moved from Clermont County to Second Creek in two wagons. We drove up the lane at dusk and didn't get the stove set up. The stovepipe was on the second wagon, that broke down. We left the stove in the middle of the room and had no fire at all that first night. There were not enough blankets so we piled in together and slept the best four people can.

The next morning dry frost ran along the fences that were yet standing on that tired place and kindled from the sun. That didn't

117

last out the day. When the second wagon pulled in with the stovepipe the rain had already washed soot into all the woman's dishes. She had the pleurisy and the boys weren't big enough to help or to stay out of the way. My brother Rolfe left after we unloaded the last of his wagon. Before he headed back to the river bottoms he looked at Old Man Leash's barn and the house with tin in the windows for glass and the yard half covered with dead leaves and blue snow from the early thaw.

"I'd like to give you a few days' work," he said.

"You better get on back," I told him. "I'll fight it awhile myself." That was in March. And we were renters.

Later on I laid awake at nights. For years after that one summer I remembered the oldest boy. And still do. I bought his colts at auction and I paid more than anyone else thought they were worth. I had in mind something to give my boy an interest in the place. He could drive them through the most narrow gate on the farm. Now, of course, you don't work a boy when he's only twelve. But that was during World War I. There were no men around. Even then he could throw on a set of harness. He was big like his grandfather's people from Kentucky.

That afternoon I sent him on to the barn. He was high up on the last load of hay with one foot curled around the horseshoe nailed to the wagon standard. He had always said he could hold them, and I never said he couldn't. He was headstrong and twelve and they were colts. (I should have driven myself.) I saw them kick up the dust. They headed for the barn. The lane was narrow. They were frightened and trotting when they ran over the washed-out place in the lane. I hadn't put a tile in there.

I thought he would jump. He could have. I yelled for him. But he would lose his load and his team: I'd made him proud of them. Or maybe he didn't hear. But I yelled.

After the hay load turned over they galloped dragging the wagon tongue and the doubletrees over rocks all the way to the barn. When I got there the reins were still wrapped like black snakes around his arms. His team was panting and chewing leaves off a young elm tree.

That was summer.

But later I went ahead and signed the papers. The Batesons and

Turner Tedrick all saw the recorder's notice in the paper. I owned the old Leash place. But the older men—now they are all gone— knew about the wet forty acres, the piece of land that always kept me from making a real crop. The hog check just paid off the bank; after threshing I had to settle with all the grocery stores. That one year I didn't know whether to buy her a washing machine against the snowed-under wheat or to wait. That Christmas morning I got a box of Havana Prince cigars and the boy that could hardly remember his brother's funeral was sixteen and he could only have a lumber jacket. And she had bought herself a pair of three-buckle galoshes. The next morning I woke up and looked out the window. It seemed that all the snow was fresh, all the way to the woods. I hated to think of spring because there wasn't quite enough snow before our icy rain to save the wheat, after all. While I was lying there in bed I started wondering all over again, when I saw the fresh snow with perhaps the wheat, underneath. And I didn't blame the younger boy when he left (he never was as big or as clever as the oldest brother) and went over to Dayton to work at the National Cash.

And that was Christmas.

Even last Sunday, when I unlocked the door from the inside, I knew that it was too hot for services. Nearly everyone came last Sunday, but the maple trees in the churchyard and the hog weeds, rank and high as a man around the old schoolhouse (deserted now), and the grass, and the old leaves tumbling, were things in water, as though on the bottom of a creek that barely flows. Inside the church the fans the ladies moved were like the fins of minnows, all in a row, churning sluggish water.

"And great waters covered the earth . . ."
"And he saith unto Him, O Lord . . . O Lord . . ."

From the vestibule you know about the service: Old Man Culberson reading the wrong lesson, in response. Spinks, who had never learned to read, gums the words. The Baker Boys thinking of work: which one this next week will stay in the house like a woman and clean the parlor and wash and cook dinner. Brother, there, between his father and his mother . . . I wonder if my oldest boy would have been perhaps like Brother. Their words are bubbles rising in

119

a deep mud-bottom pool where the dozing carp drifts through the overhanging willow roots.

"And now," Harry Shurden said from the pulpit, "while we are delaying for our young man to arrive, let us sing Number Four Four Nine."

Mrs. Bateson hit one chord on the piano. The choir stood up from straight-backed chairs.

"Let the lower lights be burning, send a gleam across the waves."

Mrs. Tedrick looked over her book and followed the song she knew but could not recall in the heat. The congregation joined in. Old Man Culberson still did not have the place. He was searching through his songbook. Russy Lee was a monotone, singing every note and every word, as though he were a mechanical piano that never could run down but could only stop abruptly. But it was too hot: eyes wandered to the pattern in the aisle rug, to the stained-glass window and the motes floating through diagonals of colored light. The eyes strayed beyond the automobiles—aimed as though driving furiously through the church—beyond the encircling woods, with Brother and me in the middle of it all.

This was last Sunday when our young man came to the vestibule. He paused at the door. He opened his mouth to sing. I saw he still wanted to walk striding down the aisle, singing revival bass. And I wanted him to: I had to want him to and that is why I nailed down the brass carpet strip again each Monday.

He took one long step inside, singing. The toe plate on his shoe hung up on the carpet strip. He always managed to drag his toe at the door. Each Sunday I hoped it would be different. I wanted him to be like the bay race horse with four white feet at the fair. That one horse who pulls up from behind at the turn and runs blowing and lathered past the stands out front and pulling a yellow sulky. The one that wins because you had to bet on him, even when you thought from the go he was in a pocket. And he was, until the turn.

As he stumbled I watched the corners of our young man's mouth to see if he had it whipped: no. But he straightened. He took shorter steps, on his toes, as though the pulpit were at the far end of a long, silent hall with closed doors on either side, eight stories up in a government building where a farmer goes for a loan. He got to the pulpit finally.

"Ahaaa," our young man said.

Oh, he was no Jeremiah. He was from Cincinnati. He preached five churches each Sunday; from Cuba to the Macedonia Grace M.E. He drove furiously from one sermon to the next. He was young, so I nailed down the brass carpet strip each Monday for him. Even while I bet on him I knew he would be ordained someday and would leave Second Creek forever.

"This morning I want to talk to you folks about Sin. Sin should always be on your mind. At least I know it is on my mind. I'll talk of Samson and Delilah. And The Flesh. I'll tell you how it was in this last Great War, in the Navy."

Brother leaned forward in his sailor suit to hear how all San Francisco was Delilah: the white teeth of women smiling at you in the darkness. How they had rooms better than your own. The Flesh. Old Lampie Fisher nodded. He remembered the load of hogs he took to Cincinnati every spring. There were the rooms upstairs over the old stockyard saloon. They would cash a hog check if they knew you. And Grandma Saddler nodded: she used to call Ed from the back field in the middle of the afternoon . . .

Now, at our show of hands, only Old Mrs. Moss leaned forward in her pew.

"Oh yes, yes," she murmured, "I've been bad, bad. I've sinned."

But she was almost ninety, and everyone knew she held up her hand to any question. The young man had his hand up, too, but you couldn't tell if it were for example or for confession. He looked down from the pulpit to her. She stared up at him. In the front row the old ones nodded.

He gathered up his notes while he talked.

"Ah yes, and that just about winds up our sermon for this morning. And remember, friends, all this I told you this morning happened in the Navy. Before I heard the call of God. Ah, the things I've seen in San Francisco."

Outside the engine of our young man's car began to sputter. Already another crowd was waiting in Macedonia.

Inside, the church was quiet. One fly buzzed in the ceiling heat and bumped against the silent lamp globes suspended as dead planets from the ceiling. But that was last Sunday.

Now, this morning, in this vestibule one hand holding this door,

waiting for the older preacher, you can know this. As an old man
staring at the year you can know this: by March even Old Man
Culberson had his plowing done. There was the right kind of a dry
spell in April, and just after every dead furrow in all Second Creek
was run out, the rain came from the east. In late July, when you
threshed out a head of wheat in your palm (reaching through the
fence, Striders' fence), you saw the grains bulged and glowing.
Grandma Moss lived through the heat of August and was up and
around again. The co-op paid a dividend. Hogs were steady at
twenty-two dollars and wheat right at parity. This season every
crop and every radish seemed to explode from the ground. I had
seen this only once, and that was years ago when I was a boy, in
Clermont County. Now I looked out on the churchyard, as you
look out upon a garden that perhaps this evening may huddle and
bunch down for Indian summer. An old man, staring at this hour.

I saw the older preacher get out of his car. You could see how
long his legs were. He came out of his car head-first, as though
he had always ridden in a storm-front buggy and not in a black
sedan. He settled the white starched collar and his black tie and
smoothed the vestment. He paused and looked around the horizon
and then at our church. As they walked toward the front steps you
could see his face had been tan once. You knew he must carry a
watch that could be snapped open, if he had wanted to get at the
heavy gold chain and the agate watch fob beneath the robe. He
nodded to me, like you would nod to a janitor. Then his back was
toward me when he paused to look inside.

He saw us all: the Striders and Tedricks, and Russy Lee and
the Batesons and the Baker Boys, and Brother. In front he saw the
gray hair and the beards and the black puffed sleeves of the old
women, and the hard of hearing; he saw Brother hulking beside his
mother, the only one of us who wore infirmity as a brace. Behind
them the business suits, the pin stripe of part in black hair, and
behind them the half-stallion boys that teased Brother if they caught
him alone. In the back were the small boys who put chewing gum
under the pews for me to clean off.

When the time came our young man stood up.

"Ahaaa. As was announced last Sunday we have with us today
one of my teachers from the seminary. And I must tell you why:

122

I know I have not been doing such a good job here. That has been on my mind. Somehow when I come down the road and when I walk in that door I know what I *want* to say . . . Uh, well, when you are up here before a crowd it's different. Anyway, it's a real pleasure to introduce as this morning's speaker the Reverend Dr. Thomas Ransome."

Behind the pulpit I could see only the black robe and one shining leather shoe. He had kept his face covered with his hands, even after our young man turned to him. Then he stood up. But he kept his head down. His hair was white almost, and his collar was white, but his tie and his vestment were black. He did not open the Bible. He placed his two large palms on the leather covers. He leaned forward, as though he were talking directly to me. That was the way he had. I saw Brother lay down his fan.

"Oh, my Brothers. Oh, my Brothers in Christ, let us pray!"

And in those words was the beginning of the greatest sermon that Second Creek ever heard. It was in the voice of this man—a voice faint as shucks rustling in a winter mattress, then a voice rolling across the gray heads bent, then back beyond the pew of small boys, as picked corn down chutes. The lamp globes overhead swayed and the sound of that voice echoed even in the vestibule where I stood. Even to me in the vestibule, who could not go inside honestly, nor yet cared to walk in the churchyard during a preaching.

"I do not need to open this book on this Sunday, oh, my Brothers. Rather let me read the text from my own heart. Let me open wide this bosom where The Word shimmers beside The Word, wherein each of us can stare at the meaning, and see.

"Do not think *me* your preacher this morning of our Indian summer in this country. Think of Saint Paul who gives us our text as he gave his epistle to another parish another Sunday morning. Remember these words, remember this:

"For the good that I would I do not:
But the evil I would not, that I do."

He paused as though in meditation on his text. But you knew that he would speak when we were with him. You could see the face wrinkles; you could see the tremble of his fingers. The vibration of his sermon made me, *even me,* know that here was Faith. He had

123

what I could not have for long and yet he was speaking to me, speaking to me in our season of gold. I knew then that this was the sermon of his life, delivered just before the hour of his own Indian summer:

". . . Nor are we perfect. That is the evil, the madness, that we do. My old heart tells me and my old mind tells me and my old conscience tells me that I should every morning of this world preach! Yet should I desert the post of guide to younger men who as yet, by their own confessions, cannot speak what must be in their hearts?

"No, I am a strawberry preacher. I come out but once a year. And yet I know I am not an evil man. I know the pulpit is not for display of learning, but for preaching God's word. To the people. Yet is not this same compromise in the midst of every life, in the midst of our ruin?"

The ruin: strap the brace on leg, for ache comes now from elbows: up from the sawmills and the river bottom, up from my father's people in Clermont County, where only briars can grow. And yet I know this sermon comes from faith greater than an elm tree spread against the summer sky . . .

"But within the very Word of God, within the Bible beneath these hands there is the good that we would do, against that which we do. Did not Eve eat of the fruit and did not Adam eat because of *love* for her? And this in the center of their unmitigated paradise?"

In Paradise: I bought the colts at auction and paid more than any bidder but the lane was narrow. I'll fight awhile myself and see her apron on the front-room couch. And snow and woods and Christmas as spring wheat perhaps beneath the snow, Havana Prince. Brother was there in front with quiet fan and did not twist the nervous sailor hat.

". . . And further Cain slew Abel: one the farmer, one the man who lived by pastures. They could not live together. There was violence, and blood fell from wounds into that receiving earth, just as blood from soldiers, in our time, soaked the blanket-lined foxholes in that forest of Alsace called Haguenau, where my own son died.

"Cain and Abel, if you will, stand for different economies and they could not both survive. And, my Brothers, how differs that from our time? Are we not in the very midst of the midnight clash of economies, opposed?"

The hour passed. I did not move. I did not take my hand from the door. No pew creaked. I looked at the bell rope. Once. The voice rising and falling seemed to catch the swing and strength of the morning breeze. Then silence, like rabbit tracks in snow.

". . . But how, O Lord, how, you are saying, can we transcend this tyranny of Heaven in which we live? Oh, I know the disappointments of the farm myself. These hands I hold before you have held the reins of unbroken colts. How many days have these feet walked behind the creak of trace and chain making upheaval of broken sod in a March wind? And even there was contradiction, for things are not simple on our farms . . ."

The words, words sudden as quail against the sun:

". . . But in this change in our lives and in this violence and in this contradiction we must find our salvation. We must embrace the contradictions of this life, by Love and not by Madness. Let us think no longer in terms of Good or Evil, let us say only we must guide us through corridors of darkness by Love.

"Therefore, let our Faith be our altar, that we may be saved from the despair of disbelief. In your hearts, in this country and in your village, and in my city:

> "Until farmers hold the old egg is not new
> Until the cobbler sews his stitches true,
> Until at store no bacon suckles mold
> Until the butcher skewers his thumb of gold,
> *Let us pray.*

> "Until the baker sells no chaff for bread
> Until the sheriff takes no bribes to bed
> Until our doctor dreams of cures, not pay
> Until, O God, I preach for You, each day,
> *Let us pray.*

"And now, my Brothers in Christ, on this Sunday morning of our Lord, shall we pray together? And let him who will come forward and kneel beneath these hands upraised toward Heaven.

> "Our Father who art in Heaven,
> *Hallowed be thy name*
> Thy kingdom come, Thy will be done,

> *On earth as it is in Heaven.*
> Forgive us our trespasses
> *As we forgive . . ."*

From the front I heard the rustle: his classroom paper slid along the seat. The handle on the red fly swatter scraped the pew. The sailor hat dropped lightly. Across the lowered heads of hair that row by row frontward changed from black to gray to white, I saw him. He was standing in the diagonal of light from the upper window. Alone. He swayed forward. I thought he would walk alone. I thought it happened this Sunday. I saw it with my own eyes. I reached for the bell rope . . . *Ring out, ring out the joy bells* . . . But he sat down. He sat down. Heavily. He knocked the black cane with the white crook to the floor. He knocked the crutch over when he reached for the cane. Both the sticks rattled on the floor. His mother fanned him. Our church was over.

Oh, there were the hands to shake, a whole line of hands to shake. Then the two preachers were together in the black sedan. The older man slumped in his vestment and rested his head in his hands and did not look ahead through the windshield. Our young man drove the sedan out of the churchyard, slowly, toward Cincinnati.

The ladies clustered around the Striders' car, at the front steps. The ladies did not look at each other squarely. Grandma Shurden finally spoke. She is a cousin to Mrs. Strider by marriage.

"The boy seemed some better, Mary."

"Well yes, he does today. I'm real sorry he interrupted our services. I hope the visiting preacher wasn't offended, and my wasn't he good?"

Brother sat hulking in the back seat. Joe and his wife did not look at each other. They got in and stared ahead through their separate windshields.

"You keep him off those feet until he gets his strength," Grandma Shurden called at her. "Yes, good-by . . . good-by."

After they were gone I heard Grandma Shurden above the noise of the starting engines. "I don't care if he was born that way. I still say he's a spoiled brat. . . ."

Old Man Culberson looked at the sky. Grandma Shurden is a cousin of his on her father's side so he knew when to keep out of her

way; he just looked at the sky and said there would be a goslin'
drowner by night. Then all the cars were gone.

But I had to put the velvet runner back on the piano and sweep
and put away the collection plates. And I wondered this: if Brother's
own mother had not reached up one brown paw, a hand brown from
working in flower beds and radishes, and in panic grabbed the sailor
blouse (*you may rescue, you may save*), would this have been the
Sunday, after all? If Brother had walked, just one step without the
black cane with the white plastic crook, would anyone or would I
have believed? Even if his own mother, from panic, had not tipped
him back in the pew (maybe she wants to bring him each Sunday
down front), could you believe your own eyes?

And all of this seen because even in the vestibule, and with my
years and all, I do not bow my head . . . hadn't ever bowed and
meant it, I suppose.

I found the fly swatter with the red handle underneath Brother's
Sunday-school paper. The ladies can never know she pulled him
down because they all bowed their heads. They heard only his noise.
His mother will never know the ladies could not see, because from
the vestibule each Sunday I know that she watches only Brother.

I carried the fly swatter with the red handle downstairs. In the
middle of the first room is the church furnace: squat, sheathed in
tin, the fire out a long time now. I hung up the fly swatter in the next
room, the storage room, where I have to live.

In my room there is one cot and there is one orange crate. In the
bottom of this upended crate are the old newspapers and magazines,
and the mystery stories from the County Bookmobile, and my old
McGuffey readers. On the center shelf of the orange crate is my own
Bible. (Oh, I know that Book as old men do.) On top of the orange
crate is one water basin. Overhead above the basin is one light bulb
that burns all the time, perhaps forever. The room is too cold in
summer and too hot in winter, with the furnace on the other side of
the partition, but somehow I manage. When I came here six years
ago I pushed back all the things in storage to make myself a room.

On the floor in my basement room all the cardboard boxes are
stacked one on top of the other, bulged and cracking at the sides.
They are twisted and piled to the ceiling; some are overturned where
people were looking for something, or where I have chased the rat.

127

The curtains for the stage and the velvet drapes, and the old costumes and worn-out aisle rugs cascade down the pile of boxes like a dirty waterfall. In the corner are the rods and sticks: broken shepherds' crooks and stars on broomsticks and stuffed lambs and old cradles and arks and masks and flats of scenery, all broken and torn and sagging. Behind the loose paper are the songbooks, dry and brown. Some stacks of books are knocked over and the leaves scattered open, the pages fluttering. But in winter the place seems dry.

I sat down on my cot. I had until next Sunday to dust. Since I'm eighty-seven next week I know some things: I know a farm I finally bought and signed the papers on and then lost it all—land and improvements—during the depression. Then I lost my wife: I came home one day and saw her apron on the front-room couch. I heard later how the doctor took her right on to Cincinnati without stopping at his office in town. And I know this: they don't need me around. They let me be janitor because they are sorry. It would be a shame for such an old man to go on the county. But I can still dust.

So I sat on my couch with my back to the cool water pipes. I looked at all that junk. Then I heard my rat. He was somewhere back in the old papers rustling as shucks in cribbed corn or rustling like a rat does under old hay in a mow. He was stirring, perhaps along the wall, behind the songbooks. Yes: a rustle behind the songbooks in the basement of this church and in my room. I'd set poison. I'd tried a cat. I bought a new steel trap but I never caught him. Yet there he was in the midst of this Sunday morning that fizzled out, still rustling among loose papers; perhaps he would stare tonight with rat's eyes from the darkness.

I threw a shoe at the pile of junk and yelled, "Suieeee!" Even so, I heard him. Even then.

Finally I went on upstairs to finish. I walked twice around the inside of the whole church. The first time I locked each window. The second time around I checked each window. Now I would not wake up at night during storm and wonder if one window were open perhaps just a tiny crack, with the rain beating in on our rugs. Then I locked the front door. Noise from the night lock reechoed through and through the church.

Starting this week it is the Striders turn to feed me. I'll sit at the far end of their table so that I can get Brother to talking. I'll tell him

128

at first how it lets me sleep at night if I always check the windows twice; I'll tell him how I've tried to catch the half-grown rat; somehow it's there, and yet he always gets away. That will get him talking, just as my own boy would have talked to me. Then I'll inquire of Brother. I'll ask him, confidential, and he will say, perhaps later when we are alone, that he could or could not have walked this morning. Then I will know, for once and for all.

I started down the road to Strider's place. We still call it the Old Leash Farm. But I understand that Strider is renting. I understand he rents from a bank or some insurance company in Cincinnati.

from the Atlantic Monthly

PEGGETY'S PARCEL OF SHORTCOMINGS

JOHN HERSEY *was born in Tientsin, China, June 17, 1914, of missionary parents. He traveled around the world with them when he was four to five years old and settled permanently in the United States at the age of ten. He received his B.A. degree at Yale in 1936 and studied a year at Clare College, Cambridge. Mr. Hersey's first job was as private secretary to Sinclair Lewis, after which he spent seven years as a writer, editor, and war correspondent for* Time *and* Life *and* The New Yorker. *During World War II he published two books of reportage,* Men on Bataan *and* Into the Valley *and a novel,* A Bell for Adano, *which won the Pulitzer Prize for 1945. In 1946 he published* Hiroshima, *which appeared first in* The New Yorker *and later as a book, and in 1950, his most praised novel to date,* The Wall. *He worked as an editor on the writers' co-operative magazine '47 and has been vice-president of the Authors' League since 1948. Mr. Hersey lives in Connecticut with his wife and four children.*

"I well remember," said Miss Peg, the pastry cook, with a coffee éclair hovering in her fingers, "the night I fell into the embrace of the United States Merchant Marine. I weighed scant two hundred eight pounds at that time. I was, you might say, thin as a shelf."

Probably Miss Peg meant to say "sylph." In fairness, you had to grant to Miss Peg that she was always willing to risk elegance, if there was any of it handy. Only sometimes her tongue slipped—especially if it was all lubricated to receive an éclair or a napoleon.

They were gathered—Miss Peg, Mrs. Manterbaum, and Johnny, the second busboy—in the pantry locker down in the basement. As pastry chef, Miss Peg kept the key to the locker, and late each eve-

130

ning, about eleven o'clock, when the clubhouse was quite deserted and lay black and junky on the Florida beach, like a tremendous shipwreck, she would ghost in through the service entrance to the basement with one or two guests, unlock the wire mesh door to her locker, light up the single bare bulb that hung down from the ceiling, get out a few good things, seat the party on the wooden crates she kept her pans in, and then she would begin to talk. Mrs. Manterbaum, whose job was to keep the cabañas clean, was notorious among the help for her sweet tooth, a regular sugar-thief, and she had worked herself into the position of being invited by Miss Peg almost every night to taste a few "extra" pastries. Miss Peg used to ask Johnny, the second busboy, about once a week, because he was good-natured about pushing her pastry cart around to the Big People in the dining room for her. If there was one thing she hated in life, it was cart pushing. That, and bending down to slide her pans in and out of her ovens.

"I was twenty-three," Miss Peg said, "and I was then doing scullery for a certain Mrs. Charles Saunders in Old Bridge Harbor, on Long Island. Mr. Saunders was in asphalt and, as we used to say, he couldn't get out. Though in truth he was prosperous. Mrs. Saunders had fourteen in help. I remember one thing about Mr. Saunders, which was, he was very particular about the way his shoes were laid out in the mornings—the laces had to be real loose and the tongues lifted out and bent forward, so he could more or less walk right into his shoes. If Mr. Saunders had any difficulty about walking into his shoes any morning, he was liable to a very bad state of mind at breakfast, and goodness knew who would feel the shock of it. You understand, I only heard these things. Small Peggety, as they called me —the 'Small' was belittling, you might say, considering my heft— never advanced beyond the Near Pantry, and had no occasion to see Mr. Saunders standing in his own shoes, laced or unlaced. Fact is, the first time I ever laid eyes on him, close by, was the day the United States Merchant Marine and I had our little heave-to.

"It happened in the following particulars. My cousin Bob, who never came across with the rest of us, lives some short distance outside Greenock, by Glasgow, and he being a familiar of certain public houses on the waterfront, travels, you might say, victoriously—by talking with those who go to sea."

"Vicariously," Johnny said.

"I beg your pardon?" Miss Peg said, very grand.

Johnny realized one of the reasons Miss Peg liked him was that he had gone through third-year high school and was, in her words, "a bookish lad"; he did read a good bit. Miss Peg had never had any schooling, and her elegance had been picked up over the years of service while she was passing the peas, so to speak. Johnny dared now and then, to catch her up on some of her errors of overreaching.

"Your cousin Bob," Johnny said, "travels vicariously."

"*Well?*" said Miss Peg, with rising tone, as if to ask why the young scoundrel felt it necessary to repeat something that had already been said. "So one evening," she went on, "Bob met this tidy, small-boned Yank, a boatswain's mate, third class, in the United States Merchant Marine, named Bufano. A swarthy sort. Talking of one big thing and another, they landed at last upon me, so it was necessary—Bob thought—to tell the fellow all about me. I will say, Bob has a straight tongue, he did not dangle any pretty marionette before this Bufano's eyes. To be blunt about it, he said his cousin Peggety was *fat*. 'So much the better,' says this Bufano. 'I always was squeamish about getting myself bruised against sharp and knobby things. I am glad to hear that you have a nice soft cousin.'

"The first thing *I* knew," said Peg, "I received a postcard written in a fine Eyetalian hand, all curlicues and scrolls on the capital letters, like a birthday cake, saying, *Meet me outside Ritz corner 46 and Mad six pm Thursday evening. Assume this is helps night out. I have grand news of your cousin Bob from other side. Bufano, Bsns Mate 3/c, S.S. Fanter.* This 'grand news'"—Miss Peg said, leaping ahead in her narrative, as she sometimes did—"was that our Bob was spending much time in the public houses and was a two-hump camel when it came to the ale: he could drink twice as much and hold it twice as long as anyone else. 'Grand news'!

"The next Thursday," Miss Peg resumed, "I got myself all frilled up, smelling like a church on Easter morning, and Mason, the chauffeur, was just about to drive the help to the station, and me, sitting there, taking up half the back seat of the car, happy as a lintie thinking about my unknown sailor boy, when out from the quarters comes a message: "Tell Small Peggety to stop by at Mr. Saunders' office, 30 Rockefeller Plaza. He has a wee errand for her.'

"Our Maggie, the cook, who if I was overweight she was a dried-up apricot of the fuzzy variety, said sarcastic, 'Write down the address. Our Peggety is in love, she's a bag of daydreams, she'll never remember.'

"Between the message and Maggie, it took quite some time for the others to dill me down to where I was calm again. Wasn't it just like Mr. Saunders to save his 'wee errands' for *that* day? Any other time, this command would have made me tingle with the fun of doing it— 'thistles in me thumbs,' as our Mum used to say when she had a thrill. But that day, it was all I could do to think of my seafaring man with the handwriting like Queen Victoria's Golden Jubilee fireworks.

"Nevertheless, when we reached the city, I went of course as directed to 30 Rockefeller Plaza and I shot up into the sky where Mr. Saunders did his work and up I went to the lady at the desk and I said, trying to be sort of saucy and mature, 'I am the Peggety. Mr. Saunders has a wee errand for me.'

"The lady looked at me and said, 'Sister, aren't you kind of dressed up for *this* errand?'

"So I replied, 'The nature of the work was not divulged, you might say.'

"The lady flicked a switch on a box, and I heard Mr Saunders' voice come out of the box, only his voice sounded like his nose had been snipped off by a crow or was pinched with a clothespin; he said, 'What is it?'

" 'Your maid,' the lady said into the box, 'has come for the carcass.'

"This gave me the goose pimples all over, and since I was a thimber sort of girl, a large skin area, you might say, there was a considerable amount of puckering up to be got done with.

"Mr. Saunders kind of laughed a noseless laugh from the box and said, 'Send her in.'

"I walked into the office whither the lady nodded, and there he was, the master, looking very wild, but with his nose, thank the Lord, quite unharmed. It must have been merely the mechanics of the box that had taken away his nose from his voice. In general the master was very wild, however. He was in his shirt sleeves and he was dressed in a big white apron and he had in his hand a butcher's knife of the largest sort, and I thought: Oh me, I thought asphalt was used to pave the roads, what *can* it be that the master does for a living?

"He said to me, 'Sit down, girl, I'll be ready in a few minutes.'

"It was then," Miss Peg said, "that I noticed another gentleman in the room, he was dressed in ordinary business clothes, though his look was rather ferocious, too, it seemed to me, but at the time, you must remember, I was only Small Peggety, twenty-three winters along, tipping the scales approximately two-o-eight, with no experience of the world beyond the Near Pantry, consequently this fierceness may have been imaginary on my part.

"I also noticed—and this hit me all of a sudden, like the sun coming out from under a cloud—a smell in the place like Fulton Street at the East River, in other words, fish in all its glory. And by following my senses, I tracked this scent to Mr. Saunders' desk, where lay, about as big as my upper arm, no, bigger yet, a whole salmon. A very substantial fish, I can assure you, Mrs. Manterbaum.

"Mr. Saunders grasped the butcher knife in both hands, and he began to stagger and struggle around the room, talking the while like that raddio fellow, Mr. Clem McCarthy, dealing with the Derby, in case you are interested in the horses, Mrs. Manterbaum—breathless he was and yet in command of the telling. I soon puzzled it out that Mr. Saunders was describing to his friend the capture of this particular salmon of his. He was using the butcher knife for his rod and reel, and I was fearful lest he would fish himself into total blindness with that sharp thing. And so we had game-fishing all up and down the office for the next half hour. They say that salmon do go upriver in order to make love, and to hear Mr. Saunders speak of the reluctance of this whopper to leave the headwaters of the Skampawam, or whatever the river would be named, in Nova Scotia, it was—to hear *him*, I believe this fish must have been engaged in the romance of the century in the salmon world. Really, the aquarium should be told about it. Well! I tell you! We *finally* landed the thing, but we were panting and giving off a deal of perspiration over it—and there the lecherous rascal was, big as life and ten times smellier, right on Mr. Saunders' desk, asphalt be damned.

" 'He's been thawing out all day,' Mr. Saunders said. 'We shipped him down in dry ice. His guts were cleaned up there, and now'—advancing on the salmon with the dreadful knife, he said this—'now I'm going to lop off his head and tail so the girl here can manage him by hand and take him out home for us, and tomorrow night, Spencer, tomorrow *night!* Well, you'll just have to wait and taste him.'

"Our creature was thawed out all right, and he gave up his head till there was salmon blood all over the newspapers on Mr. Saunders' desk. Likewise the tail, a smaller operation but also not without splashes and clots of red. By this time the odor of fish was almost a fog around us that you could see. Whew!

"More newspapers, a bundle, string; there we were. 'Now, girl,' said Mr. Saunders, who, never having been on *my* side of the Near Pantry, of course did not know me by name, 'now, girl, you may take it home. And have a care!'

"What a care I had, all that suffering night! And yet . . .

"It was now, you see, pushing six o'clock, because of the length of Mr. Saunders' description of his triumph over the poor hooked thing. Thus, if I was to meet my friend with the birthday-cake handwriting, I would have to rush right over there, with no time to park my bundle meanwhile. Right through the newspaper, through goodness knows how many layers of current events, you could not fail to smell my pink beheaded treat. Trembling I dashed to the Ritz, corner of Madison and Forty-sixth.

"I was on time but early. The Merchant Marine, being a man of the world, had decided to have a wee tease of Small Peggety, who knew nothing. So there I stood, before the most swoshy hotel in the land, waiting, with ladies going by in ermine and sapphires and curls right out of the permanent-wave machine, and me, under the marquee with all its sweet little light bulbs, me, embracing a two-and-a-half-foot stink. I was mortified to death, Mrs. Manterbaum.

"At last he came and worth waiting for. Short, stocky, and sort of pale Moorish-complected. His pants as tight as wedding gloves. He was a lovely, tiny creature. He strolled right up to me, with all the swagger of his cute bowlegs, and he said, raising his white cap, 'Miss Peggety, if I am not mistaken. I could have spotted you, my dear, from a mile away.'

"Well, he had my heart right then and there, though now in my calmer years I can see that his first remark—about kenning me from such a very impressive distance—left something to be desired as a compliment.

"Right there on the street corner, as he gazed up into my eyes, looking for my soul, you might say, and my heart like a moth by a sixty-watt lamp, I saw that the flanges of his nostrils were working away quite passionate, exactly like Mr. Rudolph Valentino's, but then I realized that it wasn't so much love at first sight as it was he had caught a whiff of something about my person. What he smelt, you already know, Mrs. Manterbaum.

"I had no doubt, in the next moments, that my Bufano was as packed full of gentility as his bell bottoms were packed full of Bufano. Because without so much as muttering, 'Hm, fishy out tonight, ain't it, Miss Peggety?'—with no such remarks, without a flicker of his lovely waxen eyelids, without even moving to windward of me, he said, 'Well, my dear, what'll it be? Shall we dance? Or is food your pleasure? A steak, Miss Peggety?' You see how well bred he was? Steak! Any lesser man would have asked me if I was in the mood for a bite of sea food.

"Timid, I said, 'First off, Mr. Bufano, I'd like to run down to Grand Central and check this parcel for the evening.'

"I could see from the way my Bufano looked at the package in my arms that he knew what I was carrying. Jaunty as you please he swung around and offered me the crook of his arm.

"At the checking place in Grand Central I just pushed the package across the brass-plated counter. The man there pulled it toward him and actually snapped the checking tag onto the string. Then (I guess his nose was tuned in by this time) he looked up and said, 'What's in here?'

" 'Just some laundry,' I said. My Bufano stiffened a little at that. The counterman thumped at the package with his fists, shook his head, unsnapped the tag, and shoved the thing back to me.

" 'Sorry, lady,' the counterman said, 'we ain't allowed to accept no carrion here.'

"I guess my feelings took a tumble that you could see and hear, because Bufano said, 'Cheer up, my dear, we'll just hurry over to Pennsylvania Station. We should have done that in the first place. You'll have to leave from there when our spree is over.'

"But the man in the parcel room at Penn Station was even quicker than our Grand Central fellow. Indeed, he looked at us at first with a dread look of suspicion, as if we were trying to dispose of the parts of a human body, one by one. I must confess, with the moisture and even some of the tint of corpuscles beginning to show through at the ends, my package might have been a man's thigh piece, from groin to kneecap. Except for the odor, which gave us an unmistakable alibi. All the man at the Penn Station counter said was, 'Uhn-uhn,' negative.

"My Bufano was a cheerful little rooster, he said we should try the Hotel Wentman, just a couple blocks over; they had a big checkroom, he said. No luck, they wouldn't take fish. We tried the Hotel Regina. No luck. We tried the Hampdon and the Marjoran. No and no. They wouldn't even let us all the way across the lobby at the St. Anselm. Mr. Bufano tried to rent a room at a little no-good place away over west, thinking we would put our salmon to bed in it, but they stopped us in the elevator.

"And so it was that at a few minutes before eight o'clock in the evening we stood on a windswept corner in western Manhattan, and the tears welled up in my eyes, and not even my pigeon, my Bufano, could comfort me. For suddenly I realized that this parcel was more than a cut-off salmon. This was all my troubles, wrapped up in shabby newsprint. This was all the things that kept me from all my desires. That package—I suddenly realized it, Mrs. Manterbaum—that package was all the unhappiness I couldn't get rid of in this life: it was my fleshiness, my unbeatable appetite for chocolate things, and my being without any learning, and no friends to speak of, and teased by such spiteful old maids as our Maggie, and couldn't even be promoted past the Near Pantry, and what good was I anyhow? And I was embracing all these things in my arms like a dear beloved friend, and smelling to high heaven of the burden.

"Then it was that my Bufano said, 'Well, Miss Peggety, three's a crowd, but let's face facts, he goes where we go.'

"And I suddenly realized, you have to live with whatever it is you have to live with, so I dried up my eyes and said, 'Suits me, Mr. Bufano.'

"'Well!' he beamed, and a gold tooth he had glistened like the planet Venus at the edge of night. 'What was it to be, steak or a little twinkletoes?'

"Now that I knew where I was, with my shortcomings folded up in a wee bundle of old papers, you might say, and my Bufano willing to accept them if I would, I grew bold suddenly and said, 'Couldn't we do both, Mr. Bufano? Eat and dance too?'

" 'Miss Peggety, you're a dear,' he said, and if I had cried this time, it would have been for other reasons than mere fishiness. My Bufano was so delicate!

"We had a grand time, I can tell you. My Bufano took me here and there, now dancing, now eating, now tippling a wee beer, now riding a Fifth Avenue bus just for the ride, as idle as you please. Soon we were used to our scaly friend and his consequences. What if everybody *did* turn and give us a stare, with tiny wrinkles at the bridge of the nose? In a way, it was gaudy, you might say. Surely Small Peggety had never in her life attracted so much attention, either from eye or nostril. I will go further. Our salmon became more than a novelty: he was, at last, a handy thing to have about the person. In a crowded situation, we could always get passageway—the mob just opened up for us, real respectful. In the eating places (my Bufano took me to some of the basement ones, away to the fringes of the great city, where, either through kinship with the proprietor or a grand little tip, there was never a question of accepting us with our third party), we used it for a little extra table, beside us, to hold an ash tray or perhaps a wee pony of spirits. There it was, squared off at both ends, like a piece of log, and it stood up steady and true, very convenient by the knee for a reach. And there our hands did brush against one another: that was when I knew that my Bufano was the nicest one of all.

"Indeed, what except my parcel of shortcomings led to the bliss of the evening? I had to be back to the Ncar Pantry by seven in the morning, which meant, at the latest, the five-thirteen from Penn Station. It was still only about three in the morning when my Bufano, with the gentlest way in the world, said, 'My dear, don't you think that your salmon needs a little ventilation? I should hate, for your Mr. Saunders' sake, to have it fester and decay. It wants aeration. I propose that we go up to Central Park, and fold back the newspapers, and give it the night air to keep it tasty.'

"That we did. We found a wee hillock, away from the paved walks

138

—'Asphalt!' my Bufano had remarked as we had gone along the walks. 'Your Mr. Saunders is everywhere'—and we set up our fish on the hill and peeled away the newsprint and let the sweet, damp night get at it. We moved away a little, to wait for the salmon to grow mellow, when, next thing I knew, as natural as the dew all around and the constellations winking up there, Bufano got his arms about me. He could just barely make it with his short little arms and my girth, which he praised. And he stood on tiptoe and kissed me."

Miss Peg's voice had fallen low; her eyelids shaded her jovial eyes in a modest downward look. Mrs. Manterbaum sighed.

"Did you catch your train?" Johnny, the busboy, asked.

"I caught my train, Johnny," Miss Peg said. "Yes, I caught my train." She paused. "I never saw my Bufano again, either. He was the hit-and-run sort, you might say. But I don't know, Johnny, it didn't matter. That night did something for me. You know, Mrs. Manterbaum, I have never been able to give sufficient worry to my faults since that night. Some would call me slack. . . . I don't know. . . . Yes, I caught the five-thirteen, Johnny."

"How was the fish next night?" Mrs. Manterbaum of the sugar tooth wanted to know.

"When they brought it out to the Near Pantry, after the second serving," Miss Peg replied, "I dared to cut away a wee snippet. I put it in my mouth. Oh, heavens, Mrs. Manterbaum! It faded on the tongue. It put this angel cake of mine to shame. And as I rested the morsel against my palate and let it warm my throat, the way the men do with their brandy, I squeezed out a sob, Mrs. Manterbaum, I'm not ashamed to tell you that, and I said to myself, 'I'm not so bad as I thought, not half so bad.' . . . *Well!*" Miss Peg said abruptly and more briskly. "Time to lock up."

Miss Peg lifted the pan of delicacies and slid it onto the shelf where it belonged. She stood up and dusted the crumbs from the front of her dress, seeming to be rather pleased with herself.

from Epoch

A SENSE OF DESTINATION

FAYE RITER KENSINGER *was born in Carroll, Iowa, in 1910 and grew up in Iowa and South Dakota. Her initial ambition was to become matron of an orphans' home, which gave way to her desire to be a newspaperwoman in New York City. She took her bachelor's degree in journalism at the University of Missouri, and became, she writes, "a Missourian by marriage." She lived in Missouri and Arkansas until 1940, whence began a trek from one air base to another, the most remote situated in the Philippine Islands. An Air Force R.O.T.C. assignment at Cornell is now providing the opportunity to work for a Master's degree in creative writing, and there is a novel almost finished. Mrs. Kensinger's stories have been published for the past ten years in* The University of Kansas City Review, *where she made her debut, in* Prairie Schooner, Decade, *the now defunct* Southern Literary Messenger, Matrix, Mademoiselle, *and* Epoch, *most of them under the name of Faye Riter.*

Grandma Westerman surrendered to circumstances after she broke her leg in a fall on the short flight of steps leading down to the kitchen. She began the descent with the righteous irritation of one prepared to reprimand the housekeeper for filching secretly from pantry stores. And, one foot catching in the hem of her long black skirt, she had fallen with all the gracelessness of her age. A leg had twisted beneath her so that brittle bones cracked and splintered.

And she lay there almost the whole morning, for the housekeeper, having heard her approach, had snatched bonnet and shawl and hurried out of the basement door to do the morning marketing. Then she had met an intimate friend, quite by chance, of course, in the fresh, meaty atmosphere of the butcher shop and had been invited to step over to the coffeeshop, where the remainder of the morning had vanished.

The housekeeper had screamed at finding her mistress lying as in death upon the floor. "Lord help me," she babbled, trying to decide whether it was best to inform first the doctor so that he could attend the old lady, or to call the eldest son, who could at once take over the responsibility of the injured woman.

"There," she soothed distractedly, standing over the quiet figure.

At that moment Grandma Westerman opened accusing eyes. "Robber," she pronounced with finality, and closed them again.

"It is good, maybe, that you fell," the doctor told her later, scratching his neck reflectively. "For once you are pinned down, and one can look at you and see that you need attention for other things."

She snorted indignantly at that.

"You were dizzy, perhaps, when you fell?" he suggested.

"What an idea! I was in absolute health."

"Just like my mother," he commented, writing out prescriptions, "never ready to admit an ailment. Why do you have such pride?"

It was at this period, more shamed by the disease of her body than by the breaking of bones, that Grandma Westerman announced to her son Albert, the eldest although the last of them to marry, that he might now move into the family home.

"It will come to you, anyhow," she said heavily from the brass bed. "I will not be in your way."

"We shall come to look after it," he agreed at once, stiffening his shoulders, "and you too," he added in haste. "It will not do for you to be here alone now."

Afterward she declared that if nothing else good came from the disaster, at least she had got rid of a corrupt housekeeper and gained the devoted Clara.

Meanwhile Albert and Leonie and the three children moved in, and Clara, whose duties were restricted to the dim bedroom and pocket handkerchief of a sitting room and to the care of the grandmother, faithfully reported the changes that the household was seeing. Since she herself was elderly, and at once in sympathy with Grandma Westerman, Clara regarded the alterations with certain suspicions and even with jealousy.

"You will not know the ground floor when next you see it. They are throwing paint upon the walls with abandon—unpractical, foolish colors that will show every touch. And the fine, heavy draperies have been taken down and packed away. There will be only glass curtains of silk, and the sun will shine in to fade the flowers on the carpet. It is too much to expect that they will close the shutters on the sunny side."

In the beginning Grandma Westerman did not feel much interest in the mysterious proceedings below. The shock of exchanging a vigorous life for a bedridden one was all she could handle for a time.

"The young do not have the solid, conservative ideas that I was brought up on," she told Clara gloomily. "Let them do what they will."

After a time, when she had reconciled herself to pain and to lying abed, she hunted ponderously in her mind for means of passing the hours when her hands were tired with the weight of the lace she was knitting, or her fingers stiffened after working with an embroidery needle and thimble on the cutwork of a bureau scarf. She would sigh and call out to Clara, "Did they leave the painting of fruit over the sideboard?"

"That was carried off long ago," Clara would respond with relish. "And in the bay that looks out on the garden She has green things growing. Likely they will die soon."

"I suppose my good tablecloths are used for everyday," the old lady would go on. "Finally they will fall to pieces in the wash water."

"No-o-o-o." Clara would shake her head. "Mats She uses for everyday. With children too. They are more practical, She says. But it keeps her girl polishing."

"I came here the same way," Grandma Westerman said abruptly one day. "I made my changes, too, though not with such speed. It is not easy to go into the household of another without seeing what might be done."

"You have good understanding," Clara approved. "They have taken out the hall trees, and your heavy carved table. They had things of their own, too, She said."

By the time they were finished with the renovation, Grandma Westerman thought, by the time the painters and carpenters were gone and every pin was in place, then they would come to sit with her longer. As it was, Leonie must answer every summons of the workmen and of Christine, the hired girl, to whom the big house was confusing. The children were at school, and Albert was gone all day. Save for the clumsy movements of the workmen, the house was quiet; it was not quite as she had visualized, living with three careless children.

Leonie, thin, sallow, sharp-eyed, her face softened only by abundant wavy hair, came in every day, naturally. She would sit down a moment, but her eyes would wander restlessly away from the bed as though contemplating brisk activity. "Do you not want these blinds opened? I myself would become spiritless in so dark a room." She might arise to straighten the bureau top that was disorderly with medicine bottles, fancywork, and newspapers. "At the pharmicist's I saw Belle Speas; she asked for you and sent word her mother would come soon. She is suffering from kidney stones—old Mrs. Bartel." And then, with a sigh, "I must hurry down and make the noodle; that Christine cannot make one fit for a pig, and Albert insists on the kind you taught me when first we were married."

In the evening Albert would come in for a short while, expansive after a heavy supper despite his thin, slightly stooped figure, smelling of cigar smoke and faintly of the cologne applied that morning after shaving.

"Well, Mama," he would say without expecting an answer, "have you had a good day? Business is something to make your eyes pop, believe me. It was not like this in Papa's day. All the forms and permits to be got!" He would shake his head and cluck his tongue, sitting down then to talk about the business for a time. "You will fall asleep if I speak longer of business, eh, Mama?" He would chuckle paternally at his own jokes.

Once she heard him reminding the children that they were to stop in every day to speak to their grandmother. "Every day, mind you," he repeated.

"I do, Papa!" Elizabeth, the eldest, cried indignantly, so that her father hushed her. "I do nearly every day, anyhow. Maria is the one who sneaks out of it, and I am quite sure Theodore doesn't go in more than once a week."

Curiously the old lady listened to the objecting young voices, and that of her son, leading them, then, like the concertmaster setting the pace and the tone, so that the three fell into the murmur habitual upon this floor of the house when one of the parents was near.

When spring bloomed into summer and she found herself promoted to a yellow wheel chair shiny with varnish, she asked Clara to push her into the carpeted hall, and it seemed that she entered another house upon leaving her own room. It was not merely the new brightness of the walls, nor the glimpse of the lower hall with its table and heavy mirror in place of the hall trees; it was that she had been gone from the most of the house so long that it was unfamiliar and no longer hers. She was a stranger, looking at the home of another.

Surprisingly it was less painful than Grandma Westerman had anticipated; she was ready to admit that the house belonged now to Leonie, whom she did not know intimately and never would, and to Albert, who lacked the vigor of his parents. And it belonged, too, to the children. A tennis racket rested carelessly in a corner, and in the upper hall a doll carriage, its hood primly up to shield the occupant, stood against the wall as though possessing perfect right to its position.

With Clara she schemed clumsily to get the children, one at a time, into her room. It was like snaring animals that were neither timid nor sly; they were all absorbed in inconsequential activities more important to them than the turning of the earth.

Elizabeth, the eldest, was first. Fidgeting in the small rocker, she frowned at fleeting thoughts as though at ease and yet forgetful of her surroundings.

"You are old enough to begin a marriage chest," Grandma Westerman suggested. "Do you embroider well? Can you knit lace?"

"That's old-fashioned, Grandma," Elizabeth explained, rocking lightly and playing with the gold locket she wore. "I can hemstitch very well; Mama says I take smaller stitches than she can."

"Maybe you would like to learn to knit fine lace yokes for your nightgowns," the old lady ventured.

"That is no longer the fashion," the girl said with pity, and smiled as though her grandparent were a child still learning the ways of the world.

Grandma Westerman would not stoop to luring any of them with gifts or promises. No bribes, no candy bowl, no coins. Gifts

144

were strictly associated with occasions—birthdays and Christmas, Confirmation, graduation.

Theodore did not know what to do with himself when he was in her room. He studied the floor, described circles on the carpet with his shoes, played tricks with one hand upon the other, and labored with a frown to think of subjects for dutiful conversation.

"I know a boy that collects birds' eggs," he said with sudden inspiration. "He let me blow one out. A swallow's egg with speckles. First you punch a needle in each end, and then you blow. You barely blow at all, or the egg breaks."

"Your grandfather collected stamps," Grandma Westerman told him. "Do you like stamps? Someday they may come to you."

"I might collect wild animals," he confided, "someday." Then the look of far-away dreaming left his eyes, and he hurried away with complicated but vague explanation regarding a ball game.

Of a cool summer morning Maria could be heard lurking in the upper hallway, passing her grandmother's door without apparent reason other than curiosity or perhaps some half-murmured and mysterious game she played with invisible companions.

If Grandma Westerman called out to her, the little girl appeared shyly in wordless question, cradling a doll with battered face or carrying scraps of paper, bits of cotton material, a fancy box, or some other subject worthless in the eyes of an adult.

"Will you let me see your leg?" Maria asked hopefully in an undertone at one of the first intimate encounters.

Grandma Westerman lifted the light cover, revealing the plump cast upon her old leg. And when Maria reached out exploring fingers to tap the cast, Grandma Westerman chuckled aloud.

"You find that interesting," she stated, watching the child's soft face, feeling a faint flush of pleasure as Maria stared long with respect and admiration.

"What do you do, now that there is no school?" the grandmother asked when the leg was modestly covered again.

"Oh—things," Maria answered vaguely, her eyes turning away and dreaming momentarily upon unseen vacancies. "Lots of things." A secret look of pleasure entered her eyes.

"All day you play," Grandma Westerman said wonderingly. "From morning till nighttime."

Maria nodded slowly in pleased agreement. "Sometimes I work, though," she spoke virtuously in afterthought.

"What work do you do?" the old woman asked indulgently.

Maria frowned in recollection. "One day I made a penwiper for Papa's desk."

"Very good," Grandma Westerman praised.

Maria shook her head in distaste. "It was ugly. Ugly, ugly, ugly. Mama would let me use only old dark cloth—so the ink would not show."

"That was sensible."

"I don't like to be sensible," Maria demurred. She rocked so hard that the chair moved over the faded carpet.

"Everyone must learn to be sensible. The earlier, the better." Grandma Westerman fell into an unexpected doze, and by the time she opened her eyes again Maria had slipped away.

It was the elusiveness of the household that caused Grandma Westerman to brood for slow stuffy hours. She was outside the magic circle they occupied, and there was no way to step over the boundary. She was outside in time and in space, in person, even. There was no way to enter but with the assistance of a spiritual hand from one within, and that hand was not offered. They saw her, but they looked with shallow, absent eyes—those people within this one small magic circle. They saw the plump, old-fashioned little woman, lips disciplined, standing soberly outside, watching, ready to speak phrases of another world, another time, phrases that were dull and stiff and hopelessly outmoded. They felt sorry for her, sorry for the detached position of her years and her physical being, but they did not feel compassion; their mental eyes could not penetrate that far.

They did not know, she would tell herself mournfully, that they were all moving with unsuspected speed toward the very position she held. The parents surmised it, perhaps, at shadowy moments in the night's midst when they lay in uneasy wakefulness, but they would never speak aloud of it. As for the children, they had not one idea in the world that they would ever proceed past a wonderful age of fresh adulthood where the universe would open like a sorcerer's ball to offer dazzling beauties.

"If they could but know," she would speak to herself in alarm. "If they could but know." And she might utter a faint sound of consternation that would rouse Clara if she were in the room, and then Grandma Westerman would have to mumble that she had merely cleared her throat.

When Albert's birthday arrived, a celebration was planned; it was as though, in taking over the family house, he had come of age or attained a position of increased prestige, at least. Grandma Westerman's other sons and their families came from their homes in nearby towns to celebrate the occasion. When the gala day arrived, two of them carried her from her room, down the steep flight of carpeted steps, through the rear hall and the tiny conservatory, where a long table was set under the chestnut trees. Her wheel chair was there, awaiting her, and Clara fussed over her, shaking out a light shawl to cover her legs, rearranging the lace collar on her black silk dress.

It was a drowsy summer afternoon; the languid wind played with the corners of the white tablecloth without intent, and the bees droned monotonously in the arbor. The families made a fine showing, ten children and the half-dozen adults, the sister of one of the daughters-in-law, and then herself, apart from the others, eating from a tray upon which Clara highhandedly placed some of the choicest morsels—the livers of chicken, the most perfectly shaped little dumplings, the tiniest of the new potatoes dripping with black butter.

Grandma Westerman's mind journeyed back to the times that she herself had been the one to plan such occasions. She it was who arose early to cook and bake, to turn out the richly seasoned dishes, to give orders to the housekeeper, choose the cloth to be used, cut the garden flowers, and lay the silver on the table. Now it was another; now it was Leonie. She had arisen when the dew still drenched the grass. The precisely decorated cake that stood before Albert now, bearing his name and birth date, was of her baking.

Albert cut it with a long silver knife, lightheartedly pretending for the children's sake to make a wish as the blade disappeared beneath the snowy icing.

"The first piece is yours," the smaller children repeated solemnly. "The first piece is yours, because this is your birthday."

He set to one side the plate holding the first slice, and when he cut a second, Clara, hovering over him, whispered in his ear. As he was about to hand her the second plate he put it aside and impulsively reached for the first. With a courtly bow in his mother's direction he announced, "To Grandma I present the first slice with the birthday wish."

As Clara with a proud smile bore the plate to her, the children all clapped loudly in approval, and the women joined in for an indulgent moment. Their clapping was flat and hollow in the sleepy summer air. It was as though for a moment they were expressing all the half-spoken excitement of the day in the wild movements of their palms meeting, parting, meeting vigorously again. It was not Albert's act or the honor accorded the grandmother they were applauding; it was the summer day, the good heavy dinner, and the expectations and secret dreams of their age.

They toasted the day with sweet, pale wine. The old woman became drowsy for a time; Albert's voice, as he arose to make a solemn speech, drew farther and farther away from her, and she awoke only when the air was quiet again.

With lazy whoops, then, the boys arose and went to assemble at the far side of the garden, and the girls followed them hopefully. Christine and Clara had cleared the table of all but the coffee cups and the wineglasses and the remains of the cake, and the parents reviewed news of the past months, relating what mutual acquaintances had died, what families had been blessed with births, describing illnesses and other misfortunes that had overtaken some. They spoke of old Mrs. Bartel dying suddenly, of the division of property, the quarrel between two of the children over certain land.

"She had nothing left," Grandma Westerman said unexpectedly.

From their positions at the table they all turned to stare at her, sitting aside in the varnished wheel chair.

"I myself am ready to go," Grandma Westerman continued calmly. "I am ready to die."

In abrupt shame and alarm the faces turned away from her again, all but those of the two older granddaughters, who, lips parted, watched her frightenedly.

"No, Mama," one of the sons murmured uncomfortably.

"It is not right to talk so," another reprimanded gently.

All were silent for moments. Then one of the women spoke hurriedly, asking Leonie about the burnt-sugar birthday cake, of which now only a thin wedge remained.

148

After a while Grandma Westerman fell into a light, restful doze. And she dreamed that the sons and sons' wives had drawn into a clandestine group at the end of the table to speak of her in deep whispers.

"Grandma is failing so fast; I could not believe it when I came yesterday. . . . She is becoming a different woman—fleshy still, but quiet and watchful, with little to say. . . . She is slipping—slipping slowly away. Leonie says she sleeps more and more—little naps here and there. . . . And what she said a while ago. 'I am ready to die,' she said; I thought my heart would turn over. . . ."

Afterward she did not know if they had really spoken such words or not. Perhaps she had not even slept, but had withdrawn into a cocoon apart from consciousness but not remote enough for unconsciousness.

The thought fretted at her brain. If she were going to die, she wanted the quitting to be abrupt, not lingering. She wanted to move rapidly from one world to another without having time to think about it, to be fearful of the moment and to conjecture as to what internal strength she might have.

Above all, she desired to be heard before departing. How could she tell them what occupied her thoughts? They did not have time to listen. They were, in addition, deaf and blind to what was to be heard and seen.

Her own mother had died without speaking of what lay within her heart, but she had been unwarned of death. One hour she had gone about household duties; the next hour she had been carried to her bed to draw final breath. Yet there had been her paternal grandmother, who lived with them for the long years of her widowhood. She had calmly bade them draw about her bedside. Grandma Westerman had huddled there with her brothers and sisters, terrified into wordlessness, yet bound by a terrible curiosity for the labored breathing, the ashen face, and the determined voice speaking solemnly, almost wistfully, but still commanding them so that the hour remained in her mind all this time.

"Honor thy father and mother," the old woman had said hoarsely to the frightened children. And to the parents, "Above all, live prudently . . ."

But it was not enough, Grandma Westerman told herself. It was

149

as though her grandparent were bidding a stern farewell before making a visit elsewhere, or merely giving reprimand for some misdeed. The young should learn what lay before them; knowledge of that kind would give purpose to their lives, contemplative wisdom to their youthfulness. How could they live prudently when the reason for prudent living was unknown to them?

And how could she tell them except at such a moment as death, when they would gather round with respect upon their faces and respect within their beings, respect for death first, and then for the one about to close her eyes forever to the world? It was too plain that she could not command from the weak position she held now. To them all she was but an ailing old woman with a crippled leg upon which she would never walk again, a sick old grandmother who was classified nearer the children than the adults.

She had lost the independent vigor of being that had been a foremost quality. It had begun slipping unnoticed from her long before she fell upon the stairs. And now she had ceased expecting its return, ceased caring even. Yet it was better that way; if she had known it was dwindling into nothing, she would have been angry and frightened. Now it was gone, and she was ready to accept the loss just as she had accepted whatever came.

Yet there remained this one desire, this yearning to reveal to her children and her grandchildren the direction in which they walked.

She began dwelling upon what she would speak to them. Beneath the sky, she must tell them, the earth turns slowly. No one feels the motion of its turning, but there it is. The seasons follow one another; the years tread softly on each other's heels; the generations are born and given maturity, and the movement is the same. The universe operates by cycle; every element depends upon a cycle.

"As I move away," she said in the darkness of quiet night hours, "you move up. We walk slowly, all of us, away from the sun, that gives life." There was another thought that caused her to digress then. Did they walk away from the sun, or did they move toward this representation of God? She could not tell. But whatever the focus, they walked blindly. They had little sense of destination until all of a sudden it appeared before them, ready to swallow them whole, to add them impersonally to all who had gone before into the vast, solemn brilliance of the unknown world after.

150

That was not all. There lay, in the invisible air, the unspoken bidding to serve the world in some manner, to extend the eye and the hand beyond the fairy circle of family and friends, to touch what seemed near untouchable. It was more than duty: it was a spiritual bidding of a universe in which all souls were equal in need. All were frail and open to pity; all must, despite weak and transparent qualities, give of themselves. She herself had not become aware of this until age had crept quietly, stiffly upon her.

She lay thinking upon all this, repeating until the thoughts wore grooves of their own upon her mind and crowded out the tiresome details of the physical world. The season changed, but she hardly noticed. She was on her way; despite the old limbs quiet in the bed, she was taking the last dragging steps. Sharply she attended to that one activity; when she could step not once more she must take a stand and speak.

The sons came regularly, one by one, to sit near her, but she scarcely noted their presence. Only Clara was left of reality, Clara whose bent shoulders and slow, steady steps appeared without being summoned. Grandma Westerman would look at her with fondness, at the patient eyes and wrinkled, ministering hands.

Sometimes in the heavy night hours, when Clara would pour her a drink of water or let medicine trickle into a silver spoon, they would speak in spare phrases with an intimacy that comforted her.

"You will have a home here," Grandma Westerman murmured. "I have spoken to Albert."

"It is wicked to imply," Clara reprimanded as a child. "You will be better one day soon. The medicine is slow when one is heavy with years."

"I see the truth," the old lady said stubbornly. "At my hour nothing obscures the eyes."

"One must always hope," reminded Clara. "There is nothing in the world if not hope."

"When the time comes," Grandma Westerman spoke, "you must call them in—Albert and Leonie and the children."

"Yes, yes," soothed Clara. "You have told me a dozen times. I have promised."

"There is something I wish to say to them," the old woman said dreamily, "something they must know."

151

Day by day a great eagerness for the hour came over her. Sometimes she feared to fall asleep, thinking it might come unbeknownst, and be lost to her. "If you see sometime," she instructed Clara, "that the time has come, rouse me. Do not hesitate."

But in her awaiting, in the alert core of her mind, she watched stealthily. The triumph of recognition was almost overwhelming. Such eagerness flowed through her that she lost awareness. In the dazzling, blinding swirl of unconsciousness she forced her way determinedly back, and held a position divided only by a dimness of physical perception.

There was confusion in the doorway; she endured it with patience, holding proudly to her command of the hour; such strength seemed to resurge she thought herself able to wait for long. Anticipation brought exquisite pleasure so that she trembled violently and Clara held to her while still crying to the family, "Hurry now!"

It was Elizabeth who was responsible for the commotion. Hysterically she tried to pull away from her father. "Don't make me," she wept.

"She is too sensitive for this," Leonie defended her daughter. "And at the delicate age too."

"Nevertheless she must enter," Albert pronounced. "This is Grandma's last wish. Slap her cheeks and bring her to her senses."

When the old lady opened her eyes again, the room was quiet but for Elizabeth's muffled sobbing as she stood pressed within the circle of her mother's arm. She could see the two small children standing beside Leonie, and she frowned at the absence of Albert.

"My stomach aches," Theodore whispered, and Maria looked at him as though he were a stranger.

At last Grandma Westerman discovered that one hand was being fondled, and that at her side was Albert, his eyes pink, his face damp. Finding his nearness distasteful, she looked at the children again. It appeared that two large tears stood on Maria's cheeks, that they had come unbidden from the round, wondering eyes to roll gently only a little way. She wished Maria were beside her rather than Albert; the child would be less disturbing than the man, but there was not time to request the change.

Clara she could not see at all, but sensed that the elderly woman was close to her. Sighing, prolonging the moment a bit, Grandma Westerman wet her lips with unwieldy tongue, and spoke.

"The universe turns slyly, and unseen," she said. In a little the church bells would be tolling ponderously for her; she and her brother had run swiftly down the street to the church when their grandmother departed.

"She is out of her head," Leonie murmured. "She does not know what words she speaks."

"As I move away," the old woman went on softly and deliberately, as if repeating a lesson, "you move up into my place . . ."

Blinking her eyelids, she looked at them long. What she had already said was beginning to penetrate; she could tell by the increasing mistiness of the faces as though the spirits had arisen to the very surface.

Exultation flowered as she bid the next phrases come to her lips and tongue, and she could not speak at all for a moment. But she had only begun. Her triumph must carry her through to the end of the precise revelation.

"We are all walking faster and faster," she wanted to say, "to our destination . . ."

But with a rude rush it all receded from her—the words, the faces, the brilliance, the universe. And she was alone.

from the Atlantic Monthly

OLD CENTURY'S RIVER

OLIVER LA FARGE *was born in New York City fifty years ago, but says he is "by descent, upbringing, and inclination" a native of Rhode Island. After finishing at Harvard in 1924 he spent a year and a half in Mexico and Guatemala working as an anthropologist. He switched from anthropology to writing as a major interest after the publication of his novel,* Laughing Boy, *the Pulitzer Prize winner in 1929, but continued to interest himself in applied anthropology, concentrating on the welfare of our Indians. He is at present president of the Association on American Indian Affairs. In 1931 his story "Haunted Ground" won an O. Henry prize. Mr. La Farge is the author of five novels, one collection of short stories, three non-fiction books, and author or editor of four scientific works. He served in the Army Air Forces during World War II, emerging as a lieutenant colonel and receiving the Legion of Merit. He is a Fellow of the American Association for the Advancement of Science and of the American Anthropological Association.*

Almost as soon as he found those two miraculous bottles of whisky he knew that they meant the end, and were to be the means of it. He did not state this explicitly to himself, but felt it below the level of worded thoughts or of admission, as a wild animal knows that its end is coming, as an old jungle hand, by the time he had reached his age, should have learned to know.

He saw the little suitcase that contained them by pure accident, because one of his awkward, improvised crutches slipped as he was turning away, after he had cut his fourth heart of palm. Four hearts of palm weren't much of a supply, but that was all he had

154

strength for now. It was better to go short, and be sure of making it back to his shelter and his mosquito net before dark. He turned slowly, one crutch slipped, he caught himself, and it was then that he saw the edge of the valise, under a low-growing *ramón* palm. His faded blue eyes studied it for several seconds while he remembered that Tolling had looked for it, and had said that, among other things, he had two bottles of good whisky in it.

He lowered himself to the ground slowly, with elaborate care not to jar his bad leg. The slightest jolt, twist, or even just wrong position meant a white swirl of pain which was not quick in going away. Presently he was on the ground, his legs out in front of him, and had pulled the little suitcase into the open.

He felt the case gently with the palm of his hand, studying it. It was about eighteen inches long and a foot wide. It had been badly scratched, probably bounced off a couple of trees when it was thrown from the plane, and one end was slightly charred. Three weeks lying on the damp ground had done it no good. Still, you could recognize its quality, the quality of the leather, very unlike the soft surface of native Mexican tanning. The brass locks were neat and solid. The initials under the handle were clear, "J.H.T." Tolling's case all right, and because he had not yet given up his fight, he could think that it was too bad that by now Tolling and McDaniels, two young and healthy men, might well be dead, and to consider with a bit of triumph and a bit of laughter that he, old, injured, his system charged with God only knew how many tropical infections, was still alive and still fighting.

An Indian would have given up by now. An Indian's reason would have told him that it was all over days ago, and very reasonably he would have given up and avoided a lot of discomfort by deliberately dying, the way Indians know how to do. A white man goes beyond reason, not with hope so much as with determination, and so a lot of times he wins out when he ought not to. Thus the first thing he got out of finding the valise was a lift, not at that moment applying to his situation the meaning of the thing he had just admitted to himself, his belief that Tolling and McDaniels had failed to make it. He thought of their probable demise only as a contrast to his own survival, with the triumph that the aged, the sick, the disreputable feel over the downfall of the young, the strong, the correct.

He remembered the ridiculousness of being hired by those two young fellows to guide them in the air. He remembered their tale of gold cached in an ancient mound, and the map and the old letter they had to prove it. He knew better, but they offered him nice work, good pay, and a cut in everything they found, to fly around and identify places from the air, later to run their camp and supply train. In honesty he'd warned them that they were starting too late, with the rains coming on; but they wanted to make a scout now, and come back the next season. That was all right with him. Anyway, he'd long wanted to know what it was like to fly.

He sure as hell found out. Sick and frightened, right from the start. And then good and lost—everything looked so different from the air. All he could do was feel awful and hang onto himself, and hang onto the gleam of the river, when he could find it.

After the crash Tolling had delayed awhile, looking for the valise, before he and McDaniels started out. He had hoped to find it, not only for the liquor, but because it contained personal papers and a large-scale map of Chiapas. Tolling set a lot of store by maps. The trouble was, he had looked too close to the wreckage of the plane. From where he sat, the old man could not see the clearing in which they had come down, but he could see, like shafts between the great trees, the glow of light which marked it. The clearing was of no interest to him. There was nothing edible growing there. Except where the plane had cut a swathe and made a scorched area, it was all oleander, high as a man.

They were dead and he was on his own, all right. He was sorry about them. It had been fine, the way they dragged him away from the burning wreckage, the way they splinted him and fixed up his shelter under his directions, and the generosity with which they divided the salvaged supplies with him. They had wanted to try carrying him out, but he knew that that would never have worked. Even then, when they stood before him, ready to go, he'd figured that forty miles of this kind of bush, with the swamp to cross, was going to be tough going for a couple of complete greenhorns. The bearing of their failure upon his own situation began to impress him. To free his mind of it, he concentrated on the suitcase. He was a

156

trifle lightheaded, not with the familiar fever of malaria, but with a giddiness and feeling of infection which came from the poisons being manufactured in his leg.

He tried the catches. The two locks snapped open. Good. He lifted the lid. The top layer of socks and some brightly striped drawers kept the rest of the contents snug. Under them were various papers in several bundles, the folded map, and the two bottles. He did not touch them, but sat studying the labels and seals. The best, bottled in bond, aged, one hundred proof, the kind of liquor the very existence of which a man completely forgot in the little towns of the back country, drinking barbed wire, *aguardiente,* most of the time, and Habanero when he was flush.

The pale golden-brown contents of the two bottles promised him pleasure and relief from pain. The continuous throbbing of his leg this last week had at first broken his sleep, and the last few nights had allowed him to doze only in snatches. With one of these under his belt . . .

Seldom in his life had he tasted liquor of this class, mostly that time he found gold and sold out, and went clear to Mexico City. It had been his plan then to go to the States, with all the cash he had, but Mexico City had everything, even blondes. He suspected that that blonde of his was synthetic, but if so she had done a job of it. She was blonde all over. He frowned over her name. Rita— Rita something, claimed to be half Polish. She was expensive as hell, but worth every peso of it. The memory of those six weeks had stayed good for years. She'd gone in for all sorts of mixed drinks, but he had mistrusted them; that was when he got onto the fine bourbon. It goes down like tea, and it's as strong as anything that ever hit your stomach.

He closed the valise. Drawing his machete, he cut a length of narrow, flexible *liana.* The act took two flips of the wrist. He handled his machete with old skill, but he paused between the strokes and afterward set the blade down as though it were heavily weighted. There was no more strength in him. With the liana he slung the valise from his shoulder. Then he sheathed the machete and went through the long, careful, effortful process of getting to his feet and onto the crutches Tolling and McDaniels had made for him.

It was about a hundred feet from where he stood to his shelter. He had come so far only because he had cleaned out everything edible nearer, at least everything that grew in places open enough for him to penetrate. Cutting a path into the really thick places was quite beyond him in his condition. As he inched his way back, he made a remarkable picture. He wore a fairly new straw sombrero, set aslant on his longish white hair. His three weeks' beard was scraggly, curly, and nearly as white as the finer hair of his head. His face was deeply tanned, of a sickly color under the tan, lined and sunken.

He wore a strong khaki shirt and slacks, purchased with the advance money the young men had given him, but these now looked as if he had had them for years. They were filthy. The shirt had several rips in it. The left trouser leg, over his bad leg, had been cut away at the knee. On his left foot the newly purchased, high-laced boot had likewise been cut away above the ankle, leaving a sort of shoe. In between was the splint, fashioned out of pieces of the wrecked plane and wrapped with materials which had become gray-black, fuzzy, rotting rags. In his left breast pocket four slender white hearts of palm stuck up like candy sticks. His machete and knife hung at his waist, the little valise, woefully heavy, slid around against his back and his side.

He concentrated on his panting progress, leaving for later the endless, rambling self-communions of a man who has been long alone.

The forest in front of him lightened, there were the same brilliant shafts and streaks ahead of him as had marked the neighborhood of the clearing. He came out on the edge of the river beside his shelter. He rested, looking at the river. It was familiar; a great part of his life had been spent along it. Its presence supported him.

Within easy distance of him were a number of traps, the simple arrangements of sticks the Indians make for catching the smallest animals. He scanned them carefully, without expectation; he'd been living and moving around here too long for the little creatures to be coming by.

His shelter was a simple affair of palm branches and a tarpaulin, a lean-to facing the river. One end was over the roots of a massive mahogany, the other was partly closed by a smaller tree. In a rise of ground between two roots was his bed, a pile of palm branches and a blanket with the mosquito net suspended above. Behind that, on the raised shelf of another root, were his rifle and his supplies. In front of the shelter was a meager pile of firewood beside the black circle of his fire. The edge of the circle was cut by a frying pan with a spoon in it and a blackened tin can, its top bent backward to form a sort of handle.

His supplies were cached in the empty tin cans beside the rifle. In one was a small bag of salt and another bag containing a handful of rice. A second was half full of carefully saved cigarette stubs, and on top of them an empty quinine bottle containing two whole cigarettes. In others were some money, some pieces of newspaper, a dozen matches wrapped elaborately in part of an oilskin tobacco pouch, and a bottle of insect repellent, nearly empty. Between the bed and the fireplace stood a badly dented army issue canteen, its upper part fire-blackened, lacking its canvas cover and its cup. Most of the cans showed the effects of fire. The rifle had a charred place on the stock. Along the barrel were a number of spots of rubbed-down rust.

After a moment's hesitation he took out one of the whole cigarettes and laid it carefully on a root. He hefted the canteen, and was relieved to find it full. It had become difficult to remember whether he had stuck to his routine of working his way to the water and filling it before he went looking for food. He tended to his fire, uncovering the coals, laying on twigs and bark, fanning gently with his hat, until he had a dependable little flame.

Daylight would last at least an hour more, but already the river was beginning to fill with shadow, while the sunlight became sharper, more emphatic, on the far bank. The occasional bole of a great tree, exposed directly to the light, turned gold. The water was a living, dull metal, moving in an oily, quiet, powerful, yet sluggish way, with blue here and there in its swirls. The Chacaljá— the river had a dozen names, Spanish, Nahua, Mayan; from among them this one, the one the Indians of the headwaters gave it, was the one which to him best meant the whole. The name Concha used for it. The hut he had lived in with Concha hadn't been far from here, when he'd been a young sprout. A doll, a kind of toy, a live toy who could love you and keep house and laugh and make you

159

laugh. He wanted not to think of her, but could not stop the sequence, first of Concha in those good months and then of how she screamed and wept when El Nopo, that bandit bastard, and the troops of his private revolution came through and took her along with them. You were a young Gringo and you worked for the oil company. You were a Gringo and strong and wonderful, and you were supposed to be able to cope with anything, and you stood there looking into the rifle barrels while they tied your girl on a saddle.

That was what started off the first big drunk. He quit his job clearing trail and got really in Dutch with the company. That was the start of a lot, he guessed. He certainly had stayed drunk a long time.

He opened the valise and got out the bottles. They were fair prey, and maybe, if he got out of here, he could use the clothing, but the papers belonged to Tolling. Some of them were handwritten letters. They ought to be sent home. Holding one of the bottles, thinking of that, he really thought out and faced the first fact. In the end of the dry season as it was now, with the bush at its driest and openest, you could figure on a couple of healthy men taking ten days to go forty miles, if they didn't hit a made trail farther down the river and if they were green at bush travel. You could figure even on two weeks. But you could not figure on three. He knew where he was, as he had told them, about five miles below El Salto, the first fall, and forty miles above Ocantán. At Ocantán there were a Swiss and a number of Mexicans, and at least two double canoes with outboard motors. They would have been here by now; the river was low and mild. Being completely green, the young men had not gotten out. There was only one answer to that one, they were dead by now. Easy enough to happen too. So here he was.

He opened the bottle slowly and smelled of it. Then he lit the cigarette. Boy, this was life. A remark he had heard somewhere came to mind: "James, serve the champagne in tin cups, the gentlemen wish to rough it." He took a pull at the bottle. It was really prime stuff. He had smoked little the last few days, because the smoke tasted foul, but now his cigarette was good. He meditated taking a swig of water, but decided in favor of letting the liquor glow in

160

his mouth and throat and stomach. He set the bottle down with care and smoked, looking out.

The old Chacaljá—a few miles above here he had lived with Concha, when he was a young sprout full of beans and had a regular job. If you could go there now, you probably could not find the spot, any more than you would be able to find any trace of his camp a few years from now. How long ago was that? He had to do a little counting to figure that this was nineteen-fifty, not forty-nine. Usually a little thing like that made no difference. He came out in nineteen hundred, the leap year when it didn't leap, the turn of the century. He liked to say that, after the lapse of time had made it impressive, "I came out here at the turn of the century, when I was a young sprout," so that back when he was hardly fifty the Americans had taken to calling him Old Century. Those two boys, Tolling and McDaniels, had called him "Mr. Century" when they first met him. The cigarette was half gone. He took another good pull at the bottle.

Pretty nearly half a century, and not much to show for it. No sign of that fortune he'd been going to make. He'd had one real friend, Whittaker, and old Whit was long gone. Up this same river too. He wished old Whit were here now to sit with him and pull at the bottle and watch the day go over the Chacaljá and night come down. It would be a pretty night, with a moon, if it didn't cloud up. There'd been a lot of clouds around lately. Be a hell of a note if the rains started tonight and ruined this binge. Old Whit had said one time, when they were both good and drunk, that it was a pity he, Century, hadn't stayed in school and gotten an education. He'd have been a poet or a philosopher, Whit had said. Funny thing, he'd felt something that way about Whit.

Apart from Whit, he couldn't say he'd had any real friends. Knew a hell of a lot of men of different kinds, yes, liked some of them, been able to work and live with a lot of them, but not friends, not really. First he guessed he was too brash, and then maybe too much of a rum-bum. Besides, the more you live in the bush and along the river, the more you want to be let live inside yourself.

There had been a variety of women, some of whom he remembered sharply, some of whom were mere whorehouse blurs, vague punctuations to drinking, but none of them had lasted. He'd have

161

liked to have had Eufemia last, but Eufemia was a Tehuana, and she ended up by going home with a Tehuano man, the way they always do. He guessed his kid was a good Tehuano, speaking Zapotec as his mother tongue. The chief thing he could say for all these years was that he'd never worked hard, not steadily that is, and he'd had a lot of fun.

Or maybe the chief thing was that here he was, sick, old, and crippled, and still alive after three weeks. Most white men would be dead by now. The grub left him wouldn't have lasted ten days. If his leg cleared up he could tough it out indefinitely, even after the rains came if he had to. And the two young men were dead. Apart from his leg there was nothing the matter with him. Of course he guessed he'd been orating to himself a lot, but anyone does that who lives much alone in the bush. He had a drink to his own mastery of the wild country.

As that drink took hold his mood changed. He thought of the great joke of being hired by those two young fellows and how, to clinch the job, he had artfully let them draw out of him every fool story he had ever heard of gold being found. Anyone knew it was all bunk. He'd seen it proven a dozen times. What a joke on them—and now on him too.

A curassow, big and black-looking, lit on a branch not twenty feet from him. He stiffened and reached for his rifle, almost tasting the meat. The bird flew off again. He swore. He had moved too soon, before it got settled. He looked at the little package of rice and his slivers of heart of palm, studying the rice for a long time. He looked at the bottles, then out over the river. The higher bank opposite was completely in shadow, and the shadow was mounting rapidly up the trees. With a manner of finality he built up the fire, poured water in the tin can, and set it to boil. He watched it in a sort of blankness until the water bubbled properly, then with the same manner of finality he poured in the last of his rice and added salt. He cut the hearts of palm carefully into small pieces and added them. The extravagance which wiped out his entire larder was committed under compulsion. As soon as the food was in, he drank again, this time following the drink with a brief chaser of tepid water. He did not want to empty the canteen and be forced to the difficult process of going down the bank to the water. Do that in the morning, on a morning drink.

If only his leg started mending he'd be all right. If he could get around even as well as he had at first, he wouldn't worry for grub or for being able to tough it out. He'd last until he could walk like a man and then, rains or no rains, he'd get out to Ocantán. They would have made sure he was dead. He chuckled. It had happened before. Old Century dead and buried a lot of times, and he turns up again. Just a bad old man, but powerful hard to kill. In one of the tin cans, underneath bits of newspaper, he still had a hundred pesos, part of the advance the boys had given him. He meditated on the simple facilities for pleasure in Ocantán, the known limits of hospitality and the extension of those limits to be made by the judicious buying of drinks all round, and he planned himself a pleasant stretch of time once he got out. The Swiss, Anthaler, set a good table.

The rice was done. The stew lacked meat, but latterly he had been eating little, both to stretch his small reserve and because he lacked appetite. Now his stomach had come magnificently to life under the influence of the whisky. The stew was delicious. Cooked, it just about filled the can. He cleaned it all out, at first greedily, then with more leisure and appreciation of enjoyment. When there was nothing left but a few inaccessible grains, with a sense of lavishness and pleasure he threw the can high. It sailed through the air, turning over on itself, and dropped beyond the bank. He listened for a splash, and was disappointed when he could not hear one. The dinner called for another good slug of bourbon and the other whole cigarette. He stretched and sighed luxuriously.

Briefly the strong light remained on the treetops across the river, while the wall of the main mass was mysteriously blue; then the light went, and almost without transition the far wall became a black strip rising to the sky while the river itself, which had been dark, acquired reflections of light. Beyond those trees, to his left, he could see indications of the moonrise. Tomorrow would be the full moon. He greeted the night with another drink.

The bottle in his hand brought his mind back to the boys and the plane ride with them. He had been pretty well lost until, just before the engine stopped working, he had recognized El Salto and

163

the S-bend of the river by the big swamp. The swamp it was mos
likely that had got the boys. Then everything had come unstuck a
once, and he hadn't done anything but pray until they pulled him
out from under the wing and brought him round. It had been a satis
faction, once he was himself, to tell them instantly just where the
were. He remembered now their look of respect, just as he remem
bered trying to tell them how to get by in the bush, and feelin
even then that you couldn't tell it to someone, it had to be learnec
You had to live it.

He could not exactly say that his leg had stopped hurting, bu
he didn't mind it much. He wished he had some coffee to go witl
his dinner and lead back into the drinks in a proper manner. H
wished Whittaker were here. There was mist in the enclosure o
air over the river now, and the moon, coming up beyond the ocea
of trees, began to reach the upper wisps of it and make them glow
As a result of light at the higher level, the river itself was lost in dark
ness. It would be nice to have Concha here now, Concha or—h
remembered a phrase—or the equivalent thereof. It was MacNamar
at Frontera who used to say that. Concha or the equivalent thereof
He could imagine it, but Whit would be better. It would be the en
of both bottles, sure enough, if he could turn up again.

.Old Century, fifty years in the bush, and what had he to show fo
it? Lying here like a goddamned sultan, looking at the moonris
over the Chacaljá, with a full belly and a rotting leg, and more o
the finest whisky in the world than he could possibly get down i
one night. That was a hell of a note. He held the bottle up to th
moonlight to see how far he had lowered it, and as it was not ever
halfway yet, he drank again.

"Or the equivalent thereof." This stuff had no equivalent. Mac
Namara, he'd gone back to the States. A lot of them had gone back
some of them had stayed here, dead. Why did they all go back t
the States? He could have gone back, two or three times, with
good bit of money in his pants, but each time, like that best o
them all, his visit to Mexico City, he got to somewhere where th
facilities were good and there he stayed until he was broke. It neve
made him feel bad, winding up broke. Who the hell wants to g
back to the States? Drinking the best whisky in the world on th

moonlit banks of the Chacaljá, when by good rights he ought to be dead a week ago.

It seemed to him that there was some connection between the lowering of the level in the bottle and the lowering line of the shadow around him. He was not able to keep pace, however, and he did not really try, because to have emptied the bottle by the time the moonlight reached him would have been to force his pace unpleasantly and bring pleasure to an end too soon. It was just one of those fool ideas that used to amuse Whit. "Don't kill the bottle, just squeeze it slowly to death." That had been Whit.

He saw the moon, just short of full. He took its light on his face. The light was a ragged silver line along the edge of the cut-bank in front of him, and shortly, or he thought it was shortly, it reached the river. The fact that each change he was watching was totally familiar did not in the least decrease his delight in it. As drunk as he was beginning to be, his appreciation was intensified and he felt, as he had when he was young, and on other drunken occasions, that there was much more in this than the eye beheld. Although familiar it was unique, it was a manifestation of something great which hovered just beyond the line of comprehension.

The thin mists lay between him and the moon, forming streaks of luminosity. The jungle on the other side was a jagged silhouette of deepest blue-black with silver edges and curious sprays and spurts of silver, or of white, ice-cold fire along the top. The river swirled black designs in the brightness of its reflections, the moon path broad and flecked, breaking up at the edges, merging into an area of blackness on each side. The ice-cold fire lay on his hand; it lay, barred and mottled with shadow, around him and between him and the edge of the bank. The thing was enough in itself—he needed no one, lacked for no company.

He drank slowly but at some length. The liquor now really did go down like tea. This is what Old Century's got, he told himself. He's got the Chacaljá River. He's got this. I got this and I got the bush, and the satisfaction of knowing that even this old and bad off I can stay alive here and have the love of it. This is what I've got and it ain't hay. He put his bottle to his lips, tilting his head well back, and felt insulted and fooled when it ran dry at the second swallow.

He looked at the empty bottle and then at the untouched one. He did not seem anywhere near drunk enough for the amount that had gone down. He hefted the empty bottle, set it down, picked up the full one, and as he did so, feeling the second bottle's weight, the inner realizations which had been working to the surface ever since he saw these two miraculous containers, which he had been holding back and denying since they began gathering days before, came to the top.

There was the simple, central fact of his leg. It didn't only hurt him like fury, it was not only swelling, it smelled. Unable to wash or change his clothes, he had gathered about him a general, ripe, definite smell, but after enough time has gone by, a man ceases to notice his own odor. This was different. He knew perfectly well what it was and what it meant. With food and shelter, still he and his leg had only a few more days to go, days of increasing pain and wretchedness. And he was at the end of gathering food. Right now he had strength and a sense of well-being out of that God-sent bottle, but he could not survive on that. He was through.

It was, of course, quite unnecessary for him to restate all the factors of his situation to himself. He knew the bush, the river, himself, and how men die much too well. He simply admitted their sum and told himself, This is what I've *had*. So now what?

The surface of the river was now entirely covered with a low-lying mist which lay in slight, irregular waves, shining white, with decorations of soft, bluish shadow. From the main body, higher elements detached themselves here and there. This soft brightness gave a new background for the silhouettes of the growths immediately in front of him, a new value to the dark, silver-topped block of the far side. This phenomenon, too, he knew well. He had been looking forward to it. He nodded his head sagely. He would go to the river, he would join the good old Chacaljá.

Slowly, with great seriousness, he peeled the wrapping off the second bottle and loosened the cork. He put the bottle down. A man should leave some kind of word. He had an idea. If he left a message in the first bottle, the chances were fair that even if it was Indians who found it, they would bring it to Ocantán. He opened

Tolling's valise once more, and searched in it uncertainly by the moonlight. He found what seemed to be a blank piece he could tear off a sheet, and a pencil. For a long time he pondered and frowned. Finally he wrote, "*Sirvase pagar al portador 1 peso*. Died drunk and happy. Old Century William Tecumseh Carpenter." He had trouble making the letters. He folded the sheet, and on the outside, on both sides, printed in unsteady letters, "*Llevase á don Alberto Anthaler—1 peso*." After a little thought, he added a cross to impress the Indians.

He rolled the paper in a squill, pushed it into the bottle, and watched it unfold. That was about the best he could do to preserve himself for posterity. It would certainly bother Anthaler and the rest as the news spread along the river to know how he came to end up drunk on such elegant liquor, in his predicament. He corked the bottle. Then he made a cigarette from a piece of newspaper out of the storage can and some of his stubs. He smoked it slowly and gravely, watching the dance of the mist strands, the very slow, dreamy, coiling flow of the main body of the mist on the river.

When the cigarette was gone, he took a short drink from the second bottle. Forcing it into a trousers pocket, he got his crutches, and pulled himself erect much more easily than he had expected. Once he was up he was quite steady, which surprised him and gave him a moment of pride. Then he set to the serious business of getting to the edge of the bank, lowering himself to a sitting position, and letting himself down to the water. Anyway, he thought with satisfaction, I don't have to make it back up again.

At the water's edge the mist reached to a short distance over his head. Around him was a soft, fuzzy, cool, gray whiteness, and above him a soft glow melting toward a defined central brightness where he faced the moon. The water took his bad leg wonderfully, cooling and easing it. He let himself in, supporting himself on his crutches. If anything, it was chilly in the river, but the sense of his body's lightness, the feeling of cleanliness, and the complete easing of his leg were sheer delight.

A down tree projected from the bank near him, one end firmly bedded near the shore, the other bobbing and weaving faintly in a slow eddy. He worked his way to it, moving slowly in the supporting, hindering water.

Under his weight the trunk sank lower, so that it was no trick to sit on it and balance with the water up to his waist. He let his crutches float away. The old Chacaljá, he thought, this is what I've got, this is what I've had. The high boot laced on his healthy leg kept the good water from washing about it as it did the other. He wished he'd taken it off, but it was too late for that now. Balancing on the log, he dug out the bottle, hoping the water hadn't got into the liquor. That was one place the river did not belong. He took a solid drink, his face raised toward the soft whiteness which covered him. Faintly here and there he could make out the outline of the black shadow of a tree. It seemed to him that he was experiencing the essence of the river.

He was sitting in the middle of a misty sphere, which in the direction of the moon contained a great, luminous circle with that brightness in the center. I sure as hell wish Whit was here, I wish he could see this. The good old Chacaljá. He felt the whole river, the vastness of it, waiting. The river and all that that term embraced in its true sense. The slow waters were waiting for him, the *lagartos*, the alligators, were waiting for him. Along the banks the countless roots which drew their life from the river waited for him, and so did the big and little fishes, the water grasses, the buzzards, the insects, and all the various and beautiful snakes, the *nauiacas*, the *masacuates*, the *culebras*, and the rest. The only people who did not form part of the river, and who therefore did not have sense enough to be waiting for him to join them, were the men who lived along it. They would be curious, perhaps even worried, about his disappearance; the others would know. The graceful animals who drank at the river and who fished in it, the deer, the lions, the iguanas, the jaguars, the big, slow-moving *dantas*, would know, the mists, and the days and nights, the bugs darting over the water, the gravels and sands and rocks. He was conscious of them all, and he embraced them.

The sphere with its area of brightness, in which he could see nothing and beyond which he could see everything, contracted and expanded. The moon spot tended to whirl, or else he was whirling. It seemed to him that he had experienced this manifestation before. He took another good, long pull at the bottle, a longer pull than he really wanted, forcing himself, because he did not think that he would get to take many more. Holding the bottle by the neck with its bottom resting on his thigh, he stared at the moon spot. It was all waiting for him. He knew it all; if Whit were here right now he thought he could explain to him what that thing was you felt in the beautiful moments, that thing that had always been just out of reach when you watched the moonrise or the dawn, and at such times. His hand fell off the bottle, letting it go into the water with a faint gurgle. Slowly, rather majestically, he followed, his eyes closed, his mouth slightly open, slipping gently, almost noiselessly, into the river, in which he drifted limply, without motion of his own.

from Mademoiselle

THE JERSEY HEIFER

PEGGY HARDING LOVE *was born in Chicago in 1920, grew up in Minneapolis, went to Swarthmore College, and married another Swarthmore graduate. "We have lived in a lot of different places," she writes, "preferably rural, including two co-operative general farms and one very co-operative dairy farm." She started writing in college, and her first published story was a third-prize winner in u* Story *magazine college contest. Since then she has had four other stories published, three in* Mademoiselle *and one in* The New Mexico Quarterly Review. *She has studied at various times under James Gray and Robert Penn Warren at the University of Minnesota, where her husband is now getting his Ph.D. in physiology, while she does free-lance editing and as much writing as possible.*

In October the cows went apple-crazy. The sweet, sun-warmed apple smell drifted down from the orchard, tempting them unbearably; and by afternoon one or the other—the heifer usually, she was the mischief-maker—would have nudged down a rail from the old wooden fence around the pasture. Once, only once, young Phoebe Matthews looked out the kitchen window and caught them in the act, but the picture stayed forever in her mind, an image of transcendent innocence and freedom. Leaping negligently, her hoofs tucked up delicately, the Jersey heifer went over the lower rails like a deer, and close behind, clumsy but with drooling haste, Daisy, the three-year-old Guernsey, stepped clumsily out, one stiff leg at a time, banging her plump udder with shocking heedlessness against the bar.

They trotted eagerly along the quiet dirt lane, turning their wary heads from side to side; and later, near milking time, Phoebe and

170

Joe, her husband, had come upon them drunk with bliss in the long grass of the orchard. Each time they were discovered there, the cows stood perfectly still, their red and tawny coats bright against the blue sky, their soft, wide eyes looking out innocently among the apple branches. Long threads of saliva trailed from their velvety muzzles and glistened in the late sunlight, and under their hoofs the crushed and rotting apples gave off a heady fragrance.

Always at the sight of them there Phoebe's heart leaped in delight. She hated to drive them out; but Joe, slapping lightly at their smooth, hard flanks, would chivvy them back to the pasture with a slow-moving, gentle stubbornness that matched their own. "Apples cut down Daisy's milk," he told Phoebe firmly. "I've got to wire that fence," but he lingered beside her, smiling to see the tipsy heifer prance off down the pasture.

"Let them go," Phoebe pleaded, begging as earnestly as for herself, "let them have a little freedom. I'll bring them back when they get out."

"Well," Joe said, musing, "well," and he looked off over the fields that were so newly theirs. "The apples will be picked pretty soon now anyway," he said, and running his thumb lightly down Phoebe's arm, he headed back to where he had left the horses hitched to the spring-tooth harrow.

By the end of October they had picked all the apples on the trees and stored them in barrels in the cellar. They were Baldwins, small, tart, and juicy, the best-flavored apples anywhere, Joe insisted; and though the trees were old and shamefully neglected, though curculio and scab had made their inroads and no one bought Baldwins any more, still Joe and Phoebe knelt carefully in the long grass, collecting even the windfalls and hauling them up the wagon ramp into the upper story of the old bank barn for cider-making.

They were pressing cider the afternoon the county agent stopped by for his first visit, and the first thing he told them was that the orchard should be cut down. Those old trees would never show a profit, he said, no matter how they were pruned and sprayed. Joe walked around the farm with him with a pocket edition of Thoreau sticking out of his hip pocket—he liked to read it while he was resting the horses or waiting for the cider to drain. Pax, their springer spaniel, raced ahead while Phoebe, trailing behind, listened uneasily

171

to the agent's suggestions. The orchard should go, the horses should
be replaced by a tractor and modern equipment, new fences should
be built, the chickens not allowed to run; and when Phoebe said in
alarm, "But we like horses!" the agent smiled like a wise, indulgent
uncle.

"You know, I'm always glad to see city folks coming back to the
farm," he said. "A fine young couple like you, not afraid of hard work,
and I can see you've done a lot here already, why, there's no reason
at all why you shouldn't have a good, solid return on your investment. But you've got to remember, first and last, farming is a business."

"We figured farming was a way of life," Joe said. For a long moment they all were silent, and Phoebe, kneeling suddenly, gave Pax a
fierce, quiet hug. After a minute Joe said: "I guess you better not put
us down as farmers. We're grateful for your advice and we sure need
a lot of it, but maybe we're aiming at two different things. We don't
want a business, or an investment either. We just want to live right
and do right by our land and animals." Joe's smile was apologetic
and a little troubled, but his voice was earnest. "Put us down as
shiftless no-accounts or crazy damn fools," he said, "but I guess we'd
rather live peaceful than make money."

"No, son, I'll put you down as two romantic dreamers and come
around again next spring." The agent got in his car and was starting
out the dirt lane when he leaned out the window again, grinning like
a paternal old tomcat and pointing to where the pasture fence rail
was down again. "Your cows are out," he called. "Who's boss around
here, you or bossy?" and, laughing slyly, he jounced away in his
dusty sedan.

For a little while Phoebe and Joe stood where he left them, quiet
and abstracted in the pale, slanting sunlight. Phoebe's hands were
cold and sticky from the apple juice, and she held them up in the
sun to warm them. At last she said, "I'd better get the cows." The
orchard was stripped now, completely appleless, so she wouldn't find
them there; but the scent of apples still hung everywhere in the air,
filling the cows with yearning, and searching restlessly for fulfillment
they still broke out of the pasture. Joe looked at Phoebe as if he
hadn't heard her. "What if he's right?" he said broodingly. "Maybe
it's all an impossible dream." But when Phoebe protested, "No, he's

wrong! We've never been so happy." Joe smiled and touched her re-assuringly, because of course it was true.

In a minute Joe went back to the barn to finish pressing the last batch of cider, and Phoebe started down the lane. "Co' ba, co' ba," she sang out dreamily, taking comfort from the sound of her voice in the quiet air. It was a call for cows she had read in a book, but of course they never came. Back in the barn she heard Joe snort with laughter, and off behind the orchard great rustlings and upheavals in the underbrush signaled that Pax was on his way. "No, not you, foolish," she cried before he even got there, but he bounded out through the sumac beside the road, grinning and panting, with dirt from his diggings all over his face and tongue and his long, silky ears matted with burs. She was going to let him greet her before she sent him back, but after a token snuffle at her legs he ignored her utterly. He zigzagged wildly across the lane, nose in the dust, and in a minute he was off again, hot after a recent rabbit.

Phoebe walked on past the fenced-in vegetable garden, nipped now by frost but still green with broccoli and parsley, still orderly and serene; past the cropped-down empty pasture that sloped gently to the stream. The woods beyond flamed with color in the horizontal sunlight, and in the pasture the fierce old pin oak stood all alone in crimson splendor among the hummocks and the browning grass. Up the lane two sets of hoofprints lay guilelessly in the dust—one set large and clumsy, moving ponderously after the smaller, dancing crescents that led the way—and among them, steaming faintly in the cooling air, three insolent small cowflops on the rutted road. "They can't have been out long," Phoebe said out loud to herself. "That minx, that little devil," and, smiling ruefully, looking all around, she walked on after them.

Ever since they moved to the farm eight months ago she had started talking to herself. She wasn't lonely—even when Joe was work-ing off in the fields she had the animals for company; but she talked to them the way she talked to herself, loving, reassuring, and scold-ing in calm, sensible words that vanquished any wayward feelings of uncertainty, any possible tremor of fear. Yet she wondered some-times—she wondered now, with an unreasoning, anxious moment of panic as she walked down the lane—why she should ever be uncertain and afraid. After the lost, dismal years when she had followed Joe from one army camp to another, the farm seemed like a paradise. Joe had been hopelessly miserable in the Army, putting in his whole three years as cook's helper in vast base kitchens in the South. With dogged non-co-operation he stayed a p.f.c. throughout the war, unable to adjust to necessary evils and ridden by a constant sense of guilt, of being party to an infinite wrong.

Phoebe suffered with him in nearby furnished rooms, clerking in five-and-tens or typing in sweltering, alien offices. On week ends they rushed together in joy and despair, and lying in some mildewed, roach-infested haven they talked with helpless longing of the North, of the small New England college where they had met, of the good life they must find away from all this. It seemed to them that love and innocence had been destroyed everywhere, and that all the values of the world they knew had become false and unreal. Without their knowing quite how it happened, the good life of their desperate Sunday longings gradually came to mean a small farm of their own, in a climate with decent, changing seasons, where they could raise their own food, earn just what they needed and no more, and live in honesty and freedom. Only there, starting a new life from scratch, did goodness and integrity seem possible. It didn't matter that they were both city-bred; the last few months before Joe got his discharge they pored in fierce absorption over the Strout farm real estate catalogues, and Phoebe took out every book in the public library on vegetable crops, dairy management, and poultry raising for profit.

They bought the farm on a GI loan—ninety rolling north New Jersey acres, a quarter-mile back from the highway and no improvements. There were plenty of reasons why it was cheap—the sagging clapboard house, the long dirt lane that drifted shut in winter and ran with mud in spring, the hand pump at the sink, and the dirt floor in the stable; but Joe and Phoebe looked at the mulberry tree and the maples, the lush curves of the hayfields, the broad, shallow stream in the pasture, the thirty acres of well-grown woods so silent you could hear the mushrooms growing. They bought it in November and moved in in February. They had a mortgage Joe felt they could handle and enough money saved up to buy some stock and tide them over the first year.

For Joe the core of the farm was the fields and topsoil and green

174

crops making their intricate, purposeful growth—he had been going to teach botany once; but from the beginning it was the animals Phoebe loved most of all. She saw the whole farm as a combination Eden and Noah's Ark, where she and Joe and Pax and the cows and horses could live together as joint tenants on equal terms, in innocence and mutual respect. In her heart she could not believe that God had made her truly different from the animals she loved, born in sin with a heritage of guilt; and she would gladly have traded all her human knowledge and foresight for Pax's trustfulness or the Jersey heifer's wild, free spirit. "There's a serpent in your garden," Joe had teased her one day in May, holding up a wriggling five-foot black snake he had found behind the barn, but Phoebe's faith had not been shaken. She knew black snakes were harmless and ate lots of rats and mice. "Or chickens or eggs," Joe added dubiously; but he had built a fine tight henhouse, and he let the snake writhe peacefully away.

Up by the jog in the road Phoebe found the cows. They were off on the edge of the woods, nosing around in the faded goldenrod and wild asters under two ancient, half-dead crabapple trees. There was nothing there but a few dried-up, worm-hollowed crabapples, and the cows seemed apathetic, sunk in depression. "Don't look at me like that," Phoebe said, "it isn't my fault." The Jersey stared at her with great accusing eyes, her long-fringed eyelashes sticking out beneath the gentle curve of her pale, sharp horns. She held her head low, petulantly, the warm black markings on the dainty face shading away to the velvety umbers of her chest and back, her broad, saucy nose thrust out and her nostrils working slowly. When Phoebe touched her muzzle, she tossed her head and leaped sharply back.

"All right, if that's the way you feel," Phoebe said. "Come on, Daisy, we'll let her sulk." Phoebe put her arm across Daisy's broad russet-patched rump, and obediently Daisy lumbered back to the dusty road. She plodded slowly back toward the farm, now and then stopping in her tracks and turning her shy, hornless forehead to look around at Phoebe. When Phoebe clapped her on the hip she went on amiably, switching her tail rhythmically behind her in the late chill air.

Before they had gone far, Phoebe heard the Jersey scrambling back onto the road and the quick, light thud of her hoofs coming after them. Phoebe smiled to herself and kept on, purposely not looking back; but in a moment she became aware of a strange, unnerving silence. The quiet struck her suddenly as deeply suspicious, even terrifying, and for a long, disoriented instant she felt herself walking down an endless alien road surrounded by unimaginable hidden dangers. She stopped, whirled quickly, and found the heifer so close behind her that her horns could not have been an inch away from the seat of her jeans. "What are you doing?" Phoebe cried sharply. "Go on, you get in front of me." But the Jersey stood her ground stubbornly, head lowered and eyes rolling with audacity. After a moment Phoebe went on, walking stiff and wary, driving Daisy before her and turning her head every minute to look distrustfully behind. "Cut it out now," she ordered fiercely, stopping, turning, and going on uneasily; but all the way back to the barn the Jersey followed a hairbreadth behind, the bracketed horns lowered and dark eyes rolling boldly while her hoofs stepped delicately in perfect silence in the soft dust of the road.

"She threatened me, she threatened me all the way," Phoebe told Joe when she got back. She was laughing, but hurt and outraged just the same, and the strange nightmare feeling had not quite worn off. She had fastened Daisy in her stanchion in the stable below, on the ground floor of the barn, brought her hay and grain, jockeyed the heifer out through the stable door into the pasture and replaced— how many times now?—the fallen fence rail. The sun was nearly gone and she was shivering in a sweater when she went up the steep, crude stairs from the stable to the upper story, through the narrow trapdoor where they threw down the hay. Joe had finished the last batch of cider and was lining up the clear amber jugs beside the door, ready for loading on the Model A tomorrow to take to town. Discarded apples and the pressed-out apple cakes lay in a heap below the haymow, and in the cavernous gloom the autumn smell of apples, sweet and sour, mingled with the summer smell, dusty and sweet, of tender-cut green timothy and clover.

"That heifer thinks she's pretty cute," Joe said, pulling on his leather jacket, getting ready to go. "I think I'll keep Daisy in tonight after milking. Maybe the Jersey won't wander without her." Leaving the wide wagon doors open to the last rays of the sun, they went out of the barn together and up the path to the house. It was time to get the milk pail from the kitchen, time to start the fire for supper. "What are we having?" Joe asked, putting his long arm across Phoebe's shoulders. "What do you think, silly?" Phoebe said wearily, dreamily. "Apple fritters, apple butter, apple pie."

It was late that night, so late it was early morning, that Phoebe woke up suddenly with her heart pounding heavily. She sat up in bed listening tensely, and in a moment she heard it, a terrible bawling cry from somewhere outside. "Joe, Joe," she cried, shaking him frantically, "somebody's crying terribly." He struggled up, and in the dark bedroom they listened for the sound. At once it came again, a strangling, agonized bawl rising hideous with pain and terror through the cold black night.

"It's the heifer," Joe said, leaping out of bed and searching in the dark for his clothes. "That's not Daisy's voice, it's the heifer, somewhere near the barn." He was putting on his pants and shoes blindly, fumbling in haste.

"Oh, hurry," Phoebe cried, "please hurry," and she scrambled wildly on the cold bare floor trying to find the place where she had dropped her clothes.

"Light the lamp first, Phoebe," Joe said. "No, baby, please light the lamp first so I can get down there fast. Then you can dress." His voice calmed her a little and in a moment she had found the matches and lit the kerosene lamp that stood on the old pine dresser. Joe's back and arms made great black shadows on the ceiling, flailing into his heavy sweater, and then he picked up the lamp and clattered out, down the narrow boxed-in stairs. Dressing as fast as she could, shivering with cold and fear, she heard Joe downstairs unhooking the big flashlight that hung in the kitchen. His footsteps strode across the kitchen, Pax's claws clicking behind, and both of them rushed out into the night. In a minute she was dressed herself and running for the barn, a lantern in her hand, through the clear, chill blackness.

The bellowing grew closer, more localized, and she headed up the wagon ramp and through the wide door of the barn's upper story. On the other side of the floor Joe's flashlight lay on the rough boards, throwing an arc of light across the shadowy loft. The apple heap was trampled, disarrayed, and the scattered fruit rolled, thumping hollowly, under her stumbling feet. Pax stood stiffly, cautious and curious, and beyond him Joe knelt beside the open trapdoor, the trapdoor for forking hay down to the stable. Phoebe saw the opening filled with a grotesque, meaningless shape, and then she saw it was the heifer, hanging head down in the narrow stairwell. All she could see was the slender rump and lower back wedged tight in the aperture, the hind legs caught on the floor boards, kicking feebly, and the long fringed tail thrashing blindly back and forth across the pitiful, terror-soiled buttocks. From below, the gasping cries came up in rhythmic agony, hushed a little but not stopped by Joe's quiet voice talking and talking to her as he crouched at the opening, trying to see how she was caught.

"The apples," Phoebe moaned, flinging herself down beside him, "she smelled the apples and came to find them." But Joe had jumped up, taking the flashlight, and was running out and around to the stable door below. Phoebe ran after, her heart hammering, the lantern swinging insanely from her hand, and Pax eager at her heels. The low, oak-beamed ceiling and thick stone walls of the stable made a warm, cozy cave, and in it the heifer hung crazily upside down, her head and one foreleg wedged at an impossible angle between two treads of the heavy, ladderlike stairs. The wedged foreleg was broken, bone thrusting through the skin, and in her struggles she was slowly strangling herself. In the lantern light her eyes rolled whitely, blindly, and the helpless, rasping cries grew steadily fainter. Beyond the plank partition the horses stomped restlessly in their stalls, and through it all Daisy stood facing the stairwell, shaking her head in her stanchion and shifting ceaselessly in troubled bewilderment on her clean straw bedding. She lowed nervously, swinging her hindquarters from one side to the other while Joe and Phoebe worked desperately with the tortured heifer.

"If we could saw the stair!" Phoebe cried in anguish. "Wouldn't that free her?"

"It's no use," Joe said. "The weight of her fall would snap her neck. Phoebe, you'd better get the gun."

"No, Joe, oh, no! Can't we lift her, can't we try again?" she begged frantically.

Joe's face was drawn and despairing. "It's no use. She's close to six hundred pounds and there's no way to lever her up." The heifer bawled again, a hopeless choking cry, and in the lantern light her

178

free leg kicked futilely in the air. "She's suffering, Phoebe. Get the gun."

Phoebe had turned, blindly, and was rushing out the door when Joe called, "Phoebe, bring a knife, too, the sharp knife in the kitchen." For a moment she didn't understand, and then she turned back whimpering in horror. "No, no, we can't, I won't!" Across the shadowy stable Joe's voice rose in furious torment. "Get the knife! You know we can't waste food." He stared at her relentlessly. "We wanted a farm, didn't we? To make our own life, our own food? We've eaten meat all our lives, now we've got to earn it."

Wordlessly Phoebe went out, Joe's voice, soft and exhausted now, calling after her, "Hurry, baby, I don't want to leave her." Running mechanically back to the house, Phoebe kept thinking dully, the gun and the knife, the gun and the knife. The .22 rifle for shooting rats, used only twice even for that, and the long, clean knife, the knife for slicing cabbage from the garden, for cutting the fresh-baked bread she was so proud of. With the flashlight she found the gun and the box of cartridges on the parlor mantel, the knife in the kitchen drawer, and not thinking at all, moving in a desperate, mindless agony, she ran with them back to the stable. Joe still stood beside the heifer, his arm under the tawny, gasping chest in unavailing support, still comforting the Jersey in a hoarse, gentle voice, while Pax lay quiet in the straw, alert and watching, and Daisy lowed uneasily.

Phoebe laid the knife, the gun and cartridges beside Joe and turned away. She went to Daisy quickly and unfastened her stanchion, turning her toward the door out to the barnyard. With clumsy hands she got the door open and Daisy out, the stiff cow legs hesitating as always before the step over the doorsill. She walked beside her down the slope of the pasture, and they were well away from the stable when Phoebe heard the shot. She stopped then, letting Daisy swing slowly on by herself into the darkness, and for a long moment she stood quiet, shaking in the cold.

She was still standing there when Joe shouted from the stable, "Phoebe, call Pax." Numbly she walked back to the door, and in a fleeting glimpse she saw the heifer hanging limp in the lamplight, a dark stain on the stairs beneath her head, and Joe shoving Pax roughly away from a bucket that stood on the floor. Pax came re-

179

luctantly when she called, and holding him wearily, detachedly, without love, she took him with her back to the house.

When Joe came in they sat in the cold kitchen for several minutes before they went to bed. At last Joe said, "I'll try and get Mr. Myers first thing in the morning to help me butcher." He looked at Phoebe sadly in exhaustion. "You know we had to, don't you?" She looked at him hopelessly, nodding slowly. "It was all my fault," she said, "all of it. I wouldn't let you wire the fence. I killed her, I killed our sweet Jersey heifer," and when Joe put his arms around her she finally began to cry. "No, baby, don't say that," Joe said painfully. "It was a crazy accident and no one's fault." But Phoebe shook her head. "I killed her. I laughed when she pushed down the fence rail, I didn't care, I liked her to be saucy. And only when she threatened me," Phoebe sobbed, "only her horns, only her horns made me afraid."

After her tears Phoebe slept, but she woke early, long before milking time. She lay quietly in bed, her body aching, her mind calm but filled with a clear despair. Beside her Joe slept deeply, and for a moment she felt a bitter, shocked wave of resentment that he still slept, escaping so easily; but turning her head stiffly on the pillow, she saw the anxious lines tensing the sleeping eyelids, the jaw clenched tight and grinding faintly in a dream of agonized effort. Looking at his sleeping face, she was washed with shame and racking love—beside his goodness, his unforced selflessness, she was a monster of childish frailty. Oh, it's easy, it's easy, her mind whispered, to scream and run and cover your eyes, but how much harder to pull the trigger in love, to bleed the dead for the sake of the living. Always, always Joe had had the hard part and she the easy mournings, the easy joys. For a moment in the cold gray light she thought hopefully: It will be different when we have children. Then the hard part will be mine, our life will be fairer; but when she tried to vision it she saw with aching conviction that even then it wouldn't change. After the painful hour of birth all would be as before, and she saw herself a wayward, feckless mother, overemotional, given to reasonless euphorias and panics, unable to provide that calm and certainty that children need.

Just before sunrise Phoebe got up and went down to start the kitchen stove. Pax slept curled tightly in his wicker chair, but when he woke he unwound happily, yawning and stretching down onto the floor, and came up wagging his wavy-haired rear. At first she looked at him with horror, unable to touch him, remembering in a flash his avid interest in the bucket in the stable. He came to her like a friendly, handsome stranger, and even when she knelt, suddenly humble, and stroked his soft liver-and-white coat and bur-brocaded ears, she went on thinking: But how can I ever really know him, know the real meaning of his life?

She went on out for firewood and kindling, and coming back from the woodpile with her arms full she stopped above the pasture, shivering in the still, gray light. Below the pin oak Daisy lay placidly on the drying grass, her head held high in quiet dignity as she chewed faithfully on her cud. The fence rail was still down where the heifer had got out last night, but Daisy ignored it, content by herself in the deserted pasture. Like Pax, she met the morning serene, untouched by tragedy, and for a long time Phoebe stood watching her from another world. Of course they can't care, she thought, watching all alone; it's part of their innocence. She thought of all the innocent ones—the horses and chickens, the black snakes and the rats—and she knew at last that she was hopelessly excluded, forever responsible. The serpent had been there in the garden all the time, a thousand apples joyfully offered and taken. She heard again the county agent's wise, indulgent voice, and already she saw the barbed wire strung along the wooden fenceposts, Daisy's next calf born and sent away, flock after flock of chickens in their biennial cycle of birth, production, and early, practical death. She turned away, lonely and chilled, but with her armful of firewood she went on resolutely through her own human cycle, up the steps and into the kitchen, to kindle once more the comforting fire for breakfast.

from Tomorrow

THE INVADERS

ROBIE MACAULEY *is a native of Grand Rapids, Michigan, where he was born in 1919. He wrote his first novel at the age of twelve,* The Boy Crusader. *He studied under Ford Madox Ford at Olivet College and under John Crowe Ransom at Kenyon. He says these two men taught him most of what he knows about writing. Mr. Macauley spent four years in the Army, doing counter-intelligence work in France, Germany, and Czechoslovakia, winding up finally in Japan. Afterward he taught at Bard College and at the University of Iowa. He began writing seriously three years ago and won the* Furioso *prize for fiction in 1949 with a story called "A Nest of Gentlefolk." Since then his stories have appeared in several magazines, including* The Sewanee Review, *and he also wrote the introduction to Ford Madox Ford's tetralogy,* Parade's End. *He is married and is teaching at the Woman's College of the University of North Carolina.*

Like bright figures on a poster they suddenly appeared at the top of the stairway, outlined against the sky. He was dark and she was blond as the summer morning around her, a tall, easy-standing girl, deerlike, trim, and nordic-faced as any printed model on a fashion page. She wore a fire-colored playsuit belted with white, blue sandals, and she carried a basket on her arm. She could not resist raising the other arm just as they reached the dune edge, as if she were demanding to be photographed by some ready camera, ever prepared for her newest step or gesture.

"Oh, how glorious!" she said.

He laid down the things he had been carrying and together they stood and looked.

That early June had been racked with storms and filled with an overplenty of rain. The doors and windows of the cottages to the right and left of them on the dune and farther back in the woods were still blind with nailed-up boards or shutters and, driving along the road to the shore, they had met no one, because it was nearly the first day of real summer weather we had that year.

The dune was tall and it was as if they looked from a high theater balcony down onto a tremendous vacant stage. Over the slightly curved shoreline the very small waves folded themselves gently while the whole expanse of water out to the far horizon glistened like a sheet of stretched blue silk.

"We have it all to ourselves," he said. "That's fine."

She made a half-circle sweep with her arm. "Is that all it means to you? Look, Gib, doesn't it suggest something? I mean, doesn't it suggest something more than just that to you?"

He had decided to pick up their things again and had managed to get most of them into his arms. "Yes, it's a nice view," he said, "but I've seen it lots of times before."

"Not *that*. Don't you see what I mean? I mean it's like our life together after we got married—no one has been there before; it's all ours to do with what we please."

"I suppose so," he said, starting down the stairs. "But I hope it won't be as empty as all that."

"Now you're being nasty, Gib."

"No, I wasn't. Now look out for these stairs. They're rotten and one good shake would knock them down."

"I wish you wouldn't snub me like that. Sometimes I think you don't appreciate things the way I do."

"I'm just busy with all this gear," he said.

She followed him down the steep stairs, and when they got to the level of the beach they went directly down to within five yards of the water. As he laid their blanket out on the sand and put their surfboard, picnic basket, and towels to one side, she stripped off the red garment; underneath it she had a bathing suit that shone green like the water in a quiet shoal. They lay down flat in the sun for a while and watched two clouds that swam like lonely white fish in the sky.

He watched them for a long time as they glided through the airy blue pool and out of sight. He closed his eyes, but after a few minutes

183

he awoke with the feeling of lying in a bath of warm honey. The sun had risen higher and it seemed to be nearly noon.

She lay on her back and he could see that she was now asleep. To his eyes she was like the elegant landscape of some familiar province as he lay there barely breathing. Sitting, he looked down on her as an aviator might look down on his own country and recognize the gentle heights, the rolling plains, and the symmetrically built town of her face. He closed his eyes and lay back again. A familiar country? Yes, something like that. When he had asked her to marry him he was not quite so aware of the borders and confines, he thought drowsily. Past the country club on one side, the suburban home on another, the good schools, the parties, the familiar names, was an unexplored wilderness, a wild Ireland beyond the pale. There was a certain dark frontier farther than which one could not go. As he fell asleep again he dreamed about riding a bicycle around an enclosed track with no exit.

In time she awoke, and she awakened him by tickling his ribs and kissing him on the forehead.

"Shall we go swimming now?"

While they were dozing a brisker wind had come up, stirring the surface of the water into rough little whitecaps that broke on the shallows about a hundred feet out. He picked up the surfboard and she followed him to the edge of the beach. Janet was somewhat afraid of the water. She had explained it by saying that someone had pushed her into a deep place once when she was a child and she had nearly drowned. She always asked a hundred questions to reassure herself before she finally put her foot in. Is it cold? It looks terribly cold, doesn't it? Do you think there's any undertow today? Now let's not go too far out, shall we? It is freezing, isn't it?

She followed by inches; he was already pushing the white board through the waves toward the spot where the breakers curled over. If you took the right moment and jumped on the board just ahead of a breaking wave it would carry you on the crest nearly to shore. He showed her how.

A wave rolled toward them, bigger than any of the others. "Now!" he said, and boosted her onto the board. She slithered her body until she got firmly settled and grasped the handholds at the side. He swung the front end around a little so the wave would catch her evenly. It was almost on them. "Hold tight!" he yelled, and dived beneath the water.

As long as his breath held out he swam beneath the surface. The ridged sand of the bottom slid under his hands and a colder current knifed along his backbone. It was quiet here; the water scarcely seemed to move. He opened his eyes and thought that fish swimming in this green silence would never realize the dash and fury of the surface. But he preferred the waves. He put his hands flat on the sand and gave himself a push that plunged him up and into the air again. He looked for her.

But he had got turned around in swimming under water and he was facing down the beach. He was suddenly aware that the beach was no longer empty. He tossed his head to throw the water out of his eyes and began a slow sidestroke.

There were two figures on the beach, two men walking along the edge of the sand about a quarter of a mile away. They were not wearing swimming suits, they were fully dressed, and, though close to the shore line, they were not wading. They walked along slowly side by side as if going down a city street. He caught the glint of the sun on skin and then he realized that one was black.

He had only a minute to wonder about them because in the next he heard Janet calling to him, "Hi! It got away from me, Gib."

She was floundering in the shallows where the wave had carried her and trying to stand up in the riptide. She got up and waved to him. In the tossing water he could see the white back of the surfboard being carried down shore. It was about halfway between himself and the two men walking along the beach.

Then she saw them. She slowly lowered her arm and even at this distance he could feel her astonishment. Not that there was anything odd about other people on the beach—it was usually crowded this time of year—or that there was anything particularly strange about these two, but they had become so accustomed in the last few hours of thinking of themselves as the only two people in the world, had so accepted and enjoyed their isolation, that anybody's coming would be a shock. He planned to remark something about Crusoe and Friday when he came up with her. But now he had to swim for the board and it was getting farther and farther away.

He went as fast as he could, but before he had gone very far he hoped that the two men had sighted it. He hadn't noticed before how strong the downshore current was. It seemed to push him along, but the board was traveling faster.

They stopped, and one of them stooped and rolled up his trousers legs. He was coming out into the water now and Gib could see him lifting the board up. Then they came on down the beach at the same pace toward the spot on shore where Janet was standing. Both of them had their arms hooked over the board.

He reached the shallow water and stood up; when he got to the shore they were just handing the surfboard to Janet. "Thanks," she said with a smile. "It knocked me over and ran away." They didn't smile in return. "O.K., lady," the white one said. "It's O.K."

They were not men, but boys. They both seemed to be about sixteen or seventeen, though they were short, shorter than Janet. He took Janet's arm and they went up and sat on the blanket and lighted cigarettes.

The boys stood and stared at the surfboard which lay near the water where she had dropped it. They turned it over and looked at the other side. Evidently it was sandy because they scooped up water in their hands and tried to wash it off. "That's O.K.," Gib said. "It'll be all right." The boys came up and sat down carefully, about four yards away from them.

The white one had skin the color of skim milk. He was either completely and prematurely bald or else his head had been closely shaven recently. He had a small bunched face with sharp features that reminded Gib of some kind of tool, a monkey wrench, perhaps. The other one had closecut hair, too, and a flat face like an imprint in some thick, warm tar. They sat close together, arms folded over their knees, and occasionally seemed to give each other a slight push or nudge, like a signal.

They were wearing high bootlike shoes, which they had put aside on the sand, but that was the only way they had prepared for the beach. Their shirts and trousers were made of similar gray stuff and the pants legs of the one who had gone after the surfboard were black from being wet. Except for the slight movements of shoulders or elbows, they sat very quietly, gazing at Janet and Gib.

Gib felt that he had to say something. "Where you fellows from?" he asked.

"Flint," said the colored boy.

The other one said something to Gib. It was a strange accent, Polish, he thought, and the words were run together. "We come up to the beach, we hitched up for the day," was what it sounded like. It might be a speech impediment, Gib wasn't sure.

"Aren't you going in swimming?"

"No, we ain't going in swimming." This was the colored boy and, though the words sounded unfriendly, the tone was soft and meaningless.

"We ain't got no suits," he finally said.

They asked about the surfboard. It was a neat board, they said. They had never heard of anything like that. Carried the lady right into shore.

After that no one said anything for a while. Janet had been rubbing suntan lotion on her shoulders, but when he started to light a cigarette, she took him quickly by the arm. "Let's go back in the water," she said, and ran into the waves, still pulling her rubber cap over her ears.

She was ahead of him all the way out to the sandbar where the waves broke. They dived through one together and when they came up she said, "Listen, I wanted to talk to you. What do those two want?"

In the trough of the wave before the next one came they stood and looked back to the shore. The two figures had moved; they were a few feet out in the water pushing the surfboard around between them. They were being careful not to let it get away.

The next wave slapped the swimmers before they knew it; it seemed to break just behind their ears, rush over them, and pull them violently toward shore. When they emerged, she took his arm with both hands.

"They're up to something, I know it. Did you notice their clothes? They look as if they'd run away from a reformatory." Her fingers gripped harder against his skin and her voice was drawn and uneasy.

He was a little dismayed by her show of nerves. "Well," he said, "I think it's obvious that they think we're in *their* way. They came up here to go swimming. They haven't any suits and they can't swim naked until we go away."

"Maybe you're right," she said doubtfully, "but they give me the shivers anyway. They don't seem like *boys,* do they? There's something awfully grim about them."

"Forget it," he said, pretending to duck her. "We'll move our things up the beach and eat lunch. They probably won't stick around long if we ignore them." He dived over the next wave and they started for shore.

A little compunction, a little guilt troubled him over his compromise with her fears. The boys had seemed only somewhat lost and lonely to him. If they lived in a crowded tenement, as he supposed, this stretch of empty sand and empty water must bewilder them more than he could understand. But he forgot about that as he raced her to the beach.

They did as he had said. The boys, now sitting close together in the same spot, watched their movements of gathering their things and going off without any question. They were still sitting there when Janet and Gib got out of sight around a place where the beach narrowed and the dune came close to the water.

"We might have offered them a sandwich," he said as they were eating. She shook her head.

"It was better not to. We'd have them around like flies all afternoon."

After they had finished eating they lay still on the blanket again, letting the sun cook them. He drifted again into the dozing state, dangling between real sleep and real wakefulness. Suddenly he was disturbed. It was nothing more than a momentary change in the light or the air, as if a shadow had passed across the sun. He felt that he must open his eyes, wake up. Slowly he did. They were sitting there less than ten feet away, staring silently at his face.

"What do you want?" he asked, and sat up. They sat together just as before, one head dazzlingly black in the sun, close to the naked blue-white one. He felt that she was stirring on the blanket, and in a minute she would see them too. It seemed impossible to explain their strange insistence, this speechless patience, in his own terms. She would be frightened when she saw them here again and a little of her panic would take hold of him, he knew—not entirely, but just a little more, and he was afraid of it.

He spoke slowly. "You fellows must be hungry?" He waited for an answer, but all he saw was a minute movement as if they had both at the same time shifted a little nearer the blanket. "Would you like a couple of sandwiches? We have some left over." They were silent.

He went to the picnic basket on hands and knees, taking care not to disturb her. He reached in and took out the leftover sandwiches, still wrapped in wax paper. The white boy extended his hand and took them. Gib was aware that she was awake now and listening.

"Why don't you go away somewhere and eat them?" For a minute he was not sure that they would pay any attention. Finally they rose slowly and went about twenty yards away; then they sat down again. They began to unwrap the sandwiches.

"*Get rid of them,*" she whispered. "They're planning something, Gib, I know it. They're after us." Her whisper was hysterical; he could see a white bloodless band running across her cheeks beneath the tanned surface. "I can tell."

"Nonsense," he whispered back, but the very violence of her exaggeration shook him.

"They have criminal faces," she said.

"Now don't be silly, Janet. They haven't done a thing. They're pests, sure, but that doesn't mean they're up to anything." But the confidence had gone out of his words and he was aware of an angry pulsing under his ribs. "By God, if I thought so . . ." he said.

"Look!" she whispered sharply.

They had stood up, dropping their sandwiches in the sand, and were looking at some spot down the beach, near the edge of the water. "What is it?" she asked. They could not tell. Gib got up on his knees to see. The two boys were going forward in an awkward stalk. They both stopped to gather something and then broke into a trot.

Gib saw what it was. There were five or six sandpipers hopping in their delicate spinsterish fashion along the edge of the shore.

The boys were running at them now and the birds took alarm. The boys stopped and began to throw the stones they had picked up as the frightened birds scattered on the beach or began to fly out over the water. One of the attackers gave a quick cut-off laugh and then they were running down to the edge of the water.

"They're coming back!" she said.

They stood looking down at Gib and Janet. The colored one laid the sandpiper on the ground as if it were an offering or a prophecy. Neither of them said anything yet; the colored boy smoothed the dead feathers with his hand and he smiled as he did so. When he smiled, Janet screamed.

"Get out of here!" The words shot out of her mouth. "Get out of here and leave us alone. You've bothered us enough today. We don't want you, understand? We don't want you; you can go wherever you're going and take your bird with you. *Go away!*" Gib realized that he had taken hold of her hand and that his other hand was clenched in a fist. His breath was pumping; he knew he was hers.

They were undecided and they both kept glancing down at the bird as if they expected it to tell them something. The colored boy made some kind of gesture with his open hand in front of him, the palm showing pink in the center. At last he said, "We . . . I don't know. We ain't bothering you."

"Get out of here," Gib said. Now he was sure of himself. "We don't want you." The white boy sat down.

Janet's face was white now; it didn't seem pretty any longer. She was gathering up their things and with no more words Gib helped her. They put everything together and started down the beach, walking close to the water so that they could move faster on the hard sand.

"Are they?" she asked after a while. He had kept glancing back. "Yes," he said.

The stairway was nearer; they had only about fifty yards to go. He looked back again.

"They're about a hundred feet behind us," he said.

They got to the bottom of the stairs and she started to climb, panting from the exertion. He went a little more slowly, shifting the things in his arms so that he might drop them easily. He looked back and saw that the two were close behind them. They were standing at the foot of the stairs now. Their faces were raised toward him, and it seemed to him for a moment that they looked only puzzled and curious.

The colored boy stood a few paces in front of the other with his hands dropped by his sides. Suddenly he made that odd empty gesture with the palm of his hand and Gib paused near the top of the stairway.

But it was the white boy who spoke in his queer accent. His voice was windy and panting.

"Mister," he said, "give us a lift out to the highway?"

"No!" she said from behind him. "Hurry, Gib, hurry and for God's sake watch out." Her voice had risen to the pitch of a bird's shrill, dying scream. "Watch out!"

Gib ran up the last few steps. He could see the boys stand there for a moment and then they came forward and began to climb the stairs. He saw the black hand and the white hand clenched on the railing. "Gib!"

He threw the blanket and the surfboard on the ground and faced around. He watched them climb until they were less than ten feet below him. "Gib!" she whispered.

They were close. He knew what he had to do from the tone of her biting whisper. He wrenched at one of the 2x4 railings and the rotted thing came away with the pull. He saw the two faces, one black, one white, tottering in front of him. He swung the club with all his force, and he saw the whole rickety structure give way. At the moment the blood splashed on his hand, the stairway fell. It seemed to burst into chunks and fragments of wood and avalanche down the steep dune. In the tangle of wood and sand and bodies he could see a raised black hand, open in the air with a pink spot showing in the center of the palm.

from Mademoiselle

THE SOJOURNER

CARSON McCULLERS *was born in 1917 and her home town is Columbus, Georgia. After finishing high school in Columbus, she studied at Columbia and at New York University. She married Reeves McCullers in 1937. She appeared in the 1943 O. Henry collection with "A Tree. A Rock. A Cloud." Her novels are* The Heart Is a Lonely Hunter, *1940;* Reflections in a Golden Eye, *1941; and* A Member of the Wedding, *1946. She was awarded Guggenheim Fellowships in 1942 and 1946 and was made a member of the American Academy of Arts and Letters in 1943. She made a play from* A Member of the Wedding *which was produced in 1950, and which won the New York Drama Critics' Award for the best American play of the year, as well as the Donaldson Award for the best play of the period. Mrs. McCullers's collected works appeared in May of this year. She is at present working on a novel called* The Clock Without Hands, *with its setting in the South. She now lives in Nyack, New York.*

The twilight border between sleep and waking was a Roman one this morning: splashing fountains and arched, narrow streets, the golden lavish city of blossoms and age-soft stone. Sometimes in this semi-consciousness he sojourned again in Paris, or war German rubble, or Swiss skiing and a snow hotel. Sometimes, also, in a fallow Georgia field at hunting dawn. Rome it was this morning in the year-less region of dreams.

John Ferris awoke in a room in a New York hotel. He had the feeling that something unpleasant was awaiting him—what it was, he did not know. The feeling, submerged by matinal necessities, lingered even after he had dressed and gone downstairs. It was a cloud-

192

less autumn day and the pale sunlight sliced between the pastel sky-scrapers. Ferris went into the next-door drugstore and sat at the end booth next to the window glass that overlooked the sidewalk. He ordered an American breakfast with scrambled eggs and sausage.

Ferris had come from Paris to his father's funeral which had taken place the week before in his home town in Georgia. The shock of death had made him aware of youth already passed. His hair was receding and the veins in his now naked temples were pulsing and prominent and his body was spare except for an incipient belly bulge. Ferris had loved his father and the bond between them had once been extraordinarily close—but the years had somehow unraveled this filial devotion; the death, expected for a long time, had left him with an unforeseen dismay. He had stayed as long as possible to be near his mother and brothers at home. His plane for Paris was to leave the next morning.

Ferris pulled out his address book to verify a number. He turned the pages with growing attentiveness. Names and addresses from New York, the capitals of Europe, a few faint ones from his home state in the South. Faded, printed names, sprawled drunken ones. Betty Wills: a random love, married now. Charlie Williams: wounded in the Hürtgen Forest, unheard of since. Grand old Williams—did he live or die? Don Walker: a B.T.O. in television, getting rich. Henry Green: hit the skids after the war, in a sanitarium now, they say. Cozie Hall: he had heard that she was dead. Heedless, laughing Cozie—it was strange to think that she, too, silly girl, could die. As Ferris closed the address book, he suffered a sense of hazard, transience, almost of fear.

It was then that his body jerked suddenly. He was staring out of the window when there, on the sidewalk, passing by, was his ex-wife. Elizabeth passed quite close to him, walking slowly. He could not understand the wild quiver of his heart, nor the following sense of recklessness and grace that lingered after she was gone.

Quickly Ferris paid his check and rushed out to the sidewalk. Elizabeth stood on the corner waiting to cross Fifth Avenue. He hurried toward her meaning to speak, but the lights changed and she crossed the street before he reached her. Ferris followed. On the other side he could easily have overtaken her, but he found himself lagging unaccountably. Her fair brown hair was plainly rolled, and as he watched her Ferris recalled that once his father had remarked that Elizabeth had a "beautiful carriage." She turned at the next corner and Ferris followed, although by now his intention to overtake her had disappeared. Ferris questioned the bodily disturbance that the sight of Elizabeth aroused in him, the dampness of his hands, the hard heart strokes.

It was eight years since Ferris had last seen his ex-wife. He knew that long ago she had married again. And there were children. During recent years he had seldom thought of her. But at first, after the divorce, the loss had almost destroyed him. Then, after the anodyne of time, he had loved again, and then again. Jeannine, she was now. Certainly his love for his ex-wife was long since past. So why the unhinged body, the shaken mind? He knew only that his clouded heart was oddly dissonant with the sunny, candid autumn day. Ferris wheeled suddenly and, walking with long strides, almost running, hurried back to the hotel.

Ferris poured himself a drink, although it was not yet eleven o'clock. He sprawled out in an armchair like a man exhausted, nursing his glass of bourbon and water. He had a full day ahead of him as he was leaving by plane the next morning for Paris. He checked over his obligations: take luggage to Air France, lunch with his boss, buy shoes and an overcoat. And something—wasn't there something else? Ferris finished his drink and opened the telephone directory.

His decision to call his ex-wife was impulsive. The number was under Bailey, the husband's name, and he called before he had much time for self-debate. He and Elizabeth had exchanged cards at Christmastime, and Ferris had sent a carving set when he received the announcement of her wedding. There was no reason *not* to call. But as he waited, listening to the ring at the other end, misgiving fretted him.

Elizabeth answered; her familiar voice was a fresh shock to him. Twice he had to repeat his name, but when he was identified, she sounded glad. He explained he was in town for only that day. They had a theater engagement, she said—but she wondered if he would come by for an early dinner. Ferris said he would be delighted.

As he went from one engagement to another, he was still bothered at odd moments by the feeling that something necessary was forgotten. Ferris bathed and changed in the late afternoon, often think-

194

expatriate - leaves country for good.
evading life; cheats time.

ing about Jeannine: he would be with her the following night. "Jeannine," he would say, "I happened to run into my ex-wife when I was in New York. Had dinner with her. And her husband, of course. It was strange seeing her after all these years."

Elizabeth lived in the East Fifties, and as Ferris taxied uptown he glimpsed at intersections the lingering sunset, but by the time he reached his destination it was already autumn dark. The place was a building with a marquee and a doorman, and the apartment was on the seventh floor.

"Come in, Mr. Ferris."

Braced for Elizabeth or even the unimagined husband, Ferris was astonished by the freckled red-haired child; he had known of the children, but his mind had failed somehow to acknowledge them. Surprise made him step back awkwardly.

"This is our apartment," the child said politely. "Aren't you Mr. Ferris? I'm Billy. Come in."

In the living room beyond the hall the husband provided another surprise; he, too, had not been acknowledged emotionally. Bailey was a lumbering red-haired man with a deliberate manner. He rose and extended a welcoming hand.

"I'm Bill Bailey. Glad to see you. Elizabeth will be in in a minute. She's finishing dressing."

The last words struck a gliding series of vibrations, memories of the other years. Fair Elizabeth, rosy and naked before her bath. Half dressed before the mirror of her dressing table, brushing her fine chestnut hair. Sweet, casual intimacy, the soft-fleshed loveliness indisputably possessed. Ferris shrank from the unbidden memories and compelled himself to meet Bill Bailey's gaze.

"Billy, will you please bring that tray of drinks from the kitchen table?"

The child obeyed promptly, and when he was gone Ferris remarked conversationally, "Fine boy you have there."

"We think so."

Flat silence until the child returned with a tray of glasses and a cocktail shaker of martinis. With the priming drinks they pumped up conversation: Russia, they spoke of, and the New York rain-making, and the apartment situation in Manhattan and Paris.

"Mr. Ferris is flying all the way across the ocean tomorrow," Bailey

alcohol , jealousy , money probl

195

said to the little boy who was perched on the arm of his chair, quiet and well behaved. "I bet you would like to be a stowaway in his suitcase."

Billy pushed back his limp bangs. "I want to fly in an airplane and be a newspaperman like Mr. Ferris." He added with sudden assurance, "That's what I would like to do when I am big."

Bailey said, "I thought you wanted to be a doctor."

"I do!" said Billy. "I would like to be both. I want to be a atombomb scientist too."

Elizabeth came in carrying in her arms a baby girl.

"Oh, John!" she said. She settled the baby in the father's lap. "It's grand to see you. I'm awfully glad you could come."

The little girl sat demurely on Bailey's knees. She wore a pale pink crepe de Chine frock, smocked around the yoke with rose, and a matching silk hair ribbon tying back her pale soft curls. Her skin was summer tanned and her brown eyes flecked with gold and laughing. When she reached up and fingered her father's horn-rimmed glasses, he took them off and let her look through them a moment. "How's my old Candy?"

Elizabeth was very beautiful, more beautiful perhaps than he had ever realized. Her straight clean hair was shining. Her face was softer, glowing and serene. It was a madonna loveliness, dependent on the family ambiance.

"You've hardly changed at all," Elizabeth said, "but it has been a long time."

"Eight years." His hand touched his thinning hair self-consciously while further amenities were exchanged.

Ferris felt himself suddenly a spectator—an interloper among these Baileys. Why had he come? He suffered. His own life seemed so solitary, a fragile column supporting nothing amidst the wreckage of the years. He felt he could not bear much longer to stay in the family room.

He glanced at his watch. "You're going to the theater?"

"It's a shame," Elizabeth said, "but we've had this engagement for more than a month. But surely, John, you'll be staying home one of these days before long. You're not going to be an expatriate, are you?"

"Expatriate," Ferris repeated. "I don't much like the word."

"What's a better word?" she asked.

He thought for a moment. "Sojourner might do."

Ferris glanced again at his watch, and again Elizabeth apologized. "If only we had known ahead of time——"

"I just had this day in town. I came home unexpectedly. You see, Papa died last week."

"Papa Ferris is dead?"

"Yes, at Johns Hopkins. He had been sick there nearly a year. The funeral was down home in Georgia."

"Oh, I'm so sorry, John. Papa Ferris was always one of my favorite people."

The little boy moved from behind the chair so that he could look into his mother's face. He asked, "Who is dead?"

Ferris was oblivious to apprehension; he was thinking of his father's death. He saw again the outstretched body on the quilted silk within the coffin. The corpse flesh was bizarrely rouged and the familiar hands lay massive and joined above a spread of funeral roses. The memory closed and Ferris awakened to Elizabeth's calm voice.

"Mr. Ferris' father, Billy. A really grand person. Somebody you didn't know."

"But why did you call him *Papa* Ferris?"

Bailey and Elizabeth exchanged a trapped look. It was Bailey who answered the questioning child. "A long time ago," he said, "your mother and Mr. Ferris were once married. Before you were born—a long time ago."

"Mr. Ferris?"

The little boy stared at Ferris, amazed and unbelieving. And Ferris's eyes, as he returned the gaze, were somehow unbelieving too. Was it indeed true that at one time he had called this stranger, Elizabeth, Little Butterduck during nights of love, that they had lived together, shared perhaps a thousand days and nights and—finally—endured in the misery of sudden solitude the fiber by fiber (jealousy, alcohol, and money quarrels) destruction of the fabric of married love?

Bailey said to the children, "It's somebody's suppertime. Come on now."

"But Daddy! Mama and Mr. Ferris—I——"

Billy's everlasting eyes—perplexed and with a glimmer of hostility —reminded Ferris of the gaze of another child. It was the young son of Jeannine—a boy of seven with a shadowed little face and knobby knees whom Ferris avoided and usually forgot.

"Quick march!" Bailey gently turned Billy toward the door. "Say good night now, son."

"Good night, Mr. Ferris." He added resentfully, "I thought I was staying up for the cake."

"You can come in afterward for the cake," Elizabeth said. "Run along now with Daddy for your supper."

Ferris and Elizabeth were alone. The weight of the situation descended on those first moments of silence. Ferris asked permission to pour himself another drink and Elizabeth set the cocktail shaker on the table at his side. He looked at the grand piano and noticed the music on the rack.

"Do you still play as beautifully as you used to?"

"I still enjoy it."

"Please play, Elizabeth."

Elizabeth arose immediately. Her readiness to perform when asked had always been one of her amiabilities; she never hung back, apologized. Now as she approached the piano there was the added readiness of relief.

She began with a Bach prelude and fugue. The prelude was as gaily iridescent as a prism in a morning room. The first voice of the fugue, an announcement pure and solitary, was repeated intermingling with a second voice, and again repeated within an elaborated frame, the multiple music, horizontal and serene, flowed with unhurried majesty. The principal melody was woven with two other voices, embellished with countless ingenuities—now dominant, again submerged, it had the sublimity of a single thing that does not fear surrender to the whole. Toward the end, the density of the material gathered for the last enriched insistence on the dominant first motif and with a chorded final statement the fugue ended. Ferris rested his head on the chair back and closed his eyes. In the following silence a clear, high voice came from the room down the hall.

"Daddy, how *could* Mama and Mr. Ferris——" A door was closed.

The piano began again—what was this music? Unplaced, familiar, the limpid melody had lain a long while dormant in his heart. Now it spoke to him of another time, another place—it was the music Elizabeth used to play. The delicate air summoned a wilderness of memory. Ferris was lost in the riot of past longings, conflicts, ambivalent desires. Strange that the music, catalyst for this tumultuous anarchy, was so serene and clear. The singing melody was broken off by the appearance of the maid.

"Miz Bailey, dinner is out on the table now."

Even after Ferris was seated at the table between his host and hostess, the unfinished music still overcast his mood. He was a little drunk.

"*L'improvisation de la vie humaine,*" he said. "There's nothing that makes you so aware of the improvisation of human existence as a song unfinished. Or an old address book."

"Address book?" repeated Bailey. Then he stopped, noncommittal and polite.

"You're still the same odd boy, Johnny," Elizabeth said with a trace of the old tenderness.

It was a southern dinner that evening, and the dishes were his old favorites. They had fried chicken and corn pudding and rich, glozed candied sweet potatoes. During the meal Elizabeth kept alive a conversation when the silences were overlong. And it came about that Ferris was led to speak of Jeannine.

"I first knew Jeannine last autumn—about this time of the year—in Italy. She's a singer and she had an engagement in Rome. I expect we will be married soon."

The words seemed so true, inevitable, that Ferris did not at first acknowledge to himself the lie. He and Jeannine had never in that year spoken of marriage. And indeed she was still married—to a White Russian money-changer in Paris from whom she had been separated for five years. But it was too late to correct the lie. Already Elizabeth was saying: "This really makes me glad to know. Congratulations, Johnny."

He tried to make amends with truth. "The Roman autumn is so beautiful. Balmy and blossoming." He added: "Jeannine has a little boy of six. A curious trilingual little fellow. We go to the Tuileries sometimes."

A lie again. He had taken the boy once to the gardens. The sallow foreign child in shorts that bared his spindly legs had sailed his boat

199

in the concrete pond and ridden the pony. The child had wanted to go in to the puppet show. But there was not time, for Ferris had an engagement at the Scribe Hotel. He had promised they would go to the guignol another afternoon. Only once had he taken Valentin to the Tuileries.

There was a stir. The maid brought in a white-frosted cake with pink candles. The children entered in their night clothes. Ferris still did not understand.

"Happy birthday, John," Elizabeth said. "Blow out the candles."

Ferris recognized his birthday date. The candles blew out lingeringly and there was the smell of burning wax. Ferris was thirty-eight years old. The veins in his temples darkened and pulsed visibly.

"It's time you started for the theater."

Ferris thanked Elizabeth for the birthday dinner and said the appropriate good-bys. The whole family saw him to the door.

A high, thin moon shone above the jagged, dark skyscrapers. The streets were windy, cold. Ferris hurried to Third Avenue and hailed a cab. He gazed at the nocturnal city with the deliberate attentiveness of departure and perhaps farewell. He was alone. He longed for flighttime and the coming journey.

The next day he looked down on the city from the air, burnished in sunlight, toylike, precise. Then America was left behind and there was only the Atlantic and the distant European shore. The ocean was milky pale and placid beneath the clouds. Ferris dozed most of the day. Toward dark he was thinking of Elizabeth and the visit of the previous evening. He thought of Elizabeth among her family with longing, gentle envy, and inexplicable regret. He sought the melody, the unfinished air, that had so moved him. The cadence, some unrelated tones, were all that remained; the melody itself evaded him. He had found instead the first voice of the fugue that Elizabeth had played—it came to him, inverted mockingly and in a minor key. Suspended above the ocean the anxieties of transience and solitude no longer troubled him and he thought of his father's death with equanimity. During the dinner hour the plane reached the shore of France.

At midnight Ferris was in a taxi crossing Paris. It was a clouded night and mist wreathed the lights of the Place de la Concorde. The midnight bistros gleamed on the wet pavements. As always after a transocean flight the change of continents was too sudden. New York at morning, this midnight Paris. Ferris glimpsed the disorder of his life: the succession of cities, of transitory loves; and time, the sinister glissando of the years, time always.

"Vite! Vite!" he called in terror. "Dépêchez-vous."

Valentin opened the door to him. The little boy wore pajamas and an outgrown red robe. His gray eyes were shadowed and, as Ferris passed into the flat, they flickered momentarily.

"J'attends Maman."

Jeannine was singing in a night club. She would not be home before another hour. Valentin returned to a drawing, squatting with his crayons over the paper on the floor. Ferris looked down at the drawing—it was a banjo player with notes and wavy lines inside a comic-strip balloon.

"We will go again to the Tuileries."

The child looked up and Ferris drew him closer to his knees. The melody, the unfinished music that Elizabeth had played, came to him suddenly. Unsought, the load of memory jettisoned—this time bringing only recognition and sudden joy.

"Monsieur Jean," the child said, "did you see him?"

Confused, Ferris thought only of another child—the freckled, family-loved boy. "See who, Valentin?"

"Your dead papa in Georgia." The child added, "Was he okay?"

Ferris spoke with rapid urgency: "We will go often to the Tuileries. Ride the pony and we will go into the guignol. We will see the puppet show and never be in a hurry any more."

"Monsieur Jean," Valentin said. "The guignol is now closed."

Again the terror, the acknowledgment of wasted years and death. Valentin, responsive and confident, still nestled in his arms. His cheek touched the soft cheek and felt the brush of the delicate eyelashes. With inner desperation he pressed the child close—as though an emotion as protean as his love could dominate the pulse of time.

from Harper's Magazine

MONTE SAINT ANGELO

ARTHUR MILLER *is a native New Yorker, now living in Brooklyn, who is one of the best known of living playwrights. He took his A.B. degree at the University of Michigan in 1938, is married, and has two children. He is the author of a novel,* Focus, *and of the following plays:* Man Who Had All the Luck, Situation Normal, All My Sons, *and* Death of a Salesman. *For the last-named play he received both the Pulitzer Prize and the New York Drama Critics' Award.* All My Sons *was also crowned by the drama critics in 1947. Mr. Miller received the Avery Hopwood Award for Playwriting in 1936 and 1937 and the Theatre Guild National Award in 1938. Early this year his version of Ibsen's* The Enemy of the People *was produced on Broadway and later published. This is his first appearance in the O. Henry collection. He has written only a few short stories.*

The driver, who had been sitting up ahead in perfect silence for nearly an hour as they crossed the monotonous green plain of Foggia, now said something. Appello quickly leaned forward in the back seat and asked him what he had said. "That is Monte Saint Angelo before you." Appello lowered his head to see through the windshield of the rattling little Fiat. Then he nudged Bernstein, who awoke resentfully, as though his friend had intruded. "That's the town up there," Appello said. Bernstein's annoyance vanished and he bent forward. They both sat that way for several minutes, watching the approach of what seemed to them a comically situated town, even more comic than any they had seen in the four weeks they had spent moving from place to place in the country. It was like a tiny old lady living on a high roof for fear of thieves.

202

The plain remained as flat as a table for a quarter of a mile ahead. Then out of it like a pillar rose the butte, squarely and rigidly skyward it towered, only narrowing as it reached its very top. And there, barely visible now, the town crouched, momentarily obscured by white clouds, then appearing again tiny and safe, like a mountain port looming at the end of the sea. From their distance they could make out no road, no approach at all up the side of the pillar.

"Whoever built that was awfully frightened of something," Bernstein said, pulling his coat closer around him. "How do they get up there? Or do they?"

Appello, in Italian, asked the driver about the town. The driver, who had been there only once before in his life and knew no other who had made the trip—despite his being a resident of Lucera which was not far away—told Appello with some amusement that they would soon see how rarely anyone goes up or comes down Monte Saint Angelo. "The donkeys will kick and run away as we ascend, and when we come into the town everyone will come out to see. They are very far from everything. They all look like brothers up there. They don't know very much either." He laughed.

"What does the Princeton chap say?" Bernstein asked. The driver had a crew haircut, a turned-up nose, and a red round face with blue eyes. He owned the car, and although he spoke like any Italian when his feet were on the ground, behind his wheel with two Americans riding behind him he had only the most amused and superior attitude toward everything outside the windshield. Appello, having translated for Bernstein, asked him how long it would take to ascend. "Perhaps three quarters of an hour—as long as the mountain is," he amended.

Bernstein and Appello settled back and watched the butte's approach. Now they could see that its sides were crumbled white stone. At this closer vantage it seemed as though it had been struck a terrible blow by some monstrous hammer which had split its structure into millions of seams. They were beginning to climb now, on a road of sharp broken rocks.

"The road is Roman," the driver remarked. He knew how much Americans made of anything Roman. Then he added, "The car, however, is from Milan." He and Appello laughed.

And now the white chalk began drifting into the car. At their elbows the altitude began to seem threatening. There was no railing

203

on the road and it turned back on itself every two hundred yards in order to climb again. The Fiat's doors were wavering in their frames, the seat on which they sat kept inching forward onto the floor. A fine film of white talc settled onto their clothing and covered their eyebrows. Both together began to cough. When they were finished Bernstein said, "Just so I understand it clearly and without prejudice, will you explain again in words of one syllable why the hell we are climbing this lump of dust, old man?"

Appello laughed and mocked a punch at him. "No kidding," Bernstein said, trying to smile.

"I want to see this aunt of mine, that's all." Appello began taking it seriously.

"You're crazy, you know that? You've got some kind of ancestor complex. All we've done in this country is look for your relatives. I mean it, you really have a lust for your history, don't you."

"Well, Jesus, I'm finally in the country, I want to see all the places I came from. You realize that two of my relatives are buried in a crypt in the church up there? In 1100 something."

"Oh, is this where the monks came from?"

"Sure, the two Appello brothers. They helped build that church. It's very famous, that church. Supposed to be Saint Michael appeared in a vision or something . . ."

"I never thought I'd know anybody with monks in his family. But I still think you're cracked on the whole subject."

"Well, don't you have any feeling about your ancestors? Wouldn't you like to go back to Austria or wherever you came from and see where the old folks lived? Maybe find a family that belongs to your line, or something like that?"

Bernstein did not answer for a moment. He did not know quite what he felt, and wondered dimly whether he kept ragging his friend a little because of envy. When they had been in the country courthouse where Appello's grandfather's portrait and his great-grandfather's hung—both renowned provincial magistrates; when they had spent the night in Lucera where the name Appello meant something distinctly honorable, and where his friend Vinny was taken in hand and greeted in that intimate way because he was an Appello—in all these moments Bernstein had felt left out and somehow deficient. At first he had taken the attitude that all the fuss was childlike and silly and sentimental, and yet as incident after incident, landmark after old landmark turned up echoing the name Appello, he gradually began to feel his friend combining with this history and it seemed to him that it made Vinny stronger, somehow less dead when the time would come for him to die.

"I have no relatives that I know of in Europe," he said to Vinny. "And if I had they'd have all been wiped out by now."

"Is that why you don't like my visiting this way?" Vinny asked sympathetically. He was ever trying to know Bernstein, whom he loved and respected, but who was closed to him.

Bernstein felt Vinny's attempt to reach into him. "I don't say I don't like it," he said, and smiled by will. He wished he could open himself like Vinny; somehow it would give him ease and strength, he felt. They stared down at the plain below, and spoke little.

The chalk dust had lightened Appello's black eyebrows. For a fleeting moment it occurred to Appello that they resembled each other. Both were over six feet tall, both broad-shouldered and dark men. Bernstein was thinner, quite gaunt and long-armed. Appello was stronger in his arms and stooped a little as though he had not wanted to be tall. But their eyes were not the same. Appello seemed a little Chinese around the eyes, and they glistened black, direct, and, for women, passionately. Bernstein gazed rather than looked; for him the eyes were dangerous when they could be fathomed, and so he turned them away often, or downward, and there seemed to be something defensively cruel and yet gentle there. They liked each other not for reasons so much as for possibilities; it was as though they both had sensed they were opposites, as only two men may know that thing of each other. And they were drawn to each other by the lure of the expression which each embodied for the other's failings. With Bernstein around him Appello felt diverted from his irresponsible sensuality, and on this trip Bernstein often had the pleasure and pain of resolving to deny himself no more.

The car turned a hairpin curve with a cloud below on the right, when suddenly the main street of the town arched up before them. There was no one about. It had been true, what the driver had predicted—in the few handkerchiefs of grass that they had passed on the way up the donkeys had bolted, and they had seen shepherds with hard mustaches and black shakos and long black cloaks who had regarded them with the silent inspection of those who live far away. But here in the town there was no one. The car climbed onto the main street which flattened now, and all at once they were being surrounded by people who were coming out of their doors putting on their jackets and caps. They did look strangely related, and more Irish than Italian. The two got out of the Fiat and inspected the baggage strapped to the car's roof while the driver kept edging around and around the car as though in fear for it. Appello talked laughingly with the people who kept asking why he had come so far, what he had to sell, what he wanted to buy, until he at last made it clear that he was looking only for his aunt. When he said the name the men (the women remained at home) looked blank, until an old man wearing rope sandals and a skating cap came forward and said that he remembered such a woman. He then turned and Appello and Bernstein followed up the main street with what was now perhaps a hundred men behind them.

"How come nobody knows her?" Bernstein asked.

"She's a widow, I guess she stays home most of the time. The men in the line died out here twenty years ago. Her husband was the last Appello up here. They don't go much by women; I bet this old guy remembered the name because he knew her husband by it, not her."

The wind, steady and hard, blew through the town, washing it, laving its stones white. The sun was cool as a lemon, the sky purely blue, and the clouds so close their keels seemed to be sailing through the next street. The two Americans began to walk with the joy of it in their long strides. They came to a two-story stone house and went up a dark corridor and knocked.

There was no sound within for a few moments. Then there was. Short scrapes, like a mouse that started, stopped, looked about, started again. Appello knocked once more. The doorknob turned and the door opened a foot. A pale little woman, not very old at all, held the door wide enough for her face to be seen. She seemed very worried.

"Ha?" she asked.

"I am Vincent Georgio."

"Ha?" she repeated.

"Vicenzo Georgio Appello."

Her hand slid off the knob and she stepped back. Appello, smiling in his friendly way, entered with Bernstein behind him closing the door. A window let the sun flood the room, which was nevertheless stone cold. The woman's mouth was open, her hands were pressed together as in prayer, and the tips of her fingers were pointing at Vinny. She seemed crouched, as though about to kneel, and she could not speak.

Vinny went over to her and touched her shoulder and pressed her to a chair. He and Bernstein sat down too. He told her their relationship, saying names of men and women some of whom were dead, others she had only heard of and never met in this sky place. She spoke at last, and Appello could not understand what she said. She ran out of the room suddenly.

"I think she thinks I'm a ghost or something. My uncle said she hadn't seen any of the family in twenty or twenty-five years. I bet she doesn't think there are any left. . . ."

She returned with a bottle that had an inch of wine at the bottom of it. She ignored Bernstein and gave Appello the bottle. He drank. It was vinegar. Then she started to whimper, and kept wiping the tears out of her eyes in order to see Appello. She never finished a sentence and Appello kept asking her what she meant. She kept running from one corner of the room to another. The rhythm of her departures and returns to the chair was getting so wild that Appello raised his voice and commanded her to sit. "I'm not a ghost, Aunty, I came here from America. . . ." He stopped. It was clear from the look in her bewildered, frightened eyes that she had not thought him a ghost at all, but what was just as bad—if nobody had ever come to see her from Lucera, how could anybody have so much as thought of her in America, a place which did exist, she knew, just as heaven existed and in exactly the same way. There was no way to hold a conversation with her.

They finally made their exit, and she had not said a coherent word except a blessing which was her way of expressing her relief that Appello was leaving, for despite the unutterable joy at having seen with her own eyes another of her husband's blood, the sight was itself too terrible in its associations, and in the responsibility it laid upon her to welcome him and make him comfortable.

They walked toward the church now. Bernstein had not been able to say anything. The woman's emotion, so pure and violent and wild, had scared him. And yet, glancing at Appello, he was amazed to see that his friend had drawn nothing but a calm sort of satisfaction from it, as though his aunt had only behaved correctly. Dimly he remembered himself as a boy visiting an aunt of his in the Bronx, a woman who had not been in touch with the family and had never seen him. He remembered how forcefully she had fed him, pinched his cheeks, and smiled and smiled every time he looked up at her, but he knew that there was nothing of this blood in that encounter; nor could there be for him now if on the next corner he should meet a woman who said she was of his family. If anything, he would want to get away from her, even though he had always gotten along with his people and hadn't even the usual snobbery about them. As they entered the church he said to himself that some part of him was not plugged in, but why he should be disturbed about it mystified him and even made him angry at Appello, who now was asking the priest where the tombs of the Appellos were.

They descended into the vault of the church where the stone floor was partly covered with water. Along the walls, and down twisting corridors running out of a central arched hall, were tombs so old no candle could illuminate most of the inscriptions. The priest vaguely remembered an Appello vault but had no idea where it was. Vinny moved from one crypt to another with the candle he had bought from the priest. Bernstein waited at the opening of the corridor, his neck bent to avoid touching the roof with his hat. Appello, stooped even more than usual, looked like a monk himself, an antiquary, a gradually disappearing figure squinting down the long darkness of the ages for his name on a stone. He could not find it. Their feet were getting soaked. After half an hour they left the church and outside fought off shivering small boys selling grimy religious postcards which the wind kept taking from their fists.

"I'm sure it's there," Appello said with fascinated excitement, "but you wouldn't want to stick out a search, would you?" he asked hopefully.

"This is no place for me to get pneumonia," Bernstein said. They had come to the end of a side street. They had passed shops in front of which pink lambs hung head down with their legs stiffly jutting out over the sidewalk. Bernstein shook hands with one and imagined for Vinny a scene for Chaplin in which a monsignor would meet him here, reach out to shake his hand, and find the cold lamb's foot in his grip, and Chaplin would be mortified. At the street's end they scanned the endless sky, and looked over the precipice upon Italy. "They might even have ridden horseback down there, in armor. Appellos." Vinny spoke raptly.

"Yeah, they probably did," Bernstein said. The vision of Appello in armor wiped away any desire to kid his friend. He felt alone, desolate as the dried-out chalk sides of this broken pillar he stood upon. Who am I? he wondered.

He remembered clearly his father telling of his town in Europe, a common barrel of water, a town idiot, a baron near by. That was all he had of it, and no pride, no pride in it at all. Then I am an American, he said to himself. And yet in that there was not the power of Appello's narrow passion. He looked at Appello's profile, and felt the warmth of that gaze upon Italy and wondered if any American had ever really felt like this in the States. He had never in his life sensed so strongly that the past could be so peopled, so vivid with generations as it had been with Vinny's aunt an hour ago. A common water barrel, a town idiot, a baron who lived near by. . . . It had nothing to do with *him*. And standing there he felt a broken part of himself; and wondered with a slight amusement if this was what a child felt on discovering that the parents who have brought him up are not his own and that he entered his house not from warmth, but from the street, from a public and disordered place. . . .

They sought and found a restaurant for lunch. It was at the other edge of the town and overhung the precipice. Inside, it was one immense room with fifteen or twenty tables, the front wall lined with windows overlooking the plain below. They sat at a table and waited for someone to appear. The restaurant was cold. They could hear the wind surging against the windowpanes, and yet the clouds at eye level moved serenely and slow. A young girl, the daughter of the family, came out of the kitchen and Appello began to question her about food when the door to the street opened and a man came in.

For Bernstein there was an abrupt impression of familiarity with the man, although he could not fathom the reason for his feeling. The man's face was indistinguishable from all Sicilian faces, round, dark as earth, high cheekbones, broad jaw. He almost laughed aloud as it instantly occurred to him that he could converse with this man in Italian. The waitress gone, he told this to Vinny who now joined in watching the man. Sensing their stares, the man looked at them with a merry flicker of his checks, and said, *"Bongiorno."* *"Bongiorno,"* Bernstein replied across the four tables between them. And then to Vinny, "Why do I feel that about him?"

"I'll be damned if I know," Vinny said, glad now that he could join his friend in a mutually interesting occupation.

They watched the man who obviously ate here often. He had already set a large package down on another table, and now put his hat on a chair, his jacket on another chair, and his vest on a third. It was as though he were making companions of his clothing. He was in the prime of middle age and very rugged. And to the Americans there was something mixed up about his clothing. His jacket might have been worn by a local man; it was tight and black and wrinkled and chalkdust-covered. His trousers were dark brown and very thick, like a peasant's, and his shoes were snubbed up at the ends and of heavy leather. But he wore a black hat, which was unusual up here where all had caps, and he had a tie. He wiped his hands before loosening the knot, for it was a striped tie, yellow and blue, of silk, and not a tie to be bought in this part of the world, nor certainly to be worn by these people.

And there was a look in his eyes that was not a peasant's inward stare, nor did it have the innocence of the other men who had looked at them on the streets here.

The waitress came with two dishes of lamb for the Americans. The man was interested and looked across his table at the meat and at the strangers. Bernstein glanced at the barely cooked flesh and said, "There's hair on it."

Vinny called the girl back just as she was going to the newcomer and pointed at the hair.

"But it's lamb's hair," she explained simply. They said oh, and pretended to begin to cut the faintly pink flesh.

"You ought to know better, signor, than to order meat today."

The man looked amused, and yet it was unclear whether he might not be a trifle offended.

"Why not?" Vinny asked.

"It's Friday, signor," and he smiled sympathetically.

"That's right!" Vinny said, although he had known all along.

"Give me fish," the man said to the girl, and asked with intimacy about her mother who was ill these days.

Bernstein had not been able to turn his eyes from the man. He could not eat the meat and sat chewing bread and feeling a rising urge to go over to the man, to speak to him. It struck him as being insane. The whole place, the town, the clouds in the streets, the thin air were turning into an hallucination. He knew this man. He was sure he knew him. But quite clearly that was impossible. But there was a thing beyond the impossibility of which he was drunkenly sure, and it was that he could, if he dared, start speaking Italian fluently with this man. This was the first moment since leaving America that he had not felt the ill-ease of traveling and of being a traveler. He felt as comfortable as Vinny now, it seemed to him. In his mind's eye he could envisage the inside of the kitchen; he had a startlingly clear image of what the cook's face must look like and he knew where a certain kind of soiled apron was hung.

And yet it was crazy, and he knew that something was happening to him that had never happened before.

"What's the matter with you?" Appello asked.

"Why?"

"The way you're looking at him."

"I want to talk to him."

"Well, talk to him." Vinny smiled.

"I can't speak Italian, you know that."

"Well, I'll ask him whatever you want to know."

"Vinny . . ." Bernstein started to say something and stopped.

"What?" Appello asked, leaning his head closer and looking down at the tablecloth.

"Get him to talk. Anything. Go ahead."

Vinny, enjoying his friend's strange emotionalism, looked up at the man who now was eating with careful but immense satisfaction.

"*Scuze*, signor." The man looked up. "I am a son of Italy from America. I would like to talk to you. We're strange here."

211

The man, chewing deliciously, nodded with his amiable and amused smile, and adjusted the hang of his jacket on the nearby chair.

"Do you come from around here?"

"Not very far."

"How is everything here?"

"Poor. It is always poor."

"What do you work at, if I may ask?"

The man had now finished his food. He took one last drag of his wine and got up and proceeded to dress and pull his tie up tightly. When he walked it was with a slow, wide sway, as though each step had to be conserved.

"I sell cloth here to the people and the stores, such as they are," he said. And he walked over to the bundle and set it carefully on a table and began untying it.

"He sells cloth," Vinny said to Bernstein.

Bernstein's cheeks began to redden. From where he sat he could see the man's broad back, ever so slightly bent over the bundle. He could see the man's hands working at the knot, and just a corner of the man's left eye. Now the man was laying the paper away from the two bolts of cloth, carefully pressing the wrinkles flat against the table. It was as though the brown paper were valuable leather that must not be cracked or rudely bent. The waitress came out of the kitchen with a tremendous round loaf of bread at least two feet in diameter. She gave it to him and he placed it flat on top of the cloth, and the faintest feather of a smile curled up on Bernstein's lips. Now the man folded the paper back and brought the string around the bundle and tied the knot, and Bernstein uttered a little laugh, a laugh of relief. Vinny looked at him, already smiling, ready to join the laughter, but mystified.

"What's the matter?" he asked.

Bernstein took a breath. There was something a little triumphant, a new air of confidence and superiority in his face and voice, as though now for the first time it was he who had the private secret and was at home. "He's Jewish, Vinny," he said.

Vinny turned to look at the man. "Why?"

"The way he works that bundle. It's exactly the way my father used to tie a bundle. And my grandfather. The whole history is packing bundles and getting away. Nobody else can be as tender and delicate with bundles. That's a Jewish man tying a bundle. Ask him his name."

Vinny was delighted. "Signor," he called, with that warmth reserved in his nature for members of families, any families.

The man, tucking the end of the string into the edge of the paper, turned to them with his kind smile.

"May I ask your name, signor?"

"My name? Mauro di Benedetto."

"Mauro di Benedetto. Sure!" Vinny laughed, looking at Bernstein. "That's Morris of the Blessed. Moses."

"Tell him I'm Jewish," Bernstein said, a driving eagerness charging his eyes, as though he were going to answer the doorbell to let in a long-awaited friend.

"My friend is Jewish," Vinny said to the man, who now was hoisting the bundle onto his shoulder.

"Hch?" the man asked, confused by their sudden vivacity. As though wondering if there were some sophisticated American point he should have understood, he stood there smiling blankly, politely, ready to join in this mood.

"*Judeo*, my friend."

"*Judeo?*" he asked, the willingness to get the joke still holding the smile on his face.

Vinny hesitated before this steady gaze of incomprehension. "*Judeo*. The people of the Bible," he said.

"Oh, yes, yes!" The man nodded now, relieved that he was not to be caught in ignorance. "*'Ebraio*," he corrected. And he nodded affably to Bernstein and seemed a little at a loss for what they expected him to do next.

"Does he know what you mean?" Bernstein asked.

"Yeah, he said, 'Hebrew,' but it doesn't seem to connect. Signor," he addressed the man, "why don't you have a glass of wine with us? Come, sit down."

"Thank you, signor," he replied appreciatively, "but I must be home by sundown and I'm already a little late."

Vinny translated and Bernstein told him to ask why he had to be home by sundown.

The man apparently had never considered the question before.

He shrugged, and laughed, and said, "I don't know, all my life I get home for dinner on Friday night and I like to come into the house before sundown. I suppose it's a habit; my father . . . You see, I have a route I walk, which is this route. I first did it with my father, and he did it with his father—we are known here for many generations past. And my father always got home on Friday night before sundown. It's a manner of the family I guess."

"Shabbas begins at sundown on Friday night," Bernstein said when Vinny translated. "He's even taking home the fresh bread for Sabbath. The man is a Jew, I tell you. Ask him, will ya?"

"*Scuze*, signor." Vinny smiled. "My friend is curious to know whether you are Jewish."

The man raised his thick eyebrows not only in surprise, but as though he felt somewhat honored by being identified with something exotic. "Me?" he asked.

"I don't mean American," Vinny said, believing he had caught the meaning of the man's glance at Bernstein. "*'Ebraio*," he repeated.

The man shook his head, seeming a little sorry he could not oblige Vinny. "No," he said. He was ready to go but wanted to pursue what obviously was his most interesting conversation in weeks. "Are they Catholics? The Hebrews?"

"He's asking me if Jews are Catholics," Vinny said.

Bernstein sat back in his chair, a knotted look of wonder in his eyes. Vinny replied to the man who looked once again at Bernstein as though wanting to investigate this strangeness further, but his mission drew him up and he wished them good fortune and said good-by. He walked to the kitchen door and called thanks to the girl inside, saying the loaf would warm his back all the way down the mountain, and he opened the door and went out into the wind of the street and the sunshine, waving to them as he walked away.

They kept repeating their amazement on the way back to the car, and Bernstein told again how his father wrapped bundles. "Maybe he doesn't know he's a Jew, but how could he not know what Jews are?" he said.

"Well, remember my aunt in Lucera?" Vinny asked. "She's a schoolteacher, and she asked me if you believed in Christ. She didn't know the first thing about it. I think the ones in these small towns who ever heard of Jews think they're a Christian sect of some kind.

I knew an old Italian once who thought all Negroes were Jews and white Jews were only converts."

"But his name . . ."

"Benedetto is an Italian name too. I never heard of Mauro though. Mauro is strictly from the old sod."

"But if he had a name like that wouldn't it lead him to wonder if . . . ?"

"I don't think so. In New York the name Salvatore is turned into Sam. Italians are great for nicknames, the first name never means much. Vicenzo is Enzo or Vinny or even Chico. Nobody would think twice about Mauro or damn near any other first name. He's obviously a Jew, but I'm sure he doesn't know it. You could tell, couldn't you? He was baffled."

"But my God, bringing home a bread for Shabbas . . ." Bernstein laughed, wide-eyed.

They reached the car and Bernstein had his hand on the door but stopped before opening it and turned to Vinny. He looked heated, his eyelids seemed puffed. "It's early; if you still want to I'll go back to the church with you. You can look for the boys."

Vinny began to smile, and then they both laughed together, and Vinny slapped him on the back and gripped his shoulder as though to hug him. "Goddam, now you're starting to enjoy this trip!"

They walked briskly toward the church, the conversation returning always to the same point when Bernstein would say, "I don't know why, but it gets me. He's not only acting like a Jew, but an orthodox Jew. And doesn't even know . . . I mean it's strange as hell to me."

"You look different, you know that?" Vinny said.

"Why?"

"You do."

"You know a funny thing?" Bernstein said quietly, as they entered the church and descended into the vault beneath it. "I feel like—at home in this place. I can't describe it."

They picked their way through the shallower puddles on the stone floor looking into vestibules, opening doors, searching for the priest. He appeared at last, they could not imagine from where, and Appello bought another candle from him and was gone in the shadows of the corridors where the vaults were.

Bernstein stood—everything was wet, dripping. Behind him, flat and wide, rose the stairway of stones bent with the tread of millions. Vapor steamed from his nostrils. There was nothing to look at but shadow. It was dank and black and low, an entrance to hell. Now and then in the very far distance he could hear a step, another, then silence. He did not move, seeking the root of an ecstasy he had not dreamed was part of his nature; he saw a vision of the amiable man trudging down the mountains, across the plains, on routes marked out for him by generations of men, a nameless traveler carrying home a warm bread on Friday night—and kneeling in church on Sunday. There was an irony in it he could not name. And yet pride was running through him like a narrow and cool trickle of water. Of what he should be proud he had no idea; perhaps it was only that under the glacial crush of history a Jew had survived, had been shorn of his consciousness, but still held on to that final impudence of a Saturday Sabbath and a fresh bread. There was a smile on Bernstein's face and he was almost laughing, but he wished he could know why he was proud and why his mind invited the feeling.

He could see Vinny's form between the walls of crypts, coming toward him with springy step. And he knew that now for the first time he would look straight into Vinny's eyes, as though he had been newly joined with something very old and work-worn and honorable.

Vinny came up to him smiling like a young boy. "It's back there! I found it!"

"That's great, Vinny," Bernstein said. "I'm glad."

They walked into the narrow corridor, both stooping, Vinny slightly ahead with the candle raised in one hand, his other grasping Bernstein's wrist. He had never liked anyone grasping him; it always seemed like an invasion of privacy. But now he wanted very much to laugh or to sing loudly, because it felt so rich and fine—a touch of the hand in the darkness.

from the American Mercury

THE BUTCHERBIRDS

ESTHER PATT *was born in St. Joseph, Missouri, November 18, 1914. She attended private schools, and also took courses in art and in radio dramatics. She studied creative writing two semesters with Alexander Cappon at the Night College of the University of Kansas City and attended two sessions of the Crossroads of America Writers' Conference at the university. In 1947 she and her mother spent six months touring the Great Smokies and the delta country. At present Miss Patt is an insurance underwriter in Kansas City. "The Butcherbirds" is her second published story. She writes that she "has many short stories crying to be written and three book lengths far in the future."*

I was just a kid when I first saw her. The iceman had been by and I was sucking ice through a washcloth. The coldness was much pleasanter than candy and imagined sweetness tasted better than any other.

I first noticed the ball fringe bobbing along her horse's side while it beat the brick with its shoe and flexed poor muscles under the fly net. The movement, complete with fanning of the tail, fascinated me, and I sucked deep into the cold and watched the ball fringe and the horse.

The horse was fixed to a wagon full of dewberries. Up on the seat, still as a robin on a nest, *she* was. "Hello," I said. Her hair was looped well above her ears before it hid under the undecided brim, but perhaps she hadn't heard me. I tried again. "Hi," I said. There weren't any kids to play with and I was ready to talk to anyone.

There wasn't any sound except the lurching of the wagon—a rebound of the efforts of the horse.

"My name's Marnie," I said. "I used to have a brother, but he's dead. He died before I was born. His name was Elvis. Do you have a brother?"

My mother called me then, but I didn't go until I was sure she wasn't going to answer. Deciding she was deaf, I went on home. At our gate—the third down—I met a man coming out. He looked so mean I turned to watch him and he went straight to the wagon. My mother was on the porch.

"Who was that?" I said.

"A huckster," she said.

I saw her every once in a while after that, but it was always the same She took no notice of me whatever, and certain she couldn't hear me, it was easy saying anything I wished to her. It gave me satisfaction I had lost with dolls and I pretended she talked back to me. She sat quiet—holding onto the reins. I don't think she even ever sneezed or coughed. Through the weeks the load shifted from berries to peas and potatoes and the like, but if her clothes varied I never noticed. I never saw her without her hat. It had such a pallid look— as though it yearned for younger years.

I was careful not to talk to her when there were passersby. Somehow I knew it might not be understood and if it got back to my mother, it might even be unpleasant. Maybe if there had been kids in the neighborhood, it would have been different.

Once when I was in the drugstore, Mr. Farrow who ran it said, "Saw you talkin' to Quare Beanblossom. What did Quare have to say?" His face wasn't big enough to hold his grin, and the bow tie twitched under pressure of the laugh that waited for my answer. I snatched my mother's medicine from off the counter and ran for the door, and the laughter rolled along the boards burning my bare heels in its fire. "Wouldn't want folks to think *you* was quare, too, would you?" he called after me.

I ran home fast, but the question chased me all the way. I put the powders on the kitchen cabinet and ran out to the boxwoods. There was a place there where they made a kind of square, and when I squatted on my knees no one could see. There against the stiffness I cried harder than a ten-year-old should know how. My folks were from north of the Ridge, and we always noticed when people said things like *hoose* for house and *quare* for queer, but I didn't know the words were wrong.

Next time I saw her I didn't say anything at all. I just sat a little ways apart and looked at her. She didn't seem to notice, but I still stood up for her, deciding she wasn't only deaf, but blind. That word *quare* would wedge into my chest and make it hard to breathe.

One evening before supper was when it happened. I guess my mother was in the kitchen—anyway she didn't see me. I was playing jacks—trying to keep the ball from bouncing between bricks. I looked up and there *she* was, motioning from on the wagon. I remember dabbing at my eyes with my wad of handkerchief, trying to rub off the imagining, but the jacks hurt squeezing into my hand and I knew I wasn't sleeping. I got up and went over to the wagon.

It was the first time she had ever looked at me. *Into*—more than at me. Since I'm grown, I recognize it for the look of those with knowing—a kind of fusing. She said, "Get in the wagon."

It didn't come to me to ask where we were going. I just climbed onto the seat. She kept looking at my house until we turned the corner into Churning Road which wasn't paved. The mood had got into the horse, and its quick beats muffled by the dust were like the poundings in my neck. Even the trees were allies, and for the first time I felt a part of everything I saw—as though everything breathed together for excitement. We were flying—the horse kept trotting, I know—but we were flying. She didn't say any more—but it didn't matter when you were flying.

We left Churning Road for another—might even have left the whole state of Virginia for a state of happiness. I shared no sense of space or time but, looking back, we could perhaps have gone five or six miles. My spine bent to the right for the curves to the south and to the left for those that sloped into the woods. It was cooler, but the sun still had a long ways to drop. When our pacing slowed to meet a curve, I heard her voice close by my ear. "Do you know who I am?" she said.

My breath was sucked away in waves that left me drowned in silence. I couldn't say her name to *her*. "No, ma'am," I said. My eyes flooded with the lie, and I wanted to beg her not to tell me who she was. "I'm Quivera Baneblaus," she said.

How *beautiful* a name—*Quivera! Mr. Farrow was a liar,* I thought.

She took off her hat and dropped it in the emptiness back of the seat, and I saw her hair braided to a crown on top her head. She wasn't pretty—not the way women were supposed to be—but she had —she had projection. She was a silent sort of spokesman for—the road —the trees—the horse—and she was—really beautiful. I didn't think it through—I only felt it with the tasting edge of any child that age.

"The first time you seen me," she said, "you asked have I a brother. I got one—he should have died before my time."

"Brothers is supposed to be fun," I said.

"Sometimes things is different from what they's supposed to be," she said, "and sometimes things oughtn't be the way they is."

We kept on going, and I tried to figure out how things were like she said, but the more I thought the harder it got, till I forgot what it was she said.

"I thought you was deaf," I said. She didn't say *anything* to that. "I thought you was blind, too," I said.

We pulled away from the road into a place where rocks had spread so long before that they were dyed with damp and moss and reddish earth. The horse shuddered and wouldn't go ahead, and I wondered if it saw the mill. It was a stooping mill with empty stares. I had to grab the seat then, till she could hold the horse.

"Mares is like most women," she said. "They don't hold with snakes."

I saw it then. I thought I was going to be sick, but I only sat there —watching the writhing and the thrashing in the air. Hanging by the neck—a snake—on a thorntree that was strung with dead snakes hanging there like ropes from spikes along the limbs. It made such vivid motion—such green and boneless efforts—and the hooking of its tail—piercing just the air——

I felt a solid tube explore my throat and gagged with such a force that she held me then, and I felt safer in her nearness even though she fought quick breathing. She held the mare to flinching, and the three of us were—all of life—all life—watching all of death.

"It's ugly," I said, pushing close against her.

"They's pretty, gentle grass snakes. Likes to play, they do—in the clearin's and the marshes same as you. And they don't never bite," she said. "It's a sorry sight—a sorry, sorry sight."

I leaned hard against the safeness that was her and looked again. I was very tired—but the sureness in her voice helped me see the things, perhaps the way they should be seen. All movement gone, they hung alike.

I counted—there were twenty-one. Some were shriveled—dry, and even black; and some were brown like grass, but mostly they were bright and green. I looked back at the mill, to see if it was there, I guess, and saw two dead snakes in another tree, and a mouse—its head was gone.

"Yes," she said, "they's all around."

Back of us were four more—even closer—and a lizard. Stuck, they were—all stuck right through the necks. My legs felt bruised—as though I'd tried to run and couldn't.

"How'd they get there?" I said.

"Butcherbirds," she said.

I'd never heard of butcherbirds, and didn't know what they were. "I *hate* them!" I said, very loud. "*Hate them—hate them——*"

I got hot and sick and started coughing—spitting up. She put the firm coolness of her hand on my forehead and wiped the sweat away, and she wiped the sickness off my dress with her petticoat. I looked back at the mill, expecting birds to fly out blackened windowholes and kill me in the dimness that was beginning evening. The wagon lurched and I cried out, but it was only that the mare was reaching grass. *She* held me close, and rocked me.

"We cain't hate butcherbirds," she said, "'cause butcherbirds ain't bad. It's a sorry sight—the snakes, it is—but it ain't bad of the butchers. It's their way," she said. She rocked me, easy. "They's just like folks—and so's the snakes.

"I broke my leg and set it once, and I had to pull and hoist. I learned respectin' for the snakes. They have a thrustin' way, and they thrust up or downhill without legs or tryin'. They love their mates, and they chin their pretty backs to tell 'em so. I *know*," she said; "I *watch* 'em."

I loved her then, I think. Loved her way—and was awed by all she knew. I'd never compared animals with people, and so I was ashamed, even of mashed anthills and all my jars of fireflies. "Tell me about butcherbirds," I said.

She looked all around, and up into the trees—and over by the mill.

I followed, clinging with my eyes to her line of power—stretching along the rope that was her vision—aiming safely—knowing that our eyes held hands, exploring forests of the leaves that were the parent trees of those small ones strung with death. But these were all we saw. "The butcher's gone," she said. "He's a *chubby* one—got a hook beak like lots of folks." She stopped talking, and just sat.

"Why does he do like what he does?" I remember asking.

"He has weak-like feet," she said, "and sticks his meat up so's he won't need hold it while he eats. Sometimes he's a-flyin' back—but mostly he goes off butcherin' again." She shook her head. "Killin' is a sorry way," she said. She looked at me—and all sadness looked—and darkness came and took the day away. I felt the sureness of her hand lift reins from off the whip hook, and I heard wheels turning on the rocks—and so I knew we'd left the snakes.

The road we came was different going back—and so was I. Maybe I discovered then that wonder rides at night along with love—and growth—or maybe that the things I saw by day I felt by night. *She,* herself, was boundless, and I warmed against her—limp—content to doze and share the slight and rhythmic movement that was life. I think we took the very pulse of night—pounding in the creek bed through the frog that felt it on his belly. I think we were the breathing core of everything that was.

The mare had knowing feet, and seemed to be familiar with flight into the night. I slept against Quivera, and woke only when we stopped. It was so cold—sitting up away from her.

"You're goin' to have some supper before I take you home," she said. "If *he* ain't here, you are."

"If who ain't here?" I said.

She pulled up to a door and didn't answer. There were dark *things* in the yard around the house, but I couldn't see just what they were.

"Wait," she said.

I sat there in the wagon, sleepy—chilling—while she went inside. She limped easily—or perhaps it was a rhythm of her own. I saw a lamp go by a window to another—then back again—and she held it at the door.

"Come, child," she said. The words were quiet, as though fearful of waking up the night. I climbed down, past the dark arm of a pump. There was a cat behind electric eyes. I was going to pick it up, but it went squirming underneath the house. She put down the lamp and motioned me to sit. My dress smelled, there inside the house. I didn't want to sit up to the table. She came—unbuttoned it down the back —slipping it off my head—and I sat in my petticoat. She had a listening way——

"What you listenin' for?" I said.

"The butcherbird," she said.

I thought that she was fooling me, and so I grinned. "What butcherbird?" I said. I let my voice coast down the hill to show I knew a joke.

"My brother," she said. She told it simply, and I knew it for a truth. At least I knew she meant it—and there was nothing more to say.

She lit another lamp and turned the wick up high. "Preserves," she said. "You like—strawberry?"

"Oh *yes*," I said. Quickly I was very hungry.

"Come with me," she said. "We'll get you some."

We went out again into the night. Her very touch had turned the lamp into a giant firefly breathing flame inside its tummy. It showed us to a mound of ground—such a swollen, rounding grave with a wooden door that moaned and lay there still and quiet when we dropped it on its side. Down along decaying stairs I hugged my arms to hide my bareness from the eyes that were reflected lamps in jars of fruits and jellies. It seemed to me they stared from out deep sleep.

She handed me a pail to carry, and a jar. She took a crock, and took the lamp back from its watch there on the floor, and we went up and out into the night—and back into the house.

The butter from the crock was sweet and sweating on the bread, and the berry juice ran pink veins in between. The milk was thick with cream, and cool. I hadn't known I was so hungry—and yet I swallowed fear with every bite. *She*—the heroine of all my life—who knew the snakes and dark—*she* was limping to the window—peering out—listening at the door——

"If *he* comes," she said, "go quiet to the wagon."

When she filled the mug again with milk, I saw the trembling of the pail. Silence cowered in the corners, and I knew it for a house that never laughed—but then I hadn't known a house that had. A cat explored the cold stove in the corner, and *she* was watching me.

I said, "Ain't you hungry?"

She moved the soaking berries closer to my plate. "They's a different kind of hungry," she said, "an' that's the kind I am."

"Ain't you goin' to eat?" I said.

She smiled. I thought maybe she was pulling jokes, and so I grinned. She was *very* pretty then—even like women were supposed to be.

"How come about your brother?" I said.

"He cain't help bein' what he is," she said.

The quiet started clattering. She was quick to stand in front of me, and I could only see the folds and folds that were her skirt. The cat came darting—pushing on my legs like bony knuckles in a glove. Quivera picked the empty pans up off the floor and put them back—up on the stove, and when she turned, I saw the fear.

"I was thinkin' it was *him*," she said. She held my dress for me and I climbed in, not breathing till my head was out—and she listened at the door—and then we went out to the wagon.

It was there we knew the safeness. Settled there against her, I wanted nothing else. Just to ride—to ride—and be forever with her—there. Once again we went, bending to the right and to the left—and the moon had such a long, long climb to make—but going back was shortest, and even when I shoved the town clear with my carried feet, I knew the mare would win. And so, like this, I saw the end of Churning Road.

Drawing to the side, she pulled up on the reins. I didn't want to go back home—I didn't want to *leave* her—but that was all there was to do. She held her hand against my cheek. "The day when you'll be hurt—will be a *sorry* day," she said. "Remember then that butcherbirds cain't help bein' what they is."

It was the *loving* in her that made me cry. She kissed my cheek. I knew that she expected me to go. I lingered though, after I was finally down—and waved until I couldn't hear the hoofing of the mare—and then I went three houses down, and started up the walk to squares of light that were my house.

I could hear my father. He was almost shouting. There was a

bursting in my chest like too much running—and I had to go to the bathroom. The screen was hooked. I rattled the little white knob.

My father came. He came to the door with his shirt off, frowning at the dark. When he passed the lamp the light came through all the hair on his chest and made it glisten. There were red marks just below his neck where he had rubbed, and he was rolling fingers the way I hated. He flipped the hook on the door.

"*Where've* you been?" he said. He grabbed my shoulders and shook me hard. "It's late!" he said. "Where've you *been?*" My mother came in from the kitchen with a powder in her hand and a glass of water.

"Shut up," she said. "The neighbors can hear you!"

"I don't give a God damn," my father said.

My mother unfolded the wrapper like chewing gum and dumped the powder in the water. She shook it in a careful circle and drank it all. She set the glass down on the table and belched. There was a moth flying around, batting the sides of the glass shade over the dining table. She looked at the moth and kept belching three or four times. When she was through she said, "Tell your father where you was."

I couldn't tell them—I *couldn't.* They wouldn't understand. I stood there looking at the moth, and the walls moved in around me—only they weren't walls. They were just remembered walls that I used to know, and they didn't matter. When I looked at them closer, I saw the gold between the roses was all tarnished, and I knew I'd been gone a long, long time. "I want to go to bed," I said.

My mother was looking at my dress. "What's that?" she said, pointing to where I had been sick.

"I got sick," I said.

"*You* got sick," she said. "*You* got sick. *I'm always* sick—and you make me sicker when you don't show up for supper."

I started to my room—but she stopped me.

"*Where was you?*"

"I was riding with the huckster woman," I said miserably.

"That *goofy* woman?" my mother said. "You went riding with that *nitwit*—in that wormy wagon?"

"She's *not* goofy!" I yelled. "She's *not* a nitwit." I was shaking all over, like the mare when it saw the snake. "*Not half as goofy as you are,*" I said.

225

My father was stocky, and my mother would have been, if she hadn't had an ulcer. They just stood there, looking—and then my father hit the side of my head with his hand.

"Don't you talk that way to your mother," he shouted.

I wanted to run away, but there was no place to run to but my room, so I ran there.

from Charm

HOMECOMING

ELIZABETH GREGG PATTERSON *was born in Newport, Arkansas. She was graduated from St. Mary's Hall in Minnesota and from Smith College in the class of 1926. Her first work was published in* American Prefaces *some twelve years ago, and since then has appeared in* McCall's, The Saturday Evening Post, Collier's, Cosmopolitan, Good Housekeeping, The New Yorker, *and* Charm. *She was a Fellow at Bread Loaf in 1932, being recommended by Connie Smith, at that time fiction editor of* McCall's. *She is married to Kenneth Patterson, and they have lived for the past twelve years in Saginaw, Michigan. There is one child, David, now eleven years old. Mrs. Patterson adds: "Last summer we were in South America, where David was bitten by a monkey, and this winter we took up skiing."*

She had not wanted to go to the party but her mother, cajoling her, and then, little by little, insisting, had at last had her way. Soft her mother was, loving, but tenacious somehow when she'd got an idea fixed in her mind.

"They're all your friends, darling," she'd said. "People you've known all your life. They'd be hurt if you didn't go; they wouldn't understand it. I saw Jane Whittaker the other day, just before you came, and she said, 'I'm dying to see Isobel, Mrs. Foster, I'm just dying——'"

"Of curiosity," said Isobel.

Mrs. Foster sighed. "I wish you wouldn't take that attitude," she said. "No one feels that way about you here. You're at home, darling."

"I know," Isobel said. "I know, Mother. It's just that I want to get my bearings first, not see a lot of people, not anybody really, but just take a breather—something like that—and then decide what I'm going to do. Because I have to decide."

She had been sitting beside her mother and, feeling cramped suddenly, oppressed by the small, overcrowded living room, she got up and walked to the window and looked out at the gray, deserted, windy street.

"Five years," her mother was saying. "And in all the time you were married to him you were home only once. If you'd come oftener, you wouldn't feel so strange now."

"It was impossible," Isobel said. "There was always something."

"I know." Still standing at the window, she heard her mother's voice change a little, harden, the way it did when she spoke or thought of Gregory. "I always said if your father had been alive," she continued, "he might have made you see. How selfish he was, I mean, and spoilt—how nothing could ever have come of it."

Isobel lifted her shoulders. It was strange, she was thinking, that even now, when it was all over, the papers signed, decree granted—that was the phrase, wasn't it?—even when it was as final as that, the necessity of concealing stayed with her, the impulse to hide the hateful, appalling scenes, to deny the failure. Draw the shades, she thought. Shut the door. Nobody can see then—nobody can hear.

"I wouldn't say that nothing came of it," she said. She turned away from the window and, coming back to where her mother was sitting, leaned her shoulders against the mantel. "It was all right at first—right at first, anyway. And then I have Toby. You can't look at Toby and say it was time altogether wasted."

"No." Her mother smiled. "When you think of Toby. Except that it's hard to raise a child alone, a boy especially. But maybe someday——" Her eyes narrowed, giving her soft little face the look of a child plotting some future pleasure.

"Mother, *please*," Isobel said, and Mrs. Foster looked up at her, her eyes innocent, artless.

"But I was just thinking of you, darling," she said. "How gay you used to be, how you loved parties."

"Oh, that." Isobel wheeled round, staring at herself in the mirror above the mantel. In Reno she had spent hour after hour in the sun, but her tan had faded quickly, disappearing, it seemed to her, almost overnight and leaving her skin just on to yellow. Her eyes looked enormous against the pallor of her face and there was a kind of rigidity in her chin and in the muscles around her mouth. For a long time now she'd been promising herself she'd relax; soon—next month, say, next week, tomorrow—and when that time came, she'd tell herself, she'd never again pretend to anyone about anything. For it was that that wore on a person—the tight, governing mask of pretense.

She forced herself to smile. "It's just that no one should be divorced in the fall," she said. "There's just such a general failing of forces at that time that one's own particular failure looms even larger."

"But you wanted a divorce, Isobel?" her mother said quickly. "You aren't sorry, are you?"

"Oh *no*." Isobel leaned over a little, her forehead resting against the palm of her hand. "Lord, no. It was the only thing I did want, finally. No, how could I be sorry? Let's not go into that again, Mother. *Please*."

"Well, all right," Mrs. Foster said. "I'm not going into anything, darling. It's just that I want things to be pleasant for you. I'd thought of having a little party here, just your old friends—but the apartment's so small. And the club—well, I didn't know about having it there. But when Jane Whittaker called, I was so happy. You used to go to so many parties at the Whittakers' house. And Andy's bought it back—the old place, you know, on Superior—and he and Jane have moved in."

"The Red Dragon?" Isobel asked.

"Well, it's still red; but the fence is gone, I think," Mrs. Foster said. "Such entertaining as they did—when Andy's mother was alive, I mean, and you were all growing up. Party after party. And then when you were off at school, and coming home for your summer and holiday vacations . . ."

Ages ago, Isobel thought, locked away in some remote period of the past; and yet, as you reckon time, as you count the years, not so long ago at that—not too long, at least, to prevent the name "Red Dragon" from coming quickly and easily to her lips or to blur the accurate, remembered vision of the house itself, the iron fence, the turrets, the red-cushioned seats in the library.

"It's their housewarming," her mother was saying. "There'll be hardly anyone you don't know. I don't think your crowd has changed much. I'd keep Toby, of course; I'd just thought it would be good for you to go out and have a nice time again. You're pretty. . . . You're young. . . . And——"

Her voice hesitated, and Isobel, turning round, saw that she was looking down, her hand fumbling against the buttons of her blouse, the fingers blunted, the veins rising in bluish knots along the back. Although her face was soft and childish still, her hand, groping a little, seemed old, unsure of itself. Remembering how easily her mother cried and wondering how often, alone in the apartment, she'd cried on her behalf, Isobel felt a wave of contrition rise inside her, dissolving her resistance.

"Look, Mother, I'll go," she said. She sat down on the couch. "Let's not make an issue of it. I'd like to go, really. I think it's only the mechanics that had me stopped; getting there, for instance—the lone woman in the taxi. And hooking a ride home with someone. I have to get used to it, of course. Six months from now I probably won't give it a second thought."

"Perhaps there'll be an odd man," Mrs. Foster said, her voice rising a little. "I don't know who. There aren't many unattached men in Bloomington—but perhaps there'll be someone."

"Predatory," Isobel said, smiling widely. "Absolutely no sense of shame. I'd run a mile from an odd man."

"I just meant someone to have a nice time with. That's all." Mrs. Foster folded her hands in her lap. "You take Millicent Forbes, Millicent's been divorced for quite a while—over two years, I think —and she seems to have a nice time. I'm always reading in the paper where she's been to the country club, or at a dance, or a dinner party. She goes with another couple—I think that's how she manages—but when I see her she always seems awfully busy and cheerful."

"Sounds wonderful," Isobel said, feeling her lips stretch wide, maintaining her smile.

"Of course that all takes time," Mrs. Foster said. "But you don't want to shut yourself off from people—not here at home where everyone knows you." Her foot tapped lightly against the floor. "Sue and Myron will ask you to go with them. You won't have to go alone."

But Isobel had had enough. The soft sound of her mother's words, offering her, out of love, out of pity, the small immediate solution, spun through her mind and she pushed back the low table that stood in front of the couch and stood up.

"I wonder if Toby's awake," she said. "I've never known him to sleep this long."

She thrust her hands into the pockets of her skirt and started for the door and stopped there for a second before she turned back, conscious only of a kind of angry necessity to deny whatever impression of dependency, of pathos, she might have given.

"I don't mind going alone," she said. "I'd like it. You've no idea what fun it is just being alone."

She wore her green dress and she thought, in spite of herself, as she put it on, how Gregory had hated green. "It's a stinking color," he'd said. "Nobody's skin is that good. And it makes my head ache." But he was wrong, of course; her skin was that good, and she'd bought the dress as soon as she'd got to Reno, letting it represent, somehow, her first overt act of freedom. She tried her gold jewelry, and then her silver; but the dress was better, she decided, with none.

Myron's voice, talking to her mother in the living room, reached her and she was ready now—there was no earthly reason for keeping him waiting, but she delayed still and turned once more to scrutinize the sweep of green outlining her figure. Slowly she sucked her underlip between her teeth and bit down upon it. And whatever's the matter with you? she hooted. Scared? Of what? Of people you've known all your life? Of Myron Kent, for instance?

When she opened the bedroom door she was smiling, the insistence of her smile helping to hold the curious little kernel of reluctance far below the surface, to squeeze it away into nothing. She heard her heels clatter down the hall and the bright note of her voice fill the living room.

"Myron!" she said. "You're an angel, you know." She kissed him as she had always kissed him on her comings and goings from Bloomington. "Are you sure you're up to this harem act? It was Sue's idea—Sue insisted you wouldn't mind."

He was fatter. He'd been a good-natured, hearty sort of boy when they were growing up, thickset even then, but now his vest seemed to strain against its buttons and she could see the little roll of flesh escaping over the tight circle of his collar. Briefly she remembered the year that he had been in love with her, his second year at Dartmouth. She'd gone to the Carnival with him and all that winter he'd written her earnest, inarticulate letters as though love, somehow, embarrassed him.

"Listen to her . . . listen, will you?" he kept saying, making each word a booming ejaculation. "Would I mind? How do you like that, Mrs. Foster? Just as though we'd let her go with anyone else. 'Isobel's here,' Sue told me yesterday—was it yesterday, was that when you got here? But, anyhow, I'd heard it already from Andy Whittaker at lunch, and it was fixed right then." He held her coat for her, still talking. "Don't wait up for her, Mrs. Foster," he said. "We have to get that house warm, you know. . . . That house has had time to cool off."

And then they were in the hall and, as he opened the outside door for her, the wind struck icily against her legs. She buried her chin in the fur of her collar and started, half running, toward the car.

"How's Sue?" she asked.

He dug his fingers into her arms, slowing her down to a walk.

"Say!" he said. "You haven't heard? We're going to have another baby! . . . After six years, how's that for luck?"

"Why doesn't Mother ever tell me anything?" she said. "A boy, I hope. But then, from the way you look, it doesn't matter, does it?"

She repeated almost the exact words to Sue as soon as they were in the car, and she saw Sue laugh and put her hand over Myron's and laugh again. "He's been impossible," she said, speaking in a high, light voice. "He started telling people almost before we were certain ourselves. Honestly, you'd think it was the only baby in the world."

It was warm in the car and Sue's coat was open, the illuminated dashboard laying a gentle pattern of light and shadow on her throat and over her slender young face. "It's not for months," she went on, "but I've made the most awful nuisance of myself—limp and exhausted, you know, and turning Myron into an absolute watchdog." She looked up at him, her voice teasing a little.

"You know what Bloomington is, Isobel," he said. "And Sue here —well, Sue never missed a thing until now. Susy was a breeze for her, and she's kept my tongue hanging out ever since. Danced me through three pairs of evening shoes since we've been married."

"Darling, I couldn't have." Sue laughed. "That's impossible." And then she turned to Isobel, her voice changing a little and losing some of its lightness. "But it's *you* we want to hear about, Isobel," she said. "How things are, I mean, and—well, how *you* are."

They had been close friends once, intimates really, trusting each other and exchanging long confidences. For a while after Isobel had left Bloomington they had written to each other—often, at first, and then less and less as their lives and their interests diverged until, finally, they had managed only an exchange of cards at Christmas. "Why don't you write?" they had scribbled hastily on the cards. "You've been owing me a letter for months," they had written.

But it was not so much the lessening of their intimacy, Isobel realized, that made it difficult for her now. It was not really that at all, but the apparent fact of Sue's and Myron's happiness, lying all safe and secure between them, as tangible, as real, as their bodies. Did they ever quarrel, she found herself wondering sharply, or scream out in anger at each other or lie awake at night filled with hate? Well, not likely, she thought. Not very likely. She looked at the solid outline of Myron's hand on the wheel, remembering Gregory's hand, trying to shut it out of her mind forever, but remembering anyway, the lamp crashing to the floor and Gregory lunging at her. She swallowed. She had not answered Sue, she realized; and she felt the silence wash up around her.

"I?" she said finally, speaking with a kind of quick impatience. "Well, I'm uninvolved. Let's put it that way. And it can be a beautiful state—after certain involvements. Confusing, though. Just at first, anyway." It didn't mean much—a hodgepodge of words—and she leaned forward, staring through the windshield. "But, look," she went on. "Catch me up on the vital statistics, will you? Who has what—as to children, I mean. And how old? Take yours, now—Sue; how old is she?"

"Six," said Sue, "can you believe it? And Toby? You know I've never laid eyes on Toby."

"Toby's two," said Isobel. "And not confused at all. Here, for instance, you'd think he was the native—not I. I'm still trying to orient myself."

"And no wonder." Sue slid her arm through Isobel's. "You've been back so seldom. Almost never. You've treated us badly."

"Tonight will fix you," Myron said. "You'll feel at home at the Whittakers' all right. It's just the same. Andy and Jane have polished it up a bit, but it's the same old Red Dragon."

"I've the oddest feeling of not wanting to go," she said. "Keep an eye on me, will you, Myron? Don't let me hide in a closet."

"But whyever should you?" Sue's hand pressed against her arm. "Everyone's dying to see you."

Isobel laughed. "I don't know exactly," she said. "I think I'm afraid we'll see all our young ghosts, playing Sardines or Murder or something. I might give mine an awful scare; it's probably a snooty little ghost—dead sure of itself."

She had meant it to be funny, and why did it sound bitter then, she wondered. Why, even now, when they were doing their best to make it easy for her, did everything she said ring hard and bitter in her mind? Ah, relax, she told herself. Try letting go. Just try. . . . She took a deep breath.

"It does make you think back, doesn't it?" she asked. "Jeff Mason and I locking little Beanie Childs in the tower room—remember? And we forgot about him. Everybody forgot about him. And Mrs. Whittaker had to phone the Masons after we'd all left; because Jeff had the key in his pocket. Poor Beanie."

She said it again later, standing with Andy Whittaker by the piano. "Poor Beanie," she said. "The life we led him."

They had arrived early. And that was different from their custom in the past, for it used to be that they would circle the block and circle it again, waiting for the cars to collect; never, for some obscure reason, wanting to be among the first. They were less noisy too; and, although they drank more, it took longer for the party to crystallize, to come together, and at the same time to drift apart and spread out through the house. For quite a while they stood in groups of threes and fours, juggling their glasses and their cigarettes, filling the living room with smoke, and stabbing around a little for something to talk about. She and Andy Whittaker and the Bannions, for instance. The house—they discussed the house, the lightened woodwork, the old stained glass in the window of the stairwell that Andy had had removed; and then tennis. Isobel had not played tennis for years, but she found herself clinging stubbornly to the subject until she thought again of Beanie Childs and, with her anecdote, evoked a sudden burst of laughter and released a flood of reminiscences.

"Darling," Jane Whittaker said, leaning over Andy and scooping up an ash tray. "You're monopolizing Isobel. You've got her backed against the piano where she couldn't move if she wanted to. . . . And everyone's glass is empty."

"Isobel looks wonderful," Eve Bannion said, her eyes sweeping over the green dress, resting for a moment on Isobel's ringless finger. "Doesn't she, Ted?"

"Isobel always looks wonderful," Ted answered. "The only trouble with her is that we don't see her often enough."

Wonderful. They kept saying it, the latecomers as well as the ones she had already greeted. Not a bit changed, they said. And how long had it been? Three years? Four, since she'd been in Bloomington? Well, for heaven's sake—and so much had happened in that time. They couldn't possibly tell her everything, not in one evening they couldn't. The fire at the country club. Old Mr. Bassett's will. And Johnny Evans—she knew about Johnny, didn't she?—going absolutely loco one night and walking naked down Superior. . . . They spoke with a kind of nervous excitement, quizzing her a little with their eyes but, for a time at least, skirting wide of any mention of her personal affairs; and not for a long while mentioning Gregory at all.

They had not liked Gregory and, on his one visit to Bloomington, Gregory had hated them. "They make me feel so cozy," he'd said. "And if there's anything I don't like . . ." "Good Lord!" he'd said. "Another dinner party? And will I draw that woman again? The one who gobbles her food?" That had been Peggy Arnold. "Peggy's an awfully good sort," she'd said, "if you'd just try getting to know her." "And why?" he'd asked, his face wrinkling with distaste. That had been long ago, before she had admitted even to herself that anything was wrong, and she had forgiven him over and over.

She took her second highball, drinking it quickly. The O'Keefes came in, and the Dalys; and the party, slow in starting, began at last to get under way. Someone turned on the record player in the library and Isobel danced with Andy Whittaker and with Myron and with Dave O'Keefe.

"Do you want me to ask you how it seems to be back again?" Dave said while they were dancing.

"Not particularly," she told him.

"All right then; I won't. You can just relax."

He had a slow, laconic way of speaking and he held her loosely, dancing rather badly and keeping a little ahead of the music, as though he were impatient with it. The record ground on. She could hear laughter now, coming from the living room, and she saw Andy go through the hall with a tray of glasses. There was gaiety enough. The house and the people were familiar to her—her mother had been right about that—and if her youthful ghost lurked anywhere around, she was unaware of it. Perhaps she should have gone out more, she thought, not lived so quietly in Reno, not stayed so much to herself there at the last in Virginia. Perhaps that would have been better and she would be less conscious now of the thin, persistent barrier setting her apart, isolating her. "You cast such a pall, Isobel," Gregory had said. "Or we do, rather. In combination, at least."

She missed a step, stumbled, and recovered herself.

"Sorry," she said; but Dave did not answer. He was looking down at her, his eyes squinting a little, his face remote.

It was after she had danced with him that Eve Bannion asked her how long she was going to be in Bloomington.

"I've got this beastly bazaar on my shoulders," she said. "And I'm always looking for new talent."

"Well, not that long," Isobel told her. "I mean if it's the Christmas bazaar, I'm afraid I'll be gone by then."

She saw Madge Daly turn a little, looking at her, her eyes moving slowly over her face; and whatever it was that had held them in restraint at first was gone now, she realized, and the way was open.

"Why, I thought you were going to stay," Madge said. "I thought you were going to live here. I don't know why—I just supposed that's what you'd do."

They were in the living room again. Dave leaned in front of her and pushed his cigarette down in the ash tray, and she smiled and moved back a step.

"No," she said, "I hadn't planned to live here."

"But where, then?" Madge persisted. "Because we're curious, of course."

Of course, thought Isobel. And why not? I'd be, too, if I were in your shoes.

"I'm not quite sure," she said. "New York, perhaps—that is if I work again. And I think I will—for a while, at least."

"Darling, I think that's terribly wise." This was Jane. She had started across the room and stopped suddenly and come back to where they were standing near the fireplace. "I think it would be the best thing in the world for you."

"Working?" Eve asked. "Oh, I don't know. I'm not sure I would if I were Isobel. I don't think I'd ever want to work again; no matter what happened."

"Eve spent two months in the library," Ted said. "It left its mark on her."

Madge was still looking at Isobel, her face intent, her lips already forming the next question.

"But what would you do about Toby?" she asked. "Leave him here with your mother? For the time he's supposed to be with you, anyway."

"I have custody of Toby," Isobel said, her voice rising a little. "And no—no, I wouldn't leave him. I'd take him with me."

"To New York?" Madge paused. "But I should think that would be hard; if you want to take a job, I mean."

It was hot in the room, Isobel realized, suddenly quite hot and airless. "I'll have to manage some way," she said. "Get somebody in to take care of him—something like that. I haven't really got it planned. . . . After a while he'll be in school, of course——" She let the sentence trail off.

Dave, who had been playing with his pocket knife, snapped it shut and put it back in his pocket.

"These women will complicate it for you if they can," he said. "How about a drink?" He put his hand on her arm.

She followed him toward the hall and, seeing Sue on the davenport, stopped there and sat down beside her.

"Don't let Madge Daly worry you," Sue said. "You know how Madge is. Always prying."

"She doesn't worry me," Isobel said. "I'm afraid I just confused her, though, trying to tell her what I was going to do. I confused myself really."

"Well, I don't see how you could have everything figured out. Not right away, at least. You've been through a lot, I know; and it takes time to get things straightened out again."

Isobel looked at her, seeing the gentle face, the eyes very clear and serene, feeling a sudden and absurd irritation at the note of sympathy in Sue's voice. How could you know? she thought fiercely. From your safe, protected little perch how could you possibly know anything about it? What it's like to live for months with somebody you hate and who hates you, trying to patch it up somehow and seeing it go to pieces again until the whole thing—your life, really—is a violent and impossible mess, whatever pride and self-confidence you had gone, destroyed. And divorce—what that's like when you finally get it; how alone it can make you feel.

Her eyes swept over the room, and she was sorting its occupants, she realized, cataloguing them neatly, couple by couple. Where's Millicent? she wondered suddenly. Millicent and I would make a pair.

"Where's Millicent Forbes?" she asked aloud; but, as if in answer to her question, she heard Millicent's voice in the hall and saw her come into the room, her arm through the arm of a tall and rather thin young man.

She looked older than when Isobel had seen her last, and her mouth was curved in a hard, bright smile.

"We're late," she announced. "We're terribly, terribly late. Blame Stephen, everybody. Stephen had to see this man, and I couldn't induce him to——" She broke off, catching sight of Isobel. "Why, Isobel!" she said, and with her arm still linked through the young man's she came over and kissed Isobel and introduced her to Stephen Dekker.

He stooped a little so that his long, sheeplike face was almost on a level with hers, and when he spoke his mouth twisted in an odd way, enabling her to see the wet pink lining of his lips.

"He's marvelous at the piano," Millicent said. "Absolutely marvelous. I don't know how we've existed without him. But he'll have to have a drink before he'll play anything. Won't you, darling?" She turned to him, pouting a little.

"I could do with one," he told her, and in an instant she had wheeled him around and was heading for the hall, smiling back at Isobel over his shoulder.

"Where on earth did he come from?" Isobel asked.

"From St. Louis," Sue said. "Or I think it's St. Louis. He took Johnny Evans' place, anyway. Millicent makes a ridiculous to-do over him; but then it's someone for her to go around with . . . I mean, of course——" She groped a little for her words, a faint blush coming up into her face. "You know what it's like in Bloomington. There aren't many——"

"Odd men," Isobel supplied.

Later, when Stephen Dekker played, a group formed around him, and Isobel went over and stood just within the curve of the piano, her arms resting on its top.

"He really is good, isn't he?" Eve whispered to her, and she nodded, although it seemed to her that he struck his bass chords needlessly hard and put in a lot of extra runs and flourishes.

He played "Lover," and some songs from *South Pacific*. And then he played some older things like "The Last Time I Saw Paris" and "Blue Skies." While he was feeling his way between pieces, running off chords, Millicent, who was sitting on the bench beside him, would suggest something to him and he'd play that.

"That was heavenly," she'd say. "I could listen to it all night."

After a little she started to sing, and everyone joined in, humming through the parts where they had forgotten the words.

He nodded his head to the music, accentuating the rhythm; and now and then he looked up, his eyes flicking over the group around him, resting an instant on Isobel's face, moving on, and then coming back, finding her more certainly the second time, looking at her longer. She did not like him. His sheep's face glistened a little in the warm room, his hair rose thick and oily from his forehead, and his eyes, rimmed slightly with red, were small and very bright. She didn't like him at all. He was ugly, she thought, and his playing was loud and stupid; yet, standing there, feeling his eyes singling her out, she felt a whisper of excitement form and mount inside her and she let her lashes fall down along her cheeks and lift again, slowly, almost reluctantly, at the moment when she knew he was looking at her.

"One more," he said. "I'm out of wind. I'm going sour."

She glanced at Millicent, and then she looked straight at him, smiling now, not much of a smile—but enough, and raising her brows so that they made a thin, questioning arch.

Someone turned the record player on again as soon as he had finished, and he got up and went out into the hall with Millicent for a dance.

They couldn't have had much of a dance, Isobel thought. He must have handed Millicent over to someone else in a hurry, for almost immediately he was back in the living room, alone this time, and she knew he was looking for her. She was over near the bay window with Myron and the Dalys, and she edged around a bit so that her back was to the door, waiting for him, feeling the little sensation of excitement fan up again.

"Like to dance?" he said, and she turned, not hurrying it, and faking a slow surprise.

"Why, yes. . . . Yes, I'd love it."

He held her closely, his pale, heavy cheek close to hers, his hand pressing hard against her spine. After a bit he began to talk, keeping his voice low so that she had to strain to hear him.

"Lousy bunch of records," he said. "Makes you wonder where they get them, doesn't it? I should have brought some of mine along. Andy asked me to, and then I came away forgetting them. I've got a couple you might be interested in. How'd you like me to play them for you some night?"

She arched a little away from him.

"What makes you think I'd like them?" she asked.

"I don't know. Just a hunch. Just the same way I knew you could dance like this." He executed an intricate series of steps and she felt her way, hesitating a little, not quite keeping up with him.

"I'm not that good," she said.

"Well, almost. . . . You could be easy enough." He started humming and stopped and bent his head a bit so that his mouth was close to her ear. "I saw you in there at the piano," he said. "While I was banging that stuff out. And I said to myself, there's a gal. Just like that. There's a gal. I always was a sucker for green."

He spun her around very fast and the room reeled before her eyes, reeled and steadied, and she was looking directly at Millicent.

240

She was at the record player with Andy Whittaker. Andy was fiddling with the dials, adjusting the volume, but Millicent wasn't paying any attention to him. She was just standing there, a little to one side, not smiling, but staring at the dancers—at Isobel, really. Her face looked shut away, her animation pinched off at its source, and her eyes were narrowed a bit as though she were trying to figure something out.

"Then I'm glad I wore green," Isobel said, turning her head so that she was looking again at Stephen, and letting her voice sound round and throaty. "Otherwise you might never have noticed me."

He laughed. "Oh, there are a couple of other colors I go for," he said. "I don't limit myself to green."

When the music stopped, he suggested that they go into the dining room. Had she had anything to eat, he asked, and she shook her head and felt him slip his arm through hers.

She took a plate from the table and put a sandwich on it and some olives. But she wasn't hungry. She rolled an olive around on the plate with the tip of her finger, listening to him say something and, when she did not answer, hearing him repeat it. She wished she were back in the living room with Sue or, better still, she wished she were at home. She thought of the way Millicent had looked at them while they were dancing, and she was tired, suddenly, annoyed at herself for simpering up at him and trying to lead him on, and tired of the whole stupid, senseless game. To what end? she thought. She didn't like him; and, even if by some amazing fluke of fortune she did, how, she wondered, would she feel then? With what sort of faith would she approach the whole delicate, tenuous procedure of male and female: the advances and withdrawals, the discovery of tastes that were like and unlike, the adjustments, the hesitancies, the doubts, the decisions?

She put her plate down on the edge of the table. "I'm not hungry after all," she said.

He had just popped the last of a sandwich in his mouth and he didn't answer, but she saw him look beyond her, and in an instant she heard Millicent's voice.

"Here you are, Isobel," she said. "I've been looking for you, darling, because I haven't had a chance to say two words to you and you've no idea how much I've thought about you lately." The color had come up in her face and her eyes were glistening. Taking a cigarette from her case, she leaned over and waited for Stephen to light it. "I told Stephen he'd like you," she went on. "I told him all about you, and I said we must see a lot of Isobel while she's here; we must cheer her up, because I know it's a hard time for her." She smiled and blew the smoke out of her mouth. "But tell me, darling, how was Reno?"

"Reno was all right," Isobel said. "Hot."

"I think you were so smart to go there. I mean things happen so much quicker there and, once your mind is made up, you want to get it over as quickly as possible and be through with it, don't you? Except, of course, with a child you never are really through with it, are you?"

It was an old game, old as the hills; and there was a way of answering her—there were any number of ways, except that, in trying to rally her forces, Isobel felt no force at all, but only a despairing inertia which, moving upward in her chest, seemed to stiffen her throat.

"Madge says you got custody of Toby," Millicent said. "I think that's wonderful. Complete custody? Is that what she meant?"

"Yes," said Isobel.

"But on what grounds, darling?"

Isobel sucked in her breath, letting it out slowly. The room had grown very still and she looked down at Millicent's hands, lifting her eyes until she saw the fat silver beads around her throat, and higher, so that she was looking at her chin, and then at her hard, brilliant mouth.

"Cruelty," she said, and, though she spoke lightly, holding the word thin and small, it seemed to bound through the room and the house, echoing up the stairway, and up again to the tower room where long ago she had played her young and heartless trick on Beanie Childs.

Someone put a glass down on the sideboard. Jane Whittaker leaned over the table and straightened a candle.

"You poor thing," Millicent was murmuring. "You poor darling. You have had a time of it, haven't you? Peter, of course, was a sot. But a good-natured sot. I guess I came off pretty lucky after all."

Isobel nodded, not answering, and when Dave O'Keefe took her hand and suggested that they dance again she followed him out of the room, walking carefully, holding her shoulders very straight.

He looked down at her. "How'd you come to marry that lug anyway?" he asked.

"I don't know," she said.

"You should have brought him out here first. Any of us could have put you wise."

She shook her head. "I wouldn't have listened."

"No, I guess not. Dead sure you were right, I suppose?"

"I suppose. It's hard to remember. I just made a mistake," she said.

"Well, chalk it up to experience. Anybody's entitled to a mistake or two."

He turned her around, lumbering through the dance steps.

"Watch those instincts, though," he said. "Take a look at our friend, the huntress, Millicent in there, and keep a curb on that sort of stuff."

"I haven't got any instincts," she said. "Not any I can be sure of, anyway. People want to know; everybody wants to know, I guess. I guess it's natural. But I haven't got any plans or instincts or——" Her voice thickened and she pulled away from him. "I'll be down in a minute, Dave," she said. "I'll be right back." And she started up the stairs, running, hearing him call to her, "Hey, what's wrong? What did I say?" but running on until she found the bathroom and, with the door locked behind her, she leaned hard against the lavatory, braced against the trembling in her legs.

What's it going to be like? And I, what will I be like? Like Millicent? Fighting tooth and nail for anybody—just anybody? Or like I am now? Like this? Remembering every bit of it? And afraid? And defeated? And lost? Lost. . . .

She shut her throat against her sobs, and after a while she turned on the spigot and began to scrub her hands.

When she went down again, Myron was at the foot of the stairs.

"I was looking for you," he said. "Say, I think we'll have to leave. Sue's bushed, but I hate to drag you off while things are still going. Why don't you stay?"

"No," she said. "It's late. I don't mind leaving now. I'd rather."

They were quiet in the car driving home. Sue rested her head on the back of the seat and Myron rolled up the window beside him.

"That all right?" he asked. "Cold?"

"No, darling," she said. "I'm fine."

"We shouldn't have stayed so long."

"We didn't stay too long. I thought it was nice, didn't you, Isobel?"

"Yes," said Isobel. "It was a lot of fun."

"How'd you like Stephen Dekker?"

"He was all right, I suppose."

• "Sounds enthusiastic, doesn't she?" Myron said.

"But, darling, nobody's very enthusiastic this time of night." Sue yawned down in her coat a little and shut her eyes.

When they reached the apartment house, Myron got out of the car and went with Isobel as far as the entrance hall. He said good night quickly.

She waited an instant after he had gone, listening to him run down the walk and hearing the door of the car slam and the tires grind over the pavement, and then she got out her key, unlocked the door, and went on into the apartment.

Toby was sleeping in a crib in the bedroom, and she stood at the foot of the crib looking down at him. He was on his back, his fat, soft arms flung up over his head, his face, in sleep, in repose, almost an exact miniature of Gregory's. No, she said to herself, thinking again of Millicent's words, with a child I guess you're never really through with it. But I won't spoil him, anyway. Not if I can help it, I won't. I won't let him be like Gregory.

She took off her coat and, throwing it across the bed, went over to the dresser. The jewelry that she had tried on and discarded still lay on the dresser top, and she picked it up and put it in the jewelry box, listening to the links of the bracelet strike tinnily against each other. She wished she had not taken that last highball. Her head had begun to ache and, although she was sleepy, she didn't feel like going to bed.

The apartment seemed very still, the room close and still around her. She remembered the way Gregory used to act after a party, kicking off his shoes, swearing at his necktie, banging at the window that always stuck. . . . She remembered Gregory; and, standing there, the appalling, the bewildering truth came over her that if he were here tonight, this minute, she'd take him back. If he came into the room, his face scowling with ill-temper, ready to quarrel, ready to find some little thing and worry away at it and build it up, she'd take him back. If he came over to her and, with the old, known gesture of certainty, put his hand on her, she'd turn to him and bury her face in his coat. Any way that he came, she realized despairingly, any way at all, she'd take him back, if only to fill for an instant the vast emptiness that was in her.

from the Virginia Quarterly Review

THE SHADOW OF AN ARM

THOMAS HAL PHILLIPS *was born on a farm near Corinth, Mississippi, in 1922. He was graduated from Mississippi State College and served three years in the Navy, part of the time as commander of an LC-1, participating in the three invasions of Anzio, Elba, and southern France. He has written nothing about the war, however. He took his M.A. at the University of Alabama, where he studied under Hudson Strode. He received a Rosenwald Fellowship and a Eugene Saxton Award for his first novel,* Bitterweed Path, *published in 1950. His second novel,* The Golden Lie, *was published in the spring of 1951. Mr. Phillips taught creative writing two years at Southern Methodist University and is at present in France on a Fulbright scholarship.*

Peane sat on a stool beside the compress and watched the cotton, like a stream of snow, slide down into the baler. In his right hand he held a short hickory rod, now worn sleek, with which he stirred the cotton so that the chute would not choke. He could not see Mr. Sid and Mr. Clark, standing on the weighing platform behind him, but he could hear them; and Mr. Clark was saying: "But Papa, that's old-timey business. If I'm going to keep books I want to pay everybody with a check every Saturday night. And if they say I never paid, then I'll have a record."

"All right," Mr. Sid said. "All right. But nobody yet ever told me I didn't pay them. Let's go on up to the house and you can write the checks."

Above the sound of the gin Peane heard Mr. Sid walking toward him. He knew Mr. Sid's walk. Then he felt the hand touch his shoulder and Mr. Sid said: "We're going to dinner. We'll be back in a little while."

"Yessuh," Peane said. He heard them go down the ladder. Then he looked around to see that Mr. Clark was the last to disappear below. He hoped Mr. Sid wouldn't let Mr. Clark start writing checks on payday. Having a check was not the same as having the bills, even the wrinkled bills; and that was another thing Mr. Clark didn't understand. But Mr. Sid did.

Peane reached out his right hand and jerked the cotton down. Sometimes he did not use the stick at all. He liked to feel the cotton just before it went into the bale. It was warm and soft then. He smiled a little. His hands and arms always looked blacker against the white blanket sliding downward. He half-closed his eyes and pictured every wheel that quivered now in a long, steady drone. He knew everything about the gin: he and Mr. Sid had built it. He knew more about it than Mr. Roy Drew, who was only the ginner. He thought of Mr. Roy because he heard laughter. It came from the suction platform at the front of the gin, and he knew it was Mr. Roy talking to Mr. Albert. They were ginning Mr. Albert's bale now, and in a few minutes Mr. Albert would come back to the compress and joke about how much his bale was going to weigh.

After a while he heard the steps he expected but he did not look up at that moment, for the chute was filling. His left hand reached out for the lever; slowly the presser went down. Then he released the lever, and with a hiss of steam the presser jolted upward again.

"Peane?"

"Yessuh." He turned. It was Mr. Albert. He was tall and heavy and red-faced now. Peane could remember when he was tall and slender and the bottoms of his trousers always struck above his ankles.

"Where's Sid?"

"At the house. For dinner." His left hand worked hard at the lever again.

"When you gonna quit monkeying with this old gin and come over to my place to grow cotton?"

"I don't know, suh." Peane laughed. Mr. Albert was a lot like Mr. Sid.

"Well, hell. I feed my hands. It's nearly one o'clock."

"Yessuh. Mr. Sid'll be back now, any time. Then I go eat."

"Has Clark come home from school to run his daddy's farm next year?"

247

"I don't know. Mr. Sid didn't say yet. But Mr. Clark's here." Peane let the press down and up again. A light cloud of steam covered his hand.

"What's it gonna weigh?"

Peane laughed. "About 490."

Mr. Albert looked over into the baler. "Now when the hell have you weighed a bale for me that didn't push the pè beyond five hundred?"

Peane reached out with the stick, for the chute was filling again. He let the presser down and the compress creaked. Mr. Albert grunted. "I'll be damned, Peane. If I brought you and Sid a six-hundred-pound bale your old compress would bust wide open. You ought to get a new all-electric outfit, like the one in Raymond. Just touch a button there and a button here . . ." They turned to the sound of steps behind them.

Mr. Sid was climbing the gin's back ladder. His big arms and shoulders were just above the gin's floor. A healthy red always showed across his face.

"Sid," Mr. Albert said. "Did you hear what I said?"

Mr. Sid was standing straight now. He was big, not fat. "No. What?"

"If you don't jack up this damned gin and put a new electric outfit under it, I'm gonna start hauling my cotton to Raymond."

Mr. Sid grinned and came on to where Peane sat. He put his hand on Peane's shoulder. "He can't tell a good gin when he sees one, can he?"

Peane laughed. Mr. Sid turned toward Mr. Albert. "You want those fancy suction motors to shoot your cotton through and cut it all to pieces? Hell no."

"I know," Mr. Albert said. "I know they shoot it through so fast it looks like it's sprinkled with pepper. And cut it up too."

"Now you're talking," Mr. Sid said. He took the hickory stick from Peane's hand. "Reckon this bale will touch five hundred, Peane? Or is this another one of those shirttail bales of Albert Bynum's?"

"A dollar on it," Mr. Albert said. "A dollar that it tips five hundred."

Mr. Sid laughed. "You better go on and get something to eat, Peane."

Peane walked toward the house with the November chill close about him. He wondered what it would be like if Mr. Clark took over the gin, though he did not believe Mr. Sid would let him change anything. He remembered Mr. Clark saying: "But you ought to switch over to electricity, Papa. You could save on cordwood, and belts, a dozen things, and cut out half the work. . . ." And Mr. Sid had said: "I'm sixty-two years old. I'm not going to tear up something I built just to do away with a little work. That's the trouble with the world. People trying to get out of work when it's the best thing I know of to keep a man happy—plenty of work and a good wife."

"But it's foolish not to switch."

"Someday, Clark," Mr. Sid had said, "it'll belong to you and Elizabeth and Karen. Then you can put in electric motors and push buttons—mirrors, if you want to."

Mr. Clark did not understand.

But Peane understood. It was something you felt, and not something to talk about. He looked back for a moment to the gin which he and Mr. Sid had built thirty years ago: the high tin top, the tall smokestack, and the silver suction pipes. He turned and hurried on toward the house.

He passed his own small house and then Etta's house at the edge of the garden. He did not see anyone nor any smoke from Etta's chimney. It seemed like a day when everything had stopped. Something was waiting.

On the back steps, at the big house, he stopped. He did not remember the first time he had gone into that house. He remembered being seven and Mr. Sid six, and together they had sometimes slept on the same pallet. Then Mr. Sid was suddenly grown—all too soon. His face was big and red, and the ridges leaped on his arms when he lifted any weight. The farm was all his. But he did not make Peane work in the fields. Together they had built the gin—though a few of the field hands helped now and then. That was why Mr. Sid didn't want the gin changed. Mr. Clark could never understand.

Peane went into the kitchen. When he did not see Etta, he called to her. He heard only a voice in the living room, and he knew it was Mr. Clark. "Mother, what time did Elizabeth and Karen go to Vicksburg?"

"While you were at the gin. They didn't know you wanted to go.

And besides, they're going to be at the high school all afternoon."
That was Miss Annie. Then she said: "Peane? Is that you?"

"Yes, ma'am."

"Etta's in the garden. She put you a plate in the warming closet."

"Yes, ma'am."

The moment his hand touched the warming closet of the stove he heard the gin's whistle, and in his mind he could see clearly the long blasts of steam rising above the boiler. His heart leaped but he did not move. His hand seemed glued to a platter. Mr. Clark's voice was quick in the living room. "Mother, something is wrong at the gin. That damned old dilapidated boiler, I guess."

Peane wanted to turn, to say the whistle wouldn't blow if there was anything wrong with the boiler. But his hand still clutched the platter.

"Peane?"

Suddenly his hand jerked to his side and he was hurrying toward Mr. Clark.

"Let's see what's the matter. I've been telling Papa that something was going to happen . . ."

They ran out of the house toward the gate and the car. Peane sat in the back seat as they raced down the driveway and turned into the road toward the gin. Mr. Clark's lips kept moving: "Damned old thing ready to fall in on his head and Papa won't change it. No telling what's happened now."

The car lurched from the gravel road on to the sawdust-covered gin yard. Peane's hands reached out and pressed against the seat when the car came to a stop near the scales. He ran behind Mr. Clark toward the ladder of the gin.

At the head of the ladder Mr. Albert towered above them. He reached down and caught Mr. Clark's arm, helping him up the last few rungs. "Over here, Clark. . . ."

Peane pulled himself up quickly to the gin's floor. His short breath was like a quick heartbeat. Mr. Sid was lying beside the compress, his bloodstained arm folded across his chest. His sleeve was hardly torn, like little rips from barbed wire. A small streak of blood crossed his lips.

"You can't stop the blood," Mr. Albert said. "Too much in the

250

shoulder. You'll have to take him to Raymond. You can't get to Vicksburg in time.".

"But there's nothing at Raymond—a two-by-four clinic."

"We can't get to Vicksburg."

Mr. Clark was kneeling. His own face was turning white. Mr. Albert reached down and pulled him up. "Go on. Go on down, Clark. Get the car started. Peane's stout. He can lift him and I'll hold his arm and shoulder."

"Where's Roy?" Mr. Clark said. His breath was fast.

"Gone after you. Go on now. . . ." He shoved Mr. Clark toward the ladder.

Peane stooped and lifted Mr. Sid, who opened his eyes and closed them again.

"Peane?"

Peane could not answer. Mr. Sid was too heavy. Mr. Albert had the injured arm and shoulder and he was saying: "Easy, Peane. You'll have to carry him down the ladder by yourself—not room for us both."

Peane's foot touched the top rung. He inched downward. His shoulders touched either side of the ladder opening. He wanted to look up, as if suddenly everything was reversed and he couldn't ask God for anything unless he looked up. He was almost saying: "God, you know I can't think of nothing with all this weight. . . ."

Then he was in the car and they were moving. Mr. Clark's right hand was cotton-white upon the steering wheel, and Mr. Albert was holding the shoulder and whispering: "You made it, Peane, and that damned ladder sagging with all your weight. . . ." And still Peane wanted to look up but he could not, he thought, for the weight in his arms. It was all a little like the times they used to wrestle—and he could throw Mr. Sid. He wanted to touch Mr. Sid's face, to wipe the streak of sweat and blood away.

Mr. Sid did not open his eyes. He said: "The press caught my shoulder. It stuck. The lever. You know how it does . . . sometimes . . . Peane. . . ."

Peane did not move though the weight was getting heavier and heavier. He wished Mr. Sid was six or seven. He could hold him then. It would be all right. For a moment Peane seemed to close his own eyes. Then the car was stopping. His body came to life again, beneath the weight.

He put Mr. Sid on the white table in the clinic. Then, without saying anything, he turned and went back to the car. He wanted to look up and say something, now that the weight was gone, but he was sick—low inside him. He got into the back seat. Then he saw the blood and got into the front seat, put his head down into his hands, and tried not to think of the dripping from the cotton which Mr. Albert had held beneath the torn sleeve. He sat a long time.

Somebody tapped him on the shoulder. "They want you in there," Mr. Albert said. "And hurry. I have to leave—to go to Vicksburg after Elizabeth and Karen."

In the hall of the clinic Peane saw the doctor and Mr. Clark and the nurse. They were in a little group. Peane knew the doctor: he was Mr. Edgeworth's boy and not much older than Mr. Clark.

"Can't we do something else?" Mr. Clark was saying. "Can't we wait until Karen and Elizabeth get here?"

"Yes," the doctor said. "We can wait. But the sooner he gets the blood the better. And they're not likely to have AB, since you didn't. He can't wait long for a transfusion."

Mr. Clark kept looking at the doctor, not at his face, but at the mask hanging around his neck. Then slowly he turned to Peane. His face was very white. "Would you give Papa a transfusion—if you're the right type?"

Peane could not answer; he had not expected Mr. Clark to ask him anything. He nodded, and again he was beginning to be sick, low in his stomach. Mr. Clark caught his arm lightly and said: "Go with the nurse." It was the first time Peane ever remembered Mr. Clark's touching him. He nodded again, and then he followed the nurse. He was trying to think about his hat, trying to remember where it was.

The room was white and the smell was sharp. The nurse took the forefinger of his right hand and washed it with alcohol. "Hold still," she said.

"Is he going to be all right?" Peane said.

"We don't know."

"Sometimes it gits stuck," he said. "The lever at the compress."

"Clench your fist, then open it."

He was afraid.

"It stuck with Mr. Sid. Then the press comes down . . ."

"Open it. Your hand."

"But it always comes down slow and you can git out of the way. Only this time it must . . ."

She pricked his finger. "Now lean back and rest awhile." She went away and he closed his eyes.

In a few minutes he was lying on a white table with the needle in his arm. It was the thought of the needle that hurt. He kept his eyes closed and tried to think that it was only somebody pinching him— like Mr. Sid poking fun.

"It was the right kind," the nurse whispered, but she did not seem to be talking to him. And he was afraid to ask anything; even his asking might make things go wrong.

After a few minutes he heard: "I'm all through now. You just lie there and rest awhile."

He lay there, trying not to remember, and the nurse went out. But the smell and the quietness did not make him afraid any more. He felt as if he had touched something he had always wanted to touch, had held something he had always wanted to hold. It was a long time before the nurse came back into the room. He was glad when she came.

"They're moving Mr. Walters now. He's awake. The doctor wants you to lift him onto the bed. They're all sick. Everybody but the doctor. Some people can't look at blood."

Peane nodded slowly. He got up.

"You know where room two is? Down the hall?"

"No, ma'am."

"Come on. I'll show you."

She went down the hall ahead of him and turned into a room. He reached the doorway of the room and stopped. His hand clutched the facing. Then he knew that Mr. Sid's arm was gone.

"Here," the doctor said. "Can you lift him by yourself?"

Peane pulled his hand away from the facing. Slowly he walked toward the bed.

"Stand between the roller and the bed," the nurse said. "And turn his head that way."

Slowly Peane nodded. He was numb with the feeling that he

might drop Mr. Sid. His whole body seemed unable to stand. Then his hands moved under Mr. Sid's shoulders and under his thighs. His arms against the white sheet were darker now—like their being against the stream of cotton in the compress. He closed his eyes, lifted, and turned. Something hurt in his stomach. Mr. Sid's shoulders touched the bed. He opened his eyes and for a moment stared. Then his lips moved slowly. "Peane . . . did you give me the blood?"

"Yessuh."

"You shouldn't be lifting me."

"You're all right now," the nurse said quickly. "You're going to be all right." Her hands moved along the sheet beside his good right arm.

Mr. Sid kept looking at Peane. "You know how that damned lever sometimes sticks. . . ."

"Yessuh," Peane said.

"You rest now," the nurse said. She motioned Peane quietly toward the door.

Peane walked home. He knew that he did not have to walk: it was something he wanted to do. He had walked for a long time when he realized that it was beginning to rain. The wind seemed to whip the low clouds down into his face. He had been thinking that Mr. Sid would be all right.

When he came within sight of the gin he thought of Mr. Clark there, so he turned and cut across the pasture and went past the barn toward the house which was dark now. When he passed the big house he wished that somebody had been there: he wanted to tell somebody something. It was a strange feeling, as if nothing had happened to Mr. Sid, but the day itself had died.

In the damp darkness inside his room he lay on his bed and waited. He did not sleep, but sometimes he would feel his arms, as if to make certain that nothing had happened to them. A little while later he heard the sound of a car, and he got up. Then he saw the light from the big house. He crossed the yard to the back door and went into the kitchen. He was not hungry. He only wanted to tell somebody something—that everything was gone and he could never go back to the gin again.

He could hear voices in the living room. Then suddenly Mr. Clark was saying: "Peane? Is that you?"

"Yessuh." He was trying hard to think how to tell Mr. Clark—he would take over the gin now.

"Did you want something, Peane?"

Peane could not answer. He could not say anything.

"Oh, you want your pay." Mr. Clark turned back into the living room. The house was silent, more lifeless than Peane ever remembered. Then Mr. Clark was returning across the dining room toward the kitchen. He held out a check before him. Still Peane could not move nor say anything. Mr. Clark reached out and pushed the check into his coat pocket, and then he quickly drew two twenty-dollar bills from his wallet. "Here's something for you, Peane. And if you don't mind, I wish you wouldn't tell anybody about giving the blood." They did not say anything else to each other. After a minute Mr. Clark went back into the living room. Peane stood and watched until the light went off in the dining room. Slowly he turned and went out into the night. He looked across the yard toward the gin, and beyond the gin toward Mr. Albert Bynum's place. But for a while he did not move. He took the check and the bills and tore them piece by piece and let the rain wash the pieces out of his hand and onto the ground. Then he began to walk, for he knew that Mr. Sid would understand. And he was thinking that he would not take all of himself: he would leave something behind.

from Harper's Magazine

CYCLISTS' RAID

FRANK ROONEY *was born in Kansas City, Missouri, in 1913. He lived there until he was twelve and a half, when he moved to Los Angeles, where he stayed until the Army took him in 1941 He went to Belmont High School in Los Angeles, and his attendance there ended his formal education. After that, he writes, he "washed dishes, sold various articles from house to house, did a little professional cooking (very little), and ended up on the labor gang at one of the Hollywood studios." After the war Mr. Rooney settled in New York, doing some stage and radio work and determining to be a short-story writer. His stories have appeared in* Collier's *and* Cosmopolitan. *He says his chief recreations are "chess, singing, and reading—none of which I do very well."*

Joel Bleeker, owner and operator of the Pendleton Hotel, was adjusting the old redwood clock in the lobby when he heard the sound of the motors. At first he thought it might be one of those four-engine planes on the flights from Los Angeles to San Francisco which occasionally got far enough off course to be heard in the valley. And for a moment, braced against the steadily approaching vibrations of the sound, he had the fantastic notion that the plane was going to strike the hotel. He even glanced at his daughter Cathy standing a few feet to his right and staring curiously at the street.

Then with his fingers still on the hour hand of the clock he realized that the sound was not something coming down from the air but the high, sputtering racket of many vehicles moving along the ground. Cathy and Bret Timmons, who owned one of the two

256

drug stores in the town, went out onto the veranda but Bleeker stayed by the clock, consulting the railroad watch he pulled from his vest pocket and moving the hour hand on the clock forward a minute and a half. He stepped back deliberately, shut the glass case, and looked at the huge brass numbers and the two ornate brass pointers. It was eight minutes after seven, approximately twenty-two minutes until sundown. He put the railroad watch back in his pocket and walked slowly and incuriously through the open doors of the lobby. He was methodical and orderly and the small things he did every day—like setting the clock—were important to him. He was not to be hurried—especially by something as elusively irritating as a sound, however unusual.

There were only three people on the veranda when Bleeker came out of the lobby—his daughter Cathy, Timmons, and Francis La-Salle, co-owner of LaSalle and Fleet, Hardware. They stood together quietly, looking, without appearing to stare, at a long, stern column of red motorcycles coming from the south, filling the single main street of the town with the noise of a multitude of pistons and the crackling of exhaust pipes. They could see now that the column was led by a single white motorcycle which when it came abreast of the hotel turned abruptly right and stopped. They saw, too, that the column without seeming to slow down or to execute any elaborate movement had divided itself into two single files. At the approximate second, having received a signal from their leader, they also turned right and stopped.

The whole flanking action, singularly neat and quite like the various vehicular formations he remembered in the Army, was distasteful to Bleeker. It recalled a little too readily his tenure as a lieutenant colonel overseas in England, France, and finally Germany.

"Mr. Bleeker?"

Bleeker realized the whole troop—no one in the town either then or after that night was ever agreed on the exact number of men in the troop—had dismounted and that the leader was addressing him.

"I'm Bleeker." Although he hadn't intended to, he stepped forward when he spoke, much as he had stepped forward in the years when he commanded a battalion.

"I'm Gar Simpson and this is Troop B of the Angeleno Motor-cycle Club," the leader said. He was a tall, spare man and his voice was coldly courteous to the point of mockery. "We expect to bivouac outside your town tonight and we wondered if we might use the facilities of your hotel. Of course, sir, we'll pay."

"There's a washroom downstairs. If you can put up with that——"

"That will be fine, sir. Is the dining room still open?"

"It is."

"Could you take care of twenty men?"

"What about the others?"

"They can be accommodated elsewhere, sir."

Simpson saluted casually and, turning to the men assembled stiffly in front of the hotel, issued a few quiet orders. Quickly and efficiently the men in the troop parked their motorcycles at the curb. About a third of the group detached itself and came deferentially but steadily up the hotel steps. They passed Bleeker, who found himself maneuvered aside, and went into the lobby. As they passed him, Bleeker could see the slight converted movement of their faces —though not their eyes, which were covered by large green goggles —toward his daughter Cathy. Bleeker frowned after them but before he could think of anything to say, Simpson, standing now at his left, touched his arm.

"I've divided the others into two groups," he said quietly. "One group will eat at the diner and the other at the Desert Hotel."

"Very good," Bleeker said. "You evidently know the town like a book. The people too. Have you ever been here before?"

"We have a map of all the towns in this part of California, sir. And of course we know the names of all the principal hotels and their proprietors. Personally, I could use a drink. Would you join me?"

"After you," Bleeker said.

He stood watching Simpson stride into the lobby and without any hesitation go directly to the bar. Then he turned to Cathy, seeing Timmons and LaSalle lounging on the railing behind her, their faces already indistinct in the plummeting California twilight.

"You go help in the kitchen, Cathy," Bleeker said. "I think it'd be better if you didn't wait on tables."

"I wonder what they look like behind those goggles," Cathy said.

"Like anybody else," Timmons said. He was about thirty, some-what coarse and intolerant and a little embarrassed at being in love

258

with a girl as young as Cathy. "Where did you think they came from? Mars?"

"What did they say the name of their club was?" Cathy said.

"Angeleno," LaSalle said.

"They must be from Los Angeles. Heigh-ho. Shall I wear my very best gingham, citizen colonel?"

"Remember now—you stay in the kitchen," Bleeker said.

He watched her walk into the lobby, a tall, slender girl of seventeen, pretty and enigmatic, with something of the brittle independence of her mother. Bleeker remembered suddenly, although he tried not to, the way her mother had walked away from him that frosty January morning two years ago saying, "I'm going for a ride." And then the two-day search in the mountains after the horse had come back alone and the finding of her body—the neck broken—in the stream at the foot of the cliff. During the war he had never really believed that he would live to get back to Cathy's mother and after the war he hadn't really believed he would be separated from her—not again—not twice in so short a time.

Shaking his head—as if by that motion he could shed his memories as easily as a dog sheds water—Bleeker went in to join Gar Simpson, who was sitting at a table in the barroom. Simpson stood politely when Bleeker took the opposite chair.

"How long do you fellows plan to stay?" Bleeker asked. He took the first sip of his drink, looked up, and stared at Simpson.

"Tonight and tomorrow morning," Simpson said.

Like all the others he was dressed in a brown windbreaker, khaki shirt, khaki pants, and as Bleeker had previously observed wore dark calf-length boots. A cloth and leather helmet lay on the table beside Simpson's drink, but he hadn't removed his flat green goggles, an accouterment giving him and the men in his troop the appearance of some tropical tribe with enormous semi-precious eyes, lidless and immovable. That was Bleeker's first impression and, absurd as it was, it didn't seem an exaggeration of fancy but of truth.

"Where do you go after this?"

"North." Simpson took a rolled map from a binocular case slung over his shoulder and spread it on the table. "Roughly we're following the arc of an ellipse with its southern tip based on Los Angeles and its northern end touching Fresno."

"Pretty ambitious for a motorcycle club."

"We have a month," Simpson said. "This is our first week but we're in no hurry and we're out to see plenty of country."

"What are you interested in mainly?"

"Roads. Naturally, being a motorcycle club—you'd be surprised at the rate we're expanding—we'd like to have as much of California as possible opened up to us."

"I see."

"Keeps the boys fit too. The youth of America. Our hope for the future." Simpson pulled sternly at his drink and Bleeker had the impression that Simpson was repressing, openly, and with pride, a vast sparkling ecstasy.

Bleeker sat and watched the young men in the troop file upstairs from the public washroom and stroll casually but nevertheless with discipline into the dining room. They had removed their helmets and strapped them to their belts, each helmet in a prescribed position to the left of the belt buckle but—like Simpson—they had retained their goggles. Bleeker wondered if they ever removed the goggles long enough to wash under them and, if they did, what the flesh under them looked like.

"I think I'd better help out at the tables," Bleeker said. He stood up and Simpson stood with him. "You say you're from Troop B? Is that right?"

"Correct. We're forming Troop G now. Someday——"

"You'll be up to Z," Bleeker said.

"And not only in California."

"Where else, for instance?"

"Nevada—Arizona—Colorado—Wyoming."

Simpson smiled and Bleeker, turning away from him abruptly, went into the dining room where he began to help the two waitresses at the tables. He filled water glasses, set out extra forks, and brought steins of beer from the bar. As he served the troop, their polite thank yous, ornate and insincere, irritated him. It reminded him of tricks taught to animals, the animals only being allowed to perform under certain obvious conditions of security. And he didn't like the cool way they stared at the two waitresses, both older women and fixtures in the town and then leaned their heads together as

260

if every individual thought had to be pooled and divided equally among them. He admitted, after some covert study, that the twenty men were really only variations of one, the variations, with few exceptions, being too subtle for him to recognize and differentiate. It was the goggles, he decided, covering that part of the face which is most noteworthy and most needful for identification—the eyes and the mask around the eyes.

Bleeker went into the kitchen, pretending to help but really to be near Cathy. The protective father, he thought ironically, watching his daughter cut pie and lay the various colored wedges on the white blue-bordered plates.

"Well, Daddy, what's the verdict?" Cathy looked extremely grave but he could see that she was amused.

"They're a fine body of men."

"Uh-huh. Have you called the police yet?"

He laughed. "It's a good thing you don't play poker."

"Child's play." She slid the last piece of blueberry pie on a plate. "I saw you through the door. You looked like you were ready to crack the Siegfried line—single-handed."

"That man Simpson."

"What about him?"

"Why don't you go upstairs and read a book or something?"

"Now, Daddy—you're the only professional here. They're just acting like little tin soldiers out on a spree."

"I wish to God they were made of tin."

"All right. I'll keep away from them. I promise." She made a gesture of crossing her throat with the thin edge of a knife. He leaned over and kissed her forehead, his hand feeling awkward and stern on her back.

After dinner the troop went into the bar, moving with a strange co-ordinated fluency that was both casual and military, and sat jealously together in one corner of the room. Bleeker served them pitchers of beer and for the most part they talked quietly together, Simpson at their center, their voices guarded and urgent, as if they possessed information which couldn't be disseminated safely among the public.

Bleeker left them after a while and went upstairs to his daughter's room. He wasn't used to being severe with Cathy and he was a little embarrassed by what he had said to her in the kitchen. She was

261

turning the collars of some of his old shirts, using a portable sewing machine he had bought her as a present on her last birthday. As he came in she held one of the shirts comically to the floor lamp and he could see how thin and transparent the material was. Her mother's economy in small things, almost absurd when compared to her limitless generosity in matters of importance, had been one of the family jokes. It gave him an extraordinary sense of pleasure, so pure it was like a sudden inhalation of oxygen, to see that his daughter had not only inherited this tradition but had considered it meaningful enough to carry on. He went down the hall to his own room without saying anything further to her. Cathy was what he himself was in terms which could mean absolutely nothing to anyone else.

He had been in his room for perhaps an hour, working on the hotel accounts and thinking obliquely of the man Simpson, when he heard, faintly and apparently coming from no one direction, the sound of singing. He got up and walked to the windows overlooking the street. Standing there, he thought he could fix the sound farther up the block toward Cunningham's bar. Except for something harsh and mature in the voices it was the kind of singing that might be heard around a Boy Scout campfire, more rhythmic than melodic and more stirring than tuneful. And then he could hear it almost under his feet, coming out of the hotel lobby and making three or four people on the street turn and smile foolishly toward the doors of the veranda.

Oppressed by something sternly joyous in the voices, Bleeker went downstairs to the bar, hearing, as he approached, the singing become louder and fuller. Outside of Simpson and the twenty men in the troop there were only three townsmen—including LaSalle—in the bar. Simpson, seeing Bleeker in the door, got up and walked over to him, moving him out into the lobby where they could talk.

"I hope the boys aren't disturbing you," he said.

"It's early," Bleeker said.

"In an organization as large and selective as ours it's absolutely necessary to insist on a measure of discipline. And it's equally necessary to allow a certain amount of relaxation."

"The key word is selective, I suppose."

262

"We have our standards," Simpson said primly.

"May I ask just what the hell your standards are?"

Simpson smiled. "I don't quite understand your irritation, Mr. Bleeker."

"This is an all-year-round thing, isn't it? This club of yours?"

"Yes."

"And you have an all-year-round job with the club?"

"Of course."

"That's my objection, Simpson. Briefly and simply stated, what you're running is a private army." Bleeker tapped the case slung over Simpson's shoulder. "Complete with maps, all sorts of local information, and of course a lobby in Sacramento."

"For a man who has traveled as widely as you have, Mr. Bleeker, you display an uncommon talent for exaggeration."

"As long as you behave yourselves I don't care what you do. This is a small town and we don't have many means of entertainment. We go to bed at a decent hour and I suggest you take that into consideration. However, have your fun. Nobody here has any objections to that."

"And of course we spend our money."

"Yes," Bleeker said. "You spend your money."

He walked away from Simpson and went out onto the veranda. The singing was now both in front and in back of him. Bleeker stood for a moment on the top steps of the veranda looking at the moon, hung like a slightly soiled but luminous pennant in the sky. He was embarrassed by his outburst to Simpson and he couldn't think why he had said such things. Private army. Perhaps, as Simpson had said, he was exaggerating. He was a small-town man and he had always hated the way men surrendered their individuality to attain perfection as a unit. It had been necessary during the war but it wasn't necessary now. Kid stuff—with an element of growing pains.

He walked down the steps and went up the sidewalk toward Cunningham's bar. They were singing there, too, and he stood outside the big plate-glass window peering in at them and listening to the harsh, pounding voices colored here and there with the sentimentalism of strong beer. Without thinking further he went into the bar. It was dim and cool and alien to his eyes and at first

263

he didn't notice the boy sitting by himself in a booth near the front. When he did, he was surprised—more than surprised, shocked—to see that the boy wasn't wearing his goggles but had placed them on the table by a bottle of Coca-Cola. Impulsively, he walked over to the booth and sat across from the boy.

"This seat taken?"

He had to shout over the noise of the singing. The boy leaned forward over the table and smiled.

"Hope we're not disturbing you."

Bleeker caught the word "disturbing" and shook his head negatively. He pointed to his mouth, then to the boy and to the rest of the group. The boy, too, shook his head. Bleeker could see that he was young, possibly twenty-five, and that he had dark straight hair cut short and parted neatly at the side. The face was square but delicate, the nose short, the mouth wide. The best thing about the boy, Bleeker decided, were his eyes, brown perhaps or dark gray, set in two distorted ovals of white flesh which contrasted sharply with the heavily tanned skin on the cheeks, forehead, and jaws. With his goggles on he would have looked like the rest. Without them he was a pleasant young man, altogether human and approachable.

Bleeker pointed to the Coca-Cola bottle. "You're not drinking."

"Beer makes me sick."

Bleeker got the word "beer" and the humorous ulping motion the boy made. They sat exchanging words and sometimes phrases, illustrated always with a series of clumsy, groping gestures until the singing became less coherent and spirited and ended finally in a few isolated coughs. The men in the troop were moving about individually now, some leaning over the bar and talking in hoarse whispers to the bartender, others walking unsteadily from group to group and detaching themselves immediately to go over to another group, the groups usually two or three men constantly edging away from themselves and colliding with and being held briefly by others. Some simply stood in the center of the room and brayed dolorously at the ceiling.

Several of the troop walked out of the bar and Bleeker could see them standing on the wide sidewalk looking up and down the street—as contemptuous of one another's company as they had been glad

264

of it earlier. Or not so much contemptuous as unwilling to be coerced too easily by any authority outside themselves. Bleeker smiled as he thought of Simpson and the man's talk of discipline.

"They're looking for women," the boy said. Bleeker had forgotten the boy temporarily, and the sudden words spoken in a normal voice startled and confused him. He thought quickly of Cathy—but then Cathy was safe in her room—probably in bed. He took the watch from his vest pocket and looked at it carefully.

"Five minutes after ten," he said.

"Why do they do that?" the boy demanded. "Why do they have to be so damned indecent about things like that? They haven't got the nerve to do anything but stare at waitresses. And then they get a few beers in them and go around pinching and slapping—they——"

Bleeker shivered with embarrassment. He was looking directly into the boy's eyes and seeing the color run under the tears and the jerky, pinching movement of the lids as against something injurious and baleful. It was an emotion too rawly infantile to be seen without being hurt by it, and he felt both pity and contempt for a man who would allow himself to display such a feeling—without any provocation—so nakedly to a stranger.

"Sorry," the boy said.

He picked up the green goggles and fitted them awkwardly over his eyes. Bleeker stood up and looked toward the center of the room. Several of the men turned their eyes and then moved their heads away without seeming to notice the boy in the booth. Bleeker understood them. This was the one who could be approached. The reason for that was clear too. He didn't belong. Why and wherefore he would probably never know.

He walked out of the bar and started down the street toward the hotel. The night was clear and cool and smelled faintly of the desert, of sand, of heated rock, of the sweetly-sour plants growing without water, and even of the sun which burned itself into the earth and never completely withdrew. There were only a few townsmen on the sidewalk wandering up and down, lured by the presence of something unusual in the town and masking, Bleeker thought, a ruthless and menacing curiosity behind a tolerant grin. He shrugged his shoulders distastefully. He was like a cat staring into a shadow the shape of its fears.

He was no more than a hundred feet from the hotel when he heard —or thought he heard—the sound of automatic firing. It was a well-remembered sound but always new and frightening.

Then he saw the motorcycle moving down the middle of the street, the exhaust sputtering loudly against the human resonance of laughter, catcalls, and epithets. He exhaled gently, the pain in his lungs subsiding with his breath. Another motorcycle speeded after the first and he could see four or five machines being wheeled out and the figures of their riders leaping into the air and bringing their weight down on the starting pedals. He was aware, too, that the lead motorcycles, having traversed the length of the street, had turned and were speeding back to the hotel. He had the sensation of moving —even when he stood still—in relation to the objects heading toward each other. He heard the high, unendurable sound of metal squeezing metal and saw the front wheel of a motorcycle twist and wobble and its rider roll along the asphalt toward the gutter where he sat up finally and moved his goggled head feebly from side to side.

As Bleeker looked around him he saw the third group of men which had divided earlier from the other two coming out of a bar across the street from Cunningham's, waving their arms in recognizable motions of cheering. The boy who had been thrown from the motorcycle vomited quietly into the gutter. Bleeker walked very fast toward the hotel. When he reached the top step of the veranda, he was caught and jostled by some five or six cyclists running out of the lobby, one of whom fell and was kicked rudely down the steps. Bleeker staggered against one of the pillars and broke a fingernail catching it. He stood there for a moment, fighting his temper, and then went into the lobby.

A table had been overthrown and lay on its top, the wooden legs stiffly and foolishly exposed, its magazines scattered around it, some with their pages spread face down so that the bindings rose along the back. He stepped on glass and realized one of the panes in the lobby door had been smashed. One of the troop walked stupidly out of the bar, his body sagging against the impetus propelling him forward until without actually falling he lay stretched on the floor, beer gushing from his mouth and nose and making a green and yellow pool before it sank into the carpet.

As Bleeker walked toward the bar, thinking of Simpson and of what he could say to him, he saw two men going up the stairs toward the second floor. He ran over to intercept them. Recognizing the authority in his voice, they came obediently down the stairs and walked across the lobby to the veranda, one of them saying over his shoulder, "Okay, Pop, okay—keep your lid on." The smile they exchanged enraged him. After they were out of sight he ran swiftly up the stairs, panting a little, and along the hall to his daughter's room.

It was quiet and there was no strip of light beneath the door. He stood listening for a moment with his ear to the panels and then turned back toward the stairs.

A man or boy, any of twenty or forty or sixty identical figures, goggled and in khaki, came around the corner of the second-floor corridor and put his hand on the knob of the door nearest the stairs. He squeezed the knob gently and then moved on to the next door, apparently unaware of Bleeker. Bleeker, remembering not to run or shout or knock the man down, walked over to him, took his arm, and led him down the stairs, the arm unresisting, even flaccid, in his grip.

Bleeker stood indecisively at the foot of the stairs, watching the man walk automatically away from him. He thought he should go back upstairs and search the hall. And he thought, too, he had to reach Simpson. Over the noise of the motorcycles moving rapidly up and down the street he heard a crash in the bar, a series of drunken elongated curses, ending abruptly in a small sound like a man's hand laid flatly and sharply on a table.

His head was beginning to ache badly and his stomach to sour under the impact of a slow and steady anger. He walked into the bar and stood staring at Francis LaSalle—LaSalle and Fleet, Hardware—who lay sprawled on the floor, his shoulders touching the brass rail under the bar and his head turned so that his cheek rubbed the black polished wood above the rail. The bartender had his hands below the top of the bar and he was watching Simpson and half-a-dozen men arranged in a loose semicircle above and beyond LaSalle.

Bleeker lifted LaSalle, who was a little dazed but not really hurt, and set him on a chair. After he was sure LaSalle was all right he walked up to Simpson.

"Get your men together," he said. "And get them out of here."

Simpson took out a long yellow wallet folded like a book and laid some money on the bar.

"That should take care of the damages," he said. His tongue was a little thick and his mouth didn't quite shut after the words were spoken but Bleeker didn't think he was drunk. Bleeker saw too—or thought he saw—the little cold eyes behind the glasses as bright and as sterile as a painted floor. Bleeker raised his arm slightly and lifted his heels off the floor but Simpson turned abruptly and walked away from him, the men in the troop swaying at his heels like a pack of lolling hounds. Bleeker stood looking foolishly after them. He had expected a fight and his body was still poised for one. He grunted heavily.

"Who hit him?" Bleeker motioned toward LaSalle.

"Damned if I know," the bartender said. "They all look alike to me."

That was true, of course. He went back into the lobby, hearing LaSalle say weakly and tearfully, "Goddam them—the bastards." He met Campbell, the deputy sheriff, a tall man with the arms and shoulders of a child beneath a foggy, bloated face.

"Can you do anything?" Bleeker asked. The motorcycles were racing up and down the street, alternately whining and backfiring, and one had jumped the curb and was cruising on the sidewalk.

"What do you want me to do?" Campbell demanded. "Put 'em all in jail?"

The motorcycle on the sidewalk speeded up and skidded obliquely into a plate-glass window, the front wheel bucking and climbing the brick base beneath the window. A single large section of glass slipped edge down to the sidewalk and fell slowly toward the cyclist who, with his feet spread and kicking at the cement, backed clumsily away from it. Bleeker could feel the crash in his teeth.

Now there were other motorcycles on the sidewalk. One of them hit a parked car at the edge of the walk. The rider standing astride his machine beat the window out of the car with his gloved fists. Campbell started down the steps toward him but was driven back by a motorcycle coming from his left. Bleeker could hear the squeal of the tires against the wooden riser at the base of the steps. Campbell's hand was on his gun when Bleeker reached him.

"That's no good," he yelled. "Get the state police. Ask for a half-dozen squad cars."

Campbell, angry but somewhat relieved, went up the steps and into the lobby. Bleeker couldn't know how long he stood on the veranda watching the mounting devastation on the street—the cyclist racing past store windows and hurling, presumably, beer bottles at the glass fronts; the two, working as a team, knocking down weighing machines and the signs in front of the motion-picture theater; the innumerable mounted men running the angry townspeople, alerted and aroused by the awful sounds of damage to their property, back into their suddenly lighted homes again or up the steps of his hotel or into niches along the main street, into doorways, and occasionally into the ledges and bays of glassless windows.

He saw Simpson—or rather a figure on the white motorcycle, helmeted and goggled—stationed calmly in the middle of the street under a hanging lamp. Presumably, he had been there for some time, but Bleeker hadn't seen him, the many rapid movements on the street making any static object unimportant and even, in a sense, invisible. Bleeker saw him now, and he felt again that spasm of anger which was like another life inside his body. He could have strangled Simpson then, slowly and with infinite pride. He knew without any effort of reason that Simpson was making no attempt to control his men but waiting rather for that moment when their minds, subdued but never actually helpless, would again take possession of their bodies.

Bleeker turned suddenly and went back into the lobby as if by that gesture of moving away he could pin his thoughts to Simpson, who, hereafter, would be responsible for them. He walked over to the desk where Timmons and Campbell, the deputy, were talking.

"You've got the authority," Timmons was saying angrily. "Fire over their heads. And if that doesn't stop them——"

Campbell looked uneasily at Bleeker. "Maybe if we could get their leader——"

"Did you get the police?" Bleeker asked.

"They're on their way," Campbell said. He avoided looking at Timmons and continued to stare hopefully and miserably at Bleeker.

"You've had your say," Timmons said abruptly. "Now I'll have mine."

He started for the lobby doors but Campbell, suddenly incensed, grabbed his arm.

"You leave this to me," he said. "You start firing a gun——"

Campbell's mouth dropped and Bleeker, turning his head, saw the two motorcycles coming through the lobby doors. They circled leisurely around for a moment and then one of them shot suddenly toward them, the goggled rider looming enormously above the wide handlebars. They scattered, Bleeker diving behind a pillar and Campbell and Timmons jumping behind the desk. The noise of the two machines assaulted them with as much effect as the sight of the speeding metal itself.

Bleeker didn't know why in course of watching the two riders he looked into the hall toward the foot of the stairway. Nor did it seem at all unreasonable that when he looked he should see Cathy standing there. Deeply, underneath the outward preoccupation of his mind, he must have been thinking of her. Now there she was. She wore the familiar green robe, belted and pulled in at the waist, and beneath its hem he could see the white slippers and the pink edge of her nightgown. Her hair was down and he had the impression her eyes were not quite open although, obviously, they were. She looked, he thought, as if she had waked, frowned at the clock, and come downstairs to scold him for staying up too late. He had no idea what time it was.

He saw—and of course Cathy saw—the motorcycle speeding toward her. He was aware that he screamed at her too. She did take a slight backward step and raise her arms in a pathetic warding gesture toward the inhuman figure on the motorcycle but neither could have changed—in that dwarfed period of time and in that short, unmaneuverable space—the course of their actions.

She lay finally across the lower steps, her body clinging to and equally arching away from the base of the newel post. And there was the sudden, shocking exposure of her flesh, the robe and the gown torn away from the leg as if pushed aside by the blood welling from her thigh. When he reached her there was blood in her hair, too, and someone—not Cathy—was screaming into his ears.

After a while the doctor came and Cathy, her head bandaged and her leg in splints, could be carried into his office and laid on the couch. Bleeker sat on the edge of the couch, his hand over Cathy's, watching the still white face whose eyes were closed and would not, he knew, open again. The doctor, after his first examination, had looked up quickly, and since Bleeker, too, had been bent over Cathy, their heads had been very close together for a moment. The doctor had assumed, almost immediately, his expression of professional austerity, but Bleeker had seen him in that moment when he had been thinking as a man, fortified of course by a doctor's knowledge, and Bleeker had known then that Cathy would die but that there would be also this interval of time.

Bleeker turned from watching Cathy and saw Timmons standing across the room. The man was—or had been—crying but his face wasn't set for it and the tears, points of colorless, sparkling water on his jaws, were unexpectedly delicate against the coarse texture of his skin. Timmons waved a bandaged hand awkwardly and Bleeker remembered, abruptly and jarringly, seeing Timmons diving for the motorcycle which had reversed itself, along with the other, and raced out of the lobby.

There was no sound now either from the street or the lobby. It was incredible, thinking of the racket a moment ago, that there should be this utter quietude, not only the lack of noise but the lack of the vibration of movement. The doctor came and went, coming to bend over Cathy and then going away again. Timmons stayed. Beyond shifting his feet occasionally he didn't move at all but stood patiently across the room, his face toward Cathy and Bleeker but not, Bleeker thought once when he looked up, actually seeing them.

"The police," Bleeker said sometime later.

"They're gone," Timmons said in a hoarse whisper. And then, after a while, "They'll get 'em—don't worry."

Bleeker saw that the man blushed helplessly and looked away from him. The police were no good. They would catch Simpson. Simpson would pay damages. And that would be the end of it. Who could identify Cathy's assailant? Not himself, certainly—nor Timmons nor Campbell. They were all alike. They were standardized figurines, seeking in each other a willful loss of identity, dividing themselves equally among one another until there was only a single mythical figure, unspeakably sterile and furnishing the norm for hundreds of others. He could not accuse something which didn't actually exist.

He wasn't sure of the exact moment when Cathy died. It might have been when he heard the motorcycle, unbelievably solitary in the quiet night, approaching the town. He knew only that the doctor came for the last time and that there was now a coarse, heavy blanket laid mercifully over Cathy. He stood looking down at the blanket for a moment, whatever he was feeling repressed and de- layed inside him, and then went back to the lobby and out onto the veranda. There were a dozen men standing there looking up the street toward the sound of the motorcycle, steadily but slowly coming nearer. He saw that when they glanced at one another their faces were hard and angry but when they looked at him they were respect- ful and a little abashed.

Bleeker could see from the veranda a number of people moving among the smashed store fronts, moving, stopping, bending over and then straightening up to move somewhere else, all dressed somewhat extemporaneously and therefore seeming without purpose. What they picked up they put down. What they put down they stared at grimly and then picked up again. They were like a dispossessed minority brutally but lawfully discriminated against. When the motorcycle appeared at the north end of the street they looked at it and then looked away again, dully and seemingly without resent- ment.

It was only after some moments that they looked up again, this time purposefully, and began to move slowly toward the hotel where the motorcycle had now stopped, the rider standing on the sidewalk, his face raised to the veranda.

No one on the veranda moved until Bleeker, after a visible effort, walked down the steps and stood facing the rider. It was the boy Bleeker had talked to in the bar. The goggles and helmet were hang- ing at his belt.

"I couldn't stand it any longer," the boy said. "I had to come back."

He looked at Bleeker as if he didn't dare look anywhere else. His face was adolescently shiny and damp, the marks, Bleeker thought, of a proud and articulate fear. He should have been heroic in his willingness to come back to the town after what had been done to it but to Bleeker he was only a dirty little boy returning to a back fence his friends had defaced with pornographic writing and calling atten- tion to the fact that he was afraid to erase the writing but was de- termined nevertheless to do it. Bleeker was revolted. He hated the boy far more than he could have hated Simpson for bringing this to his attention when he did not want to think of anything or anyone but Cathy.

"I wasn't one of them," the boy said. "You remember, Mr. Bleeker. I wasn't drinking."

This declaration of innocence—this willingness to take blame for acts which he hadn't committed—enraged Bleeker.

"You were one of them," he said.

"Yes. But after tonight——"

"Why didn't you stop them?" Bleeker demanded loudly. He felt the murmur of the townspeople at his back and someone breathed harshly on his neck. "You were one of them. You could have done something. Why, in God's name, didn't you do it?"

"What could I do?" the boy said. He spread his hands and stepped back as if to appeal to the men beyond Bleeker.

Bleeker couldn't remember, either shortly after or much later, exactly what he did then. If the boy hadn't stepped back like that—if he hadn't raised his hand. . . . Bleeker was in the middle of a group of bodies and he was striking with his fists and being struck. And then he was kneeling on the sidewalk, holding the boy's head in his lap and trying to protect him from the heavy shoes of the men around him. He was crying out, protesting, exhorting, and after a time the men moved away from him and someone helped him carry the boy up the steps and lay him on the veranda. When he looked up finally only Timmons and the doctor were there. Up and down the street there were now only shadows and the diminishing sounds of invisible bodies. The night was still again as abruptly as it had been confounded with noise.

Some time later Timmons and the doctor carried the boy, alive but terribly hurt, into the hotel. Bleeker sat on the top step of the veranda, staring at the moon which had shifted in the sky and was now nearer the mountains in the west. It was not in any sense romantic or inflamed but coldly clear and sane. And the light it sent was cold and sane and lit in himself what he would have liked to hide.

He could have said that having lost Cathy he was not afraid any longer of losing himself. No one would blame him. Cathy's death was his excuse for striking the boy, hammering him to the sidewalk, and stamping on him as he had never believed he could have stamped on any living thing. No one would say he should have lost Cathy lightly—without anger and without that appalling desire to avenge her. It was utterly natural—as natural as a man drinking a few beers and riding a motorcycle insanely through a town like this. Bleeker shuddered. It might have been all right for a man like Timmons who was and would always be incapable of thinking what he—Joel Bleeker—was thinking. It was not—and would never be—all right for him.

Bleeker got up and stood for a moment on the top step of the veranda. He wanted, abruptly and madly, to scream his agony into the night with no more restraint than that of an animal seeing his guts beneath him on the ground. He wanted to smash something—anything—glass, wood, stone—his own body. He could feel his fists going into the boy's flesh. And there was that bloody but living thing on the sidewalk and himself stooping over to shield it.

After a while, aware that he was leaning against one of the wooden pillars supporting the porch and aware, too, that his flesh was numb from being pressed against it, he straightened up slowly and turned to go back into the hotel.

There would always be time to make his peace with the dead. There was little if any time to make his peace with the living.

from the Pacific Spectator

SLOW JOURNEY

SYLVIA SHIRLEY *is a native of New York City where she now lives with her husband, Harry Jackel, and an eleven-year-old daughter. Her first published story was "The Red Dress," which appeared in* Harper's Magazine, *and was anthologized in 1947. She has published several short stories since, and is at present working on a novel. She was awarded a Fellowship to the Bread Loaf Writers' Conference in 1949, sponsored by Harper and Brothers.*

Mr. Rapheal sighed wearily, refolded his newspaper, and, with his usual seeming absent-mindedness, fitted it into his coat pocket. He had looked at all the columns of print methodically but had read nothing. He leaned back in his subway seat between the comfortable warmth of the two people who pressed on either side of him and closed his eyes. He was coming home, as he would any other night, from a day's work in the factory. He wondered why he should.

Was it home, now that his daughter was no longer there? Home, he thought sadly, was the time and the place where a man could remember his mother. But the remembrance of his parents and the things he had promised himself for them turned his nostalgia to bitterness. The old insidious crawling shame swarmed over him, and he tried to think of something else.

He would like a game of pinochle, cards always diverted him; but his friends were bound for their homes just as he was. Maybe they sat down to their tables with less grief. In his own house, even in good times, there was always the gloom, the foreboding, the fear of relentless evil. Still, you went to visit in a friend's house, and you didn't pry under the curtain of hospitality. He always said to Mrs.

Rapheal, when she envied others their good fortune, "Who can tell what's in his heart?"

He moved his lips now, remembering. He could see Mrs. Rapheal nod her head significantly. She knew. A person weighted down by sadness could not show a merry face. Mr. Rapheal did not remember when his wife had not been weighted down by sorrow. She had even accepted him with ironic resignation, twenty years before, when neither of them was any longer really young. But she had been a good wife, and if a little on the parsimonious side, it was only for his interest. . . .

The man in the next seat suddenly heaved up his bulk and pushed toward the door. Mr. Rapheal shifted slightly, experimentally, but the woman who had been standing over them plunged into the vacancy and rearranged herself a half-dozen times before she settled her prodding elbows.

"Women," thought Mr. Rapheal, and suddenly he was remembering Anya, a girl he had not permitted himself to remember in years. But now with his daughter Toby gone, this was a day set apart from all others of his life. It seemed natural that the specters of his past should come to dwell within him now, with more reality almost than when they actually motivated his life.

Anya was three years older than Mr. Rapheal. She would be elderly and certainly fat, just as her mother had been before her. He had such a sudden vision of the young Anya now, her heavy blond plaits, each as thick as a man's wrist, swinging as she ran up the path before him to their hilltop farm, that he half rose from his seat. He must have looked peculiar, too, because the people around him stared. "What station is this?" he asked, to cover his confusion.

Mr. Rapheal settled back again, but not so comfortably because the woman in the next seat had confiscated some of his space. He had still another twenty minutes to ride.

He thought of his wife waiting to give him his dinner. Probably she had spent the day in mourning the departure of their daughter with her young husband. He would endeavor not to notice her red-rimmed eyes as she served the meal, because if he said to her, "Have you been crying?" she would answer, "Is there something to rejoice over?" And if he said to her that he could not eat, because there was grief in him also, she would be brusque and say, "Never mind and eat. You need strength to bear your troubles." But if he made an effort to down his food in the silent room, while she fetched and carried, she would surely say, "How like a man, to be so unfeeling. A father is, after all, not like a mother. . . ."

Ah yes, how well he understood her, this Mrs. Rapheal he had married instead of Anya. He knew her thoughts before she had them, her words before she hung them in the stifling air around him. He knew her so well that he understood how impossible it would be even to attempt an explanation of his own feelings. Sometimes he could not explain to himself. The feelings were just there, and he touched his heart.

His son-in-law had said to him last night, finally and irrevocably, "I don't expect you to understand. You are too far away from it." Mr. Rapheal dug his chin a little farther down and sighed.

Mrs. Rapheal was a good wife. He was past forty when he married her and she had kept his home and his life and even his living from anger and confusion. She didn't like him to play cards with his friends. "See," she would point out, "I walk an extra few blocks to save a little on the marketing and you squander hard-earned money on gambling."

True, she had saved his money so that it had stretched over the slack times in his trade. Only four years ago he had had a chance to rent part of a loft with several machines, so that now he manufactured shoulder straps for ladies' underwear, and Mrs. Rapheal had provided the money out of her miraculous savings. He had bought her a cocktail ring with part of the first year's profits and she had wept.

"I wish you might have had something like this when we were younger," he said shyly. And she had said, wiping her eyes, "I didn't need it then, and I don't need it now. You should have put the money by for Toby."

Nevertheless, she wore it on holidays and when they went visiting: the clumsy, fan-shaped ring with its semiprecious stones. The rest of the time she wrapped it in a chamois bag and carried it in her bosom.

That's how it had always been with Mrs. Rapheal. Everything for Toby. Their first child had been stillborn and a boy, and Mr. Rapheal believed that she blamed him for that in her heart. After the baby girl there had been no other. All the hopes they had not realized in their own lives, all the dreams that the exacting drabness of their lives had not permitted them to pursue, were fixed on Toby. And now she had left them, to follow a dream of her own—one that they had not dreamt and in which they could point the flaws, but to no avail.

In the beginning it had been the music lessons; Mrs. Rapheal had so wanted Toby to play the piano. A violin had been cheaper to buy and Toby had squeaked and sawed away obediently for a year and a half until the man who taught her said he'd rather beg in the courtyards than earn his bread by such a pupil.

So they bought an old pianola from one of their neighbors and had it geared for manual playing. The tone was loud and brassy and Toby played louder and longer, and just as patiently, giving no thought to the sounds that came out. She even sang off key. Mrs. Rapheal liked to hear her.

Then there had been the Hebrew lessons. Mr. Rapheal said for what did a girl need to know Hebrew—her mother could teach her her prayers—people weren't so religious anymore, anyhow. But perversely Toby liked the language and she learned it so well that she sometimes carried the idioms over into her ordinary speech. It startled her father to hear the ancient tongue he had learned for its holiness used so expertly and so casually in speaking. She even liked to argue interpretations with her tutor, to that old man's despair, and to her father's secret delight. Neither he nor her mother had dreamed where it might lead.

Her mother thought it would be nice if Toby married a businessman when she grew up.

"So why do you spend so much time teaching her to be a thrifty housewife?" he teased as he watched them over their sewing in the evenings.

"Well," said his wife righteously, "a person needs to know how to do many things."

"And should be required to do nothing," Toby finished softly, laughing at both of them. She had her mother's talent for sarcasm, but a little humor of her own.

"A businessman," said her mother, "lives well. He doesn't have

278

to break his head about where his next week's money is coming from."

"No," Toby prompted. "He has a dozen workmen breaking their backs making money for him," and her laughter trilled in the room until her mother smiled.

"What, then," she said, "a businessman like your father who has to know what's doing in his workmen's heads? Whoever has a headache in the shop brings it to him. Little King Solomon."

"Poor Papa." Toby bit off her thread. "He should sell headache powders, and then we'd be rich."

Well, that kind of teasing was over and done with. They would neither of them hear Toby's laughter again. And the thought tore at him with such relentlessness that Mr. Rapheal got up from his seat and made his way to the middle of the subway car. He held onto the enameled bar and squeezed his eyes shut, holding his breath, as though in doing that he could squeeze away the pain.

They had known for weeks that Toby and her husband would go to Israel to live. They had known it and not believed. Even when the young couple had gone to the farm schools for their orientation, the Rapheals had not believed the day would ultimately come.

Only last night, Toby's husband said, "I see how *you* feel about it, and I don't expect you to understand how *we* feel about it. What we want is no longer important to you. You are older. You've had it too easy! You come and go by the same route each day, you see the same people and share their language. Even on vacations you go to the old places, tried and true, where there is no fear of being snubbed!"

Words, words, Mr. Rapheal thought. Impassioned words, and yet without meanings for the hearts who were listening.

"Please," Toby was saying to her mother in her strained voice. "Don't come to see us off in the morning if you're going to stand there and weep. All my life you've cried over me. When I scraped my knee, when I couldn't learn one song from another, you cried. You cried at my graduation and you cried at my wedding as though it were my funeral . . ."

Mr. Rapheal held up his hand, just as he had last night. "Stop it Toby, dove. You're talking to your mother. How can you leave her like that?"

She had swung on him then. "When you left Europe to come here, wasn't it much the same thing? Were your parents glad to see you go? Did you think you'd ever see them again? How did you leave your mother?"

Her questions swung him back across the years with a kind of ferocity that was quick and so deep-cutting it was bloodless for the instant.

"My mother was dead," Mr. Rapheal said slowly, "and to tell the truth, I was frightened to come so far alone." He did not tell her how necessary it was for him to come, nor how his family had pinned their hopes on him. He couldn't tell her that any more than he could tell her husband that he never did have it too easy, that the only friendly face he had found here in the beginning was poverty.

"I'm not going alone," Toby said. The excitement in her voice was still humming in her father's ears as he turned to the window, but he sensed the jagged little arrows of worry and doubt that lived under that excitement.

Toby's husband said, "Look, we've been over this a thousand times. We're going, and this is hardly the time for anger or bitterness. We need your blessings. Someday, perhaps when things are quieter, we'll be together again. You'll come to us. . . ."

Mrs. Rapheal said, "This is the best place to live. Ask us, we know. You're the one that has had it too easy. You have not our difficulty, you can go out in the great world. You are Americans. Who hems you in? Why can't you be satisfied with life in America?"

"Because here I am a Jewish American, no matter how I distinguish myself. Not just plain American," Leo said. "And there is always something or someone who will point a finger and say that *at* me."

"And what will they say to you there? This is the Jewish American, and that one over there is the Polish Jew or the German Jew, and so on. There are always distinctions. What is the difference?"

Leo took a deep breath. "The difference, Ma, is this. The Jews that are now coming to Israel are all there for the same purpose, to make a permanent place for those who have no homes and for those who cannot feel at home elsewhere because they are made unwelcome.

"Even here, which should be home for me and for Toby, because we have been born here, there are those who resent us because we look and act like non-Jews. If we stick to the traditions of our fore-fathers they say we are clannish and can never make good Americans . . . because we don't *assimilate*.

"My God, how I hate that word. Even the historians make us out a rootless, wandering people. With God's help and with Toby's" —here he made her a little bow—"no one will ever say that of my children. They'll have roots that will not easily be displaced."

"Speeches," Mrs. Rapheal said. "Always the speeches." She turned to her husband, "Why can't you say something to him, instead of looking out the window? What do you see there that is more im-portant than here in this room?"

Mr. Rapheal heard her, but he continued to stare out of the win-dow. He would have liked to tell them that he had made a life here. He got on all right. What if his life was bounded by his flat and his shop and the same could be said of his friends? So he didn't go to places where his kind was not wanted. What did it matter? There were other places. In the long run things ironed out. He was fond of that last phrase; he used it again and again, things ironed out. You needed only a little more patience. The young now . . .

"The young are always off to the wars to remake the world," his wife seemed to lift the words from his brain, "and it's the same world in the end!"

"It's the same world," Leo went on patiently, "because the war is fought each day to keep it the same. Somebody thought up a thing called freedom; they even teach it in the schools. Every sunrise the battle is begun again to re-establish it, because during the night a devil has been at work to undo the work of the day before."

Mr. Rapheal nodded. He remembered one bitter pogrom after another. How many times had Anya's mother sent the girl flying down the hill with the news that their town was next for the on-slaught . . . they could hide in Anya's hayloft . . . One afternoon his young stepmother had sent the little sisters back with Anya, but the rest had stayed at home. Everybody kept to their houses, Jew and Gentile alike. But those of the villagers who were always ready for mischief were waiting for the signal to come from the raiding parties. His father took his prayer shawl and his book, as the day lengthened into twilight. He put his hand on each boy's head and then slipped out of the door, down the long, winding lane. They thought he was going out for the evening prayers. All night they waited for his return, the bread dry in their throats; the drinking water in the urn was stale.

In the room behind him Mr. Rapheal heard his wife call him back; she was saying that he was without feeling, as uncommunicative as the surrounding walls. But Mr. Rapheal was remembering the daybreak in that little town which had changed hands so often that it was possible for grandfather and grandsons to be of different nationalities though born in the same house. His own father had come back with the dawn, an armful of freshly printed posters under his tunic. The elders of the town had been placed at strategic points, waiting for the bulletins to be hung. As each miscreant slunk off in the darkness, the elders had torn them down, so that in the morning no one would know that the signal had been given.

The children read the posters before shredding them carefully, and the words were branded deeply, so that in later life it seemed to them a kind of foreknowledge that they'd always had. "Rise up against the Jews!"

Mr. Rapheal turned back from the window and looked at his wife with her wringing hands, at his son-in-law with his young face so stern and distressed at the same time, and at Toby, who was looking so much the brave young wife, echoing her husband's phrases. They all seemed so childish to him. Leo was talking about dignity and the human spirit and Toby was helping him out. "Somebody thought up a thing called freedom and it's worth fighting for over and over."

Mr. Rapheal said, "You are going into danger. You'll be separated." Toby, who had never done anything more than wash her own stockings at home, would work on a farm in a settlement for the common good, and Leo would probably join the army.

"Aha," said Mrs. Rapheal. "Let's hear. The wooden image is speaking at last. Well, go ahead, speak."

Mr. Rapheal tried to ignore her sarcasm, but it was difficult to find words now that they were all looking at him. He was conscious, too, that what he had to say might seem irrelevant. "My eldest brother," he began, "had been so brutalized by service in the Czar's army that my father took a vow that no other son of his would ever serve again. Little bands of people were weekly making the dangerous trip across the border. My father sold the two cows, and the stepmother's ring. There had been nothing in my life to make a brave lad of me, so I was frightened." Besides, he added to himself, he had loved Anya, blond and brown-eyed, her braids thick as a man's wrist.

"I left because I had to, with a promise on my lips," he went on. And another in his heart. "I would send for my father one day." Mr. Rapheal wrinkled his face because the memory filled him with shame. He had sent for Anya instead, who had married someone else before a year was out.

"Somehow," he continued aloud, "I never got enough money together for my family, and when I had the money, time had run out. Twenty-five years later the Nazis killed them all. My old father slaughtered like an animal, without prayers, without tears . . . all the goodness in him come to naught. The evil from which he had protected me had triumphed over him." He kept wrinkling up his face.

"Ach," said his wife. "We are not talking about you or your old father, may his soul find peace. We are talking about the young!"

Mr. Rapheal knuckled his mouth cruelly. "What I meant," he pointed out, "was that I fled from danger. Leo is going into it."

"I understand that," Leo said simply. "And I understand what you are telling me."

"Ah," Mr. Rapheal nodded. "You understand, but does she?" and he indicated Toby with a hopeless gesture.

"We decided long ago. I go where my husband goes," Toby said. Her father looked at her dear familiar face for a long moment. That, of course, was as it should be. But why should it happen to her and why so far away? Was it not odd that these children who had been born here and educated here, Leo who had fought for his country, should still feel alien and unwanted here? This business of roots. It was too confusing. People should be people wherever they were. It was hard enough to make a living, raise a family without all this troublesome theorizing. . . .

He looked for words, something that would somehow communicate his immeasurable grief, that would reveal to them that the pursuit of dreams was without fruit. He sighed and moved his lips.

"Better be quiet," Mrs. Rapheal said callously. "There's nothing to hear when you speak. You don't help. Sometimes it is hard to believe that you are capable of civilized emotion."

He let her rant against him, and when Leo tried to interrupt, Mr. Rapheal made a little deprecatory gesture. He was used to her and it was better that she vent her bitterness on him.

"Freedom belongs everywhere, not only to us. If you must fight for it, you can do battle for it here." Mrs. Rapheal would not give over.

Leo began again with his calculating patience. "Look," he said, making little shelters with his bent fingers, "over here we have those who suffer, and over there we have those who make them suffer, and not so far away we have those who sit and let them suffer. Which is the worst offender?"

"Listen," Mrs. Rapheal said, "a dead hero is cold comfort to his wife."

Mr. Rapheal bit his lips. "All right," he said. "Enough. You are leaving in the morning and God knows if we shall ever meet again. Let's have no more words."

His wife whipped up her head at him, the furious tears blinding her, and as she ran from the room, Mr. Rapheal thought: she hates me. Sometimes he hated himself, but he could not flee from the oppression of his incommunicable emotions.

The train had come into the open air several stations back. As the door slid open, a rush of cold air fell upon Mr. Rapheal still standing in the center of the car, buffeted by the people who had pressed past his unheeding figure. He realized suddenly that the next stop would be his. He was going home. Why home?

This very morning he and Mrs. Rapheal had gone to the pier to see the young people off. Toby wore a pair of corduroy slacks and a ski jacket, a little blue hat to match her scarf on her short hair, and Leo wore his aviator's jacket dyed dark brown, all the buttons replaced. There were eight young people, all newly married, all traveling light and by freight boat. "We came by steerage and they go by freight," Mr. Rapheal thought. He kissed his daughter with dry lips, felt her convulsive fingers on his, and would have pressed her close to his heart, but he relinquished her to her mother's grasp. He held out his hand to Leo, who took it firmly and then to his immense surprise stooped and kissed him, so that his heart was twisted in a quick moment of agony.

"Go now," Toby whispered. "Don't stay behind to wave. Let me see you go, and remember that I love you."

And he had led her weeping mother back down the pier into the open street. They passed the markets where the trucks were being loaded for the trips through the city, and the workmen looked at them curiously. There were some grapes on a fruit stand, and they seemed to Mr. Rapheal to be the biggest, most luscious grapes he'd ever seen.

"Wait," he said, and he stopped to buy some. When he came back with the paper bag, she brushed his hand aside.

"You are impossible," she said. She did not let him come home with her, and so he put her on the train going uptown and took the bus to his shop. There would be little to do there—it was a slack time. He spent the whole day sweeping scraps of silk and threads together, covering the idle machines, running his hands over their hoods as he walked by again and again. He stayed long past the ordinary workday.

The train came to the last stop and he shuffled out behind the remaining passengers, but so slowly he caught his arm in the closing door.

In the street he watched the trolley take on a load of people and start its clanking way up to the end of the city line. The trees were dark and bushy against the lighter sky. He turned in the opposite direction and walked down his own street.

His wife said, "What took you so long, did you walk home?"

He did not say that he felt just as tired as if he had. After all, his thoughts had taken him back and forth, back and forth, all the weary hours. He said instead, inadvertently, "You have been crying."

"What then? Is there something to celebrate?"

He sat down to his supper and said nothing more. He could not bear to hear her start on her grief again, and there was nothing he could say to avert it. He ate because he did not wish to hear her make remarks about his lack of appetite; he did not ask her if she had eaten.

At last she said, "I have no more tears," and as she spoke they fell out afresh.

285

He stood up abruptly. "I'm going," he said.

She looked at him incredulously. "Where are you going?" He put on his hat and went to the door. "To your friends, to your card-playing friends at a time like this!" She called upon heaven to witness her humiliation, to alleviate her fate.

Mr. Rapheal did not mean to slam the door, but it was too late. He went back under the elevated structure. Another trolley was waiting for its fill of passengers before starting toward the outskirts. Mr. Rapheal went past it.

He would have liked to join his friends. He would have wondered with them where the freight boat was now, and whether any of them would be able to weather an ocean voyage again. Most of them had come across in the steerage maybe thirty, forty years ago. Boats were different now. But if he went to his friends, even they might have wondered how it was that he could leave his wife alone on such a night.

Remembering the ocean, he went back further and remembered crossing the inlet . . . and the woman with the crying baby. Mr. Rapheal started to walk more rapidly than he had ever walked before. He imagined Leo and Toby were with him. He told them the story he had never wanted to recall to his own mind.

"Moral courage," he said to Leo, "is not enough. Nor is your intellectual courage enough. Listen this once to me. When I left my own country to come here, we were a small band being guided by the bribed guards to a place where we could safely cross the border. During the day we had to hide, and in the night we had to go quickly, blindly, and in silence wherever we were led. On the second night, something went amiss, and we were forced to lie down in a ditch, all eight of us. Quickly we were covered over by canvas and dried leaves.

"We were forbidden," Mr. Rapheal hurried on, "even to whisper, nor did we dare. We could hear the rumbling of passing wheels around us, there was the gentle sound of water from near by. The baby in the arms of the woman who huddled next to me began to whimper. In the darkness the faces of the others glowed with terror as they strained their eyes toward us. She pressed the baby to her breast to feed it. But the baby kept whimpering. One of the guards lowered himself into the ditch and hissed that all our lives and his, too, would be worth less than nothing if we were overheard.

"The woman held her baby closer," Mr. Rapheal whispered to the trees, clasping his hands. He had already passed the cemetery and was now on his way to the suburbs, and there was nothing but the darkness listening to his story.

"The people huddled closer, closer. The baby began to cry louder and the guard made a threatening movement toward us. The woman looked about her, from one glistening face to another; the smell of fear and expectancy was in that tension." Mr. Rapheal paused, and faced the wide expanse of the woods on his left. The trees strained forward and listened. "Very slowly," Mr. Rapheal said, "the woman pressed the baby's head into her bosom. I could feel her elbow crush my chest. The crying ceased.

"In a little while we were ordered out into the open. The coast was clear. In relays the little rowboat took us down the little inlet. The woman dropped the dead baby into the water. The moving oars swished on." Mr. Rapheal stopped speaking. He did not see Leo or Toby any more. He wondered about the woman. How had she gone on living? He thought of Toby when she was little and when she had cried in the night, and he was there to comfort her. Would Leo be there to comfort her children, or would they cry in the night unheard? . . .

Why should he stay here? he thought frenziedly, and how had he come so far? He would go home and say to his wife, "Let us go to Israel too. I'll sell the shop. We have nothing to keep us here." And as he crossed over to wait for the trolley, because he didn't think his feet would carry him back all the long way, he heard his wife's voice quite clearly.

"What do they need *you* there for? Once old people dreamed of going to Palestine to be buried in the holy ground. Now it is for the young. What will you build, old man?"

The trolley came back, going too fast because it was empty. It almost didn't stop, but Mr. Rapheal ran out on the road. He wavered crazily as he got up on the step, and the motorman helped him get his balance.

"Whatsamatter, Pop? Had a little too much?" He grinned.

Mr. Rapheal grinned back as he dropped the coin in the box. But when he sat down, he was an old man weeping unashamedly, letting

287

the tears fall like warm balm where they would. Toby was going to fight, whereas he had run away. Was that to be his contribution to life? And he wept partly because he had left his father to die, and partly because Anya had not kept faith with him, and for the dead baby and its mother, and because his daughter had left him without speaking her fears, and partly because his wife would not understand what was in his heart. But mostly he cried because he was old in his loneliness and because Time had overwhelmed him . . . as whom would it not?

from The Yale Review

WHO TOO WAS A SOLDIER

JOHN CAMPBELL SMITH *was born on December 7, 1924, in Scranton, Pennsylvania. He received his B.A. at the University of Pennsylvania in 1950, and is now doing graduate work in English there, where he holds a university scholarship. He entered the Army in 1943, after being graduated from high school, and served three years, part of the time as an instructor in tank gunnery at Fort Knox. For two years he was in Europe as a tank commander, with the rank of sergeant, in the 634th Tank Destroyer Battalion, an attached unit of the First Infantry Division. He has published two stories in* The New Yorker *and one in 1948. Mr. Smith is married.*

Lieutenant Morse sank wearily into a chair at a table in one corner of the room. He was a tall, thin man in his early thirties, with a long and rather mournful face. He watched the proprietor bustle across the room toward him. Herr Friedmann wore his professional host's smile, an odd mixture of joviality and timid obsequiousness.

Morse had been to the *Gasthaus* once before, with another lieutenant who was stationed permanently in the area. It was a big place, much frequented by Americans, most of whom Herr Friedmann knew by name. "He'll make a point of proclaiming as soon as he sees you that he was a staunch anti-Nazi," the other lieutenant had told Morse. "The surprising thing is that it's true. He spent six months in a concentration camp toward the end of the war. But don't let that fool you. He's still a German."

"What will the lieutenant have?" Herr Friedmann asked, clasping his hands together and inclining his head slightly.

"Beer," Morse said.

"Beer. *Jawohl.*" Herr Friedmann beckoned to a nearby waiter. "Beer for the officer." All his waiters, he explained, turning toward Morse, spoke English, naturally. Then his fat, pale face became apologetic. He was sorry that there were no other Americans present, but it was early. Generally the Americans arrived later and then the Germans left, except, naturally, those who were the officers' guests. He smiled. Would the lieutenant prefer some American music?

The orchestra, if the six shabby men with their battered instruments at the other end of the room could be called that, were playing a medley of German songs popular before the war. The thin, bittersweet music sounded lonely and a little lost, the faster pieces saddest of all because they tried to sound gay.

"No," Morse said. "That's all right. I like it."

The brisk artificiality went out of the little man. His head on one side, his gaze far away, he listened to the music, the pale line of melody traced by the violinist who caressed his instrument as though lost in a world of his own, dreaming. Ah yes, it was nice. The lieutenant was right. "It is like old times. Before the war," Herr Friedmann sighed.

Morse lit a cigarette.

"You will excuse me?" Herr Friedmann asked, with a jerky little bow, becoming again the host, the proprietor.

Morse nodded. Waiting for his beer, he idly surveyed the room. It was dark and old-fashioned; despite its shabbiness, it had a certain melancholy charm, like the town itself. Morse had been in the area for two weeks, investigating an anonymous report that the former mayor of the town, a Nazi wanted in connection with the murder of some American airmen, had recently been seen in the vicinity. He had felt the charm of the place, the peaceful, rolling countryside, the town with its crooked cobblestone streets winding between high, twisted Gothic houses that belonged to a remote and innocent past. It was like an old print or the illustration to a fairy tale. Against that setting, so absurdly peaceful, seemingly so little changed by time, the man he was looking for had come to seem a phantom, a figment of his own imagination, and his search purposeless and unreal. There was no Spiermann. There had been no murders. The people he questioned looked at him as though he spoke out of an absurd phantasy. No such thing could ever have happened, they seemed to say, not here, not among us. It had left Morse with a baffling sense of frustration. He preferred Nürnberg with its ruins to this place whose serenity denied that there had been any war.

His beer arrived. On an impulse Morse laid three cigarettes on the table. The waiter, an old, somewhat stooped man with a bony face, looked at them. Then his hand reached out. "*Danke.*" Morse heard the sharp click as he brought his heels together. "*Danke schön.*" The man slipped the cigarettes into his pocket.

"Hell," Morse thought, watching him glide away. "I'm getting sentimental." It was the music and the sight of the Germans in the room, men mostly, sitting in twos and threes, sipping their beer and listening to the music as though they, too, were held by a spell that the sounds cast, waiting for the moment when the Americans would begin to arrive in force and they would leave. He raised his glass and tasted the flat coldness of the beer.

"The lieutenant is very generous," a woman's voice said.

Morse lowered his glass and looked at her, his eyes narrowing as he tried to place her.

"You remember me?" She smiled. "At the swimming pool." Her English was surprisingly good.

"Yes," Morse said.

She had been lying on a German Army blanket some distance from the pool, and Morse had paused in passing to look at her, impressed by the tanned smoothness of her body in the scanty bathing suit. She had had a handkerchief over her face, but as though she felt his eyes she had flicked it away and sat up. She was a very pretty blonde.

Her stare had been half mocking. Finally she had said, "It is very hot today. Perhaps the lieutenant would care to swim? It is permitted."

"*Nein, danke.*"

He had felt her amused eyes on him as he moved away, and when he turned she had smiled.

Now he asked, "Won't you sit down?"

She sat down in the chair opposite him. "I would like a cigarette. Please," she added with a charming little grimace.

Morse handed her a cigarette. "Something to drink too?"

She laughed, leaning forward to take a light from him. "No, thank you. I have a drink at my table."

"Your table?"

She nodded to the other end of the room, where three men and another woman were sitting around a table.

"Oh, I see," Morse said.

She said, "My name is Ilse." She waited.

"Lieutenant Robert Morse."

He was amused and found her attractive. Quite a few Americans, he thought, must have found her attractive. Her eyes were a startlingly light gray and in the setting of her thin face gave an impression of childlike innocence. She must have been about twenty-three or -four.

"Won't you join us, Robert?" she asked. "My friends would be glad to meet you. You could buy everyone a drink."

Morse was intrigued. In the morning he would leave for Nürnberg and he supposed he might just as well make the most of his last night in the area. He did not really expect anything to come of it, but there was always the possibility.

"Or better still," she said, "we will buy you drinks and you can supply cigarettes. Good?"

He grinned. "Good," he said.

The initial awkwardness of everyone at the table passed more quickly than Morse had expected. All of them had been drinking. After a time Ilse suggested that they dance. A small space in front of the orchestra had been cleared for the purpose, in deference to the American officers who frequented the establishment, but Morse and Ilse were the only ones on the floor. He felt a trifle odd holding her in his arms. She danced with an easy, supple grace. It seemed to Morse that every German in the room consciously avoided looking at them.

"We will leave in a little while," Ilse murmured. "All of us. Would you care to come? Soon this will be crowded."

Morse smelled a faint perfume that seemed to come from her hair. She was wearing a low-cut blouse from which her throat and shoulders emerged with a smooth loveliness.

"Before we go you could buy a bottle of cognac. Herr Friedmann would be glad to sell it to you. You and Hans and I could drink it and

Hans will play the piano for us in his apartment. He lives beneath me. Yes?"

Hans was a tall, extraordinarily thin young man with a scarred face who had been introduced to Morse at the table.

Morse considered. "Yes," he said.

"You are very nice, Robert." Her arm tightened around him and she moved closer. "And we could dance some more perhaps."

He looked down at her. Her eyes were closed.

Herr Friedmann supplied him with the cognac at the bar. "You will have a nice time, I hope," he said with an air of jovial complicity. He gave Morse a sly, good-humored smile as he slipped the bottle into a bag.

"Thanks," Morse said dryly.

They separated from the other three, the two men and the woman, in the street.

"It is not far," Ilse said to Morse. "You and I will go ahead. Hans goes slowly. He will follow."

When they had risen from the table to leave Morse had realized that the gaunt young man had only one leg, that the other was artificial. He protested against going on ahead of the limping man.

"Go," Hans said. "I will come."

Ilse tugged at the lieutenant's arm. "Please. He does not like us to wait."

As they reached the end of the block Morse looked back. Hans was progressing jerkily, his head bent, keeping close to the buildings, one hand extended as though to help in maintaining his balance. He had no cane.

The apartment was located on the second floor of a tall, old building. The stairs were narrow and dark. "This is where Hans lives," Ilse said, pushing open the unlocked door. "I am above." She pressed a light switch.

Morse hesitated in the doorway. The room was large and surprisingly well furnished, comfortably untidy. A door at the other end obviously led into a bedroom.

"Give me the cognac." Ilse took his arm and drew him into the room. "Here we are. See?" she said. She put her arms around him and kissed him. "See?" she said again, laughing up at him.

She put the cognac on a table and then went over and turned on the radio in one corner. "We can dance. We will not open the bottle before Hans comes. That would not be fair."

On the piano that stood at the far end of the room Morse saw the picture of a handsome, fair-haired young man in uniform. He had difficulty in relating those smiling features to those of the man he had just left. The photograph showed a fuller, more youthful face—and no scar.

Ilse manipulated the dial of the radio until the strains of a dance band came in. She moved toward him, her arms extended.

They danced. Morse, if he closed his eyes, could imagine himself back in the States, at an officers' club. The station they had picked up happened to be playing American records and he saw himself back home, moving softly to the music.

"That will be Hans," Ilse murmured. Morse, too, had heard the sounds on the stairs, the heavy, dragging footsteps. She disengaged herself. "I will open the cognac."

There was a knock and then the door opened. Hans was pale. Sweat beaded his forehead. He came in with a faint smile and dropped into a chair beside the door. "Go on. You were dancing?"

"Yes," Morse said.

"Now we will drink." Ilse, holding the bottle triumphantly, filled the three glasses she had fetched from a cabinet.

"You have a very nice place here," Morse said.

"Thank you."

"For you." Ilse handed Morse a glass, then handed one to Hans. "And for me," she said.

Hans drained almost half of his at once. The hot, stinging liquor seemed to revive him. His cheeks flushed slightly and he sat up. "That is good." He nodded to Morse. "*Danke.*"

Morse sat with Ilse on the couch. She was humming softly.

"You are not stationed here?" Hans asked.

"No. Nürnberg."

"Ah. It is nicer here."

"Much nicer."

The scar traversed all of Hans's forehead, a jagged, ugly red line that narrowly missed his left eye. He noticed Morse's stare and said, "Shrapnel. In Russia. Before Rostov."

Morse said nothing. The radio was still playing, music that had been popular back in the States a year before.

"I did not fight against your forces," the German said. "I fought the Russians. But it is all the same, eh?" He seemed to take Morse's silence as an assent. "All the same," he murmured.

"We are not being very cheerful," Ilse said. She took the lieutenant's hand. "Let us not talk about the war."

The conversation became desultory. Ilse returned from the table with the bottle of cognac and put it on the floor beside the couch. Finally she said, "Now Hans will play for us." Her second glass was almost gone.

Hans rose stiffly. "Have you any preference?" He regarded the lieutenant. "Do you wish me to play?"

"If you like," Morse said.

Carrying his glass, Hans crossed the room and turned off the radio. He smiled as he sat down at the piano, reached out and lightly caressed the keys. For a moment the smile transformed his face. Then he began to play. It was Schumann, and despite the handicap of the artificial leg, he played like a concert pianist, not like a gifted amateur but like a highly trained and almost brilliant performer. The music stole gently through the room, sad and searching. Hans sat erect, his face set and blank. He might have been alone. He finished and reached for his glass.

"Go on. Please," Morse said.

"I am not so good any more. I was once a student of the piano. Before the war." He flexed his hands and then began to play one of Chopin's Nocturnes.

Morse felt Ilse press very gently against him and her lips on his cheek.

He was surprised at how quickly the time passed. They alternated between the radio and Hans's playing. To the radio he and Ilse danced. "I love to dance," she told him. Morse was beginning to feel the cognac. Nothing seemed strange. When he wasn't at the piano, Hans watched them, sitting in the same chair by the door, his legs extended stiffly. The only effect the cognac seemed to have on him was to make him close his eyes when he played.

"Come," Ilse whispered. They were dancing very slowly, hardly moving. Hans did not look at them as they passed him. She led

Morse up the narrow stairs, holding his hand in hers. As he entered the dark room he felt her arms about him and the warmth of her lips.

Hans was still sitting in the same place when they re-entered the apartment. The radio was playing. Nothing had changed except that the amount of cognac in the bottle had diminished appreciably.

Ilse blinked as though confused by the light, then without a word crossed to the couch, curled up on it, and fell asleep. Standing in the center of the room, Morse watched her. He felt a little dazed. His head was heavy.

"You want me to play?" Hans asked.

"Not if you don't want to," Morse said. He sat down in a chair opposite Hans.

Hans's face was flushed and his eyes were bright. The scar stood out lividly. "Cognac?" He gestured toward the bottle.

Morse shook his head. "I'll have to go."

"Yes," Hans said. He looked at Morse. Then he asked, "Since how long have you been in Europe?"

"Six years." Morse closed his eyes. He felt very tired.

"You fought then in the war?"

"Yes."

"I too. In Russia," the German said, as though he had forgotten that he had already mentioned it.

Morse opened his eyes again as he heard him rise. Hans lurched over to a bureau, fumbled through a drawer, and then returned. (How thin he is, Morse thought.) His hands were trembling slightly as he extended them to Morse. He held a number of snapshots.

"Pictures," he said. One by one he handed them to the lieutenant. "My tank. I was a Panzer officer." It was a Tiger, Morse recognized, squat and ugly. He had served with the 10th Armored Division and the sight of the Tiger brought back many memories. "And here, these are pictures taken in Russia."

Some of them were just scenic snapshots, of a rolling, unfamiliar-looking landscape, of Russian villages, quaint and peaceful. Some had been snapped during combat. There was a picture of the tank in action, with German troops dashing past it, bent double, into an invisible rain of fire. Other pictures showed burning villages, Russian prisoners. One of them was a close-up of a burned-out Russian tank from the turret of which the tank commander protruded grotesquely like a black, charred doll. Morse felt a little sick.

"This," Hans said. "This was my crew."

Morse looked at them. He had seen similar pictures; in fact, he had one of himself and the crew he had served with during the war, smiling into the camera. They were all much the same. Hans stood out, tall and blond. They were posed against the tank. Hans leaned negligently against the long, ugly 88, his head bare.

Hans sat down. "All dead. Only I was saved. Blown clear." He looked at Morse, and the lieutenant suddenly realized that the man was asserting something, that they shared a common bond, the two of them, demanding sympathy perhaps, or understanding. "You? You were in the infantry?" Hans asked.

"No," Morse said, "I was in tanks too."

"Ah!" Hans leaned forward.

Morse rejected the situation, rejected the demand he felt in the other man. He remembered his fruitless search for Spiermann, the attitude of the people, that there had been no war, no guilt. To avoid having to meet Hans's eager stare, to avoid saying anything, he glanced down at the pictures he still held in his hand, those he had not seen. He sat staring at them. They showed the handsome, blond young man and a girl. Hans was in civilian clothes. They must have been taken before the war, some of them at a beach, some in the country. The girl, Ilse, looked very young.

There was a moment's silence.

"Yes. We were to have been married," Hans said to him.

Silently Morse shuffled the pictures together and handed them to Hans, rising as he did so.

"You must go?"

"Yes."

"It is too bad. There is still some cognac."

Morse glanced over at the girl on the couch. She slept peacefully, curled up on her side, and her face, sleeping, was as innocent as that of the girl in the pictures, touching and very lovely.

"I will take care of her," Hans said. His eyes had followed those of the lieutenant. He grimaced. For a moment Morse was afraid that he was going to cry. Then a smile twisted the long, gaunt face.

"I am sorry that you could not stay longer. It would have been good to talk over the war with someone who, too, has been a soldier."

Morse could taste the cognac he had drunk, flat and coppery. He tried to think of something to say.

Suddenly Hans's face twisted again. Tears and hate spilled into his eyes simultaneously as though too long repressed. He spoke in German. "*Offizier. Ich war auch offizier. Ja, ich auch.*"

Morse left the room without looking back, descended the dark, narrow stairs. In the street it was cool. He walked quickly, his footsteps sounding lonely in his own ears, thrown back at him from the darkened buildings. "*I, too, was an officer. I too . . .*" Hans's voice seemed to follow him. In the morning he would leave for Nürnberg. He was glad of that, at least. He wished, wished desperately, that he had been going home instead.

from The New Yorker

A COUNTRY LOVE STORY

JEAN STAFFORD *was born in Covina, California, in 1915, and was
reared and educated in Colorado. She spent a year in Germany
after college, then taught in Missouri for a year. Since then she
has lived in Massachusetts, Louisiana (where she worked on*
The Southern Review), *Tennessee, Maine, New York City, and
Westport, Connecticut, her present home. Her first novel,* Boston
Adventure, *was published in 1944. Her second,* The Mountain
Lion, *appeared in 1947. Miss Stafford's short stories have appeared in* Harper's Magazine, The Kenyon Review, Harper's
Bazaar, The Sewanee Review, The Partisan Review, Mademoiselle, *and* The New Yorker. *Two of her stories have appeared in
this collection, "The Hope Chest" in 1947 from* Harper's Magazine, *and "A Summer Day" in 1949 from* The New Yorker. *She
was awarded Guggenheim Fellowships in 1945 and 1948, and in
1945 she also received an award from the American Academy
and National Institute of Arts and Letters. She is married to
Oliver Jensen.*

An antique sleigh stood in the yard, snow after snow banked up
against its eroded runners. Here and there upon the bleached and
splintery seat were wisps of horsehair and scraps of the black leather
that had once upholstered it. It bore, with all its jovial curves, an air
not so much of desuetude as of slowed-down dash, as if weary horses,
unable to go another step, had at last stopped here. The sleigh had
come with the house. The former owner, a gifted businesswoman
from Castine who bought old houses and sold them again with all
their pitfalls still intact, had said when she was showing them the
place, "A picturesque detail, I think," and, waving it away, had

turned to the well, which, with enthusiasm and at considerable length, she said had never gone dry. Actually, May and Daniel had found the detail more distracting than picturesque, so nearly kin was it to outdoor arts and crafts, and when the woman, as they departed in her car, gestured toward it again and said, "Paint that up a bit with something cheery and it will really add no end to your yard," simultaneous shudders coursed them. They had planned to remove the sleigh before they did anything else.

But partly because there were more important things to be done, and partly because they did not know where to put it (a sleigh could not, in the usual sense of the words, be thrown away), and partly because it seemed defiantly a part of the yard, as entitled to be there as permanently as the trees, they did nothing about it. Throughout the summer they saw birds briefly pause on its rakish front and saw the fresh rains wash the runners; in the autumn they watched the golden leaves fill the seat and nestle dryly down; and now, with the snow, they watched this new accumulation.

The sleigh was visible from the windows of the big, bright kitchen where they ate all their meals and, sometimes too bemused with country solitude to talk, they gazed out at it, forgetting their food in speculating on its history. It could have been driven cavalierly by the scion of some sea captain's family, or it could have been used soberly to haul the household's Unitarians to church or to take the womenfolk around the countryside on errands of good will. They did not speak of what its office might have been, and the fact of their silence was often nettlesome to May, for she felt they were silent too much of the time; a little morosely, she thought, If something as absurd and as provocative as this at which we look together—and which is, even though we didn't want it, our own property—cannot bring us to talk, what can? But she did not disturb Daniel in his private musings; she held her tongue, and out of the corner of her eye she watched him watch the winter cloak the sleigh, and, as if she were computing a difficult sum in her head, she tried to puzzle out what it was that had stilled tongues that earlier, before Daniel's illness, had found the days too short to communicate all they were eager to say.

It had been Daniel's doctor's idea, not theirs, that had brought them to the solemn hinterland to stay after all the summer gentry had departed in their beach wagons. The northern sun, the pristine air, the rural walks, and soundless nights, said Dr. Tellenbach, perhaps pining for his native Switzerland, would do more for the "professor's" convalescent lung than all the doctors and clinics in the world. Privately he had added to May that after so long a season in the sanitarium (Daniel had been there a year), where everything was tuned to a low pitch, it would be difficult and it might be shattering for "the boy" (not now the "professor," although Daniel, nearly fifty, was his wife's senior by twenty years and Dr. Tellenbach's by ten) to go back at once to the excitements and the intrigues of the university, to what, with finicking humor, the doctor called "the omnium-gatherum of the schoolmaster's life." The rigors of a country winter would be as nothing, he insisted, when compared to the strain of feuds and cocktail parties. All professors wanted to write books, didn't they? Surely Daniel, a historian with all the material in the world at his fingertips, must have something up his sleeve that could be the *raison d'être* for this year away? May said she supposed he had, she was not sure. She could hear the reluctance in her voice as she escaped the doctor's eyes and gazed through his windows at the mountains behind the sanitarium. In the dragging months Daniel had been gone she had taken solace in imagining the time when they *would* return to just that pandemonium the doctor so deplored, and because it had been pandemonium on the smallest and most discreet scale, she smiled through her disappointment at the little man's Swiss innocence and explained that they had always lived quietly, seldom dining out or entertaining more than twice a week.

"Twice a week!" He was appalled.

"But I'm afraid," she had protested, "that he would find a second year of inactivity intolerable. He does intend to write a book, but he means to write it in England, and we can't go to England now."

"England!" Dr. Tellenbach threw up his hands. "Good *air* is my recommendation for your husband. Good air and little talk."

She said, "It's talk he needs, I should think, after all this time of communing only with himself except when I came to visit."

He had looked at her with exaggerated patience, and then, courtly but authoritative, he said, "I hope you will not think I importune when I tell you that I am very well acquainted with your husband, and, as his physician, I order this retreat. *He* quite agrees."

Stung to see that there was a greater degree of understanding between Daniel and Dr. Tellenbach than between Daniel and herself, May had objected further, citing an occasion when her husband had put his head in his hands and mourned, "I hear talk of nothing but sputum cups and X rays. Aren't people interested in the state of the world any more?"

But Dr. Tellenbach had been adamant, and at the end, when she had risen to go, he said, "You are bound to find him changed a little. A long illness removes a thoughtful man from his fellow beings. It is like living with an exacting mistress who is not content with half a man's attention but must claim it all." She had thought his figure of speech absurd and disdained to ask him what he meant.

Actually, when the time came for them to move into the new house and she found no alterations in her husband but found, on the other hand, much pleasure in their country life, she began to forgive Dr. Tellenbach. In the beginning it was like a second honeymoon, for they had moved to a part of the North where they had never been and they explored it together, sharing its charming sights and sounds. Moreover, they had never owned a house before but had always lived in city apartments, and though the house they bought was old and derelict, its lines and doors and window lights were beautiful, and they were obsessed with it. All through the summer they reiterated, "To think that we own all of this! That it actually belongs to us!" And they wandered from room to room marveling at their windows, from none of which was it possible to see an ugly sight. They looked to the south upon a river, to the north upon a lake; to the west of them were pine woods where the wind forever sighed, voicing a vain entreaty; and to the east a rich man's long meadow that ran down a hill to his old, magisterial house. It was true, even in those bewitched days, that there were times on the lake, when May was gathering water lilies as Daniel slowly rowed, that she had seen on his face a look of abstraction and she had known that he was worlds away, in his memories, perhaps, of his illness and the sanitarium (of which he would never speak) or in the thought of the book he was going to write as soon, he said, as the winter set in and there was nothing to do but work. Momentarily the look frightened her, and she remembered the doctor's words, but then, immediately herself again in the security of married love, she caught

302

at another water lily and pulled at its long stem. Companionably they gardened, taking special pride in the nicotiana that sent its nighttime fragrance into their bedroom. Together, and with fascination, they consulted carpenters, plasterers, and chimney sweeps. In the blue evenings they read at ease, hearing no sound but that of the night birds—the loons on the lake and the owls in the tops of trees. When the days turned cooler and shorter, a cricket came to bless their house, nightly singing behind the kitchen stove. They got two fat and idle tabby cats, who lay insensible beside the fireplace and only stirred themselves to purr perfunctorily.

Because they had not moved in until July and by that time the workmen of the region were already engaged, most of the major repairs of the house were to be postponed until the spring, and in October, when May and Daniel had done all they could by themselves and Daniel had begun his own work, May suddenly found herself without occupation. Whole days might pass when she did nothing more than cook three meals and walk a little in the autumn mist and pet the cats and wait for Daniel to come down from his upstairs study to talk to her. She began to think with longing of the crowded days in Boston before Daniel was sick, and even in the year past, when he had been away and she had gone to concerts and recitals and had done good deeds for crippled children and had endlessly shopped for presents to lighten the tedium of her husband's unwilling exile. And, longing, she was remorseful, as if by desiring another she betrayed this life, and, remorseful, she hid away in sleep. Sometimes she slept for hours in the daytime, imitating the cats, and when at last she got up, she had to push away the dense sleep as if it were a door.

One day at lunch she asked Daniel to take a long walk with her that afternoon to a farm where the owner smoked his own sausages. "You never go outdoors," she said, "and Dr. Tellenbach said you must. Besides, it's a lovely day."

"I can't," he said. "I'd like to, but I can't. I'm busy. You go alone."

Overtaken by a gust of loneliness, she cried, "Oh, Daniel, I have nothing to *do!*"

A moment's silence fell, and then he said, "I'm sorry to put you through this, my dear, but you must surely admit that it's not my fault I got sick."

In her shame, her rapid, overdone apologies, her insistence that nothing mattered in the world except his health and peace of mind, she made everything worse, and at last he said shortly to her, "Stop being a child, May. Let's just leave each other alone."

This outbreak, the very first in their marriage of five years, was the beginning of a series. Hardly a day passed that they did not bicker over something; they might dispute a question of fact, argue a matter of taste, catch each other out in an inaccuracy, and every quarrel ended with Daniel's saying to her, "Why don't you leave me alone?" Once he said, "I've been sick and now I'm busy and I'm no longer young enough to shift the focus of my mind each time it suits your whim." Afterward there were always apologies, and then Daniel went back to his study and did not open the door of it again until the next meal. Finally it seemed to her that love, the very center of their being, was choked off, overgrown, invisible. And silent with hostility or voluble with trivial reproach, they tried to dig it out impulsively and could not—could only maul it in its unkempt grave. Daniel, in his withdrawal from her and from the house, was preoccupied with his research, of which he never spoke except to say that it would bore her, and most of the time, so it appeared to May, he did not worry over what was happening to them. She felt the cold old house somehow enveloping her as if it were their common enemy, maliciously bent on bringing them to disaster. Sunken in faithlessness, they stared, at mealtimes, atrophied within the present hour, at the irrelevant and whimsical sleigh that stood abandoned in the mammoth winter.

May found herself thinking, If we redeemed it and painted it, our house would have something in common with Henry Ford's Wayside Inn. And I might make this very observation to him and he might greet it with disdain and we might once again communicate. Perhaps we could talk of Williamsburg and how we disapproved of it. Her mind went toiling on. Williamsburg was part of our honeymoon trip; somewhere our feet were entangled in suckers as we stood kissing under a willow tree. Soon she found that she did not care for this line of thought, nor did she care what his response to it might be. In her imagined conversations with Daniel she never spoke of the sleigh. To the thin, ill scholar whose scholarship and illness had usurped her place she had gradually taken a weighty but unviolent dislike.

The discovery of this came, not surprising her, on Christmas Day. The knowledge sank like a plummet, and at the same time she was thinking about the sleigh, connecting it with the smell of the barn on damp days, and she thought perhaps it had been drawn by the very animals who had been stabled there and had pervaded the timbers with their odor. There must have been much life within this house once—but long ago. The earth immediately behind the barn was said by everyone to be extremely rich because of the horses, although there had been none there for over fifty years. Thinking of this soil, which earlier she had eagerly sifted through her fingers, May now realized that she had no wish for the spring to come, no wish to plant a garden, and, branching out at random, she found she had no wish to see the sea again, or children, or favorite pictures, or even her own face on a happy day. For a minute or two she was almost enraptured in this state of no desire, but then, purged swiftly of her cynicism, she knew it to be false, knew that actually she did have a desire—the desire for a desire. And now she felt that she was stationary in a whirlpool, and at the very moment she conceived the notion a bit of wind brought to the seat of the sleigh the final leaf from the elm tree that stood beside it. It crossed her mind that she might consider the wood of the sleigh in its juxtaposition to the living tree and to the horses, who, although they were long since dead, reminded her of their passionate, sweating, running life every time she went to the barn for firewood.

They sat this morning in the kitchen full of sun, and, speaking not to him but to the sleigh, to icicles, to the dark, motionless pine woods, she said, "I wonder if on a day like this they used to take the pastor home after lunch." Daniel gazed abstractedly at the bright silver drifts beside the well and said nothing. Presently a wagon went past hauled by two oxen with bells on their yoke. This was the hour they always passed, taking to an unknown destination an aged man in a fur hat and an aged woman in a shawl. May and Daniel listened.

Suddenly, with impromptu anger, Daniel said, "What did you just say?"

"Nothing," she said. And then, after a pause, "It would be lovely at Jamaica Pond today."

He wheeled on her and pounded the table with his fist. "I did not ask for this!" The color rose feverishly to his thin cheeks and his breath was agitated. "You are trying to make me sick again. It was wonderful, wasn't it, for you while I was gone?"

"Oh no, no! Oh no, Daniel, it was hell!"

"Then, by the same token, this must be heaven." He smiled, the professor catching out a student in a fallacy.

"Heaven." She said the word bitterly.

"Then why do you stay here?" he cried.

It was a cheap impasse, desolate, true, unfair. She did not answer him.

After a while he said, "I almost believe there's something you haven't told me."

She began to cry at once, blubbering across the table at him. "You have said that before. What am I to say? What have I done?"

He looked at her, impervious to her tears, without mercy and yet without contempt. "I don't know. But you've done something."

It was as if she were looking through someone else's scrambled closets and bureau drawers for an object that had not been named to her, but nowhere could she find her gross offense.

Domestically she asked him if he would have more coffee, and he peremptorily refused and demanded, "Will you tell me why it is you must badger me? Is it a compulsion? Can't you control it? Are you going mad?"

From that day onward May felt a certain stirring of life within her solitude, and now and again, looking up from a book to see if the damper on the stove was right, to listen to a rat renovating its house-within-a-house, to watch the belled oxen pass, she nursed her wound, hugged it, repeated his awful words exactly as he had said them, reproduced the way his wasted lips had looked, and his bright, far-sighted eyes. She could not read for long at any time, nor could she sew. She cared little now for planning changes in her house; she had meant to sand the painted floors to uncover the wood of the wide boards and she had imagined how the long, paneled windows of the drawing room would look when yellow velvet curtains hung there in the spring. Now, schooled by silence and indifference, she was immune to disrepair and to the damage done by the wind and snow, and she looked, as Daniel did, without dislike upon the old and nasty wallpaper and upon the shabby kitchen floor. One day she knew that the sleigh would stay where it was so long as they stayed there. From every thought she returned to her deep, bleeding injury. He had asked her if she were going mad.

She repaid him in the dark afternoons while he was closeted away in his study, hardly making a sound save when he added wood to his fire or paced a little, deep in thought. She sat at the kitchen table looking at the sleigh, and she gave Daniel insult for his injury by imagining a lover. She did not imagine his face, but she imagined his clothing, which would be costly and in the best of taste, and his manner, which would be urbane and anticipatory of her least whim, and his clever speech, and his adept courtship that would begin the moment he looked at the sleigh and said, "I must get rid of that for you at once." She might be a widow, she might be divorced, she might be committing adultery. Certainly there was no need to specify in an affair so securely legal. There was no need, that is, up to a point, and then the point came when she took in the fact that she not only believed in this lover but loved him and depended wholly on his companionship. She complained to him of Daniel and he consoled her; she told him stories of her girlhood, when she had gaily gone to parties, squired by boys her own age; she dazzled him sometimes with the wise comments she made on the books she read. It came to be true that if she so much as looked at the sleigh, she was weakened, failing with starvation.

Often, about her daily tasks of cooking food and washing dishes and tending the fires and shopping in the general store of the village, she thought she should watch her step, that it was this sort of thing that *did* make one go mad; for a while, then, she went back to Daniel's question, sharpening its razor edge. But she could not corral her alien thoughts and she trembled as she bought split peas, fearful that the old men loafing by the stove could see the incubus of her sins beside her. She could not avert such thoughts when they rushed upon her sometimes at tea with one of the old religious ladies of the neighborhood, so that, in the middle of a conversation about a deaconess in Bath, she retired from them, seeking her lover, who came, faceless, with his arms outstretched, even as she sat up straight in a Boston rocker, even as she accepted another cup of tea. She lingered over the cake plates and the simple talk, postponing her

return to her own house and to Daniel, whom she continually betrayed.

It was not long after she recognized her love that she began to
wake up even before the dawn and to be all day quick to everything,
observant of all the signs of age and eccentricity in her husband, and
she compared him in every particular—to his humiliation, in her eyes
—with the man whom now it seemed to her she had always loved at
fever pitch.

Once when Daniel, in a rare mood, kissed her, she drew back involuntarily, and he said gently, "I wish I knew what you had done,
poor dear." He looked, as if for written words, in her face.

"You said you knew," she said, terrified.

"I do."

"Then why do you wish you knew?" Her baffled voice was high
and frantic. "You don't talk sense!"

"I do," he said sedately. "I talk sense always. It is you who are
oblique." Her eyes stole like a sneak to the sleigh. "But I wish I
knew your motive," he said impartially.

For a minute she felt that they were two maniacs answering each
other questions that had not been asked, never touching the matter
at hand because they did not know what the matter was. But in
the next moment, when he turned back to her spontaneously and
clasped her head between his hands and said, like a tolerant father,
"I forgive you, darling, because you don't know how you persecute
me. No one knows except the sufferer what this sickness is," she
knew again, helplessly, that they were not harmonious even in their
aberrations.

These days of winter came and went, and on each of them, after
breakfast and as the oxen passed, he accused her of her concealed
misdeed. She could no longer truthfully deny that she was guilty,
for she was in love, and she heard the subterfuge in her own voice
and felt the guilty fever in her veins. Daniel knew it, too, and
watched her. When she was alone, she felt her lover's presence pro-
tecting her—when she walked past the stiff spiraea, with icy cob-
webs hung between its twigs, down to the lake, where the black,
unmeasured water was hidden beneath a lid of ice; when she walked,
instead, to the salt river to see the tar-paper shacks where the men
caught smelt through the ice; when she walked in the dead dusk

308

up the hill from the store, catching her breath the moment she saw the sleigh. But sometimes this splendid being mocked her when, freezing with fear of the consequences of her sin, she ran up the stairs to Daniel's room and burrowed her head in his shoulder and cried, "Come downstairs! I'm lonely, please come down!" But he would never come, and at last, bitterly, calmed by his calmly inquisitive regard, she went back alone and stood at the kitchen window, coyly half hidden behind the curtains.

For months she lived with her daily dishonor, rattled, ashamed, stubbornly clinging to her secret. But she grew more and more afraid when, oftener and oftener, Daniel said, "Why do you lie to me? What does this mood of yours mean?" and she could no longer sleep. In the raw nights she lay straight beside him as he slept, and she stared at the ceiling, as bright as the snow it reflected, and tried not to think of the sleigh out there under the elm tree but could think only of it and of the man, her lover, who was connected with it somehow. She said to herself, as she listened to his breathing, "If I confessed to Daniel, he would understand that I was lonely and he would comfort me, saying, 'I am here, May. I shall never let you be lonely again.'" At these times she was so separated from the world, so far removed from his touch and his voice, so solitary, that she would have sued a stranger for companionship. Daniel slept deeply, having no guilt to make him toss. He slept, indeed, so well that he never even heard the ditcher on snowy nights rising with a groan over the hill, flinging the snow from the road and warning of its approach by lights that first flashed red, then blue. As it passed their house, the hurled snow swashed like flames. All night she heard the squirrels adding up their nuts in the walls and heard the spirit of the house creaking and softly clicking upon the stairs and in the attics.

In early spring, when the whippoorwills begged in the cattails and the marsh reeds, and the northern lights patinated the lake and the tidal river, and the stars were large, and the huge vine of Dutchman's-pipe had started to leaf out, May went to bed late. Each night she sat on the back steps waiting, hearing the snuffling of a dog as it hightailed it for home, the single cry of a loon. Night after night she waited for the advent of her rebirth while upstairs

Daniel, who had spoken tolerantly of her vigils, slept, keeping his knowledge of her to himself. "A symptom," he had said, scowling in concentration, as he remarked upon her new habit. "Let it run its course. Perhaps when this is over you will know the reason why you torture me with these obsessions and will stop. You know, you may really have a slight disorder of the mind. It would be nothing to be ashamed of; you could go to a sanitarium."

One night, looking out the window, she clearly saw her lover sitting in the sleigh. His hand was over his eyes and his chin was covered by a red silk scarf. He wore no hat and his hair was fair. He was tall, and his long legs stretched indolently along the floorboard. He was younger than she had imagined him to be and he seemed rather frail, for there was a delicate pallor on his high, intelligent forehead and there was an invalid's languor in his whole attitude. He wore a white blazer and gray flannels and there was a yellow rosebud in his lapel. Young as he was, he did not, even so, seem to belong to her generation; rather, he seemed to be the reincarnation of someone's uncle as he had been fifty years before. May did not move until he vanished, and then, even though she knew now that she was truly bedeviled, the only emotion she had was bashfulness mingled with doubt; she was not sure, that is, that he loved her.

That night she slept awhile. She lay near to Daniel, who was smiling in the moonlight. She could tell that the sleep she would have tonight would be as heavy as a coma, and she was aware of the moment she was overtaken.

She was in a canoe in a meadow of water lilies and her lover was tranquilly taking the shell off a hard-boiled egg. "How intimate," he said, "to eat an egg with you." She was nervous lest the canoe tip over, but at the same time she was charmed by his wit and by the way he lightly touched her shoulder with the varnished paddle.

"May? May? I love you, May."

"Oh!" enchanted, she heard her voice replying. "Oh, I love you too!"

"The winter is over, May. You must forgive the hallucinations of a sick man."

She woke to see Daniel's fair, pale head bending toward her.

310

"He is old! He is ill!" she thought, but through her tears, to deceive him one last time, she cried, "Oh, thank God, Daniel!"

He was feeling cold and wakeful and he asked her to make him a cup of tea; before she left the room he kissed her hands and arms and said, "If I am ever sick again, don't leave me, May."

Downstairs, in the kitchen, cold with shadows and with the obtrusion of dawn, she was belabored by a chill. "What time is it?" she said aloud, although she did not care. She remembered, not for any reason, a day when she and Daniel had stood in the yard last October wondering whether they should cover the chimneys that would not be used and he decided that they should not, but he had said, "I hope no birds get trapped." She had replied, "I thought they all left at about this time for the South," and he had answered, with an unintelligible reproach in his voice, "The starlings stay." And she remembered, again for no reason, a day when, in pride and excitement, she had burst into the house crying, "I saw an ermine. It was terribly poised and let me watch it quite a while." He had said categorically, "There are no ermines here."

She had not protested; she had sighed as she sighed now and turned to the window. The sleigh was livid in this light and no one was in it; nor had anyone been in it for many years. But at that moment the blacksmith's cat came guardedly across the dewy field and climbed into it, as if by careful plan, and curled up on the seat. May prodded the clinkers in the stove and started to the barn for kindling. But she thought of the cold and the damp and the smell of the horses, and she did not go but stood there, holding the poker and leaning upon it as if it were an umbrella. There was no place warm to go. "What time is it?" she whimpered, heartbroken, and moved the poker, stroking the lion foot of the fireless stove.

She knew now that no change would come, and that she would never see her lover again. Confounded utterly, like an orphan in solitary confinement, she went outdoors and got into the sleigh. The blacksmith's imperturbable cat stretched and rearranged his position, and May sat beside him with her hands locked tightly in her lap, rapidly wondering over and over again how she would live the rest of her life.

from Tomorrow

IT'S A NICE DAY—SUNDAY

R. E. (ROBERT EMMETT) THOMPSON *is a graduate student at Stanford University. He has lived most of his life in Los Angeles, where he was born in 1924. He is married. After three years in the United States Infantry, Mr. Thompson returned to Yale and received his bachelor's degree there in 1949. He spent a year in the Stanford Law School before entering the graduate English Department of the university. Most of his writing has been directed toward the stage, and in the spring of this year he was working on a new play. While taking courses at the Yale Drama School, he wrote a prize-winning play in 1948. Mr. Thompson's first published story appeared last year in* Charm *and another has been sold to* Prairie Schooner.

Like all stations, it was prosaic in its bareness—empty where the wind swept in eddies under the arches, stirring bits of paper and gum wrappers and commuter stubs, hollow-feeling and tinged gray with smoke and soot. Only two others had gotten off with me. A girl in a green tweed suit and a peaked hat with a long red feather that curled up from it and waved gently as she walked and a slim middle-aged man in a dark blue suit with the faintest of pin stripes and a precisely centered Homburg. It was that kind of station.

When I gave the cabdriver the address, he nodded his head slowly, making a slight sucking noise between his front teeth.

"First time I seen you going out there," he said.

"Yes."

"I get most the fares that go out there. That's cuz I got the regular shift on Sunday afternoon."

I didn't answer, and he turned again to driving. We went past the main part of the town and then turned off onto a narrow road. Immediately we were in the country with only a house here and there, half hidden by shrubs or gleaming white for a moment through the arching branches of willow trees.

He glanced over his shoulder at me as we were going down a slight rise in the road. "Used to take an old gentleman out here every Sunday. Maybe four years I guess. He never missed once. His only kid was out here. Maybe you seen him?"

"No."

"Don't know him, hunh?" It seemed to bother him. "You couldn't come out often or I'd a got you sure."

"This is the first time."

"Sure, that figgers. I'd got you otherwise."

The taxi turned again, and then, after a moment, stopped by a break in the long line of high, stiffly bending cypress trees that bordered one side of the road. A thick stone wall was hidden behind the cypress trees, and a gate of slender, twisting iron rods arched over with ornamental spikes bridged the gap.

I rattled the gate slightly and then waited until a thin man with thick glasses and a stained gray sweat shirt stuck his head out from the small shack that stood just inside the gate. I told him who I'd come to see and then waited while he phoned. After a moment he opened the gate and let me through.

"Just follow this path," he directed with a slight nod of his head. "You can see it from here."

The path wound beneath thick, low trees through the neatly clipped grass. A few scattered people, mostly couples or small groups, sat casually about on the grass and one larger group was silently engrossed in a game of croquet. It was very much like a park.

The house itself rose impressively from the long expanse of level green. Pseudomodern additions nestled incongruously against it, yet it still maintained an air of quiet pride.

A short, bald man with a shapeless gray suit and a wilted collar met me on the steps. He smiled, his lips stretching almost painfully in a thin line.

"You're Mr. Carlson?" He put out his hand.

"Yes."

"Well, well, yes. We've been expecting you." He looked up across the grounds and beyond the line of cypress trees. "Lovely day. Lovely, isn't it, Mr. Carlson? Well, come in. This way."

We passed through the high brass-hinged doors and turned right. His office was at the end of a narrow, thickly carpeted hallway. It was very bare—only an oak desk and a leather-upholstered chair in one corner. There was a picture of Venice on the back wall—a gondolier pushing a boat along one of the canals. He turned and leaned back against the desk, half sitting on the edge of it.

"I'm Mr. Sandborn, you know."

We shook hands again, and he motioned me toward the chair.

"No formality here, you know. This is a friendly place. Well, you've come to see our little sister, haven't you?"

"Elizabeth Jansen."

"To be sure." His short arms hung down across his body and his hands closed upon each other in the attitude of prayer, only pointing downward. He tapped his fingers together in a steady rhythm. "I thought we might have a short talk first," he said.

I nodded.

"Well, then, you're a friend of Elizabeth's?"

"It's been some time since . . . Yes."

"Good. Yes, good. Well, a special friend?" He smiled slightly, looking up at me from beneath his eyebrows.

"We were quite close once."

"Ah!" He rose, folding his arms loosely across his sloping chest. "We face facts here, Mr. Carlson. She's not well. Not in your sense. But then who's to say what is well in this sort of thing and what is not? We're humble here. You'll find some differences, of course. Nothing startling. But differences, I'm afraid."

"I know."

"Yes." He walked to the window and stood looking out, his hands clasped behind his back. He slowly tapped the back of one hand in the palm of the other.

I wanted to leave then, and I couldn't imagine how or why I had made myself come. Because when something dies, you let it die. Because it's no good coming back and turning it over and prodding it with your fingers until they become sticky with it. It wasn't because of the differences there would be, I think. Or maybe it was. A thing stays one way for a long time and if it's a bad thing you

314

don't want to stir it. The way a half-broken piece of furniture can grow to the corner of a room. Partly it's what you gauge the differences against, I guess. The last time I had seen her was on a September afternoon in Danbury, Connecticut, as she had been getting on a bus, pulling up her bag with one hand and wiping at tears with the other, and then just the blurred picture of her face pressed against the back window, stained and distorted by the cheap glass, receding always beyond the faint swirls of dust.

"About the letters, Mr. Carlson?" He had turned and was leaning now against the window sill. "Sometimes she gets confused about things, you know. But then I enclosed her letter with mine so you could see exactly . . . yes. We're forced to read our guests' letters. I can assure you I don't *like* to do it. Not at all. It's an unpleasant duty. But there *are* precautions. Yes. There *were* some letters?"

"Yes."

"I see. You . . . you have them with you?"

"Yes."

"Ah!" He walked again to the desk and sat on the edge nearest to my chair. "We feel here that our guests are always right. I like to think of it as a motto, so to speak. But of course, you understand, there are things and then again there are things. As you know from my letter, I thought it might be good for Elizabeth to have you visit her but, as for the letters, no. No, I think perhaps we had better not let her have the letters."

"I see."

"Fine; then we're in agreement. Now she'll ask you for them, of course. You can tell her you're too attached to them or some such thing. You'll work it out, I'm sure." He pressed a buzzer on the desk. "I'll have Mrs. Price take you in."

Mrs. Price was an extremely large woman, heavy-boned and broad, with steel-gray hair turned neatly up on top of her head. In her blue uniform she seemed almost military in her bearing.

"Mrs. Price will take you in. You'll remember our little talk?"

"Yes."

"Fine." He shook my hand firmly again.

"If you'll follow me, Mr. Carlson," Mrs. Price said.

"How is she?" I asked. "Miss Jansen, I mean."

She shrugged—a sort of brisk, chopping movement that fitted into the rhythm of her strides. "She doesn't give as much trouble as some of them."

We passed through an anteroom and then into a large sitting room. It was very dark. The walls were mostly covered by walnut paneling and heavy velvet drapes shut out most of the light. A thick oriental rug covered most of the floor and there were only a few pieces of furniture—high-backed chairs and ornamental floor lamps. After a moment I saw Jan. She was sitting primly in one corner of a sofa on the far side of the room.

"You have a visitor, Miss Jansen. This is Mr. Carlson. You remember Mr. Carlson?"

"Oh yes."

"Half an hour only. No more."

"Yes, Mother."

"Hmph!" Mrs. Price said. She turned squarely and moved away with the same brisk stride.

"The mother seems very tired," Jan said. "She's only been with us a few weeks. She's new, you know. The Mother Superior before her was very nice. She used to give me my beads at night sometimes. I don't like Mother Price as well." She looked about the room and then down at the sofa. "But I shouldn't say that."

She sat motionlessly, her hands folded in her lap, like a little girl sitting stiffly in the best living-room chair. She was wearing a plain, dull gray uniformlike dress and she had a small white skullcap fitted firmly across the whole of her head. A long, wide piece of sheer, filmy black lace was pinned to the top of it and hung down over her shoulders and across the front of her dress. It cast a thin shadow that wavered slightly with the undulating of the cords in her neck.

It was a shock seeing her like that. More than I had expected. It was her hair mostly, I think. Because I couldn't see any of it. And not seeing it, I wanted to touch it and feel the weight of it in the palm of my hand and crumple it. But it was trussed tight and hidden underneath the white cap.

We sat for a while on the sofa, keeping our distance and each waiting for the other to say something. I touched the cushion between us with my hand. It was a very dark blue frieze, almost pur-

316

ple really, with raised rose patterns in it. It was old but clean and not worn at all.

Finally she looked up. "You look well, Ralph."

She had never called me that that I could remember. It sounded very strange. "I'm healthy," I answered.

"Are we going to the play? My green dress, the one with the little—— No, that's not it, is it?" She looked about the room again, knitting her eyebrows together fiercely. Then she smiled. "Did you bring them?"

"The letters?"

"Yes."

I took them from my coat pocket and put them on the sofa between us. "They're only seven," I said. "One got lost somewhere." She began to pick them up, and I touched her wrist, restraining her. "Not yet."

She sat back, glancing away from my face again, then she folded her hands in her lap and sat looking intensely at them. Wholly surrounded by folds and sloping curves of black lace, they seemed lifeless and disembodied things, slender and white and cold, like single sprays of spindrift frozen to an evening ocean.

"Are you happy?" I asked.

"Very."

"Oh."

"I have a love now." She smiled. Only the very slightest of smiles. "I love God now," she said.

"Jan, do you——"

"They've changed my name, you know. It's Teresa. That's the one I wanted. You should call me Sister Teresa now."

"Oh!"

She smiled again. "Do you still frighten people, like you used to?"

She meant was I still a claims adjuster. I was, though I'd advanced a little, but I said I wasn't. Once I had taken her along with me to settle a claim in the Negro section of Chappel Street in New Haven. It was just a routine matter—a dented fender, I think—but it had frightened her terribly. She'd almost become hysterical and begged me to quit the job. I promised her I would. I had promised her almost anything when she was like that. Except to marry her. I had never promised that. She asked me what I did now, and I told

317

her public relations, which wasn't a lie really because I had a friend who thought he might be able to get me something in that line.

She nodded and relapsed again into silence. She sat absolutely still, like a bird frightened by some very slight noise or movement somewhere. When she moved suddenly, turning toward me on the sofa, it startled me.

"My family came to see me," she said. Her eyebrows knit together again and she searched my face. "Last week?" She nodded. "Yes. They don't come very often. The rules. It's very strict, especially when you begin. They asked about you. No. But you never met them, did you? Do you remember how I used to ask you to come up to the house—just for a week-end even? We have our own tennis court. My father laid it out. And there's a lovely little room in back all to itself. They gave it to me when my brother went off to Andover. And the bay. We could swim. No, that's the Cod. That's different. But there's a lake. They used to beg me to bring you even for . . . No, they didn't know about you, did they? I didn't tell them."

"Do you need anything?" I asked. "I mean anything I could send to you."

"Oh no, no. There's everything here I need. I'm very happy. Will you come again?"

"Sometime."

"You should see my room. I have such a lovely room. It's all pink almost and I made little satin sashes for the curtains. And there's the most wonderful taffeta spread with roses all up on top of it. When you pull it up to your chin, it's all soft and silky against your neck. Sometimes, when it's warm, I just sleep with the spread because it's beautiful against my skin. And they never bother me." She looked hastily about the room, then reached into the pocket of her dress and took out a small jagged piece of yellow cellophane. "This is my window," she said. "Not really, but I call it that. Because I look through the window with it. It changes everything. All the sky and the grass and the trees—they're all golden then. Sometimes I look at them all day." She reached out and touched the back of my hand very gently. Her eyes seemed very soft. "Will you take me away, Ralphie? Please. We could go anywhere. I'll make puddings for you and candies and little cakes. Please, Ralphie." She settled limply against the sofa arm again. "But I can't go, can I?"

318

"Not yet." Looking at her then, she seemed different only in externals. When she looked up at me with her wide brown eyes, I knew it was the same Jan. Her eyes didn't look. They begged mutely. Like a fawn frightened by the side of a road or some tiny animal caught in a trap, whimpering a little. It had always been like that. You could never say no, it's no good. Because I don't love you. Because I don't love things. There were always the eyes. Oh, there were times, a thousand times, when I'd said, no, it's all over. But then there were the tears and the long, violent sobs contorting her body and all the threats of killing herself or running away. Once even she had swallowed a whole bottle of aspirins and I'd spent an hour walking in a hospital corridor, while they pumped her stomach. Not that it would kill her. Because you don't die of things like that, of love. But something else that it does. I don't know what exactly, but it frightened me always, everything. Still it ended always by stroking her head and saying it was all right now. Because she was soft and young and hurt. Because you can never be wholly brutal to something that loves you.

"It's so much better now," she said. "So peaceful."

"What?"

"To love God." She looked toward the ceiling, sighing deeply, then she turned toward me again, clapping her hands together, like a little girl suddenly seeing a rainbow weaving between drops of rain. "And I have a secret, you know. God is golden, like the trees."

Almost suddenly I realized that Mrs. Price was walking silently over the thick rug toward us and I stood up, feeling embarrassed in some way.

"It's time," she said. "Two minutes over, in fact."

"Yes."

She stepped away and stood waiting, rubbing the toe of her shoe impatiently against the nap of the rug.

Jan started to pick up the letters again, and I stopped her. "Maybe I'd better keep them," I told her. "They aren't the sort of things to have in a place like this. The Mother Superior might find them. You wouldn't want that."

"No, she doesn't like us to have things she doesn't know about."

"Well, then, I'll keep them. That'll be better."

"All right." She started to move away, then she stopped and looked

319

at me again. Her voice half breaking in a sort of urgent whisper, she said, "Burn them, Ralph. Please."

She waited for me to answer, moving her lips as though to answer for me. I felt as if I were answering, as if the sound had taken shape and hung between us, undraped and assured. But I said nothing.

Mrs. Price returned and tapped Jan softly on the shoulder. "We'll have to go now," she said. "You can see Mr. Carlson again."

The tension left her body slowly. "All right," she said. She meticulously smoothed the lace over her breast, spreading out each crease and fold, and then stood up. She touched the sleeve of my coat lightly and looked imploringly at me again. She seemed very lost, like a lost child waiting patiently with strange people for the return of its mother. "You can always come on Sundays. You'll come?"

I said yes that I would come, but I knew that I wouldn't. I knew that that was all. That I wouldn't come again. Not ever. I knew it suddenly and wholly, as I had known it once before, cutting into a lamb chop at a lunch counter in Danbury, Connecticut, on a September afternoon.

She smiled. "I like Sunday," she said. "It's such a nice day."

Mr. Sandborn offered me a cigarette on the steps. He shook my hand vigorously again. "We'll see you here again, I hope."

"I don't know." I started to step away from him, then I checked myself. It wasn't that his breath was bad or that there was anything strange about his eyes. I think that it was just that it seemed wrong somehow to be talking to him where there was clean air.

"You mustn't let yourself be frightened by the bars on the gate, you know. They're only symbols, as I like to call them. A line has to be drawn someplace, even if we don't quite know where to draw it." He laughed slightly. "I think it might do her a great deal of good to see you. It's not at all hopeless. No, no, not at all."

"Yes," I said. I knew what they were thinking—all of them. That I should help her get well and someday take her away and marry her and make her happy again. I don't say they were wrong. No. You should pay for things. Even if you're not sure you owe anything. Because you're alive. Because you're breathing. Because things have to be paid for. I know they were right. I should come every Sunday, and then one Sunday Mr. Sandborn could say, You can take her out now. Then wake up one night with her screaming and throwing an empty aspirin bottle across the room. Or come home some quiet, smoky afternoon and find her gazing silently out of the window through a piece of colored cellophane. No, I don't say they were wrong. There are things to be paid for.

"You're always welcome, Mr. Carlson." He shook hands with me again and then ponderously pushed open the heavy door and went inside.

I waited for a moment on the steps, finishing the cigarette and looking at the place. Now in the twilight it seemed even more lovely and at rest. The cypress trees were all quivering with the slight breeze. They were blended in together, the branches bending a little with the wind, thick with blues and purples merging into the rich dusk green. They stood like a wall against the town, letting only corners and bits of rooftops jut above them. I crushed out the cigarette and started to walk over the soft grass and past the wall and back to town. It seemed a long way.

It was cold on the platform waiting for the train, and I leaned against a pillar out of the wind. I patted my coat where the letters were and I thought about burning them again and I knew that I wouldn't. That's wrong, too, I know. I'm not arguing that. It wouldn't have cost me anything to tell her at least that I was going to burn them. I don't know why I wanted them. So many things get mixed up—pride and desire and doubt and perverseness and things you can't quite name. I've heard of people loving old chairs or bits of cloth or smooth stones. Maybe that's it. Because you have to love something, I think. Well, so she loves God and that's fine too. I'm not mad at anybody and it's no good being jealous of God. I haven't lost anything really and maybe she's found something. But I don't know—I remember once we were in a little hotel in Bridgeport. It was July and very hot. I remember it was July because it was the week end after the Fourth. She was standing by the window and looking out, her hair with little red lights in it jiggling with the breeze from the fan, blowing in little tufts along the curve of her neck, soft and full and sharp against the clean white of her skin. She was like an entranced little girl, peering out at a strange world, tiny and shy. Then I asked her, "What do you see?" She turned and smiled and walked over to the edge of the bed. She didn't answer. She just smiled and touched the calf of my leg very gently. Then she bent over and kissed my foot. When she looked up at me, she wasn't smiling any more. But as though she were going to cry because there was just too much of everything. "Because that's the way I feel about you," she said.

APPENDIX

List of Prize Stories in the *O. Henry Memorial Award Prize Stories*, 1919–1950 inclusive.

BLANCHE COLTON WILLIAMS, EDITOR, 1919–32

1919 1st, ENGLAND TO AMERICA, Margaret Prescott Montague; 2nd, FOR THEY KNOW NOT WHAT THEY DO, Wilbur Daniel Steele.

1920 1st, EACH IN HIS GENERATION, Struthers Burt; 2nd, CONTACT!, Frances Noyes Hart.

1921 1st, THE HEART OF LITTLE SHIKARA, Edison Marshall; 2nd, THE MAN WHO CURSED THE LILIES, Charles Tenney Jackson; special prize for best work in 1919, 1920, 1921, and for THE MARRIAGE IN KAIRWAN, Wilbur Daniel Steele.

1922 1st, SNAKE DOCTOR, Irvin S. Cobb; 2nd, INNOCENCE, Rose Wilder Lane; SS. (short short story), GOLD-MOUNTED GUNS, F. R. Buckley.

1923 1st, PRELUDE, Edgar Valentine Smith; 2nd, A FRIEND OF NAPOLEON, Richard Connell; SS., TOWERS OF FAME, Elizabeth Irons Folsom.

1924 1st, THE SPRING FLIGHT, Inez Haynes Irwin; 2nd, MARGARET BLAKE, Chester T. Crowell; SS., RACHEL AND HER CHILDREN, Frances Newman.

1925 1st, MR. BISBEE'S PRINCESS, Julian Street; 2nd, SPLENDID WITH SWORDS, Wythe Williams; SS., PAPAGO WEDDING, Mary Austin.

1926 1st, BUBBLES, Wilbur Daniel Steele; 2nd, DEATH IN THE WOODS, Sherwood Anderson; SS., COMMAND, Albert Richard Wetjen.

1927 1st, CHILD OF GOD, Roark Bradford; 2nd, THE KILLERS, Ernest Hemingway; SS., THE SCARLET WOMAN, Louis Bromfield.

1928 1st, THE PARROT, Walter Duranty; 2nd, THE PECULIAR TREASURE OF KINGS, Marjory Stoneham Douglas; SS., BRIDAL POND, Zona Gale.

1929 1st, BIG BLONDE, Dorothy Parker; 2nd, THE HOMESICK LADIES, Sidney Howard; SS., HIM AND HER, Katharine Brush.

1930 1st, DRESSING-UP, W. R. Burnett; also 1st, NEITHER JEW NOR CREEK, William M. John; 2nd, THE SACRIFICE OF THE MAIDENS, Elizabeth Madox Roberts; SS., CORONER'S INQUEST, Marc Connelly.

1931 1st, No prize given, CAN'T CROSS JORDAN BY MYSELF, Wilbur Daniel Steele; 2nd (first money), ONE HEAD WELL DONE, John D.

Swain; 3rd (second money), THE FIVE-MINUTE GIRL, Mary Hastings Bradley; SS., HAUNTED GROUND, Oliver La Farge.

1932 1st, AN END TO DREAMS, Stephen Vincent Benét; 2nd, FAREWELL TO CUBA, James Gould Cozzens; SS., A TRIP TO CZARDIS, Edwin Granberry.

HARRY HANSEN, EDITOR, 1933–40

1933 1st, GAL YOUNG UN, Marjorie Kinnan Rawlings; 2nd, THE FRILL, Pearl S. Buck; SS., TO THE INVADER, Nancy Hale.

1934 1st, NO MORE TROUBLE FOR JEDWICK, Louis Paul; 2nd, OLD RED, Caroline Gordon; SS., THE DARING YOUNG MAN ON THE FLYING TRAPEZE, William Saroyan.

1935 1st, THE WHITE HORSES OF VIENNA, Kay Boyle; THE HOME PLACE, Dorothy Thomas; SS., JOHN THE SIX, Josephine W. Johnson.

1936 1st, TOTAL STRANGER, James Gould Cozzens; 2nd, SUITE 2049, Sally Benson; SS., A SUM IN ADDITION, William March.

1937 1st, THE DEVIL AND DANIEL WEBSTER, Stephen Vincent Benét; 2nd, TO THOSE WHO WAIT, Elick Moll; 3rd, THE FURY, Robert M. Coates.

1938 1st, THE HAPPIEST MAN ON EARTH, Albert Maltz; 2nd, FIRE AND CLOUD, Richard Wright; 3rd, THE PROMISE, John Steinbeck.

1939 1st, BARN BURNING, William Faulkner; 2nd, BAT FLIGHT, James Still; 3rd, CALVES, David Cornel DeJong.

1940 1st, FREEDOM'S A HARD-BOUGHT THING, Stephen Vincent Benét; 2nd, DON'T GET ME WRONG, Roderick Lull; 3rd, THE KILL, Edward Havill.

HERSCHEL BRICKELL, EDITOR SINCE 1941

1941 1st, DEFEAT, Kay Boyle; 2nd, A WORN PATH, Eudora Welty; 3rd, EIGHTEENTH SUMMER, Hallie Southgate Abbet; Special prize for a "first" story, THE VISIT, Andy Logan.

1942 1st, THE WIDE NET, Eudora Welty; 2nd, TWO RIVERS, Wallace Stegner; 3rd, WINDWAGON SMITH, Wilbur L. Schramm; "first" story, A LONG WAY TO GO, Jeanne E. Wylie.

1943 1st, LIVVIE IS BACK, Eudora Welty; 2nd, THE KNOT HOLE, Dorothy Canfield; 3rd, THE FISHERMAN OF PATZCUARO, William Fifield; "first" story, TWO LITTLE BLACK BOYS, Clara Laidlaw.

The prize stories from 1919 through 1943 are included in The Pocket Book of O. Henry Memorial Award Prize Stories, published in 1947.

1944 1st, WALKING WOUNDED, Irwin Shaw; 2nd, HOME IS A PLACE, Bessie Breuer; 3rd, THE STAGECOACH, Griffith Beems; "first" story, HEALTH CARD, Frank C. Yerby.

1945 1st, THE WIND AND THE SNOW OF WINTER, Walter Van Tilburg Clark; 2nd, GUNNER'S PASSAGE, Irwin Shaw; 3rd, OLD BILL BENT TO DRINK, Ben Hur Lampman; "first" story, FLESH AND BLOOD, Laurence Critchell.

1946 1st, BIRD SONG, John Mayo Goss; 2nd, THE INNOCENT BYSTANDER, Margaret Shedd; 3rd, SOMETIMES YOU BREAK EVEN, Victor Ullman; "first" story, WAVES OF DARKNESS, Cord Meyer, Jr.

1947 1st, THE WHITE CIRCLE, John Bell Clayton; 2nd, REST CAMP ON MAUI, Eugene L. Burdick; 3rd, THE NIGHTINGALES SING, Elizabeth Parsons; "first" story, LITTLE VICTOR, Robert Lewis.

1948 1st, SHUT A FINAL DOOR, Truman Capote; 2nd, BEYOND THE GLASS MOUNTAIN, Wallace Stegner; 3rd, POWERHOUSE, Ray Bradbury; "first" story, SPARROW'S LAST JUMP, Elliott Grennard.

1949 1st, A COURTSHIP, William Faulkner; 2nd, THE WATCHMAN, Mark Van Doren; 3rd, THE WHITE HOUND, Ward Dorrance.

1950 1st, THE BLUE-WINGED TEAL, Wallace Stegner; 2nd, THE MAGNOLIAS, Gudger Bart Leiper; 3rd, BE NICE TO MR. CAMPBELL, Robert Lowry.